# Monticello

ALSO BY SALLY CABOT GUNNING

*BENJAMIN FRANKLIN'S BASTARD*
(as Sally Cabot)

*THE REBELLION OF JANE CLARKE*

*BOUND*

*THE WIDOW'S WAR*

# Monticello

✳

*A DAUGHTER
AND HER FATHER*

SALLY CABOT GUNNING

*wm*

WILLIAM MORROW
*An Imprint of* HarperCollins*Publishers*

HarperCollins books may be purchased for educational, business, or sales promotional use. For information please e-mail the Special Markets Department at SPsales@harpercollins.com.

FIRST EDITION

*Designed by William Ruoto*

Library of Congress Cataloging-in-Publication Data has been applied for.

ISBN 978-0-06-232043-8

16 17 18 19 20    OV/RRD    10 9 8 7 6 5 4 3 2 1

*FOR MY TOM*

*I wish with all my soul that the poor Negroes were all freed. It grieves my heart when I think that these our fellow creatures should be treated so terribly as they are by many of our country men.*

    —LETTER FROM MARTHA JEFFERSON, AGE 14, TO THOMAS JEFFERSON, MAY 1787

<br>

*On the subject of emancipation I have ceased to think because [it is] not to be a work of my day.*

    —LETTER FROM THOMAS JEFFERSON, AGE 83, TO WILLIAM SHORT, JANUARY 1826

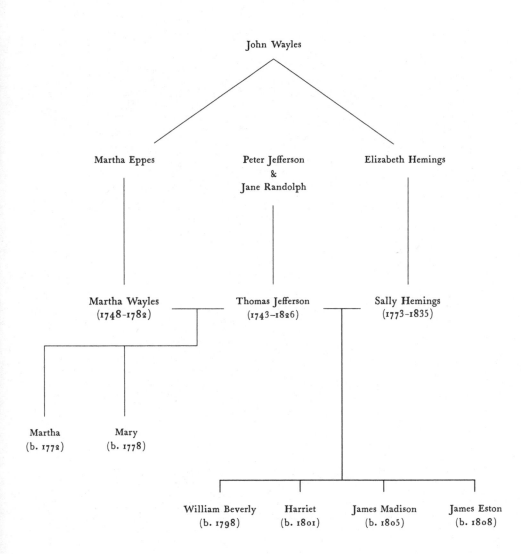

John Wayles

Martha Eppes

Peter Jefferson
&
Jane Randolph

Elizabeth Hemings

Martha Wayles
(1748-1782)

Thomas Jefferson
(1743–1826)

Sally Hemings
(1773–1835)

Martha
(b. 1772)

Mary
(b. 1778)

William Beverly
(b. 1798)

Harriet
(b. 1801)

James Madison
(b. 1805)

James Eston
(b. 1808)

# PART I

## Varina

*1789–1800*

# 1789

---

MARTHA JEFFERSON HAD DREAMED OF MONTICELLO all through the five years she'd spent in a French convent while her father served as America's minister to France. In her dreams Monticello had loomed above her as if it were the earth's ultimate height, its brightest palace, its most fruitful garden. Always in her dreams the forest was so green it shimmered, the vegetable garden sat heavy with melons and cucumbers and cabbage and squash, the orchard dropped blushing apples into her lap as she passed, sunflowers reigned over the lesser hyacinths and sweet peas and primrose in the flower beds, while curling around their little kingdom, the Blue Ridge Mountains formed a mystical, protective wall. Now, as the carriage took the first turn in the roundabout, Martha saw nothing but bare red earth, naked branches, bitter wind, and after five years of absence, more than one untended, sagging fence.

The mountain had also grown dark. Sprinkled over these outer edges of the plantation sat the slave quarters of the field workers, and as Thomas Jefferson's carriage ascended, pockets of slaves began to approach it, to follow it as if escorting him homeward, their laughing, weeping, joyful black faces pressing closer and closer to the carriage. Martha never saw such masses of Negroes in Paris—the few she had seen were free citizens of France—and the sight disconcerted her. The twelve-year-old who'd left America for

France might have thought these slaves' affection for their kind and generous master prompted this welcome, but the seventeen-year-old now returning had to wonder if what she saw might in fact be relief. What if Thomas Jefferson had never returned? What if the poor creatures had gotten sold away from their families, sold out of the county, sold to the slave hell of a West Indian sugar plantation? Or maybe what Martha saw around her was hope. Just before they'd sailed for France, Virginia had passed a law that had, for the first time, allowed a master to free his slaves. These slaves would have heard of that law; did they imagine that the man who had freed America from bondage might now free his slaves?

In Paris Martha had overheard her father telling his secretary, William Short, of his plan to convert certain of his choice slaves into free tenant farmers, and Short had leaped to endorse the scheme. The two men had talked it this way and that until it had seemed a real plan, prompting Martha to ask her father on the ship home which slaves he'd decided to set off on their own farms.

"This is an idea that will require greater thought," her father had said.

Martha drew her mind from William Short and her gaze from the fearful hope she now believed she read in the faces outside the carriage. She stared instead at the two faces that sat in the opposite seat—her eleven-year-old sister, Mary, whom they'd begun to call Maria in France, and the sixteen-year-old Negro Sally Hemings— but this sight couldn't cheer her either, as the two girls shared a similar face. Thomas Jefferson had inherited the Hemings family on the death of his father-in-law, John Wayles. Their privileged status before and since had only confirmed rumors that these pale Negroes were indeed the offspring of John Wayles and his slave Betty Hemings, which made Sally Hemings Martha's and Maria's aunt. Yes, Maria's skin was linen white and her curls auburn, while

Sally's skin was the color of dusk and her hair long and straight and black, but both shared the same delicate, symmetrical features of Martha's dead mother. Martha glanced sideways at her father. Did he see his wife's face in these two sitting opposite? Did he ever think of Sally as his wife's sister? His face showed little beyond an increased tightening around the mouth.

Maria squeezed Sally's arm as the carriage lurched through the crowd and up to the house. "See how the Negroes love you, Papa!" Martha watched Sally to discover what she might think of Maria's comment, but as was ever the case, Sally's eyes remained averted. According to French law, Sally might have stayed in Paris and lived free instead of returning to her slave life at Monticello, and so too her brother James, whom Martha's father had trained in the art of French cookery. James could easily have found work as a pastry chef in any nobleman's house in France, and Sally, a competent seamstress, could certainly have found herself a place. Instead, brother and sister had chosen to return to Virginia and their slave state. Could it be that these Negroes *did* love Thomas Jefferson as much as Maria believed they did?

Martha's eyes drifted from Sally's profile to her hands, where they lay cupped in her lap, as decorous—*more* decorous—than the women Martha had come to know and both envy and despise in France. That more than all the rest reminded Martha of her mother, and as the graceful, stately house that her mother had so loved rose in the distance, Martha's eyes filled. Her mother had died in that house. How easy to see again the darkened room, her mother's still shape beneath the coverlet, her father bending over it in shameless weeping that racked him head to foot. He'd risen only to crumple to the floor in a swoon that set the Negroes running; they'd carried him to his adjoining cabinet and laid him on the pallet where he'd insisted on sleeping through his wife's long illness. Martha had hovered, awash in her own tears, until her nurse, Ursula, circled her in sinewy, strong arms. "You cry," she'd said. "And then you brace up. Your mother's made your father promise never to marry again just so there won't be any stepmothers bossing your life. Now you pay back. Now you be your father's comfort."

When Martha's father had emerged from his room weeks later, he'd taken to his horse, riding through the Monticello woods day after endless day, until Martha begged to ride with him. In time he agreed, allowing her to witness the freshets of grief that continued to overcome him for months. And here they were again, the carriage climbing through those same woods, her father no doubt even more leveled by grief than Martha was. She'd done her best to comfort her father while they lived in France, but Paris had offered its own distractions, and Martha had been off at the convent, too often out of touch. Now back at Monticello, with fresh reminders skulking behind every shadow, it would be that much harder to fill the empty places her mother had left, to be, as Ursula had instructed, her father's comfort.

But as Martha strained to see through the carriage window every angle and bend of the old house, every tree no matter how bare it was, and every familiar peak of the distant mountains, all Monticello's darkness vanished. Yes, Paris glittered and shone, its art, architecture, and theater unmatched, but also unmatched was its stink, its beggars, its mud. Martha was home. Her father and sister were home. This was where they should be in life, and once her father puzzled out what to do about the slaves, all would be right. Martha groped sideways on the seat till her hand touched her father's, waited until his turned over and clasped hers. "'Tis lovely to be home, isn't it, Papa?"

Martha's father didn't seem to hear; he remained silent, his eyes sweeping continuously over the bare fields, no doubt taking note of every rundown outbuilding, untended fence, and peeling column in front of the house. It didn't matter, Martha wanted to tell him; it was Monticello, their beloved Monticello, and what it had lost by five years of neglect could be regained by a single year of devotion. And what devotion Martha could give it now, older and more sensible of the role she was to play, not only as comfort to her father but as steward of the house. She was no longer the young girl she'd been when she'd left Virginia for France; she was mistress of Monticello now, and it would fall to her to direct the Negroes in shaking out and pressing her father's clothes, in making sure his sheets were fresh and his chamber aired, in overseeing the dinner preparations. With no mother to guide her, Martha had been trained in none of these things; her education, overseen by her father, had thus far consisted of books, music, art, and pleasant conversation; she'd worked hard to master all these things in order to please her father, but to please him now, she knew, she must master the rest.

The carriage drew up to the walk; in the seconds it took the wheels to stop spinning Martha jettisoned her fine Paris training, grabbed her sister's hand, tumbled out, and bolted up the steps. *Don't run,* her mother used to chide her, but even the fine young Paris lady couldn't slow her feet.

"Look, Maria, our ash tree! And the rail we walked on. And our window. Do you see our window above?"

Maria pulled back.

Sally spoke from behind them. "Elle ne se souvient pas." *She doesn't remember.*

Martha looked to her sister, hoping she would see what she needed to see in order to counter Sally's pronouncement, but the great doors had already swung open and the house servants, mostly Hemingses, had swarmed out. Some of the male Hemingses had been allowed to go off and work for their own wages while the

Jeffersons were in France, and their master greeted them now as if they'd returned to him out of nothing but love; yes, looking at the eager faces around them Martha could almost believe it herself. Behind them came Betty Hemings, the concubine of Martha's grandfather; Sally fell into her mother's arms and broke into tears, surprising Martha until she remembered that mother and daughter had been apart for two years. Why, of course, thought Martha, an odd relief overcoming her; surely that was why Sally chose to leave freedom behind in France—here was the whole of her family. Thomas Jefferson always kept his slave families together wherever he could, and James and Sally no doubt understood that they could count on finding not only mother and siblings but nieces and nephews together at Monticello where they'd been left.

But oh, dear Lord, here came Ursula, pushing through the Hemingses, as tall and wiry as Martha remembered her, Ursula who had nursed Martha when her own mother's milk had dried up, Ursula who'd switched her when she'd caught her trying to walk on that rail, Ursula who'd held her while she cried for her dead mother. Ursula was not a Hemings but another illustration of the same point: Thomas Jefferson had inherited Ursula along with the Hemingses, but Ursula's husband and son had been left to his sister-in-law. Martha's mother begged her new husband to get them back, so he'd ridden fifty miles and spent two hundred dollars to reunite the family at Monticello. Perhaps *Ursula* loved her master because of this? Martha had seldom contemplated such things when she lived in France. They'd called Sally *Mademoiselle Sally* and James *Monsieur James* and their master paid them a wage and Martha forgot they were slaves. But did *they* forget?

Martha drew free of Ursula's embrace and moved deeper into the house, going from parlor to dining room to tea room, only peeking into her father's chamber and the room that he called his cabinet, afraid of restarting her tears, unwilling for her father to see her in such a state. She galloped up the steep, narrow stairs to the four rooms above, to her room. Oh, how faded and small it seemed, compared to the room that she'd occupied in memory! And how bare, as bare as her French convent! But eighty-six crates of all that they'd accumulated in France were traveling behind them—furniture, busts, paintings, curios of every size, and crate after crate of books in seven languages, all of which her father could and did read, although he never could speak French as well as his daughters.

Or Sally.

Maria stepped hesitantly into the room, her eyes shadowed and blinking against the clear mountain light. She'd been away from Monticello most of her life, having spent those first years after their mother's death with an aunt and uncle farther south, and no wonder she should look so bewildered now, so out of place. Martha crossed the room to her sister, took her hand, and drew her to the window. "See the mountains? Aren't they the loveliest thing on earth?"

"I like the river best."

The river. The Appomattox River, which ran through their uncle's plantation, which to Martha had always offered a far less interesting prospect than her mountains. "Come; let's see if Papa's spyglass is still here. And the clock, and the checkerboard. Surely you remember those." Martha led Maria down the stairs, planning to distract her with as many objects of interest as she could until the girl's things were unpacked, but as they reached the parlor, it was Martha who was distracted by one of her father's trunks, riding into the parlor on James's shoulder. The trunk reminded her of her new role.

"Take the trunk to my father's chamber," Martha said, but James had already set off with it, for indeed, where else *would* he take it? Martha turned next toward the kitchen steps, but before she'd gone far, her father appeared, beckoning to her from the door of his cabinet.

"Martha, dear, come. I should like to speak with you a minute."

Martha hastened to her father's door and stepped into the room after him, noting that it appeared well aired and recently swept and dusted, even without her directing it. Her father stood examining a bare spot on the shelf. He looked well after their journey, as straight and strong as a Virginia pine, his eyes clear, the angles of cheek and jaw unobstructed by any sagging flesh, but Martha would not be fooled by his supposed strength; he would need her here far more than he'd ever needed her in France. "I shall put my new biscuit statuettes here," he said. "Venus and Hope, side by side." He paused, turning to Martha. "As we touch on the subject of Hope, I'd *hoped* not to have to take up this matter with you just yet, to allow you to refamiliarize yourself with your heritage in peace. But you spoke in the carriage . . . I now see the unfairness in my original course. Martha, my dear, I'm to join President Washington in New York. I've been offered, and I've accepted, the post of secretary of state."

Such new words, thought Martha. Such thrilling words. *President. Secretary of state.* But New York! To fall so violently back in love with Monticello only to be asked to leave it again! She struggled to keep her heartbreak from her face. "'Tis a very great honor, Papa," she said. "And perhaps 'tis best you've told me now, so I might think as I unpack my trunk how best to repack it for New York."

Her father turned even graver, shook his head. "Only I move to New York, Martha, my love. You and Maria move to Eppington and enter into the care of your aunt and uncle Eppes."

---

## CHAPTER 2

MARCH. MARTHA HAD ALWAYS BEEN FOND OF MARCH, signaling as it did the time when Monticello shrugged itself awake and burst to life, new and old together—the orchard, the gardens, the forest, even the slave quarters and the smithy and the joinery coming alive with the fresh activity of the season. But now March signaled the start of her father's term of office, flagging the day when he would leave for New York, and Martha would climb down from her glorious height and descend into the river world of her aunt and uncle Eppes.

As Martha and her father took up their old pastime of riding out over rediscovered bridle paths, she found herself gazing at the mountain ridges in an effort to memorize them, to fix each pine tree in its place, to capture every ripple of mockingbird song. She also spent a good deal of her time attempting to memorize her father's face. She was often told that along with her father's height she'd inherited that face, but she could never see the likeness as others saw it; in her father it presented a near-perfect blend of strength and sensitivity; in her it presented a bland collection of parts that apparently turned lovely only when she laughed or fumed, or so she'd been told by her father's secretary, William Short. But oh, how she could laugh and fume! And oh, the constant struggle to keep such excesses in check! This art of concealment had been the first and last lesson taught her by her mother, and it had been reinforced by her father throughout her Paris life.

"Never let another see your anger," he would say with a heart-easing smile but a smile that never burst out with enough exuberance to actually show his excellent teeth. And there lay the other lesson, one that she'd managed to hone to a keen edge at her father's Paris dinner table: No matter how bold or silly or pretentious the other women at the table became, Thomas Jefferson's daughter must never follow suit. She must neither flaunt nor cower; she must perfect the art of dishing up substantive but uncontroversial pleasantries whenever the conversation turned her way, always remaining fleet of wit and, at times, when she could bear no more, fleet of foot.

But now the only art she cared to perfect was the art of reading her father's face. What could she see there? Easier to ask what she wished to see. The old grief, yes, grown familiar as an old coat and binding father and daughter as no other memory ever could, but perhaps a new grief too, born of the thought of leaving Monticello, at the thought of leaving his daughters. Yes, she would read these things in her father's face as they rode. He was a wonderful rider—strong and straight with that imperceptible, seemingly effortless control over the paired bodies of master and beast, forever humming or singing the Scottish tunes he so loved, no matter the fractiousness of his mount—and his mounts did tend to the fractious. Conversely, Martha was seated on the gentlest of horses, "for my daughter, only a horse so gentle it might be ridden without a bridle," her father ordered the Negro who tended the horses, a policy which left Martha little to do but think and remember and study her father's face.

Martha's father spoke. "I've always found the best cure for body and spirit to be exercise and fresh air. You would seem to subscribe to this maxim. Alas, your sister does not."

"No, she does not." Nor had Maria inherited their father's interest in horses, as Martha had. Martha had grown up watching her father run his handkerchief over his horse's immaculate back before it was saddled, watched him slide to the ground and walk at the first sign of lameness no matter how far he might be from the house, watched him wander to the stable to check on the animal at least once a day until it had fully recovered. She'd also watched him lay the whip into more than one glossy hide at the first sign of restlessness.

Martha loves horses, yes, but even more she treasured those companionable rides, the mountains with their false lure of closeness, the slumbering gardens and orchards so full of promise, the scarred and pocked house looking more and more like its old self the farther away they drew. Every childhood memory those rides awakened was a rediscovered treasure, and yet nothing was just as she'd remembered it. In her mind all her father's carefully planted trees stood in ordered rows; now their branches wound into each other in a hopeless tangle. She and Sally had once followed Sally's brothers up an apple tree that stood far enough beyond their mothers' eyes to make sure they wouldn't be caught; now Martha couldn't sort out which tree that was. They'd made babies out of pinecones and put them to bed in a needle-lined hollow log that had been long buried—or rotted—under the forest floor. She'd had to remind her father of the spot where she'd been ejected from a stumbling horse only to land on a patch of moss as soft as her own bed. Had her father really slipped out of the saddle and stretched out on the moss, crossed his arms, closed his eyes, and feigned sleep till she shook him "awake"? If he had, he didn't remember it. If he hadn't, she'd only wished it.

Soon Martha began to treasure the shared rides even more for their rarity, for on their return from Paris, Thomas Jefferson was seldom left at peace. Visitors arrived in a steady stream: friends, relatives, politicians—and as word spread of the upcoming political appointment, parasites in search of an open vein to power on which to suck. Martha saw it all and marveled at her father's ability to smile his way through it, even as she smiled and smiled in answer to the gaping "How tall you've grown!" or "How like your father!" as she towered over men twice her age and half her wit.

Perhaps that was why the tall, scowling Tom Randolph stood out, that and—she would admit it—his dramatic looks. A distant cousin to the Jeffersons, he was more apt to brag of his descent from the Indian princess Pocahontas, a fact Martha accepted as truth whenever she gazed at his black hair, black eyes, and rich complexion. These things made him stand out, yes, but that first day the scowl drew Martha as much as the rest, for it allowed her to relax her own face at last, there being no need to smile in answer to it.

There were others in the crowded parlor the day the Randolphs appeared, including family favorite James Madison, who at five feet six inches tall should have appeared comical next to the six-foot-two Thomas Jefferson but somehow never did. Madison caught Martha's eye and flushed—in his late thirties and still with the look of a child, with wide eyes and delicate chin, he'd been briefly engaged to a fifteen-year-old who'd left him for another, leaving him blushing at the sight of every young woman since. Martha tipped her head in a half curtsey, but her mind had already flitted to the real problem Madison presented—the Randolphs, father and son, had come all the way from Richmond and were naturally expecting to stay the night; add Madison and the fact that all their possessions hadn't yet arrived from France, and Martha would have to scrounge linens from the servants.

Fixed on her escape, Martha didn't see or hear a strange woman approach until she was enveloped in her arms, but the woman soon broke away to gaze at Martha. "Why, child, how fine you look! Paris has made you an elegant lady, and all quite behind my back. You must tell me all I need to know of you, everything I've missed." But before Martha could struggle to meet such an unmeetable demand, the woman gripped her again, this time by the shoulders, and turned her around to face her father. "Will you look at him! How he revives all around him! Tell me, child, what is it in him that immediately steals one's heart? Is it his manner? His voice? His countenance?"

Another unanswerable demand, but thankfully, of a type that Martha had learned to dodge with grace. "'Tis *his* heart," she said. "But now you make me look about, I see I've neglected the carafes. Excuse me, please, I must see to them at once." She broke away, in truth to chase out a servant to sort Madison's linens, and found herself nose to nose with Tom Randolph's scowl instead.

Like Martha, Tom Randolph was fresh from abroad, having been at school in Edinburgh, a fact Martha knew because Tom had written to her father in Paris for advice on his course of study. Martha needed little more information than that in order to set this one guest at ease, at least. "How lovely to find you home," she said. "Are you finished with your course?"

But Randolph's scowl only deepened. "I returned with my brother when my father called him back. I've decided to read law."

Yes, Martha remembered now—a rumor of financial difficulties that had caused the father to withdraw the younger son from school, the elder son deciding to postpone his studies and come home to work and do his part. Martha studied Tom's scowl a bit longer and thought she could see something familiar in it, something that went beyond disappointed hopes—was he wondering what to do with Edinburgh now that he was back, just as she was wondering what to do with Paris, when so few around them could begin to understand the experience?

"Tell me of Scotland," she said.

Yes, she was right—the scowl disappeared and such eagerness spread across Tom Randolph's features that Martha anticipated a longer delay than she could afford before getting to the matter of the sheets. But there Tom Randolph astonished her by shifting the talk from him to her.

"No, you must tell me first of Paris. What struck you the most? What will you miss the most? What the least?"

"The people," Martha answered at once, as if she'd long thought the question out. "And that also answers the second: the people. But for the third I must say I shall not miss the decadence, the filth. And yet everything around it so lovely! Paris was another world. But I believe I only realized how remarkable it was when I came away from it."

"How extraordinary you should say that. Those were my own words when I first returned from Edinburgh."

"Which is of course the usefulness of travel, is it not? To discover things undiscoverable at home, yet to reclaim an appreciation of our home once we get back."

Tom Randolph looked around. "To return to a home such as this, a family such as this—" He began to peer at her in a silence so intense Martha felt compelled to break it before it became an embarrassment. "I should like to talk more, but at this minute—"

In an instant the lively, engaged Tom Randolph faded. "You have more important tasks to occupy you. As do I. I've yet to pay my duty to your father."

He moved away so quickly he left Martha standing like a startled horse temporarily set back on its heels. She recovered and went in search of the servants only to find them well prepared for both Randolphs and Madison with linens, firewood, and candles. Martha returned to the parlor and found the carafes had been replenished and the sconces lit, leaving her nothing to do but glide from visitor to visitor and try not to watch her father and Tom Randolph engage in what appeared to be animated talk. *As do I.* Martha chose not to hear the offense in that remark but to take it as a case of wounded pride—after all, she knew something of that.

Her father's secretary, William Short, had stayed with the Jeffersons on and off throughout their Paris tour, and for most of the previous summer Short and Martha had seen each other daily. That she should fall in love with the popular secretary with the somber brown eyes and nimble mouth seemed as inevitable as the Paris mud; that he appeared to return the affection seemed at first miraculous and later tragic, when Martha's father asked for a six-month leave to return his daughters to America and the care and instruction of their aunt. "You're a young woman now," he said. "You must be educated in the duties of your own culture." What he meant, of course, was that she was now of marriageable age, and he wanted her away from the looseness of Paris life.

When Martha told Short, he cried out, "Your father told me he would be back in six months! He arranged a wonderful position for me here! He said nothing of leaving you behind for good! No, no, no, you must give me time to sort my affairs. Mrs. Fortier adores you; she has extra rooms. You must ask if you might stay with her till I've arranged my affairs."

It all came out in such a hot rush, Short dashed out so abruptly after he said it, that Martha sat in some confusion over what he'd actually said. *Had* it been a proposal of marriage? What affairs must he sort? How long would the sorting take? Martha knew and liked Mrs. Fortier well enough, but she did have French ways to which Martha would have to adapt, and then, of course, if she were to live for years in France . . . Martha thought of her father, and of Monticello.

When Martha's father called her to his study, his face looked the color of paste. "Mr. Short has spoken to me. I have no specific reason to distrust him, but I can feel no joy in this plan of his. I wish to do nothing to diminish your happiness—mine must not enter into the case—but I would feel remiss were I not to tell you that I foresee several conditions that might make my stay in America considerably longer. To part from you for six months is a small enough grief, although one I would never choose to experience. To part from you longer is something I can't bear to contemplate. And should something unforeseeable occur—poor health, financial responsibilities, changed political obligations, something that would keep me from returning to France at all—"

Martha left her father in a distressed state. He might not want her to weigh his own unhappiness but even so he might as well have drawn it out in ink, so clearly could she now see him roaming Monticello in his loneliness and grief. It had been true what Ursula had told Martha at her mother's deathbed: Martha's father had promised his dying wife never to marry again, as she wanted no stepmother ruling her children as harshly as she'd been ruled. How ungrateful of Martha to abandon him now! And what did he mean, *no specific reason to distrust* William Short? Of course Martha loved William, but what in fact did she know of him? Should she even trust a man who would ask her to make such a decision so fast, who hadn't even waited for her to answer, who would without qualm put an ocean between her father and herself?

When Martha told Short of her decision to return to America, she said nothing of her lack of trust in him but spoke at length of her father's loneliness and grief. She was startled when Short barked out a humorless laugh.

"I suggest you look around you. Perhaps your father grieves less than you think."

"You can't know because you didn't see him. He was rendered insensible at the loss of my mother. He needs me by him. He went pale as death when I spoke of staying behind in France."

"Of course he did. I love no man as I love your father, and yet I've loved you more for refusing to contain your life to suit his. And now you would entomb yourself in his mountain crypt."

There Short chose to say no more. Even now, Martha could make a long list of all the things he could have chosen to say, but instead he'd left the Hôtel de Langeac and had not returned to it. Martha had sent a letter just before she left, urging him to visit America soon, but Short never wrote back. And so Martha had packed up her pride and her French way of thinking and left with her father, sister, and two Hemingses for a life that, along with her old shoes and gloves, no longer quite fit.

*CHAPTER 3*

———

MARTHA HAD DECRIED THE DECADENCE and filth of Paris to Tom Randolph, but in truth, there was something as decadent about Monticello, although in a different way—the slower pace of life, perhaps, or the way her father's French wines and more elaborate French furniture, just now beginning to arrive from France, seemed out of place. And the Negroes. They crept about in an unnerving, pantherlike silence that Martha hadn't noticed before she left for France. What did they hear as they moved about? And why hadn't Martha ever before wondered about that? Martha puzzled over what seemed such a great change, either in her or in life at Monticello, she truly didn't know which. She asked Maria, pointing as Sally's sister Critta whispered out of the room after stirring up the fire, "Were they always so quiet?"

"Why shouldn't they be quiet? Ursula just hushed *me* so I wouldn't disturb Papa and Mr. Madison in their talk. Do you ever wonder what they talk of, so long into the night?"

Martha knew what they talked of—Madison's efforts to get the Bill of Rights added to the new Constitution, her father's upcoming appointment, the next year's crops—only a few passes by the library door had gleaned that much. She picked up the bell to ring for Critta as the fire was still throwing off very little heat, but changed her mind and got up to stab at the logs herself.

———

TWO WEEKS AFTER THE RANDOLPHS' DEPARTURE, Martha was standing in her room in her usual pose, hand against the window frame, gazing out at the clouds that draped her beloved mountains, when a rider burst into view on the roundabout. He was too far away for her to recognize him, but a certain rashness in style made her think of Sally's brother James Hemings and how he dared to ride so only when her father was unable to observe his approach. As mistress of the house now, Martha should speak to him—whatever mission he was on didn't give him leave to dash up the mountain in such a way that it strained the horse—but since their return from France there was something new in James that didn't encourage being spoken to. In France Martha had begun to take more notice of James, no doubt because he was the only male Negro occupying her father's house. There were no unhandsome Hemingses, but Martha had decided that James was handsomer than most, and under her surreptitious glance he'd seemed to grow bigger and stronger each day, to hold his chin higher, to meet her eye with new boldness. Back at Monticello among the other slaves his impact on Martha had lessened, but he continued to meet her eye in the same way he had in France. In France Martha had learned to simply give James a steady look back, but to look was one thing, to speak was something else.

As the rider drew closer, Martha detected a complexion only just darker than white and grew surer of James, but as he entered the first roundabout she began to doubt. This man was a fine rider, tall and straight in the saddle but never straight enough to disconnect from the movement of his horse—or rather, Thomas Jefferson's horse—and there was the problem: This was not Thomas Jefferson's horse. As he neared the house, the unknown rider slowed the animal to a walk; it fought the bit and danced sideways, but the rider expertly drew him in a small circle and spurred him into the corrected path; once man and beast were again in complete accord the man looked up, saw Martha in the window, and swept off his hat.

Tom Randolph.

The recognition gave Martha an uncomfortable jolt. Why? Because she'd thought at first that tall, straight, skillful rider was James? Or because she was so glad it was not? But was she glad it was Tom Randolph? She couldn't say that she was. He wasn't easy to talk to; he was thin skinned and perhaps even moody if his last visit could be taken as the usual case; she tried to remember the Tom Randolph of her youth, but the best she could recall was his habit of disappearing as often as he could. Martha didn't return Randolph's salute, but neither did she step back from the window until he'd disappeared from sight. She turned to her sister.

"Maria, 'tis our cousin Randolph. Come."

Maria, who'd taken advantage of her father's absence to lay aside Robert's *History of America* and pick up Eliza Haywood's *Love in Excess,* only shook their mother's auburn curls and turned her back. Martha should speak to Maria too, of course, but in her own small rebellion she left her sister to her reading and took the last few stairs with a single jump. The childish act called up another: a small Tom Randolph crying after a whipping he hadn't deserved—or so Martha had thought—then drying his face on his sleeve, dashing up a tree, and refusing to come down till after dark. When he did come down he got a second whipping, of course, but he bore that one dry eyed and defiant.

Remembering the young Tom Randolph brought Martha into the parlor smiling, which appeared to be all that was necessary to draw forth a like smile from her guest.

"I'm sorry to say my father is away from home until quite late," she said.

"I don't care. That is to say, of course I do care, but I'm only here to return the book he lent me at my last visit. And to thank him, of course. I'm staying in Charlottesville with my father and it was no great trip."

"Well then, let me carry your book and your thanks to him when he returns, and assure him of the very little trouble you took."

Even skin descended from Pocahontas could blush, and Martha instantly regretted the fresh remark, but Tom Randolph might have said he'd come in hope of seeing Martha, and she would have said a kinder thing in response. She considered and decided she might as well try out the kinder thing to see what it called up. "Must you rush back or can you stay for cider and perhaps just a few words about Scotland and Paris?"

"Oh, speak, then! Speak!"

Had anyone ever barked so gleeful a command at Martha? She thought not. She rang for a servant and began to speak. When Critta came in with a bowl of nuts and two glasses of cider, Martha fell silent, but once they were alone again she took it up, and word by word, sentence by sentence, eager question by eager question, Paris came back to life.

They'd only just begun on Scotland when Martha's father entered the room, Tom's eager leap to his feet putting the lie to his supposed disinterest in seeing his host. For a young man intent on studying law, any conversation with the author of the Declaration of American Independence must be counted a superior gift, but one of Thomas Jefferson's greatest conversational talents was to make it appear that the greater pleasure was always his. Martha kept her seat—and her silence—but more than once found her father's eye on her, which told her she must have looked excessively interested in their talk. How not? This was no worn-out sermon from older man to younger man, no parochial questioning from younger to older, but a mutual engagement on topics that interested Martha in their own right—the difference in climate between Scotland and Virginia, the level of education in their children, what the average Scotsman thought of American politics. When the talk began to drift into the corrugated ruts of the law, Martha excused herself, but at the door she turned to look again at the pair of tall, slender men standing before the fire like mismatched bookends, one dramatically fair, the other exotically dark. Just as she was about to turn away, her father uncrossed his arms and lifted a hand to stop her.

"Perhaps, Martha, you'd like to invite our young relation to dine."

Tom's scowl returned. "I thank you sincerely, but I'm afraid my father expects me to join him."

"That you honor your father over us is only to your credit, lad. Perhaps another time, and soon, I might hope."

Tom brightened. "Thank you, sir. As to whom I honor, obligation might demand it for the one, but inclination calls it toward the other. The great attention you paid me with your letters from France—"

Martha's father lifted his hand again, as if to wave away Tom's effusion, but halfway through the gesture he appeared to change his mind and dropped the hand onto Tom's shoulder instead; only Thomas Jefferson could make a single gesture serve for benediction and dismissal at once.

Tom gazed at the door through which his host had exited. "You can never be an hour in his company without something of the marvelous," he said.

Martha studied her cousin. How had she neglected to notice in the boy the seeds of the man's fine intellect?

## CHAPTER 4

AT THE END OF DECEMBER the Jeffersons traveled down the mountain and continued seventy miles east to Tuckahoe, the Randolph plantation just outside Richmond, to attend the wedding of Tom's seventeen-year-old sister, Judith. Judith and Martha being of an age, they'd maintained what Martha thought of as a diffident friendship, conducted mostly by letters that had managed to survive Martha's crossing the Atlantic. Allowing for the months-late responses to no longer current questions, Martha had still managed to piece together the chronology of Judith's courtship by her distant cousin Richard Randolph. Judith's mother hadn't approved of the entanglement of her sixteen-year-old daughter with a kinsman only eighteen years old himself, and Judith had enclosed a portion of her mother's lecture in one of her letters: *Any decision to wed is fraught with peril, but doubly so in the young. When the delirium of love is over, and reason re-ascends her throne, if they find no qualities to excite esteem and friendship, they must be wretched, and without a remedy.* Judith had answered Martha, and no doubt her mother, that the only wretchedness she could ever know would be a life without Richard. Martha, her head dancing with images of William Short, had answered Judith's letter with great empathy.

When Judith's mother had died the previous spring, the road to marriage had been cleared, as Judith's father hadn't shared his wife's objections. Arrangements for the property settlement were made and the date soon set. By chance the Jeffersons had arrived home from France in time to attend the wedding, which pleased Martha on two counts—she wished to share in her friend's joy, of course, but she also wished to see Tom Randolph.

Tom had now visited Monticello three times, and each additional time the sight of his dark, powerful form had an increasingly disturbing effect on her. In the throes of a middle-of-the-night debate with herself she couldn't account for her fascination with the man, beyond the common travel experience that set them apart together, and his openness—this face, at least, she need not struggle to read. But as the Jefferson carriage approached Tuckahoe and Tom rushed out to meet them, reaching first for Martha to help her down, she thought there might be a third reason for her fascination. She could not claim Tom suffered from the "delirium of love" that his mother had described to Judith, but she could claim to see in him an interest that appeared to at least match, if not surpass, her own. Martha had continued to struggle to push William Short out of her mind, but now, as Tom's smile blasted her, as solid arms lifted her, she realized she no longer needed to push against William Short at all.

Tuckahoe held a special place in Martha's father's heart, as he'd lived there as a boy, a fact which had always created an added draw for Martha, but the plantation itself was one of the finest in its county, and the Randolphs one of Virginia's oldest, most respected families. The house was built in the unusual shape of the letter *H,* and in season, at least while Tom's mother lived, it had sprouted some of the loveliest gardens in the area, framed by impeccably manicured, sweet-smelling boxwoods. Its famous walnut paneling and expansive carved staircase were talked of throughout the county, and on this occasion especially, fine carriage after fine carriage rolled up the drive to pay homage to the Randolph family. One entire wing of the house had been added strictly to accommodate visitors, but even so the house was packed to its seams, leaving

Martha to share a bed with Judith and her younger sister Nancy, while Maria shared with the two youngest girls.

As they prepared to sleep, Nancy's voice piped across the dark. "How does it feel, Judith, to be getting wed on the morrow? Does it feel like a dream?"

"It feels settled," Judith answered.

––––––––––

MARTHA SLEPT POORLY amid the unaccustomed creaks and sighs and ponderings and was one of the last to the dining room, catching only the tail end of the breakfast bustle; even so, Tom Randolph had lingered in wait for her, apparently intent on touring her about the property.

Tuckahoe was better tended than Monticello, but no river view could match the prospect from any direction at Monticello. Tom guided Martha to his favorite spots—the south terrace that was always first to warm in spring, the neat outbuilding where their fathers had attended school as boys, the view of the James River from the bluff. Martha had seen Tuckahoe before, of course, but this time, with Tom as guide, it felt laden with a new, unidentifiable emotion. They paused at the boxwoods. "My mother's favorite spot," Tom said with a hint of melancholy that Martha found contagious—at her last visit to Tuckahoe her mother had been with her—but more than absent parents filled the air around them. Something had begun to germinate in Martha during that latenight talk between the sisters, and here in the boxwoods with Tom Randolph it continued to grow; still, Martha couldn't name it.

Tom led Martha to the bluff overlooking the James River. He put his hands on her shoulders and turned her full circle. "All that you see will be mine someday," he said, and there Martha began to understand the sadness that had borne down on her since the previous night. She

and Judith had been young girls when Martha last visited Tuckahoe—
she could remember them racing over the lawn with the other children,
her mother hissing as she drew up, "For heaven's sake, Martha, will you
look where your hem is!" Martha had obediently pulled down her skirt
but had soon torn off again to charge down the bluff with the others.
This then was what she was grieving while Judith talked of marriage
and Tom talked of his future responsibilities: the end of her childhood.

"In truth I should prefer a smaller place," Tom said now. "Perhaps a hundred acres, just enough to provide for my family's needs,
without dependency on the Negroes. My intention is to spend the
majority of my time on the law and not on farming. I should like
to know what you think of such a plan."

The weight of the question so thrilled and alarmed Martha together that she couldn't answer. The river sped away below her, free
and strong; on impulse borne of old memories, she hitched up her
skirt and careered down the bluff toward the water, arms and legs
pinwheeling. She felt Tom's heavy descent behind her in the quiver
of the earth, felt her wild propulsion checked by his arms snagging
her waist and swinging her wide. She might have kept her feet;
Tom might surely have kept his; instead they gave way to the pull
that brought them to earth in a pile of limbs. Even then Martha
might have—should have—hurried to her feet, but instead she lay
there for just that instant, feeling the heat of Tom's body through
her clothes, the press of hard muscles and bones, and as the instant
drew out, the touch of surprisingly soft lips. She pulled back, but
already her viewpoint had changed, as if she could actually see the
last of her childhood whirling away in the froth of the river.

———————

MORE GLISTENING CARRIAGES ARRIVED, more pressed and pow-
dered people flowed through the doors to join the crush already

positioned in the parlor. At noon Judith and Richard took their places before the minister, Judith in new blue silk, Richard in fawn breeches and cinnamon jacket. Were there no unhandsome Randolphs either? The minister read from the Book of Common Prayer, although likely he had the passage well memorized: Marriage vows were not to be undertaken unadvisedly, lightly, or wantonly merely to satisfy men's carnal lusts and appetites, like brute beasts that have no understanding. Marriage was ordained first for the procreation of children; second as a remedy against sin and to avoid fornication; third for mutual society, help, and comfort both in prosperity and adversity.

Those principles assumed to be understood by all, Richard promised to love, comfort, honor, and keep Judith, forsaking all others, and Judith promised to obey, serve, love, honor, and keep Richard. Martha pondered those orders, aware of the distinction between them—that only Richard must comfort, that only Judith must obey and serve, but soon she found herself thinking not of Judith and Richard but of her parents. As her mother lay dying, it was her husband who fetched her books and her shawl for her, her husband who fed her and bathed her forehead; he never said *I needn't obey, I needn't serve*—he'd done those things because he'd loved her. Honored her. Pondering the semantics, Martha missed the minister's declaration that the couple was now man and wife and only realized that the task was done when the guests began to applaud. Martha studied Judith's face to see if she could detect a change in her and believed that indeed, Judith had found her own best word the night before: she looked settled.

The feast presented that day gave no hint of the Randolphs' rumored financial distresses. Roasted chicken, beef, venison, pork, mutton, ham, duck, goose, rabbit, pheasant, partridge, and quail loaded the tables, with eels, oysters, pies, custards, and puddings interspersed between. Wine, ale, punch, and cordials were poured, downed, and poured again; only when the guests' intake began to slow were the tables cleared away for dancing.

Tom was a fine dancer. Martha wasn't. Her limbs had grown too long too young before she'd learned the proper method for controlling them, and yet when Tom called her a jack rabbit, she laughed, liking the description. She hopped merrily up and down until she spied her father, her tall, stately father, standing against the wall talking with one of the court justices from Richmond as he watched her dance. Her step faltered, but by then it was time to stop anyway—Judith and Richard were preparing to depart in their carriage, and the gentlemen were swarming outside to fire their pistols in the air to mark the celebration. Martha noted that her father chose not to break away from his discussion. He spied Martha and smiled; she'd just returned that smile when Tom came in from firing his pistol, and when their eyes met, he beamed at her. When Martha's father smiled at her she felt loved; when Tom smiled at her she felt lovely.

MARTHA'S HORSEBACK RIDES with her father ceased. He had much to do, first in settling Monticello's affairs after five years in France, and next in preparing for his move to the capital at New York. Then there were the conferences with those influential men in Virginia politics and numerous letters to be written to those at a greater distance. With a large portion of what little time remained he continued to do as he'd taken to doing in Paris, declaring his chamber and cabinet as inviolable private space and retiring behind their doors into solitude and quiet. Little wonder that an imposed emotional distance began to grow between father and daughter even before the physical distance should demand it.

Maria barely seemed to notice, occupying herself well and happily in her preparations for Eppington. Martha couldn't seem to begin on the task, weighed down by a lassitude the cause of which she understood well enough; how much easier to plan and pack for a welcome event than an unwelcome one! She wandered about the house refamiliarizing herself with all its corners, poking into the servants' doings in an effort to master the workings of the household, refusing to admit that soon enough none of those efforts would matter to anyone.

Tom Randolph wrote soon after the wedding. *I must see you. Answer agreeably to this suggestion and I shall find my way there.* Martha had just settled herself at the table in the small parlor and begun a reply that any mother should approve: *My father and sister and I are happy to welcome you to Monticello at any time,* when Sally Hemings came into the room unsummoned. She appeared startled to see

Martha and paused at the door, silhouetted against the light, drawing from Martha once again the unwelcome thought: *how like my mother.*

"What is it, Sally?"

"Your father sent me for his book. He thought he left it here."

Martha looked around. "Yes, 'tis there, on the mantel."

Sally crossed the room, pulling her skirt clear of the hearth as she collected the book; Martha looked and looked again—with Sally's skirt still drawn back tight against her legs, Martha could clearly see that the slave was pregnant. The sight of a pregnant slave was common enough and no cause for distress, but this sight did distress Martha. Why? It would be Sally's first, and perhaps that was the significant factor, signaling as it did another generation about to be trapped in a lifetime of bondage. Sally was Martha's age, and that too could be a factor—one more piece of evidence that Martha's childhood was indeed behind her. But no, there was something new in Sally, and as Martha stared she began to understand that this change in the slave wasn't new, that today only indicated a change in degree but not of fact—the original change had begun in Paris.

Near the end of their stay, Martha's father had taken his daughters from the convent school where they'd been boarding and brought them to live with him at his home at the Hôtel de Langeac, the move prompted by Martha's announcement that she would like to join the convent. Martha's father never argued the matter with her, he simply removed her, and never again discussed the subject; this was her father's way. Along with the move came a flurry of new dresses and accessories that Martha supposed were intended to distract her, but in truth life at the Hôtel de Langeac had served as sufficient distraction already. There Martha saw her father's talents at work nightly instead of weekly; there she learned to sit at a table and converse with Paris's most influential ladies and gentlemen; there she saw enough of William Short to understand all she'd been reading in school—in four different languages—about love. And there she saw a new Sally Hemings, grown older and lovelier as if overnight, gliding over the polished floors with the kind of confidence Martha had never seen in her before, as if she'd woken up one morning and realized how beautiful she was and how polished she'd become, or, Martha thought in a kind of epiphany, that she could be free in France. Yes, it had begun there in France, just as it had with James, in a look a slave seldom gave a master—a look of new-discovered power. Martha had grown up with Sally. They'd played together and learned to sew together and even kept each other company when they were sick, but Martha would gladly have seen her stay behind—free—in Paris.

Yet Sally had chosen to come home to her enslavement.

Pregnant.

*Perhaps your father grieves less than you think.* A slow flush crept up from Martha's chest, along her neck and across her cheeks. "Do stir the fire for me while you're here," she told Sally, but the girl hesitated. Hesitated! After a time she did drop her skirt, take up the poker, and give the fire a half-hearted nudge before sweeping out of the room, her master's book clutched in her hand.

Martha returned to her letter and tried to focus on her last thought before Sally had interrupted her. *My father and sister and I* . . . Ah, yes, her mother-approved letter, but her mother was dead, and her father and sister and she were to leave Monticello in March. Martha folded the letter and sailed it into the fire, taking up a clean sheet. *Come,* she wrote. She paused, taking a deep breath to expel the excess heat that continued to inflame her skin, but the exercise accomplished nothing. Sally. Pregnant. And pregnant enough that it must have begun in France. Martha collected her pen and began to write. *If you act solely to please me,* she added, *come as soon as you are able.*

Two days later Martha learned that Sally's household duties had been reduced to care of her father's chamber and wardrobe only, that she'd been moved out of the Hemings house on Mulberry Row and into the small room under the stairs, the only Negro so accommodated in the main dwelling.

———————

TOM ARRIVED THE FOLLOWING WEEK. As Martha watched him dismount his horse, she marveled that she'd ever mistaken the elegance of his form for another, that she'd ever thought him a scowling, unpleasant creature. Her father seemed to think him a fine enough fellow too, for he made considerable effort to keep in his company despite the demands of his schedule, in fact leaving Martha less time alone with their guest than she'd hoped. It began to press on her, this lack of time, this advance of time, this idea that all was slipping away from her; Tom had arrived bubbling over in what seemed a like impatience to be alone with her, but even so, he'd been eager enough to linger with her father, where much advice was given and taken, many books recommended and reviewed, even pored over page by page, judging by the amount of time they spent above-stairs in the library.

This should only please Martha, both in the specific and the general—first at finding her father and Tom so in tune, second at the idea of an aspiring young lawyer being mentored by so fine a mind as her father's—but over dinner she found her emotions oddly somersaulting. She took her usual care to add her voice to the conversation in such a way as to be considered augmentation instead of distraction, but a second voice kept harping at her with its own distraction: What was it all in aid of? What conversation would she find at the Eppes table worth either augmenting or distracting? The recent lay of the hens. The size of the cucumbers. The heat. The rain. The drought.

Martha came out of her private conversation to find her father gazing at her with a particular look that she *had* learned to read—

one that signaled an abrupt change in thought direction. But Martha had a thought of her own, and suddenly it seemed of the greatest importance that she use this moment to air it.

"At Tuckahoe, Tom talked to me of an idea for a small plantation he might run without such dependency on the Negroes. It draws me to think he should like to hear of your plan to establish free tenant farmers here at Monticello."

Martha's father studied Tom for some time before he spoke. "We must all make effort to ameliorate the condition of those in our care." He pushed back his chair. "And now I must say good night. I have three letters to write before I sleep. Martha, our guest's glass is empty, but I believe he might enjoy his wine in greater comfort in the parlor. Maria, I'm quite sure you'll find your greater comfort in your bed—I've seen you yawn twice within the last half hour."

And so the household was arranged, as was the usual case, to the exact specification of Martha's father, but as was also the usual case, in such a way that it displeased no one, not even Maria, who was still too young to find a young man's company as agreeable as a book.

As soon as they were alone in the parlor, Tom clasped Martha by both hands. "'Tis so lovely to see you. I feared you'd escape to Eppington before we had another chance to meet."

"We don't leave till March."

"March! Good God! What is March? Two months, no more. We must make haste. Quick, then, tell me how you miss Paris, or don't miss Paris, or love Virginia, or hate Virginia, or miss me, or don't miss me, or perhaps, dare I say, think of me, as I do you, each night and morning?"

Martha pulled her hands free, already damp with Tom's impetuosity. "I love Virginia."

That a face could travel so quickly from alive to dead dismayed her. That her hands remained damp even after she removed them from Tom's dismayed her. She stood and shifted away from the fire but turned and saw Tom standing so forlornly in the middle of the carpet that she found herself taking a large step closer, and even so little a thing lightened him. What power was this in her? "I have thought of you, indeed," she said. "If I hadn't, how could I have written so bold a letter? Or do you forget my letter already?"

"I forget nothing. I trust nothing put in letters. Perhaps you wrote on the impulse of the moment and regretted it every day thereafter. Perhaps you meant it for some other man and mixed up the direction. Perhaps you intended only to tease me."

"To tease you! You could think such a thing of my nature?"

Tom closed the distance another foot between them. "Tell me, then. Am I the only one who feels he's found a friend?"

"No."

"Or more than a friend?"

"No." Oh, who was this wild creature? What was it in her, or him, that made her speak so? And who was it who closed the last foot of carpet between them? It didn't matter. There they were again, just as they were that day on the river, connecting flesh to flesh and mouth to mouth, the mix of hard and soft in him still a wonder. She should step away, she knew she should step away, but indeed, what matter if one of the servants walked in and saw them standing so? Already Martha was relearning the knack of seeing black eyes as blind and black ears as deaf. And besides, the will to step away from Tom had by now escaped her, despite the fact that her wits hadn't entirely quit her. Time, she thought. This is the fault of time, which only telescoped March nearer and nearer, while through the other end Paris—and William Short—grew smaller and smaller.

———

TOM STAYED ON THE MOUNTAIN SIX DAYS, dividing his time in near equal measure between Martha and her father. After three days

Martha's father began to join them after dinner in the parlor, which expanded the range of the conversation but truncated their growing intimacy—her father's intention, surely. To compensate, they took to touring the plantation together during the day, beginning, at Tom's request, with his host's latest innovation: new, smaller slave cabins, designed for individual families, that would replace the larger communal quarters. Martha took Tom to a cabin on Mulberry Row where some of the Hemingses lived; Tom looked over the bare walls, tiny window, dirt floor, lone bed with white counterpane, small table, hearth that held a single pot stewing a chicken carcass, the rectangular hole dug into the earth to store the vegetables they grew for their own larder. Pegs on the walls held a straw hat and a man's shirt; four crockery plates, a tin box, and two jugs sat on the mantel.

"Far superior to ours," Tom exclaimed.

Even so, as they entered Monticello Martha felt a French unease at the contrast that greeted them: light, air, space, and smells from at least a dozen different concoctions luring them to the dinner table.

---

THE NEXT DAY THEY RODE OUT ON HORSEBACK, taking Martha's favorite path through a swath of loblolly pines toward the spring, the pines more commanding than ever, no longer overshadowed by their bright-leaved deciduous neighbors. They slid from saddle to ground where they stood side by side, Tom's arm tight around her. Below them, out of sight beyond the pines, lay Shadwell, her father's birthplace, now one of his quarter plantations, but Tom was pointing north of it.

"Three miles hence—there—do you see it? There lies my father's Edgehill plantation. Sixteen hundred acres. Were it but a hundred—"

"Without dependency on the Negroes," Martha said, finishing Tom's old thought aloud.

Tom removed his arm and swung to face Martha so abruptly

she took a stagger-step backward. He grasped her by her shoulders. "Martha. I must have it settled before I go. Please tell me that you agree with me, that we would make a fine husband and wife. Need I argue my case before you, or is your understanding what I think it is, your feeling what mine hopes it to be? We're alike, you and I. Together, we would go forward a greater sum than our parts. Why, already I can't bear the thought of leaving you tomorrow, of going deeper into my life without you by me. How terrified that idea makes me! Tell me. Are we in accord? We'll find us a small place nearby, I'll go hard at the law; I have such ideas of how I might be of use to my country—never, of course, so great a use as your father, but use enough to make the both of you proud of me. Say this plan suits you, say I suit you, and I'll speak to your father this evening."

Martha heard the whole of Tom's speech as if it were a song, but with certain words coming louder to give weight to certain lines: *Settled. Agree. Alike.* She could subscribe to each of those words alone and together . . . Yes, there was another word: *Together.* Only hearing the word now did she realize how *not* together she'd begun to feel since her return from Paris. Until this past week. Until Tom. They *were* alike. They did agree. And to be settled instead of cast adrift, yes, her understanding and her feeling could unite behind each of those words. But what of that other word, *terrified,* and the permanence of an act "without a remedy," as Judith's mother had cautioned? It hadn't terrified Judith, and yet it caused Martha to long, again, for her own mother's advice, a mother who had been so cherished in her marriage that her husband had never recovered from the loss of her. But there—Martha did have her father, a father always sure of the proper course for her, a father ready to protect her happiness even above his own. This, then, was all Martha need answer. "Speak to my father."

———————

## CHAPTER 6

CRITTA WENT UP THE STAIRS AND DOWN, back and forth between the men talking in the library and the sisters sewing in the parlor. As she hurried down the stairs Martha looked hard at her, hoping to discern in the woman's features some idea of how the talk was going above-stairs, but she could detect nothing readable. Critta was considered married to a free Negro farmer whom she visited every Saturday night and Sunday, but of course no slave marriage was in fact legal. For a moment Martha pondered the advantage to the system—the built in "remedy" that had eluded Judith's mother—but when Tom appeared, beaming, Martha forgot Critta altogether.

"Your father wishes to speak with you," Tom said.

———————

MARTHA'S FATHER SAT in his usual odd, slouching position, shoulders against the chair back, knees higher than his hips, shirt-sleeves rolled up, corded forearms draped over the chair's arms, books littering the floor. He smiled at her as of old, but early in her childhood Martha had learned that her father's smile was never the whole story told. He'd once smiled when he caught her playing with the puppies instead of practicing her French, but then came the letter:

> *With respect to the distribution of your time the following is what I should approve:*

*From 8 to 10 o'clock practise music.*

*From 10 to 1 dance one day and draw another.*

*From 1 to 2 draw on the day you dance, and write a letter the next day.*

*From 3 to 4 read French.*

*From 4 to 5 exercise yourself in music.*

*From 5 till bedtime read English, write, etc.*


And if for a minute Martha might have fooled herself into thinking little was at stake, out had rolled the terrifying conclusion: *If you love me then, strive to acquire those accomplishments which I have put in your power, and which will go far towards ensuring you the warmest love of your affectionate father.*

Now, Martha's father leaned forward with an eagerness that first touched and then alarmed her as he launched with uncharacteristic abruptness into the subject she'd expected them to arrive at more tentatively.

"As I suspect you know, young Randolph has spoken to me this evening on the subject of marriage."

Martha nodded.

"I anticipated such a thing but didn't like to express my opinion, preferring to leave it to the pair of you to determine. Now, however, I feel comfortable in saying that Tom Randolph would have been my first choice. Indeed, I couldn't be more pleased to find my daughter so happily settled."

*Settled.* Judith Randolph's word. But how quickly, how easily her father had come to it! She looked at him again and saw that he'd allowed her to see his mind as he so rarely did, that he was more than eager, that he could only be called light with relief, that he smiled on her with real joy; this was not the somber pro and con discussion she'd predicted.

"I've paid close attention to the pair of you," he continued, "and I've observed a degree of feeling that would have caused me some anxiety if it hadn't led in such short order to a straightforward offer. There was another situation . . . but we need say nothing more of that. I may now leave for New York secure in the knowledge that you who, along with your sister, are dearer to me than any creatures on earth, will now be amicably disposed of. I need not fret over you in my absence." He paused, seeming at last to note something unmoored in her features. He took her hand. "Martha, child, the happiness of your life depends now on the continuing to please a single person. To this all other objects must be secondary, even your love of me, were it possible that that could ever be an obstacle."

"Oh, Papa." Martha dropped to the floor and laid her other hand on her father's knee. "Never can you come second, nor need you. Tom would ask no such thing of me. Indeed, his affection for you is only less than mine by its being newer."

Martha's father touched her cheek. "Neither of you can ever have a more faithful friend than myself, or one more willing to make sacrifices for you. Do only this for me, and cherish the affection of your husband." He paused, seemingly lost in some memories of his own. He broke out of it with a laugh. "Good God, I gave you nine chances in ten of marrying a blockhead! Now go to that lucky fellow and leave me to write my letter to his father."

———

THAT EVENING Martha's father left them alone in the parlor, but such was Tom's elation he could barely conjure words to address her. He pulled her into his arms, buried his face in her hair, and held her so tightly she couldn't have spoken if *she'd* been able to find words. She was just as glad Tom couldn't see her face either, as she didn't wish him to discover the sudden confusion in her. How fast it had all happened! How abruptly her life had altered! How *un*settled she felt!

––––––––––

Tom left monticello in such a mix of high and low spirits that he made Martha laugh, as he first reveled in his future prospects and next despaired at their parting, but as soon as his horse had vaulted out of sight, Martha sobered at the lack of him. It frightened her how abandoned she felt, how quickly she'd come to count on his attentions; with them so abruptly removed she felt only half a being. Her father had long before abandoned her, immersed in his preparations for New York; now Martha wandered about Monticello alone, rode out alone, once even traveled down the mountain as far as the Edgehill plantation, taking care to screen herself in the pines as she studied the lay of the place—overseer's cottage, slave quarters, barn, and acre upon acre of dormant fields, framed by the gray twist of the Rivanna River.

––––––––––

After tom left, Martha received her first letter from Judith, now settled in Cumberland County at another Randolph plantation called Bizarre. *Richard comes along,* Judith wrote. *He meets my every wish and dotes most handsomely.* Tom's first letter from Tuckahoe came soon after, informing Martha that his father planned to deed him his nine-hundred-acre Varina plantation, located in the lowland along the James River, twelve miles south of Tuckahoe, near Richmond. Along with the land came the forty Negroes residing there, the existing stock and farm utensils, and a twenty-nine-hundred-dollar mortgage. Tom explained that his father was eager to have his eldest son residing near him. Martha did a quick calculation based on her trip to Judith's wedding and concluded that Varina lay a three days' ride from Monticello.

Martha took the letter to her father where he sat in his library, a half dozen sealed letters piled at his left hand, at his right an unopened bottle of wine. He tapped the bottle with his quill.

"I write to Mr. Short to ask that he send us more of this fine wine from the Hermitage—you recall the Hermitage, just outside Paris?"

"I do, Papa." In fact, Martha and William Short had taken a clandestine journey there together. Had Martha flushed thinking of it? Her father paused, looking at her with more attention than seemed necessary. "Please send Mr. Short my regards," she said with new carelessness, as if it mattered little whether or not her regards were appended, and before her father could drop his gaze to his own letter, Martha handed across Tom's. Her father read it, frowning.

"Such a debt on so small a parcel will not be cleared soon." He looked up. "But all gifts need not be accepted. He does me the honor of respecting my advice. Perhaps if I wrote him—"

Martha nodded, the wash of relief swelling her throat and keeping her speechless.

———

AT THE END OF THE FOLLOWING WEEK, Martha's father summoned her to the library again. He waved a letter at her, written in a hand whose grace and clarity had already become intimately familiar. "The gift of Varina has been accepted," he said. "Tom didn't feel it was politic to refuse his father's offer." He set down Tom's letter and picked up another paper, written in an equally familiar hand, albeit a less graceful one since a wrist injury in Paris. "This document I've drafted passes to you the deed to one thousand acres at my Wingo plantation. The title to the six Negro families in residence there also passes to you. The property is tenanted, but the rents will now go to Tom, although none of these possessions can be sold without your permission. You understand my purpose?"

Martha did—her father didn't trust Tom to make a profit at Varina, and here was her security going forward—but more concerning were those six families of Negroes, doubling the number already passed into Tom's hands through Varina. And lying ninety miles to the south, even if they wished to evict the tenants and remove there, they would be no closer to Monticello. Martha could say nothing else, however, beyond, "I'm grateful, Papa."

---

MARTHA WROTE TO TOM, informing him of her father's gift. Tom answered Martha and her father in separate letters that arrived the same day; Martha's said only *I've written my duty to your father* and shifted to the subject of his great impatience to see her again.

Nothing more was said of one hundred acres without dependency on the Negroes.

---

THEY WERE MARRIED at the end of February 1790 in the parlor at Monticello. With none but the immediate family present, it little resembled the Tuckahoe affair, but Martha's ecru silk was Paris made, Tom wore a new suit of lead gray that expertly hugged his frame, and the wedding feast included many delicacies perfected by James in France: a ham in Calvados sauce; a capon stuffed with truffles, artichokes, and chestnuts; macaroni made with a machine brought home from Europe and baked with a Parmesan cheese sent by William Short; a beef round roasted with onions, carrots, bacon, thyme, and parsley; James's specialty of fried potatoes. All was followed by a tower of confections that included macaroons and meringues, accompanied by another special James concoction: vanilla ice cream wrapped in a still-warm puff of pastry. As for the wines, the Hermitage white began them, followed by a Montepulciano with the capon, Chambertin with the beef, and champagne with the sweets. No pistols were fired, but Martha's father's toast was one that she would long remember, reminding the young couple that while they held each other's love, respect, and trust they held all the earthly things that mattered. Was that rare moisture in his eyes for Martha or his own dead wife? It didn't matter. Martha took it and treasured it as hers. Even the elder Randolph's remark that the feast was "passable if one cared for sauce," didn't distress her, nor did Judith's absence, excused in a letter that arrived the day before the event, claiming an unnamed illness.

That night Maria was sent off to sleep with her Randolph cousin, and Critta helped Martha prepare for bed, tying the satin ribbon on her nightgown, pulling the fine cotton into soft folds, smoothing the sheet over her after she lay down. Critta left; Tom came in carrying a single candle which he courteously snuffed as soon as he'd caught his bearings. Martha heard the rustle of a man's heavy clothes settling to the floor, and Tom slipped in next to her in his nightshirt, collecting her to him. They lay still, pressed tight together, Martha trying to sort which heart was pounding hardest, or even which heart was hers. Tom moved first, but he moved in ways that were already familiar to her, his hand in her hair, his mouth on her mouth, until he moved in unfamiliar ways, lifting out her breast, dropping his mouth to it until something tugged at Martha deep in her womb. How odd, she thought, that her body should know what it wanted of this man before Martha quite knew it. She'd wanted things of William Short—vague yearnings that his touch had only exacerbated—but now she knew why he'd never kept on, although she'd made little effort to stop him; beyond a point—this point—there could be no turning. "Oh," she said, and "*oh,*" until she remembered Critta sleeping on a pallet in the hall and clamped her mouth closed.

Later, as she lay awake taking stock of new sensations in new places, thinking of how this new knowledge must forever change her, thoughts of Sally Hemings ambushed her—Sally, so changed in Paris. Sally, at Monticello, so pregnant.

And yet Sally was not changed. Sally was still a slave. Somehow, on her wedding night, Martha felt compelled to mark the difference.

———

THEY STAYED AT MONTICELLO until the new secretary of state left for New York, taking the first leg of their journey with him as far as Richmond, where Tom and Martha were to stop a fortnight with Tom's aunt and uncle. The wound caused by leaving the mountain throbbed, uncertain as it was when Martha would return to it; every bloodflower and lantana and oleander blossom tore at her as if full of thorns, but those marks were superficial compared to the great rent caused by the parting from her father. Martha had cried over her mother's death, of course, but she had never cried over her childhood cuts and bruises, or, in fact, over William Short's absent letters. She was not by nature the crying sort. But oh, how hard it was to leave her father! They'd never been separated by such a distance. Her father talked of a visit to Monticello in the fall, cheering Martha briefly until she remembered that she would be far off at Varina. She could douse her father in every admonition she knew regarding safe travel, healthy eating, and not overworking, but how was she to fulfill Ursula's order to comfort him in his loneliness when he was in New York and she was at

Varina? She hugged him long and watched him longer through the tears that now refused to stay contained despite her fiercest efforts; once her father had vanished from sight, she turned to find an anxious husband at her shoulder. Martha could see the effect of her tears on Tom, but she could do nothing to ease his concern; and it would appear he could think of no means to ease hers. Martha had hoped to have a private moment with her loss, but Tom seemed determined to keep by her; they stood tense and awkward side by side until Martha gave up and turned for the house.

---

M ARTHA WAS WELL FAMILIAR with the Virginia custom of newly married couples beginning their life together by visiting their relations, and she found Tom's relations as kind as she'd ever found her own, but she wished she could learn this role of wife without such a knowing audience. Additionally, Martha disliked Richmond, a city lacking the advantage of either of her two known worlds—the quiet of Monticello and the elegance of Paris. The carts and carriages and dust, the commotion around the docks, the improperly clad women hanging from tavern windows all disturbed her equilibrium, and, for some inexplicable reason, caused her to think—again—of William Short.

Martha was glad enough to leave Richmond and head for Eppington, where she and her sister were to stay with *her* aunt and uncle, while Tom readied the house at Varina. They passed field after field of fresh-turned earth, miles of timber forest, and the Appomattox River, winding beside them as if guiding them to the Eppington plantation. Aunt Eppes took Maria and Martha into her arms as any surrogate mother should, a hug that Maria could melt into but Martha could not; their uncle Eppes could be called nothing but kind, but he had no conversation beyond crops and weather and stock. Martha discovered her favorite time of the day was at its end, when she and Tom could escape behind their closed door to take comfort in each other. When Tom left for Varina, Martha found herself in tears again.

---

BUT AS THE WEEKS PASSED Varina began to seem farther and farther away, Tom more and more a stranger or a figure in a dream from which Martha had now begun to waken. She wrote her father: *I am much averse to this idea of Varina.* He answered: *Your new condition will call for an abundance of little sacrifices, but they will be greatly overpaid by the measure of affection they will secure to you.* Tom's first letter followed shortly after: *Already I am lost without you.*

By April the newspapers were full of the death of Thomas Jefferson's dear friend and mentor, Dr. Franklin. His accomplishments filled the newspapers and the conversation at the Eppes dinner table.

"Martha," her uncle said one night. "You came to know the great man in France. Have you no stories to tell us?"

A just-purchased young slave came through the dining room doors and began to collect the plates from the table. The night before, Martha had listened to her uncle complain of the boy's irksome tears when scolded, of his incessantly inquiring where his mother and sisters were, of his general inability to adapt to a new life at a new plantation. "I have many stories of Dr. Franklin in France," Martha said. "I prefer one from his return. He freed his two Negroes and was elected president of the Pennsylvania Society for the Abolition of Slavery."

The table fell silent.

---

IN EARLY MAY a letter arrived from the overseer at Monticello, accompanying some seeds Martha's uncle had requested. It included the Monticello news, which Martha's uncle read aloud to his nieces as they sat after dinner in the parlor: The corn was planted; the cherries were being harvested; the new peas had come to table. Martha's uncle paused, continued: Sally Hemings had been delivered of a boy she named Thomas.

That night Martha composed a new letter to Tom: *I've never known such loneliness. When may I join you?*

---

MONTICELLO HAD ITS SUMMER HEAT, but Eppington had more of it, hovering that much nearer the lowland. Maria didn't seem to mind, wrapped up in her cousins and reacquainting herself with her old life, a life clearly more real to her than the few years she'd spent at Monticello. Of one thing Martha was glad: She'd begun to suspect that she was to have a child, and to be near her aunt and sister as she contemplated this new situation was a comfort. Her mother had suffered greatly with the birth of each of her children, only two of six surviving, her mother sinking lower with each travail until with the birth of the final child she'd succumbed herself, and Martha couldn't help but fear a similar fate.

As Martha's situation became certain, Maria, too young to have connected her mother's death with the pending event, chittered on about her plans for the niece she was convinced Martha would bring her. "You must keep her here with us till she tumbles about like Nell's baby and makes us laugh. Till she calls me Aunt Maria. Till I've sewn a cap for her."

Aunt Eppes added her own wish that Martha keep near until safely delivered, and cheered her by adding, "You're not built like your mother. You're tall and strong. You'll not have the troubles that plagued her."

But at the end of June they received another letter from Monticello: Sally Hemings had lost her son, and Sally herself remained gravely ill since her confinement. On hearing this news, Martha's emotions began tumbling again—even as her heart could ache for Sally, something deep inside her, something shameful, eased; there would be no slave boy conceived in France named Thomas. But next came the old, uncomfortable acknowledgment that Sally and Martha's mother shared a common father, that Sally was, in fact if not in law, Martha's mother's half-sister and therefore Martha's aunt, that despite Aunt Eppes's claim, the family predilection for troubled pregnancies continued. Martha walked about Eppington cradling her womb, Maria trailing after, now and then sensing that Martha needed a hug and wrapping her arms around her. Martha began to think she was indeed glad to be where she was, to regret the letter she'd sent after her husband begging to join him.

## CHAPTER 7

---

Tom wrote to Martha's uncle, asking him to deliver Martha to Varina on his next trip to Richmond. When Martha's uncle read Tom's letter out loud, Maria burst into tears, causing Martha's eyes to dampen; the thought of parting from her sister now felt like tearing out one of her organs. As Martha packed for travel she continued to feel that alien well of tears and beat them back with determination, unwilling to have her stoic aunt observe such weakness in her. Never had she felt the lack of her mother so fiercely.

How fast their departure; how endless their journey! How far away Varina seemed from all Martha knew! She looked without interest as her uncle pointed here and there, already depressed by the utter flatness of the landscape and wetness in the air that made breathing more like drinking. The carriage finally turned off the road into a guttered track; Martha closed her eyes, a childish thing to do and not useful, as it allowed a vision of Monticello to imprint itself against her eyelids, a vision so real she believed she could feel the cool, spiced air. She opened her eyes on flat, brown earth; decayed fences; and half a dozen tiny, dilapidated buildings.

Tom came running from a low, squalid-looking outbuilding, jacket absent. By the time he reached the carriage, his shirt was transparent with sweat but Martha didn't care. As eagerly as he reached up she reached down, as thrilled with the smell of him as with the sight and touch, her relief in feeling such things providing her greatest comfort. How could she have begun to think of Tom as a stranger? How could she have forgotten how he came so alive at the sight of her? How could she have pictured herself alone at Varina when Tom would be with her? She'd once crossed an ocean to a country that spoke differently, dressed differently, ate differently, and she'd adapted to it as if she'd always lived there; she would not allow this little journey down a mountain to undo her.

"Here, Ned!" Tom called. One of the Negroes left picking up wood scraps and trotted over to help with the luggage. He was young, perhaps twelve, young enough that he actually smiled shyly at Martha, and out of that smile Martha found her own courage. She straightened herself and began to take better note of this new home of hers; she saw that a good portion of the rotted trim on the outbuildings had already been replaced, a new well had been dug, a kitchen garden had been set and new fencing surrounded it. On this second look she saw too that all was not brown earth—of course it was not—large swaths of it had been neatly hilled and each hill was now topped with the glossy green leaves of a flourishing tobacco plant. But she also saw what her father had managed to keep better hidden at Monticello: Negro men and women bent double in the fields, topping and priming the tobacco plants, the Negro children following behind picking over the leaves for worms.

Tom returned to collect her, the old scowl back as he followed her gaze over the fields. "There's much to do."

Martha took his arm, closing her other hand over it. "But what a great deal you've already accomplished."

Tom's scowl softened. "Come see your new house," he urged her.

———

OR HOUSES. A parlor and bedroom occupied one building, the kitchen and pantry the other. Tom walked Martha and her uncle over the rest of it, half proud, half nervous, but Martha pulled out her courage and admired it all—the overseer's cramped dwelling, the silent blacksmith's shop, the empty smokehouse, the unused dairy, the turkey trot, the barn. The threadlike branch of the James River flowed past but without any bluffs or breeze, the lowland beyond lying flat and still to the horizon.

After Martha had squeezed out every pleasant word she owned, they returned to the house, where the cook had set out a cold platter for their dinner. Martha's uncle left them soon after. Tom had brought a girl in from the fields to serve as Martha's maid, but Martha found it harder work to instruct the untrained slave than to shake out and hang her own clothing. When she'd dispensed with both clothes and girl, she tumbled into her bed, but as was always the case when she was most worn out, she lay awake. The sounds and the smells of Varina attacked her through the open window—a watery breeze, a distressed rabbit, the peaty smell of turned lowland earth so close and pungent she felt it would bury her.

Tom came in and slid under the sheet beside Martha; she remembered the feel of his skin, his long-muscled limbs, his gentle mouth—perhaps not as gentle as she'd remembered, but they'd been long apart, and indeed, her own eagerness overcame her in such a rush it shocked her. She'd heard of women shying away from this part of their marriage and was glad—quite glad—she needn't count herself among them. Afterward they lay and talked, Martha of her journey, Tom of the accomplishments and failures that seemed to have collected in equal number. Finally Martha's body overtook her mind—she gave up both speaking and listening, and fell into a deep sleep.

Martha woke startled by Tom's touch, struggling to come alive in harmony with him but too deep in her dreams to catch him; she'd only just begun to spark when he rolled away and began to list his cares for the day ahead. He needed to repair all the outbuildings before winter, he was behind on the tobacco, he had little cash. "It will be all right," Martha whispered low, for already she'd heard the field girl rustling about outside the door.

———

Martha's first full day almost defeated her. She could order neither the unfamiliar household nor the strange Negroes to her liking, not knowing what orders should be given. The field girl was clumsy in the house, the cook was unused to another woman lurking, and Martha couldn't find the smiling Ned anywhere. But that night Tom lifted her spirits by simply being glad of her, and the next morning she came upon Ned, filling the wood box in the kitchen, still smiling at her. She thought of her uncle's young slave; if this Ned could make something pleasant of *his* constricted life, shame on Martha for bemoaning her condition! By the end of the week she'd sent the field girl back to the fields and sorted her own linens and cupboards; she drew up and many times amended a pantry list, discovering that if she lingered in the kitchen pretending to count her utensils, Cook could teach her the kind of menu her husband favored.

———

Martha's father sent her a french cookbook, and cloth and patterns to make her servants new clothing; Martha tucked the cookbook away but set in at once to cut and sew the cloth. She wrote her father, knowing what he would wish to hear: *I would call myself content in all things were I but nearer you.* Yet she couldn't help adding: *I fear the climate here is quite unhealthful.*

Her father answered: *Nothing in my life could please me more than knowing you are content in yours.*

Martha's father also wrote to Tom, but Martha waited two days for Tom to share his letter with her. It appeared just as they were about to disrobe for bed, coming out of Tom's jacket pocket as if he'd forgotten its existence, but Martha already knew her husband better—he'd been pensive since its arrival. No, she must say the truth of it—he'd been worse than pensive, down to a place she would call morose. He waved the letter before Martha. "You might find an idea in here that will interest you."

She read, and as she read her heart began to climb upward in her chest. *I received a letter from your father in which he talks of selling his Edgehill property,* Martha's father wrote Tom. *Perhaps you might find the climate there more healthful. The cost of such a purchase might be offset with the profits from Varina.*

Martha refolded the letter. She didn't understand her father's statement that Varina could pay for Edgehill, since he'd once doubted Varina's ability to pay for Varina, but she thought it best to say nothing of that part of the letter. Edgehill was not Monticello, but oh, to lie only a few miles south of it! She might see Monticello perched atop its glorious mountain from the doorstep of Edgehill! She looked at Tom and saw he'd at once read her excitement, but he came far from matching it. Of course, she thought. Edgehill contained sixteen hundred acres. And how many Negroes?

"What of the smaller parcel you've talked of?" Martha asked. "Will your father sell you a lesser piece of it?"

"I have great doubt of it. Why make the remaining land less profitable, more difficult to sell? And I would then owe less, but I would owe it on a parcel too small to clear the debt at Varina."

"Could we not sell Varina?"

"And lose what little profit I now make?" He reclaimed the letter, returned it to his jacket, and said nothing further.

———————

As THE SUMMER and Martha's pregnancy advanced together, so did her growing unease over Tom's continued silence; where before she'd enjoyed the confidence that his most important thoughts were shared, now she felt equally confident they were not. In this she carried her own guilt; she looked out at the Varina Negroes bent over the tobacco plants and felt the shame of it but wouldn't speak of it to Tom; if they bought Edgehill from Tom's father, they would by necessity have to keep working the Varina and Wingo Negroes while adding even more. And yet she longed for her mountain. She wrote to Maria: *Please write and tell me how you fare, how fares Aunt and Uncle, what news comes your way of Monticello . . .*

Thinking again of Monticello called up thoughts of Sally. What had caused her child to die? Was it the same thing that had caused Sally to fall ill? Or had the boy died from some fault of Sally's, some lack of care or vigilance? This had been Sally's first child and she might have made some terrible mistake, such as leaving him unswaddled or overswaddled. Perhaps she'd had no milk, as Martha's mother had not, with no conveniently lactating Ursula to nurse her child for her. Martha pushed thoughts of Sally away.

———————

As THE SUMMER HEAT INTENSIFIED, Tom developed a galloping rash that tormented him through the night. Cook taught Martha to mix a balm of cucumber, chamomile, mallow, and clover; proud of this new accomplishment, Martha carried the salve to Tom where he sat outside, cooling himself and slapping away mosquitoes.

"I have something that might ease you," she said.

Tom batted her hand away. "There is nothing that can ease me. Leave me be."

———————

At the end of the month, Tom received a letter from his father. He read it, thrust it at Martha, got up, and kicked his bootjack across the room with such force that it put a deep gash in the door. Martha took the letter with less than steady fingers and read: *I write to share with you the great good news of my impending marriage to Colonel Harvie's daughter, Gabriella . . .* and Martha at once understood the violence inflicted on the bootjack. Gabriella Harvie was a year younger than Martha. A new wife was threat enough, but a new wife young enough to bear children might considerably dim Tom's expectations regarding his inheritance. Martha waited for Tom to say something of any of this, but he said nothing.

———————

Relief—of everything—came via a letter addressed to Tom from his father-in-law. This one Tom shared with Martha more promptly. *It appears I shall be able to leave here in the fall for a brief respite at Monticello. I plan to arrive around September the first and stay the month—nothing would suit me better than if you and my daughter could join me. Perhaps you might collect Maria on your way.* Martha read the letter and returned it to Tom without comment, but she could feel her heart erupting all over her face. Could Tom see it?

He could. He came to her and kissed the corner of her mouth. "I think we know where we shall be come September."

This time Martha did leap up and wrap herself around him. Tom continued, "Varina really doesn't agree with my health. This blasted rash and this incessant congestion. It will be curative for me to get into the finer air of Albemarle County." He paused. "Perhaps with a tobacco year as good as I've predicted, the extra debt of Edgehill could be managed."

"Yes," Martha answered, again willfully ignoring her doubts about their finances, but perhaps Tom was likewise doubtful. Martha woke in the night amid damp sheets bloodied from his scratching to find him standing at the window in the dark, staring out at the invisible fields of tobacco.

———

Martha kept on working through her days, growing more skilled at planning their meals, learning how to properly bleach their linens, adjusting to the cramped quarters, but it seemed each time she passed the window she would find Tom standing motionless at the edge of the field, staring at the Negroes as they worked their way back and forth, cutting the tobacco plants, laying them out to wilt in the sun. After a few hours of wilting, the plants would be hung in the tobacco house to cure for several weeks until the leaves turned the color of leather; next the leaves would be stripped from the stalks, bundled into "hands," and packed into barrels for shipment. Martha knew why Tom watched; there would be no Edgehill without a good crop, and in fact, until Tom was assured of a good harvest, there would be no trip to Monticello. Martha took to standing at the window watching Tom watch, imagining she could actually see the leaves begin to wilt under the fierce sun. She watched the Negroes move up and down the rows, bending and grasping, slashing and straightening, heaving and hauling under that same sun. She turned away from the window and went to the garden, where a Negro woman too old for the fields sat filling a basket with vegetables. Martha had learned from Ned that Tom's father had sold away the old woman's family but had been unable to sell her. Martha picked up the basket and carried it to the house.

---

## CHAPTER 8

THE TOBACCO WAS GOTTEN IN—A GOOD CROP. They set off for Monticello, traveling through hard brown fields shorn of their tobacco until the spring plantings; they left behind the mosquitoes, the damp, the earth smell, and arrived at Eppington to collect Maria. They stayed at Eppington only a single night, leaving in such haste that it provoked more than one look between aunt and uncle, and it was true that Martha's frenzy to get to her mountain cost her some of her politeness, but God's breath! She'd been polite for seventeen years—couldn't she be forgiven the occasional lapse?

From Eppington they climbed bit by bit into the dark green pines of the mountains, the ash and maple adding a softer palette, occasionally casting a stray gold leaf into their path. And the air! Here was the secret to the mountain air, Martha realized—cooler, yes, but that was only part of it—no damp! No weight! Martha reached over and gripped Maria's hand as they ascended the final roundabout; one last turn and Monticello burst through the trees, its simple lines and angles lovelier than the finest cathedral in Paris. Last winter Martha had been quick enough to spot the decay, but this time she saw none of it until Tom began to harp on its flaws.

"The cherry trees are winter killed. And where are the new fences your father talked of? And the road—'tis near impassable. He was to grade in August."

Martha listened without listening, leaning out the window to better study the forms gathering on the front steps, none of them the height of her father. Was he ill? She recognized Ursula first, and as the carriage drew closer, the Hemingses collecting behind her. She searched for Sally's petite form and long, straight hair, but couldn't find her either, causing Martha to wonder if the girl were still suffering from the birth—or death—of her son, but as soon as her father appeared Martha forgot Sally. She tumbled out of the carriage and rushed to her father, his strong arms enfolding her too briefly before necessarily moving on to Maria. She continued to fix her eyes on him and saw that he did indeed appear thinner than before, but this often happened to him while away, his problematic digestion suffering under the onslaught of haphazardly prepared food. As he stepped back from Maria to greet Tom, she also noticed the stretched look around the eyes that often preceded one of his periodical headaches.

"Father, are you well?"

"Only fatigued with concern for my family. But as you contribute to the cause, you also provide the cure. Such a bloom of health you present us!" He peered around her. "You carry no maid with you?"

"I have none."

"Then I shall lend you Molly while you're here. Come. Eat. Rest. Make it your home."

*Make* it your home? Was it not already her home?

Not anymore.

———

THE POINT WAS UNDERSCORED as Martha followed Molly, not to her old room but to the room that Martha had so often prepared for James Madison. *She* was the guest now. Her trunk had already been delivered and opened, and Molly set to work at once hanging Martha's clothes. But who *was* this Molly? Martha pondered and finally sorted: Molly's mother, Mary, a sister of Sally's, had been hired out to work for a Charlottesville merchant while the Jeffersons were in France. The sister had been allowed to take her daughter Molly with her; while there she bore two more children, rumored to be the merchant's, but last winter, on the Jeffersons' return from France, Mary and her now three children had been summoned back to Monticello.

Martha gazed at Molly as she stood with her back turned, still fussing at the clothes. The girl was young and stick straight, like Martha before her pregnancy rounded her, her hair cropped off above the shoulders and blown back from her face as if she stood on the bare peak of a mountain taller than Monticello. Her eyes were amber, her skin the color of an oiled oak floor, but beyond that Martha saw little of her aunt Sally in her. Martha refused to examine why this should please her.

———

Martha's first meal at Monticello marked another dramatic change from Varina. Her father had made arrangements with William Short to send him his favorite French wines and those cooking ingredients not found in America, and already James had covered the dinner table with salad in vinaigrette, oyster stew, blanquettes of veal, and chicken à la merengo. No traveler so nourished could fail to come to life again, and they sat at the table talking long, relaying all the important news that had seemed too trivial for letters, until Martha's father said, speaking to Tom, "I fear my daughters refuse to admit of their weariness," a signal Martha knew meant the men wished to talk alone.

The sisters retreated to their respective rooms, Maria to her old bed, Martha to what she continued to think of as James Madison's, but she was so tired she collapsed into it, remembering only a few deep breaths of cleansing air before falling asleep like a child.

She woke when Tom came into the bed; she reached out to touch his skin, still inflamed from the heat of Varina. "You talked long," she said. "It must have been a subject of great interest."

"We talked of Edgehill." Tom opened his arm and pulled Martha into him; she lay still, afraid of diverting Tom from his subject. *What* did they say of Edgehill? It seemed Martha waited a long time for Tom to resume. "Your father's talked to my father," Tom said at last. "My father has agreed to our purchasing the place for seventeen hundred dollars. He has business at the court in Charlottesville and will combine it with a visit to Monticello to settle the papers. Dear God, how tired I am."

Tired! And here Martha wanted to leap up and dance, her heart already bouncing around in her chest. But, "Sleep, then," she said.

Tom rolled away and slept, or so Martha thought—it took her some time to settle herself, but she did at last fall asleep, only to wake when Tom slipped out of bed and lit the candle on his desk. For a time Martha watched her husband as he sat writing, but when the candle had reached the stump end and he still didn't return to the bed she rose and went to him. She looked down at his paper, expecting to see a letter to his father, instead finding a blotted page drawn in columns, lined with sums. Two words headed the page: *Varina. Edgehill.*

She dropped a hand to his shoulder and felt the damp of it through his nightclothes. "What worries you most?" she asked.

"The Negroes. The debt."

"Does my father think—?"

"Your father thinks both things a temporary but necessary inconvenience." Tom barked out a laugh. "But to whom?" He set down his pen and stared at the empty wall before him. "Do you know the things your father has done, Martha? When he first came to the bar he sued—pro bono—for the freedom of a grandson of a white woman and a black slave, arguing that under the law of nature, all men are born free. The court refused to allow him to even make his argument. Next, not only did your father advocate for the emancipation of the slaves, he advocated for their enfranchisement. Did you know this, Martha? Their enfranchisement! In his first draft of his Declaration he called slavery *a cruel war against human nature itself,* but others in the Congress obliged him to delete the passage." Tom paused, breathed, the damp shirt under Martha's hand rising and falling with his effort. "And yesterday he showed me his figures calculating the greater long-term profit from child-bearing versus non-child-bearing Negroes."

Tom fell silent. Martha stayed so. What could be said to that? What could be said to any of it? Well, she knew one thing that could be said: *Leave Edgehill and its slaves to our fathers' generation. Turn your attention to the law. Let us manage at Varina.* Perhaps Martha might have said it if she hadn't just then recaptured a vision of Tom kicking the bootjack across the room, the gash it had left in the door. She recalled the sting as he batted away her hands and uttered those frozen words, *Leave me be.* She thought of Varina, so far away from those she loved and trusted, from a father who already spoke of retiring to Monticello as soon as he was able, a father who would certainly do something about the slaves as soon as he came home and had time to think longer on the matter.

She said nothing.

———

LIFE AT MONTICELLO MOVED ON, never static; work continued at converting the communal slave quarters to smaller cabins, the cabins nearest the house, in the shade of the Mulberry trees, reserved almost entirely for the Hemingses. Plans were laid out for a washhouse, two meat houses, a new stable. Whatever dreams

Martha had of leisurely horseback rides with her father were not to be, but Martha didn't mind as much as she might have, since soon she would be living at nearby Edgehill.

Sally had finally appeared, looking gray and thin, and consequently little was asked of her; indeed, it appeared to Martha that Sally came and went as she pleased, and even Martha's father, still too thin himself, seemed to now and again cast a worried eye over her. But Martha's greater concern was for her father, that worry he couldn't seem to hide now, the way his coat hung loose from his shoulders. No one could blame her for wishing to live nearer to him, to care for him as he'd cared for her. No one could blame her for wanting to be where she and Tom could keep watch over her father's treasured Monticello. Besides, the slaves were already here, whether or not they belonged to Tom or to another.

So Martha argued with herself in the darkness.

One night Martha woke in the middle of that dark and found Tom again at his desk, this time indeed writing to his father. Martha rose and went to him just as Tom scooped up the letter and waved it in the air as if to dry it, but not before Martha's eye had picked out a single short sentence that bore her name: *I do this only to gratify Martha.*

———

Tom's father arrived at Monticello in fine humor. He greeted his son with a firm grip on both shoulders, as close as Martha had ever seen him come to an act of affection; he greeted Martha and Maria each with a kiss and her father with a handshake that lingered as he spoke. "You're looking well, my old friend. But then, you always do when you're up here on your mountain."

Indeed, Martha realized, her father looked far better than he had in recent days, likely fully recovered now from the strain of his travel. In fact, they all looked better—Tom, Martha, Maria, even Sally. For all but Sally the mountain could be credited with the cure, as the senior Randolph claimed, but for Sally it could only be the passage of additional time since the birth and death of her child, or perhaps the lightened work assignment. She still appeared seldom, and when she did she managed to find excuses for any work that was asked of her; in truth, Martha was the only one who appeared to ask it.

"Sally, would you find Molly for me, please."

"At this moment your father summons me to change the buttons on his jacket."

"Sally, this basket of linens needs to go above-stairs."

"Critta comes now to fetch it."

"Sally, the wick on my lamp needs trimming."

"Shall I ring the bell?"

Martha's father being present at this last, he chimed in with, "Yes, Sally, both our lamps need trimming. Ring the bell, would you?"

Martha chose not to ask a fourth thing, in part because she was still trying to decide—or not decide—why her father would summon Critta to trim a pair of lamps instead of Sally.

———————

THE ELDER RANDOLPH HAD PLANNED TO STAY at Monticello four nights, but on the second night raised voices burst through the doors of the library. When Martha heard the first voice, she thought it her father-in-law; she only realized it was Tom after she caught more of the words.

"Two thousand dollars! You raise your price to two thousand dollars now? To your *son*?"

"And what kind of son will you be to me off in these mountains? Harvie offers two thousand and you'll pay two thousand or it goes to Harvie. Indeed, I decide it now; it goes to Harvie."

Thomas Jefferson's lower-pitched voice interjected between them, the words indistinguishable, its effect to dampen the volume of Tom's answer, but little else—Tom stormed out of the library soon after.

Tom's father left Monticello that evening.

———

THEIR TIME AT MONTICELLO DISSOLVED TOO FAST; again, the secretary of state prepared for his return, this time to the new capital at Philadelphia, Maria for her return to Eppington, Tom and Martha for their return to Varina. "What a skimpy thing a month is," Martha said one night at dinner. No one answered her, but Martha observed her father making a quiet study of her. Later that night he called Tom into his library.

Martha lay awake as she waited for Tom, listening to the sounds that had lulled her to sleep throughout her childhood: the tick of the clock, the *shoosh* of the wind in the pines, the nighttime chatter of the mockingbirds. Tom came in carrying an oil lantern so blazing it smoked the chimney and livened the room to its farthest corner. He smelled of spirits, more so than he usually did after a meeting with her father. He set the lantern down and pulled off his clothes piece by piece—shoes, jacket, shirt, breeches, stockings— for one brief moment the whole, ropy length of him gleamed white against the shadows thrown by the lantern, but as his nightshirt descended it was as if a giant hand had snuffed him out. He came to the bed but didn't extinguish the lantern; he found her body and first pressed it to him, then held it away, searching her face.

"Martha, you are all to me. You know this?"

"I do. And you are—"

He rode into the space her own words might have filled had she been as quick as he was with them. "I know you've some worries over your travail. Your father worries also."

"My mother—"

"Yes, I know; no doubt this is also why your father's suggested we stay on at Monticello until your confinement in February—he has great faith in this Dr. Norris who tends your family. He's also asked me to oversee his various work projects at Monticello while he's in Philadelphia."

Martha's heart accelerated. "And what did you answer?"

"I accepted his offer."

Oh, the weight of it as it slid away! Martha flung her clumsy body at Tom and kissed his hot neck—why was there always this feel of fever to him? But he pushed her off, worked his way to the table beside the bed, and came back to her holding the kind of rolled paper that signified a formal document. He handed it to her, drawing the lantern closer. Martha unfolded the paper and read. She looked up at Tom. "My father has deeded me Molly."

"She'll travel from Monticello to Varina with us once you're safe delivered."

And what will *Molly* think of the move? Martha wondered. But *no,* she could not—would not—think of it that way. Molly would likely think the same thing Martha thought when Tom had carted *her* so far away from her family.

## CHAPTER 9

MARTHA TURNED EIGHTEEN at the end of September. Her father ordered up roast venison and oysters and wrapped her mother's emerald ring in one of his finest Irish handkerchiefs, embroidered with his initials by his wife, Martha's mother. Father, daughter, and son-in-law sat late in the parlor talking of Paris and Scotland, but when Martha asked again of the Paris plan to convert some of the Monticello slaves to tenant farmers, her father said, "Universal emancipation must come through legislation," and turned the subject to the price of tobacco.

Soon afterward Martha's father left for Philadelphia and Tom stepped in, riding out each day to every location undergoing change, writing long letters to his father-in-law at the end of the week, reporting on his successes and failures at filling his father-in-law's shoes. He wrote the overseer at Varina every other week and took the long trip back at the end of the month to finish some business he was unable to conclude via correspondence. As much as she felt the absence of the two men, Martha seldom found extra time on her hands—she had matters of her own to attend to. Sally's aging mother, Betty Hemings, had been retired to her private cabin set at a quieter location farther down the mountain, and Sally continued to do no real labor; with no Jefferson children to nurse, Ursula was now kept busy helping James with the cooking, leaving Critta and Mary to do for the rest. Besides, more of their goods had arrived from France, and only Martha could oversee the unpacking and arranging. She took charge with more confidence than she'd managed to summon at Varina, sorting china, counting spoons, disbursing furniture, but soon she began to extend her sphere, making frequent visits to kitchen, smokehouse, and garden, selecting menus, counting hams, overseeing the harvesting of seeds from the fall garden for the next year's planting.

And Martha wrote her father begging that he allow Maria to come to Monticello. She laid out her case: She would school Maria herself, having learned the fine art of educating young women from the nuns at the convent outside Paris; she had her father's excellent library at hand, a resource that far exceeded any available to Maria at her aunt and uncle's; the sisters had already been separated far too much in life. Martha's father agreed to the plan, and Maria arrived happily enough, now too interested in the coming child to think of missing her aunt at Eppington. With Maria in the house, it grew less quiet and Martha grew less conscious of the silent tread of Negro feet. With Maria in the house, Martha's fears began to shrink, and she grew lighter with it— the sisters shed their shoes and stockings and ran across the Monticello lawn together as they'd done so often as children.

———

EACH MORNING AND AFTERNOON Martha settled her sister into almost the same program of study her father had once set out for her, but with certain changes: a reduced session of dancing and drawing, as Martha excelled at neither; more time for walking and dinner; and any reading after six was to be done only for pleasure. They sang when they played their music, Martha taking the male part and Maria the female when the verses required it:

*Oh say bonnie lass, can you lie in a barrack, and marry a soldier and carry his wallet? Oh say can you leave both your mammy and daddy and follow to the camp with your soldier laddie?*

*Oh, yes, I will do it and think nothing of it, I'll marry a soldier and carry his wallet. Oh, yes I will leave both my mammy and daddy, and follow to the camp with my soldier laddie.*

When they practiced their dancing, the clumsy swell of Martha's child often collapsed them into the old childhood laughter.

---

TOM RETURNED, exuberant at the sight of Martha and at the sight of the shimmering mountain, which in his absence had burst into all the shades of a flaming log. Martha left her sister to work alone as she rode out with Tom to examine the state of affairs at Monticello. They took the carriage, Martha's weight now too cumbersome for the saddle, and at Tom's insistence Ned rode ahead to keep watch for unexpected potholes. Tom looked sideways in amusement as Martha pointed out which fence needed new bars, reported on the new joiner, and informed him that six hogs were ready for butchering.

"I should have sent *you* to Varina," he said.

"I might report on Varina from here: It needs a new tenant."

Tom laughed. Martha laughed. She sat close to him and tucked her hand inside his arm, not just for warmth but because she'd learned to treasure this new freedom that marriage allowed her—the freedom to touch a man in public. She'd learned an even more basic thing about herself as well: She *liked* to touch this man and she liked to be touched by him. But she'd also learned that this man could be quixotic, even volatile, and she must take care around him.

---

BY MID-DECEMBER the glorious flame that was Monticello in fall had died down to the black-and-white ash of Monticello in winter.

Martha had reveled in the flood of color but she also welcomed its shedding, allowing her to admire the graceful shapes and lines of the bare tree trunks and branches that had been her close friends since childhood. As she grew in size, she clung more to Tom, not only because she needed him to balance her over rough ground or steep stairs, but because his strength gave her the illusion of her own strength, almost convincing her she had little to fear.

As with the dancing, Martha's having to push the harpsichord bench farther and farther back as they practiced their music made Maria laugh, which made Martha laugh and further eased her. She sat as near to her sister as she could, with her arm around her annoyingly slender waist, tapping out the even tempo of their music and their days together.

*Oh, yes, bonnie lad, I will share all your harms, and should I be killed, I will die in thy arms.*

———

TOM'S FATHER MARRIED GABRIELLA HARVIE at the end of December. Tom declined to attend. Martha had by now become too heavy for travel and Tom too worried for her delicate health, or so Martha suggested Tom write his father. In truth, Martha had never felt—or been—stronger; nor had she given up entirely on the idea of Edgehill. After pondering for months her father's reluctance to further discuss turning slaves into tenant farmers, after recalling his statement that emancipation should come via legislation, Martha found herself engaged in what she cynically called her own small "slave trade." If Tom purchased Edgehill, they would need to take on more slaves, but the slaves were already here and the legislation emancipating them wasn't. In that case, wouldn't their condition be bettered under Tom than under any other master? Tom had forbidden whipping at Varina. He'd bought turkeys to pick the worms from the tobacco plants in order to spare the children. He'd removed a young girl from the fields and put her to helping the old slave with the garden. And besides, Ursula's commandment aside, wasn't the oldest daughter obligated to keep near her parent, especially a parent whose health was as unreliable as her father's? The "periodical headaches," as he called them; the "digestive troubles" that descended at times of stress; the rheumatic complaints that arose during extended travel or bouts of foul weather—no one knew her father's frailties as she did. And likewise wasn't Martha obligated—as her father had felt obligated to purchase Ursula's husband and son and bring them to Monticello—to keep Molly Hemings as close to her family as possible? Here Martha's argument with herself faltered, for in fact she was the one who had excused carrying Molly away to Varina in the first place, by comparing it to Tom carrying Martha away from Monticello.

But Martha could quibble with the two sides of herself all day until—like now—both sides were so worn out she had to push them from her, the good and the bad together, and focus on resurrecting her dreams of Edgehill. She told Tom, "Might you include a word in your father's letter about your regret at your manner of parting?"

Tom lifted his eyes from the paper over which he'd been struggling. Could he see all she was thinking? Did he know of this little game she'd been playing with herself, was, in fact, playing again as he looked at her? Tom was a good man, Martha argued; he'd managed to work the Monticello Negroes successfully using her father's system of incentive versus disincentive, and surely such a system could work equally as painlessly at Edgehill. This did not mean that the Jeffersons and Randolphs and others of their like-minded Virginians couldn't continue their efforts toward eliminating slavery forever by lobbying for that emancipation legislation.

And then there was Martha's father's voice in her other ear. *Take life by the smooth handle,* he'd always told her; whether or not they managed to purchase the Edgehill property, there was nothing to be gained, either practically or emotionally, by staying at odds with Tom's father.

Tom considered his wife a moment longer. He picked up the pen, added a few words, and handed Martha the letter, grinning at her like a small boy proffering his first Latin translation to his tutor.

*My wife sends her affection and duty to you, as do I, who adds his heartfelt regret at so rude a parting from you. I remain your humble and obedient servant, TMRandolph Jr.*

---

PARADOXICALLY, as the year turned the corner into 1791 and Martha's expected confinement drew closer, as she felt the strength of the life within her, she grew calmer. Tom grew edgier. Martha didn't expect to be delivered of the child until late February, but by the third week in January Tom could no longer keep himself in place; on the twentieth of the month he set out after his Richmond aunt to install her at Monticello where she could assist with Martha's travail and aid the new mother. Martha suffered their good-bye in fair control; she watched the carriage negotiate the roundabout and felt the first ache for him, astoundingly fierce, although the second was worse when she sat down to dinner with none but Maria to join her.

Two days later, while letting out the waist of a new gown her father had sent her, Martha's womb gripped and released. She was a month before her time and paid it little notice, or rather, she made a great effort to pay it little notice, but it gripped again exactly half an hour later.

———

Ursula kept with her while Mary, Molly, Critta, and Maria busied about making the household arrangements that an infant and convalescent new mother would require; at what proved to be the eleventh hour, Martha, wanting her absent mother, cried out to Ursula. Strong hands gripped her shoulders.

"You can do this simple thing," she said. "For heaven's sake, you don't do anything we didn't all do before you."

It was true, thought Martha—all these living women and their living children surrounded her—except for Sally's dead son. But Martha barely had time to veer off in hunt of that new terror when it was over, and Sally, who had appeared from nowhere, took the tiny girl from Ursula and begun to wash her. Of course there had been pain, but already as she reached for her daughter Martha could only remember the fact of the pain and not the actual feel of it.

"What name do you give that girl of yours?" Ursula asked her.

"I shall follow Virginia custom," Martha answered. "My father shall have the honor of naming our firstborn." Only afterward did she wonder if Tom would approve.

———

Tom, wild that his daughter had sneaked into life the minute his back was turned, haunted her cradle as if unable to believe in her without seeing her for himself; he happily agreed that they should honor Martha's father by asking him to name the child. The letter was dispatched and the answer came full of concern for the health of mother and child, only in its last sentence suggesting a name: Anne for both Tom's late mother and Martha's aunt. In a burst of love for her enraptured husband, Martha insisted on adding Tom's mother's family name in the middle. Anne Cary Randolph. Their daughter.

MARTHA DID NOT INSTINCTIVELY ADAPT to the job of mother, but Ursula taught her as she needed, and her blond, blue-eyed daughter thrived in black arms or white, making little distinction between them. Anne was a placid, healthy, good-natured baby, and Martha, thinking again of Sally, acknowledged the gratitude she should feel, while wondering what use her Paris education might serve with feeding, changing, dressing, bathing. Indeed, if she'd wished, any number of Hemingses might have taken on all but the feeding, and even for that a wet nurse might have been found readily enough among the field slaves. But Martha's father had sent her a book on the advantages of breast-feeding for both mother and child, one of which was its apparent success at delaying conception. Martha loved her infant daughter, but the idea of another close on her heels was not to her liking.

Anne only caused her mother trouble at night, when Martha dreamed of the infant lying abandoned in the tobacco fields at Varina, swarmed by worms and mosquitoes. Martha woke each morning after such dreams searching for signs that either she or the infant was unfit for travel, but by March no one could ignore the glowing health of both mother and child. They were deep in travel preparation when a letter came from Tom's father. *I am agreeable to your purchase of Edgehill,* he wrote his son.

When Tom showed Martha the letter, she clapped her hands, but Tom held his up to stop her.

"What is it, Tom? He now agrees! We may purchase Edgehill, the thing we've talked of so long."

"I know, only—"

"*What?*"

"'Tis the Negroes, Martha. 'Tis my aversion to increasing the number of my Negroes."

"But, Tom! You were agreeable to the purchase only last—"

"I'm sorry, I cannot. 'Tis as if they stand chained before me, forming an insurmountable obstacle."

Oh, how Martha wished she could argue against such an objection, but she could not. Nor could she fail to respect her husband for the courage only he had managed to summon.

They left for Varina a week later.

———

THE PRICE OF TOBACCO DROPPED. Tom planted wheat, a more profitable venture and easier on the Negroes, or so he believed, and the new crop came on well. He continued to supervise the overseers at all of his father-in-law's plantations, dictating which crops and trees to plant, where the drainage canals should be dug, supervising the ongoing construction of slave cabins and blacksmith and sawmill operations. Letters flew back and forth to Philadelphia.

For Martha, she made her finest effort to make Varina home. She'd learned from her time at Monticello among the Hemingses how her household *should* run and grew more effective at supervising Cook and Molly in their cleaning, laundry, sewing, and cooking. She asked Tom for two cows and a dozen chickens, adding milking, churning, cheese making, and egg collecting to the tasks that fell under her supervision. But she soon discovered that the task she'd in fact been trained for came in the evening, when Molly carried Anne off to her cradle and Tom sat down at his corner table, talking to her as he sorted the day's correspondence, bills, crop records, and newspapers. Martha had been raised to serve as a fit conversational partner for Thomas Jefferson; she was likewise a fit conversational partner for Thomas Randolph, and soon discovered if she weighed her words just so, she could be of use to all of them.

"I dislike interfering with my overseer," Tom said, "but he missed the market high this year."

"Then he can't resent your closer attention next year."

"He started a nine-year-old girl in the field yesterday."

"I would agree with you—no one under twelve should be in the field."

"The wheat does well."

"You must suggest it to my father."

At night they shared other comforts, other words that came easier now there was no cross-current between them. But when Tom was forced to spend a month in Richmond on business, Martha found her new determination faltering, reminding her of how far off her father was, her sister. She wrote letters twice a week to her father, her sister, Judith. She opened her father's answering correspondence with the greatest eagerness, but he wrote only questions to her. *How is dear Anne? How is your health and that of Mr. Randolph? Do you have strawberries?* Maria, fourteen now, filled her letters with the doings of her cousin Jack Eppes. Judith wrote that she'd been delivered of a fine boy. Martha answered each letter the day it arrived, if more than one in a day, always taking her father's first, dashing out brief lines on Anne's and her fine health but sparing no words over Tom's continued struggles with what she now called "the Varina rash," and the ongoing, inexplicable fevers. *As for strawberries,* she wrote, *I must dream of yours at Monticello.* She decided to offer no comment on Jack Eppes to Maria; the girl was but fourteen. To Judith she wrote, *I take comfort in hearing we travel in step with life events,* and yet wondered if Judith ever felt as displaced as she did.

When Tom returned from Richmond, he brought Martha a gift—a small looking glass framed in tortoiseshell. Martha looked at her image and saw her long, slender nose; her fair skin; her lively hair; her sad eyes. The eyes surprised her—she looked past the sadness until she found the old kindness, the hope; only then did she set down the mirror.

## CHAPTER 10

Oᴜᴛ ᴏꜰ ᴛʜᴇ ʙʟᴜᴇ, with no interim discussion, Tom began to talk again of purchasing Edgehill; despite missing peak market, he'd drawn enough profit from Varina their second season to give him confidence in their future. Apparently all qualms about Negroes were now forgotten; Martha's own qualms were due, in the main, to this increasing evidence of her husband's quixotic nature. But at the first of the year, Martha became certain of another child, due in September, and her desire to have the family settled overrode all other concerns. Tom's father began to press too, his own debts closing in, the Harvies apparently having lost interest in possessing Edgehill. When Tom's father wrote a second time asking Tom to come to Tuckahoe to settle the matter, Tom agreed. At the next letter the senior Randolph's urgency became clearer.

Martha came upon her husband crumpled over the letter as if with cramp. "He wipes me away," Tom said. "He replaces me with another."

Martha took the letter and read, sure of finding something less dramatic than Tom had described, but she did not. Gabriella had given birth to a son they named Thomas Mann Randolph, exactly as if they would erase the first Tom and begin again with another. As Martha read she determined they should secure Edgehill as soon as possible to put more distance between the Randolphs, but even as she settled this in her own mind, Tom lifted his head and lurched in another direction.

"My sister Nancy has moved to Bizarre to live with my sister

Judith, unable to keep under Gabriella's roof any longer. Richard and my sisters plan to visit Tuckahoe at the same time I plan to be there. You and Anne must come; let them see how my *mother's* namesake thrives." He barked out a laugh. "We'll tell them our first boy is to be named Thomas Jefferson. They may guess what I think of my father's name then."

"Perhaps we'd do best not to discuss names until we've settled about Edgehill."

Tom pulled a folio of papers toward him. "If next season's profits match the last, I'll be able to start work on the dwelling. If your father allows, we might stay at Monticello while we await your travail and the construction together. As to the Negroes—"

So Tom had not, after all, forgotten the Negroes. He pulled a sheet of paper from the pile before him and pushed it across the table at Martha. Two columns again, two headings again: *Varina. Edgehill.* This time the columns were filled with the names of Negroes, grouped by brackets into families. "I believe I might shift some from Varina to Edgehill and keep both plantations going without adding too greatly to our total."

Martha studied the paper. The two short columns of names occupied only the top half of the paper, the white space extending below them empty of ink. That white space comforted her. And yet what might be asked of those listed at the top of the paper, to make up for the white space at the bottom? Yet Martha knew she would ask it of them, in order to move closer to Monticello.

Tom fumbled his papers together and pulled out a second letter, one Martha hadn't seen, addressed to Tom from his father-in-law. "I wrote him of the pending purchase. Here is his answer."

*This is a fine tract that will furnish you a pleasing occupation,* Martha read. Apparently nothing more was to be said of Tom's becoming a lawyer.

———————

Tuckahoe was tuckahoe no longer. Gabriella Harvie Randolph had covered the fine old walnut paneling with white paint, covered the gleaming front hall with a pea-soup floor cloth, and replaced the rich brocade furniture with hard gilt chairs. To Martha's relief, Tom managed to enter his old home affecting high spirits, the falseness of it evident only to Martha and perhaps his sisters, but both sisters appeared preoccupied with their own distresses. Judith's "fine son" was now a year old and abnormally unresponsive; Nancy complained of a persistent colic. Both sisters' faces had aged, deep shadows underlining their eyes, their cheeks hollowed, but perhaps Martha viewed them so only in relation to the plump and unlined Gabriella.

———————

Gabriella, gabriella, gabriella. Through dinner Tom's father called up his young bride's name and voice so often that all other parties soon gave up any effort to enter the exchange. Martha's head had begun to ache from the thumping bass of one voice and the piercing soprano of the other, when Nancy, possessed of a sprightlier disposition, managed to divert the stream.

"Well now, Gabbie—"

"Gabriella," Gabriella said.

"Oh, yes, of course. However shall I remember? I have it. Like umbrella without the pause, just add the *gab,* and there you have it!"

A single laugh exploded from Richard. Tom's father stood up, eyes scorching the table. "Gentlemen, we have business in the library."

The women retired to the parlor, but by now even Gabriella had fallen silent; all three women looked to Martha to start them again. She concluded that Gabriella's thriving son would be a poor choice of topic, comparing him as they all must do to Judith's lethargic child. Martha focused instead on the useful topic of health, choosing Nancy's colic as her target, and a discussion of the various remedies revived the group.

"A purge of salts," Judith said. "But beware excessive use—it can cause weakening and fever."

"I find salts of little use," Gabriella countered. "A tincture of warm wine, ground clove, and ground cinnamon, taking care not to inhale the cinnamon."

"Gum guaiacum," Martha contributed. "Although it poses danger to a fetus."

"Well then," Gabriella said. "Only our spinster Nancy is safe to use it."

"Yes, and as Nancy is the one with colic—"

"Oh, dear Lord!" Gabriella said. "Find her some of the vile stuff and be done with it! Or do you plan to keep us talking colic all evening?"

"No," Martha said, rising. "I do not. In fact, I don't plan to keep talking at all, as I find I'm quite exhausted."

She departed for her room. Judith followed close after her.

"I always thought you so clever," Judith said. "And here you let that fool woman get the best of you."

Martha, startled by the cut in Judith's tone and in fact utterly exhausted, found herself snapping back. "I rather thought Nancy got the best of *her*."

"Nancy only angered our father, which placed Gabriella even more in his favor. This is why we took her away to Bizarre, before she disinherits the lot of us."

"'Tis kind of you, Judith. And Richard, of course."

"Oh, Richard will do anything I ask."

"You're fortunate."

"Don't despair over *your* husband, Martha. I acknowledge Richard to be uncommonly agreeable."

*Oh, indeed,* Martha thought, thinking of Tom's efforts over Edgehill on her behalf, but she was too tired—and too sensible—to argue husbands with this new, sharp-tongued Judith.

———

TOM HAD NO BETTER REPORT TO MAKE of his meeting with the male Randolphs. As soon as the Edgehill papers had been signed and witnessed, the senior Randolph expressed his disdain over Tom's plans for managing his properties. Richard had been at best distracted and unhelpful, at worst rude, harping on Tom's poor timing in getting his crop to market. Both Tom and Martha slept poorly, and even Anne woke through the night as she never did at either Monticello or Varina. They decided to leave in the morning.

———

FOR THE FIRST TIME Martha was glad to see Varina. They delved into happy plans for the three fall events: their coming child, the work on the new house at Edgehill, the trip to Monticello. Not yet weighed down with the child, suffering little this time from the effects of her condition, Martha found herself taking up her father's habit of humming as she worked, although the song The "Coffee Song," was one taught her by Ursula. *Oh! Fare ye well, my bonny love, I'm going away to leave you, A long farewell forever love, don't let our parting grieve you.* Yes, now that she was to leave it, Martha could make her peace with Varina. She wrote her father brimming letters and he answered her in kind, full of nothing but praise for her husband, his plans, their future together on their neighboring plantations.

Then it began to rain, the kind of rain Martha never saw in

the mountains—a sea of rain, pounding into the fields in waves, flattening everything.

———————

THERE WERE NO PROFITS FROM VARINA, as there were no crops to send to market. They traveled to Monticello in the early August heat, anxious to be in place long before Martha might expect to be confined, but she could feel little of the joy of her previous arrival. Tom's spirits hadn't recovered from his financial reversal; he seemed to plunge lower as they arrived at Monticello. Even Martha grew dispirited at the downtrodden look to her old home, worse than it had appeared the previous winter, and this despite Tom's oversight. Or was it because of it? The disloyalty of the thought only plunged Martha's own spirits lower, but she couldn't ignore Tom's habit of dashing from plan to plan. Even Martha's joy at seeing her father was lessened by *his* distractions—incessant meetings with his friends Madison and Monroe, his long hours cooped up in his rooms writing letters, a new tendency to retire earlier and earlier to his chamber.

The anticipated reunion of Molly and her mother also disappointed. Mary had asked to be sold to the Charlottesville merchant who'd fathered two young children by her, and Thomas Jefferson had obliged her, sending her and the two youngest off together, leaving Sunday visits the only time Molly could spend with her mother. The single thing that roused them as a household was the birth of Thomas Jefferson Randolph, brought into being with an almost shameful lack of indisposition on the part of his mother.

———————

THOMAS JEFFERSON RANDOLPH—Jeff, as they called him—was dark haired and dark eyed like his father, his skin the color of pale brick. Already he possessed a more boisterous nature than his sister;

in the early morning, waking incompletely and momentarily forgetting where her life had taken her over the past two years, Martha would look at him and wonder who might have spawned him. She wrote to Judith, determined to overlook her friend's rudeness at Tuckahoe the previous spring: *I've been delivered safe of a boy we name for my father,* but for the first time in their long friendship, Judith failed to answer.

———

TOM'S SON APPEARED TO CHEER HIM. His confidence returned. Martha overheard him talking to her father regarding a replacement for an overseer who had proved too severe. "I know a man who possesses the valuable art of governing slaves that sets aside the necessity of punishment almost entirely. You'll find nothing but contentment among them."

Martha's father asked if Tom might stay on at Monticello to oversee the transition, and Tom agreed. Next Tom spoke to Martha of an idea for a new kind of horizontal plowing that might forestall the kind of loss they'd suffered over the past season. At Martha's urging he took that idea to her father, who was full of admiration. The men spent long hours discussing the best plows, the best crop rotation, the best schedule for planting.

When the time came for Martha's father to leave for Philadelphia, he pulled Tom aside to impart some last instruction, but Martha noticed her father's mind had already switched from farming to government; his final words were rich in principle and scant in specifics.

Yet Tom seemed full of optimism. "Once their work here is done, your father plans to lend us his carpenters for Edgehill," he said one evening. "With my new method of plowing and a new plow design your father has come upon, I expect next year to be a fine one."

## CHAPTER 11

T HE FIRST RUMORS came through the Negroes at a plantation called Glentivar, in Cumberland County where Richard, Judith, and Nancy were visiting. When the news reached the Monticello Negroes, Martha saw the change in them before she knew the cause—the way they looked at Tom and at her, the way they gathered around corners engaging in lively talk that broke off as soon as Martha appeared. Next, the new overseer made a rare appearance at the house, and spent two hours closeted with Tom in the small parlor.

When Tom finally came to their room, his usually rich complexion had gone the color of paper. He dropped into the chair as if his legs could take him no farther, and as with his legs, his speech seemed to have given out—it took him some moments to gather his words. "'Tis beyond crediting," he began finally. "Even now it doesn't bear repeating without the utmost incredulity, and yet I must repeat it to you, for you alone will find what sense there is in it. Here's the short of it: One of the Negroes claims he found the body of a white infant behind the main house at Glentivar, among a loose pile of shingles. They now claim Richard got the child on my sister Nancy and they accuse him of its murder."

"Richard and . . . *Nancy? Murder?*"

"You must remember this came only from the servants. They add the kind of detail that expands with the imagination: screams from Nancy's room, only Richard allowed to enter, a man's tread going down the stairs soon after, droplets of blood on the stairs.

They say 'twas Richard disposing of the infant. When the maid was finally allowed above-stairs, she saw blood on the sheets, although an attempt had been made to wash them in the basin. At dawn another servant, out for firewood, found the corpse on the shingles, but it was gone by midmorning." Tom fell silent, breathing heavily, his hands gripping and releasing the coattails of his jacket. "Well? Can you credit it?"

Martha, her mind still flying from sentence to sentence, found she could not credit it, until she considered what Negro would ever dare fabricate such statements, and to what purpose. If for vengeance, it would be doubly wrought, come back tenfold on the heads of those who dared pass the story forward.

"What is said of your sisters' and brother-in-law's response to the rumors?" she countered.

"They say 'twas only Nancy's usual monthly ills, that Judith asked Richard to tend our sister as she was herself unwell, that Richard brought Nancy some laudanum and that was the end of it. If such be the case, if I discover the author of this rumor—" He leaped up, wild eyed. "But God's breath! If this foul tale be true, if Richard Randolph has done this thing to my sister . . . to *both* my sisters! I'll have his blood for it! I promise you, I'll have his blood!"

"Tom, you must do nothing. You must leave it lie. To do anything else will make it so much worse. Say nothing to anyone until some person of substance makes mention in your presence." Which Martha fervently hoped no person of substance would ever dare do.

But Tom only grew more agitated as Martha watched, rising to measure the length of the room in long paces, going outside, wandering in again to exclaim over and over, "If such a thing be true! If he does this to my sisters!"

To calm him Martha turned back the conversation to the original question. "But of course, as I think more on it, I *can't* credit such a thing. What have we here but some silly gossip among the Negroes? Let me write Judith a general inquiry as to everyone's health and while we wait for her answer we'll go on as if we've heard nothing of the matter. This is the best way to proceed, I'm quite sure of it."

Martha's certainty appeared to subdue Tom. Martha crossed to the desk and began her letter at once—news of Monticello in the main, closing with the usual affection to be passed to Nancy and Richard.

Again, Judith didn't answer.

———

BY JANUARY the talk had left the Negroes and moved on to friends and even relations of the Randolphs. At first Martha refused to believe it, thinking the new talk borne of Tom's overly sensitive nature only, for who would dare challenge a Randolph, the oldest and most influential family in Virginia? But it soon appeared that some resentments had been running steadily underground, for years if not for an entire century. The more Martha listened, the more she began to understand that Richard Randolph was not in fact as generally popular as his wife made him out, and that the mercurial Thomas Randolph Senior was not someone people would go out of their way to protect from trouble. Certain visitors to Glentivar that weekend began to think backward and tell their own tales: Richard and Nancy had been seen kissing; Nancy refused to allow the ladies to see her undressing; she insisted on wearing a heavy cloak even in September. They only told their tales, of course, in full confidence that they would never be repeated.

———

THE TALES WERE REPEATED SO OFTEN they traveled all the way to Monticello, where Tom and Martha still hunkered, Tom attempting to keep control of the many construction projects and the new overseer, Martha arranging her father's household to better suit him when he returned to it. One of the guests at Glentivar now put it about that it was no wonder, as Judith had turned so shrewish she'd driven Richard to seek out the livelier sister. Another guest claimed to have heard Nancy's screams, to have seen the bloody stairs, to have wondered at Richard's proprietary air around his wife's sister, ministering to her alone in her bedchamber. A third claimed she'd observed Nancy's weight gain in July and suspected then that she was pregnant.

It was true that some countertalk began to travel: How could any of this be true if Judith remained so affectionate to both husband and sister? Why would Richard, Judith, *and* Nancy have just traveled to Williamsburg together? How was it Nancy was seen a day after the supposed event without the usual drain a birth would have inflicted upon her? And lest anyone forget, no *white* person claimed to have seen a corpse, although the host was rumored to have been shown some blood on a shingle.

With each rumor that reached them, Tom's control dwindled. He wrote letter after letter that Martha persuaded him to let her read, and, usually, to send into the fire instead of off for delivery. Martha tried to soothe him by directing his attention to his own farm, but he could take no comfort there. He'd counted on three thousand bushels of wheat from Varina and harvested just eight hundred; the corn was still out in January; the pigs had yet to be slaughtered. Tom finally decided to fire the Varina overseer and hire a new one. In her own case, Martha attempted to turn her thoughts to her son and daughter but found it little helped her. How might *their* future suffer if this cloud continued to hover over the Randolphs? Tom talked of traveling to Bizarre, of confronting Richard, of convincing him to do what was required to exonerate

Tom's sister, but Martha couldn't feel sure of such a course. Judith had at last written to *share the happy news of another child expected in summer,* as if to prove that affection yet remained between husband and wife, displaying little evidence of the need of a supportive shoulder. Perhaps better to keep their distance until the talk died away. Or was that only Martha's selfishness talking? She wrote to her father, seeking advice. He answered:

> *People are too rational to blame one person or family for the acts of another . . . Feel no unease but for the pitiable victim, whether it be of error or slander. If there is guilt here it is in but one person and not her.*

But not all Virginia gentlemen—or ladies—were so generous toward the victim; Martha took what pains she could to hide Nancy's vilification from Tom, convincing him to allow Martha to manage his correspondence for him. That he agreed spoke to his distress even more than the slow but steady increase in his brandy consumption.

───────────

ONE PIECE OF CORRESPONDENCE ESCAPED MARTHA. In April an open letter from Richard appeared in the *Virginia Gazette,* an obvious effort to bluff his accusers silent:

> *I will on the first day of next month appear at the Cumberland Court to answer any charge of crime anyone shall allege against me . . .*

Perhaps it might have soothed Tom had Richard stood up alone to face down the rumors, but in his next sentence he chose to include Tom's sister:

*Let not a pretended tenderness towards the supposed accomplice shelter me. That person will meet the accusations with a fortitude of which innocence alone is capable.*

Reading it, Tom began to tremble. "Oh, the wretch! The bloody wretch! That he would dare speak of her in the newspaper!" Martha rose and laid a hand on Tom's shoulder. He shook her off, his face now beyond its richest hue. He grabbed ink, pen, and paper.

"Who do you write?"

"Richard." He sat with his tools and wrote furiously. Martha stayed as she was, reading over his shoulder.

*I will wash out with your blood the stain on my family.*

"Perhaps better to appeal to Richard's honor as a gentleman—"

Tom ignored her. He snatched up the letter, folded it, sealed it, and called for Ned to hand-deliver the letter to Richard Randolph. As Ned entered the room, Martha noticed his limbs had begun to fill with muscle, but perhaps a truer sign of his maturity was the fact that his smile had lost some of its conviction. When was it that a slave first realized he was a slave, that the relative freedom of his childhood was understood to be nothing but illusion? Martha envisioned Ned's long ride to Bizarre, his delivering Tom's letter, Richard picking up his cane and striking blow after blow on the innocent messenger.

---

ALL WAS BEHINDHAND, Tom too distracted to properly tend to the farmer's calendar. They had yet to leave for Varina, and ordinarily Martha would have rejoiced in her Monticello reprieve, as spring on the mountaintop was unlike any other spring anywhere: The woods and meadows were freshly green, the fields newly turned,

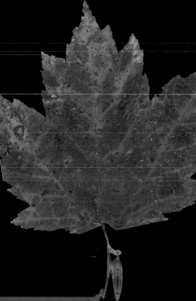

the garden hoed and ready for planting, the lantana and oleander and poppies all blooming. Martha would have dearly loved to stay on to oversee the setting of the new plants and the sowing of the vegetable garden were it not for her fresh understanding of just how much depended on a successful season at Varina. Were it not for Tom's distraction.

They were still at Monticello when the news came: Richard had arrived at the courthouse on the specified date, and much to his astonishment was met by the sheriff with a magistrate's warrant, charging him with "feloniously murdering a child said to be borne of Nancy Randolph."

For the first time, Tom's rage caused Martha to grow fearful for her husband. She would not say *of* her husband. He paced the parlor and the west lawn, but when pacing no longer contained his fury he ordered his horse, galloping down the mountain so incautiously that Martha expected a messenger to arrive with a report of his broken neck. But this Martha had learned: In such an advanced state of mental turmoil, any words from her were sure to go unheeded; she waited for night, where the dark quiet and her gentling touch might bring Tom peace, but even after he fought his way into sleep he continued to mutter and kick and sweat through his nightshirt.

On the third day of such sleeplessness, Martha's summons arrived, erasing any hope of sleep far into the future: The sheriff of Cumberland County wished to know the particulars of a conversation she'd held with Nancy Randolph on the subject of gum guaiacum the previous April.

---

IT OCCURRED AT TUCKAHOE," Martha explained to Tom. Again. "We discussed Nancy's colic, as she said it was. I gave her my remedy, adding at the mention of gum guaiacum that caution must be used as it could harm a fetus."

"Dear God in heaven! Who could have told the sheriff of such talk?"

Martha considered. Judith? She'd continued to insist, in public and in private, on the innocence of both husband and sister; she'd continued to deny that any pregnancy had existed or that any event had occurred that might cause a pregnancy in her spinster sister. Why would she then turn about and attempt to convince the court that an abortion had been attempted? But who else had been present?

Of course. "Gabriella," Martha answered.

———

Tom rode off to tuckahoe to confront his stepmother. He returned in a new rage, one that showed another glimpse of his father's nature. Gabriella Harvie Randolph had indeed offered up the details of their April conversation to the sheriff, and as in accordance with Virginia law, Negroes weren't allowed to testify in court against a white person, Martha's testimony would prove critical.

———

A week later the Randolphs arrived in Cumberland—Tom, Martha, Jeff, Molly, and Ned, with the weaned Anne left behind in the care of Ursula. The tiny court town bustled with carriages, horses, oxcarts, and pedestrians, rich and poor come together to see the mighty Randolphs brought low, or this was how it appeared to Martha; the small, brick courthouse was as packed as any Paris theater. Martha didn't know the five justices or the county prosecutor, but the names if not the faces of the defense lawyers—

Patrick Henry and John Marshall—were indeed familiar to most of Virginia. Entering the courtroom, seeing Nancy and Judith and Richard for the first time since the events unfolded, Martha faltered. She gripped Tom's hand. "Speak only the truth," he whispered. "'Tis *our* honor we guard here."

Martha was on the one hand proud of Tom that he could speak so, yet she did ponder how much easier it might make things if she claimed to forget that Tuckahoe conversation. Gabriella would say one thing, she would say another . . . And unless she was more skilled at fabrication than she felt herself to be, no one would believe her. Tom's advice was the advice she must follow if she wished to keep her branch of the Randolph family above suspicion.

———

THE PROSECUTOR BROUGHT OUT an impressive array of witnesses, including several Randolph cousins, who testified to Nancy and Richard's "unseemly fondness," their "imprudent familiarities," their "excessive attentiveness." When they spoke of the screams, the smells, and the blood, the courtroom as a body shuddered. Martha's testimony might have been considered less sensational, but she was the daughter of Thomas Jefferson, and the courtroom hummed as she stepped forward. As she spoke she focused not on Judith or Nancy or Richard but on Tom, standing tall at the rear of the room so she could see him more clearly than any other. Her statement was brief and honest: She'd told Nancy of a colic remedy using gum guaiacum last April.

"Did you include any caution regarding the dangers of gum guaiacum?"

"I did."

"Did you include in your caution that the use of this remedy might be harmful to a pregnancy?"

"I did."

The aging Patrick Henry had no questions, which Martha found peculiar, but she was happy enough to be excused with so little trouble. Richard's aunt Page followed, testifying that Nancy Randolph had asked her for gum guaiacum on her return from Tuckahoe the previous April, that she had given it to her without thought of anything beyond Nancy's ongoing complaint of indigestion.

Patrick Henry took up the defense soon after, parading a fine display of other Randolph relations who offered up as evidence the continued amicable relationship between the sisters and husband and wife, Nancy's history of "monthly ails," the fact that none of them had seen any blood on the stairs or any remains in the woodpile or any blood-stained shingles. Henry concluded that there being no witnesses to a corpse, let alone a crime, Richard must be declared innocent.

He was.

———

Back in their rooms, after Molly and Ned had been sent to the kitchen to find their supper, Martha dared to ask it. "What if the Negroes who claimed to see the corpse had been allowed to bear witness?"

Tom, ashen with exhaustion, shook his head and opened his mouth but appeared unable to speak, a thing so unlike him that Martha hurried to add, "What matter now? 'Tis over."

———

But of course it wasn't. The public believed as they'd believed before, and only Judith, having heard for the first time the whole of the evidence against her husband and sister, began to change her thinking on the matter. Although she continued to allow Nancy to live with them at Bizarre, reports of quarrels between the sisters followed Tom and Martha to Varina. In May Judith miscarried, but Martha's first letter to her, and later a second, again went unanswered.

———

NEITHER TOM NOR MARTHA COULD DWELL on the Randolphs' saga long; too much was happening in their own world. In June, true to his practice of keeping Tom informed on all legal matters pertaining to his property, Martha's father sent Tom a copy of the document manumitting Sally's brother Robert, his freedom purchased by his wife's owner, thus enabling Robert to move to Richmond to live with his wife and children. The accompanying letter was bitter, uncomprehending of the slave's desire to leave a master who had given him such great liberties over the years, who had allowed him to go out to work and keep his wages, who had treated him with such affection, who had expected a like affection in return. Isn't it enough that we demand their sweat? Martha wondered. Must we demand their love too? Is this how we soothe ourselves? *See how the Negroes love you,* Maria had declared, fresh on their return from Paris. And yet as Martha wrote out her answer to her father's letter she found only sympathetic words coming from her pen:

> *My dearest Papa, please know that Robert would never have left you for anyone other than his wife and children . . .*

———

IN JULY an unidentified insect invaded the Varina tobacco. In August heavy rains decimated the corn. In October Tom's father-in-law asked him to oversee construction of a nailery at Monticello, the nail workers to be made up of the younger boys spared from the fields, although as Martha listened to Tom's description of incessant hammering and constant smoke she doubted *spared* was the word she would have applied to the new employment. But in November came the greatest blow of all—Tom's father died in what his doctor described as a "tormenting state of mind," leaving life use of Tuckahoe to Gabriella, title to the property to Thomas Mann Randolph the Third, and sixty-four thousand dollars of debt to Thomas Mann Randolph the Second.

The blow was so overwhelming that it temporarily unbalanced Tom's mind. He walked around Monticello referring to his father as if he still lived, lashing out at Martha when she attempted to draw his attention to the wealth of accumulated mail.

"Why do you disturb me at my work?" Tom shouted, when in fact he'd been sitting in a darkened room, staring at a cold hearth.

When Martha's father wrote that due to "opposing views among certain members of the cabinet I am resigning as secretary of state and retiring to Monticello for the remainder of my days," Martha was so overcome with relief she burst out of doors and walked all the way to the spring, even as an icy rain descended.

---

TOM WOKE FROM HIS FUGUE to find the new debt weighing on
him like an avalanche of snow; he insisted on hastening his family
back to Varina so he might set out at once for Richmond to consult an attorney, so when private citizen Thomas Jefferson arrived
at Monticello, his daughter wasn't there to greet him. *The bloom of
Monticello is chilled by my solitude,* he wrote to her at Varina. Martha
answered, *I never think of your solitary fireside but my heart swells.* She
was able to conclude with happier news—that she was to have another child in September and should like to await the event, as had
become her tradition, at Monticello.

Richmond did little for Tom's spirits. He'd learned that a portion of the debt was to be shared with his brother, but that still left
a sum so large he would never discharge it in a decade, especially
considering what he already owed on Edgehill and Varina. And
while Martha had come to think that the management of her father's numerous properties had been an excessive load, now that
the load had been removed with her father's return to Monticello,
Tom appeared to have more time than he knew how to order. He
drifted from smithy to barn to smokehouse; he retired early and
rose late; he took little interest in his children; Martha could only
break the silent lock on his jaw by asking questions that demanded
answers, and even those he dismissed with as few words as possible.

Eight days after Tom's return, they woke to a desperate cold.
Martha got up with Jeff's first whimper, Molly soon followed to
rouse the fire, but neither the clank of the logs nor the babble of

the children roused Tom. Martha nursed Jeff while Molly dressed Anne and then assisted Martha, but still Tom didn't move. Unable to contain her concern, Martha crossed to the bed, smoothed down the spikes of Tom's hair, and laid a hand against his cheek. Tom swatted the hand off, much as he'd done that day on the porch when she'd attempted to treat his rash, and spoke the same words that had so distressed Martha then.

"Leave me be."

Martha let him be, but two hours later, after feeding Anne, laying out the plan for the day's meals, and ordering Molly's work, Martha returned to the bedroom to find Tom as before. She sat on the edge of the bed tick and gripped his shoulder, firm enough to signal she would not be swatted off again. "Tom, what is it? Are you ill?"

Tom opened his eyes, saw her, and closed his eyes again. "I suspect I am."

"What ails you?"

"A great ache."

"Where?"

"Generally." He would say no more.

The cold, Martha thought, and set in to wait for better weather.

———

BUT A WEEK LATER, in considerably warmer air, Tom was much the same, describing his troubles as all-consuming fatigue and odd pains that never seemed to settle in a particular location. Another week the same, and over Tom's objection she sent for the local doctor, a young man in a stained jacket who plunged Martha into instant longing for the dignified and gentle Dr. Norris at Monticello. Martha's father had taken great care in choosing Dr. Norris, select- ing a man old enough to have gathered some experience but young enough to welcome Martha's father's ideas on the detrimental effects of bleeding and purging an ill patient. This new doctor would not allow Martha in attendance and in fact would not address her at all until he was already at the door, attempting to make his departure.

Martha interposed herself between the doctor and the outdoors. "What ails my husband?" she demanded.

The doctor took a trial step forward; as Martha didn't move, he found his nose uncomfortably close to hers. He stepped back. "His troubles are rheumatic in nature," he said, speaking with the kind of conviction that persuaded Martha of nothing but his youth.

"And how do you propose to treat him?"

"I've given him a liniment."

Martha left the doctor and returned to the patient. She spied the jar on the bedside table and opened it. It smelled of camphor, turpentine, pepper, perhaps some vinegar—nothing that could hurt, which was always Thomas Jefferson's first rule. Martha sat down on the bed, jar in hand. Tom opened his eyes. She eased him out of his nightshirt and began to rub—shoulders, elbows, wrists, hands, knees, feet; she began to draw his nightshirt back down over his head but thought of a better plan.

"Perhaps if you were dressed, the confinement of the clothes might accelerate the effect of the liniment."

She collected a shirt and handed it to him. Tom sat up, and as he pulled it on she found breeches, stockings, shoes, jacket.

It worked as it was supposed to work; dressed, upright, Tom roused. "I must speak to the overseer about replacing the horse trough."

———

A GOOD DAY; A BAD DAY; a terrible day after Tom rode out to a second meeting with the lawyer. He had little to say of the lawyer, but a pouch full of newspapers, all folded back at advertisements for northern health clinics touting success with rheumatics and general malaise, occupied the main of his conversation for the next several days. As Tom read advertisement after advertisement, Martha calculated the expense, finding her only respite from worry in the constant, joyful stream of letters from Monticello.

> *March 1: This day we sowed our peas, lettuce, and radishes.*
> *March 23: The new peach trees are in blossom.*
> *April 1: We're now at work planting twenty-four hundred cuttings*
> *from the weeping willows; I estimate one hundred cords of wood*
> *just from their loppings.*

He wrote of the beauty of the Blue Ridge covered in snow, of enjoying his first dish of asparagus, of purchasing some acreage on the near side of the neighboring mountain and his plan to graze sheep there "to improve our view." He closed every letter:

> *My affections to Mr. Randolph and kisses to the young ones. To*
> *yourself my tenderest love.*

Martha read these letters to Tom, in part to keep him from the newspapers for at least those few moments, and in part in the hopes that her father's contentment would divert Tom's thoughts to a brighter future at Edgehill. Instead it caused a lower turn.

"How do you bear my presence, Martha? I hold you here when you wish to be on the mountain."

"I wish to be with you."

He studied her, seeming to find the conviction he looked for. "It doesn't make the other any less true, does it? We must go to Monticello soon."

Oh, the swift change in the air, the light, the very heat of the sun! Monticello. Soon.

———————

SUMMER ON THE MOUNTAIN MEANT all the richness of color that Varina lacked: the ancient green of the woods contrasting with the youthful green of the fields, the knife-sharp blue of the sky, the translucent river below. As they drew closer to Monticello, the pinks, purples, reds, and yellows of the columbine, roses, poppies, sweet William, and foxglove her father had resurrected danced in the breeze as if inviting the visitor to dance too. And there were other changes now that the master was home for good: a new stable, a coal shed, and a brick kiln had been built at the end of Mulberry Row, while at the great house the noise of wheelbarrows, hammers, and saws drowned out the sound of the Randolphs' arrival. Tom eased his family to the ground and set off to examine the kiln; Critta appeared and helped Molly carry the children above-stairs; Martha headed toward the noise coming out of the parlor.

The solitary fireplace Martha had envisioned her father sitting beside was the center of turmoil, the carpenter John Hemings ripping out the mantel, his master on his knees examining the bricks in the hearth, Sally hopping and laughing and brushing plaster dust from her sleeve. Martha had heard from the new overseer that three more of Sally's siblings had recently been bought or sold at their request, a brother asking to be sold after a disagreement with the new overseer, a sister asking to be sold to unite her and her five children with her husband at the Monroe plantation, another sister asking to be bought back from Martha's aunt to avoid her pending sale out of the county. Additionally, Sally's nephew Burwell had been taken out of the nailery and brought into the house to serve as Thomas Jefferson's personal servant; already his favored treatment had caused jealousy among the others. No wonder Sally could hop and laugh; no wonder John Hemings could talk to her father as he did now, as if he were the equal—or better—of any white workman. To be a Hemings at Monticello was to be as close to free as a slave could dream.

*Close to free.* Martha had been about to step through the door and into the room that contained her father and his two slaves when her words echoed back at her. How could such a thing ever be? Sally's brother had given them so much trouble her father was likely glad to be rid of him, but the man had been forced to take a place far from his kin; Sally's sister was with her family now but must always live in fear of her children being sold away from her; Martha's father may have borrowed the money to buy back Sally's other sister, but he hadn't borrowed enough to buy back the woman's fifteen-year-old son. And yes, Burwell Colbert was pampered, but he was pampered with a calculation Martha was only beginning to understand, caught young enough so that every special gift and privilege only inspired that much more devotion to his master. What on earth could *close to free* mean to any of them?

Martha stepped into the room, interrupting her father's questions, John's explanations, and Sally's brushing away more dust, this time from her master's knees.

"Martha, my dear girl!"

Sally's toe caught the loose brick as she rose and her master caught her arm to steady her, but he released Sally at once and came to Martha with arms extended; Martha fell into them, her eyes smarting with tears she refused to spill.

"My dear girl," Martha's father said again.

———

MARTHA'S RESTLESS LIMBS and tumbling head found no comfort in Madison's bed that night; exhausted, she'd retired early but lay awake turning the bolster over and over until Tom came in from yet another late talk with her father.

"Why do you lie awake?" he asked. "Here's some good news for you to sleep on. Your father's extended me a loan to finance my trip to the Boston clinic."

This was what Tom had come to call good news—more loans—while to Martha it only meant more debt. But it also meant that while Tom was in Boston, Martha could remain here, safe at Monticello, awaiting the birth of their child; even as the thought began to ease her, the disloyalty of it alarmed her. Tom undressed, slipped between the sheets, and reached to draw Martha into his arms, as always. She went to him as always, but not eagerly, her body too occupied with that other paramount task of nurturing life, her mind too cluttered with worries. And out of the thoughts of debts and crops and children rose the image of Thomas Jefferson's hand clutching his slave's arm as he had often clutched his wife's arm. Sometimes Martha's mother would drop her hand over her husband's; sometimes the husband would drop a kiss on his wife's brow.

Martha wrenched her eyes open and sat up.

Tom jerked awake beside her. "What, my love?"

"Do you remember my mother?"

"Of course. I always thought of her as a lovely, gentle, fragile bird. I suppose I thought *fragile* because she was so often ill."

"With the bringing of her children."

Tom sat up and enclosed Martha in his arms again. "I shan't go to Boston if you prefer me here."

Martha did prefer him with her. Of course she did. And yet how promptly she could answer him, "Go to Boston. I'm safe here at Monticello. Your family needs you well."

## CHAPTER 13

T OM RETURNED FROM BOSTON so improved in health and spirit that Martha stopped fretting at the expense. She gave birth to a daughter in September, again with such little trouble that she blushed to think of how she'd fretted over *that,* of the concern she'd raised in both father and husband. Following her father's earlier lead, she suggested a name found in both family trees—Ellen—and Tom happily agreed.

Martha watched this third child with care—as reluctant as she was to come forth as critical of her children, Anne, now almost four, showed little signs of the quickness Martha had expected to find in her children, or more correctly put, in the grandchildren of Thomas Jefferson. Martha would admit to being grossly under-trained for the job of housewife, but she'd assumed her exemplary schooling would allow her to do a superlative job of educating her own children. And here was her first child, slow at her words, slower at recognizing shapes and symbols, still unable to recognize the *A* in her own name. At first Martha attributed Anne's intellectual dullness to her placid temperament, but there was nothing placid about Jeff, and yet he showed himself no brighter than his sister.

But Ellen. Her dark eyes, so like her father's, traveled inquisitively around her world, and she touched everything she could touch; she did her infant best to replicate every sound she heard, and she answered every smile with a smile. Even Martha's father remarked on this child's unique awareness, her obvious desire to know. But he doted on all the children in equal measure, lavishing equal gifts on all; he even convinced Tom to leave his two oldest at Monticello with him when Tom and Martha and the infant returned to Varina. Or perhaps he'd seen the same thing that Martha had and wished only to ease the burden on his son-in-law: Tom's Boston "cure" had not held.

The trip to Varina exacerbated Tom's ills. On the road he didn't sleep, blaming a noisy inn that was in fact quieter than Monticello; the lack of sleep in turn exacerbated Tom's impatience with Molly, Ned, the horses, and any unfortunates they happened to pass with insufficient buffer along the road. Once back at the farm, Tom thrashed all night, roaming uselessly from building to building during the day, declaring them all gone to rot, although to Martha's eye nothing had changed. When the talk of aches returned, it came accompanied by talk of a spa in Virginia called Warm Springs.

After a time Martha saw that even the season's planting could not dislodge thoughts of Warm Springs from Tom's mind. "You must go," she said. "You must get yourself strong. You must write to my father and ask for another loan."

"But I cannot get strong—how can I get strong—when I receive such care only by leaving you behind? Are we not best together? The children thrive at Monticello; leave them with your father and come."

"The babe's still at breast."

"Of course Ellen comes. I speak only of Anne and Jeff."

"But such a trip for an infant!"

"She's ten months. She traveled to Varina at four months, and with aplomb."

She had; this Martha could not deny. Nor could she deny the sense of what Tom said—with each day he counted on her more and more, not just in regard to his health but in regard to the plantations, the Negroes. At first he'd managed to keep Edgehill going with no addition, but even Martha saw the cost in the poor yield and supported him in his decision to purchase four more slaves. Her case ran thus: Which was worse, to overwork the slaves they already had for a crop insufficient to pay the mortgage, or to take on extra slaves and thereby insure health and greater security for all? But Martha's reasoning only carried Tom to the brink and not across. He continued to labor over the decision, waking and sleeping—or not sleeping. She would find him at his desk night after night, drawing columns, adding numbers, subtracting numbers, throwing down his pen and going out into the dark to pace and mutter alone. Martha came to believe it was this lack of sleep in him that caused the spike in his physical ills and began to rise with him, talking to him of other subjects until he grew calm and returned to his bed to fall asleep at last. At length Martha came to see that perhaps if she joined him at Warm Springs, this next cure *would* hold. She wrote to her father explaining the need for the two of them to travel. Tom enclosed his own letter in the same mailing, and his father-in-law answered before the month's end, agreeing to the increased loan.

———

TRAVELING THROUGH VIRGINIA in summer was hot and dusty, the views not quite as lovely as in spring and fall. The ripened fields had a withered, insect-riddled look to them, the dust they kicked up bleached out the foliage on either side, the mountains seemed to grow more distant behind and no closer ahead. Molly and Ned again accompanied them, Ned growing more solemn now, as if he'd taken the Randolph worries as his own. Indeed, were they not his own? Were Tom to fail, Negroes would be sold. Even Molly buried her face in Ellen's hair more often than she used to.

Halfway through the trip Ellen grew cantankerous, but so would Martha if her breeding had permitted it; she didn't grow concerned until the infant fell quiet. They were three-quarters of the way through their journey when the child grew listless and gave up Martha's breast; by the time they'd reached the next inn, she lay slack and dull in Molly's arms.

"Hot," Molly said.

"We're all hot," Tom said.

"'Tis uncommonly hot," Martha agreed, but as soon as they reached their room, she asked Molly to get her fresh, cool water for the basin and began to sponge Ellen down.

Tom came up and felt the child's brow. "Cooler?"

"Yes, some."

They left Ellen with Molly and went below to dine, quick bites and swallows that lodged restlessly halfway down; they returned to the room and sent Molly for more cool water. An hour later they sent Ned for a doctor.

The doctor was the physical opposite of the doctor at Varina— neat, cheerful, chatty—but he insisted on bleeding the infant from the heel despite Martha's objections; he left them with drops and a promise that the child would be recovered by morning. They went to bed, Ellen cushioned between her parents, but Martha never slept beyond a minute; sometime before dawn she could feel the tiny form beside her begin to cool and she dozed. When she opened her eyes to the new, yellow light, Ellen was limp. Cold. Gone.

———

Tom sobbed, railed, cursed himself for insisting Martha and the infant travel with him, cursed the doctor, cursed the fates that plagued him. But when he'd exhausted his tears and his curses, he sat next to the numbed Martha, holding her while she held the still-cold Ellen wrapped in her shawl.

"Martha, my love. What to do?"

"Go home and bury our child."

"Indeed. 'Tis my first thought as well."

He stood up, walked about the room. "But I must share a second thought which comes to me now. 'Tis your father's money that carried us here, and to put it to waste—"

"You can't think to go on!"

"I'm no use to my family as I am. Our babe's gone beyond recovery; could we not find our infant a sound coffin, send her back into your father's good care, and continue as planned?"

He talked on. How little he cared for himself in the face of their loss, how difficult it would be to proceed, how his heart pulled him homeward. He didn't know what was right and what wrong but it seemed there was little to be gained and much to lose—including her father's investment in his health—if they turned back now. Had he turned back *before,* had he never been such a bloody fool as to set out with so young a child at all . . . Martha could hear Tom's self-hatred building and felt something unholy rise in her, an urge to join him in his curses against himself. Tom was right—he shouldn't have insisted she come, travel with so young a child. But above all Martha wanted peace in which to mourn her Ellen, and no such thing could happen as long as Tom stormed about her decrying his flaws.

"Go," she said. "Find your daughter a coffin; send her body to my father to be buried with my mother; let us get on." *Just go and leave us alone.* But oh, that she could think such a thought at such a time, that she could prefer to grieve for her child without her husband by her side!

## CHAPTER 14

––––––––––

THE ROAD INTO THE MOUNTAINS was hellish, even dangerous, but Martha little cared, taking the jolts and bumps as their due. She took note of the changed air, the familiar pine fragrance, but felt none of her usual delight in it; even the crudeness of the hut that awaited them failed to alarm her. Tom made a few halfhearted apologies that she waved away, just as she waved away his explanations, descriptions, incantations. He talked of the subterranean furnace, the bubbling baths, the blanket sweats, the wonders of nature's laboratory, but all she wished of him was his silence. She begged fatigue and went to her bed—or cot, better called—grateful for its narrowness, for the chance it afforded her to lie alone.

How long did she sleep? A day? A week? She woke, or so it seemed, in the bath, the warm, bright bubbles of gas creeping up her body through the flannel gown that she and the other women wore. She looked around at her fellow bathers and saw young and old, healthy and emaciated; she saw a woman near her age sitting on the bath steps where the attendant had deposited her, her legs shrunken and twisted. She saw another young woman supporting a disfigured, misshapen child. She heard a pair of strong, healthy women laughing and calling back and forth, here only for the delightful society, they proclaimed, but what joy the bath! *Joy.* So foreign a word to Martha now.

But every day when the white flag went up signaling the women's time in the baths Martha continued to partake, to plunge into the cold spring afterward, to traipse to the large hut for the blanket sweat where they wrapped her tightly in more flannel, piled blankets on her, left her to lie till her pores opened and the poisons in her discharged. Did she poison the very air? Surely she must. The soakings had opened her mind to the truth of her actions. She was a being possessed of her own will. She might have refused to accompany Tom to the springs and stayed home safe with her child. She might have refused to allow the doctor to bleed the weakened infant, as her father would surely have done. She might have stayed awake through the night and tended better to her child. The hut attendant who came to dry and rub and wrap Martha couldn't notice her tears among the sweat, but the girl kept quiet around Martha even so; they all did. They knew who she was, what she'd done. Not done. Martha sat in the bath among twenty other women, alone.

More days passed and Martha discovered ways to be truly alone, to walk the mountain trails that reminded her of Monticello. She ventured out of the usual path, walking among the rubbish heaps, the weeds, the hogs, stumbling by accident upon the graveyard; they all came in hope of a cure, but of course some of them died. She thought of Ellen, buried in the Monticello earth with no parent as witness, alone. She visited the Warm Springs graveyard again and again and cried for Ellen over strangers' bones.

One day, as Martha returned from her solitary walk, Tom accosted her on the steps to their cabin. "My love, this place has no cure for you. You look more despondent every day. Do you wish to go home?"

"No." The answer came too fast, too hard, forcing Martha to understand something else in her nature. These springs were her luxury, the place where she could succumb to her grief; as soon as they returned home, she must put on the expected smile and become the mother, the daughter, the wife of old.

IN TIME MARTHA BECAME MORE ATTUNED to her surroundings, to the card parties, the group picnics, the dancing, the choicest young men serenading the loveliest young women under their cabin windows. Even the married women without husbands in attendance were escorted here and there by unaccompanied married or single men, the flirtatious nature of their conversations wafting openly in the breeze. Martha also began to notice how finely dressed everyone was, how this was a "cure" that only the rich appeared able to enjoy. When Tom came to their cabin that night, she accosted him.

"How much do we spend here?"

"Not above two hundred dollars."

Two hundred dollars. A sum that might have purchased Sally's fifteen-year-old nephew, left behind when his mother came back to Monticello.

But indeed, Martha could not call the money wasted; already Tom had regained some of his energy and his spirits. He began to participate in the men's activities like hunting and billiards, and even faro and poker, which they could ill afford. At first Martha welcomed the chance for increased solitude and retired early each night while Tom played, but she soon discovered that if her mind was left to itself, it would follow the same old path, and that the old path had begun to tire her.

One night after dinner she found herself responding to a gentleman who'd stayed behind as the men departed for their cards. His easy, comfortable manner, his lovely, warm eyes reminded her of William Short; he'd been to Paris, which of course assisted with the feeling of recognition, as did a melancholy that she believed she saw in him which mirrored her own. They talked of Parisians they'd known, a shocking number having been dispatched by mob or guillotine, a conversation so at odds with the general tone of the place and yet a suitable one, considering how difficult it was for Martha to leap into the general cheer. But later, when she discovered the same gentleman turning chameleonlike into a laughing, gay partner for another unaccompanied married woman, and later saw them depart together for the cabins, she realized what kind of fool she'd almost become. Tom was well. Martha had soaked herself in her grief until she was saturated with it. It was time to go home.

———————

HOME, SHE'D SAID TO TOM, but of course she meant Monticello. Ellen. She fell into the consoling arms of father and sister, and when Critta appeared with Martha's children, their small arms unwittingly consoled her as well. When she could bear to let them go, she and Tom walked to Ellen's grave, clutching tight to each other's hands. She'd been wrong to blame Tom. To blame herself. Any decision made of love, divided only by love, could not be called wrong. The children who survived needed them whole and united, devoted to the tasks to which they were born.

———————

THE NEXT DAY Martha was able to look about and see her family with clear eyes: her father home where he was meant to be and finally growing strong there; her sister, now seventeen and so like their mother it pained Martha to look at her; Anne, soft and affectionate and delighting in her grandfather's arms; Jeff, sturdy, mischievous, leading his aunt Maria in repeated chases across the lawn. And always nearby the ever-reliable Ursula, the efficient Critta, the still-lovely Sally . . .

The still-lovely Sally, again heavy with child.

---

THE CORN AND PEACHES WERE GATHERED, the fodder harvested, the potatoes dug, and Martha and Tom were still at Monticello when Sally gave birth to a girl—light skinned, amber eyed, with touches of auburn fire in her hair. She was named Harriet, a name no Hemings had ever claimed before but an easy name to recall, it belonging to a favorite Jefferson cousin.

Tom and Martha said nothing to each other about this pale child with the Jefferson family name, but later that night Tom said, " 'Tis time for us to go home."

*Home,* he said, and meant Varina.

## CHAPTER 15

WITH THE ONSET OF WINTER, Tom's symptoms returned: fatigue, migrating pains, an inability to concentrate on a task long enough to complete it. Martha had continued to open and sort Tom's letters, making sure crucial responses went out in good time; thus she was first to read the copy of the manumission document freeing Sally's brother James, and the letter accompanying it in which Martha's father explained that he had given James thirty dollars and transport to Philadelphia. She also learned that her father would be unlikely to free any other slaves soon—he reported to Tom that he'd mortgaged the remaining one hundred to make a two-thousand-dollar payment that had come due. Martha had already given up querying her father about his slaves-turned-tenant-farmers plan; now she gave up thinking of it.

Via Tom's correspondence Martha also learned that Richard Randolph had died. Martha wrote at once to Judith, but held out little hope of an answer. A second correspondence brought Tom a copy of Richard's will, which Martha read with great interest. In it Richard specified that his slaves be freed once his mortgage on them had been cleared, and that four hundred acres of his land be distributed among them. His widow was charged with helping them establish themselves as free men, *yielding them up the liberty basely wrested from them by my forefathers and beg, humbly beg, their forgiveness for the manifold injuries I have too often inhumanely, unjustly, and mercilessly inflicted on them.* The news of Richard's death had left no visible mark on Tom, but the will did, although not in a way Martha might have predicted. "You understand, do you not?" he asked Martha. "This impoverishes my sister. I must do what I can for her now."

——————

WITH THE FIRST CLEAR WEATHER Tom left for Bizarre, entrusting Martha, now five months' pregnant, to supervise the crucial setting of the tobacco plants at Varina. After the first good rain, she issued the command to the overseer, but she took to walking the fields herself to see how he fared. She watched the slaves separating the delicate young plants from the seed bed with gentle fingers that worked around the roots to free the plants before cushioning them in their palms, carrying them to the raised hills, and tucking them into the freshly loosened earth, a single plant at a time. Every day thereafter slaves primed the plants by pulling off any wilted or yellow leaves, then suckered and topped them by removing new buds and new growth to keep the plants from flowering. Until the plants were established, the children again picked worms.

Once her fascination with the process wore off, Martha found tobacco work unpleasant; at least once a day she was forced to remonstrate with someone. That first week she spoke to the overseer for keeping the children too long in the field; the second week she chastised a young slave for stretching out on the grass the minute the overseer stepped away; the third week—for Tom had not yet returned—she barked at Ned for sneaking into the garden and pillaging her radishes.

When Tom arrived Martha took a step back at the sight of the tall, strong man with the snapping black eyes coming through the door, his good health evident. He scooped her up, all six months' pregnant, five feet eleven inches of her, kissing her breathless right there in the door. Behind Tom Ned grinned at Martha the same way he'd done as a boy, and Martha's spirits lifted high as the ceiling. All would be right. Even later in their bed, wound together too tightly for the hot, damp air, as Tom explained he'd managed to rescue a few thousand dollars for each of his sisters by assuming more of the family debt, even then Martha wouldn't let go. Of Tom. Of Ned's smile. Of that moment on the ceiling.

---

IT HAD BECOME A TRADITION NOW, the trip to Monticello to await the birth of their child, their stay on the flaming mountaintop Martha's reward for her travail. Martha's father looked fit and contented, his face thinner and his features more finely drawn, but in Martha's eyes this only made him more handsome. Her single complaint might have been that he seemed less eager at the sight of her than she was at the sight of him; in fact, his mind seemed to be elsewhere a good deal of the time. Soon enough, however, he was hovering appropriately, waiting his turn to meet his newest grandchild. The second girl named Ellen was born in October, dark haired and dark eyed like her father and brother, hair and eyes darker, in fact, than that of Sally Hemings's year-old daughter. Jeff, Anne, and Harriet Hemings played with the sheepdog together, little Harriet chortling and gabbling no matter how many times she fell over and got picked up; the infant Ellen, on the other hand, screamed if her mother put her down in the softest cradle.

Tom too seemed unable to settle, spending most of his day on horseback, bolting out of the parlor in the evening soon after the family gathered. Even at night, in Madison's bed, he uncharacteristically kept his distance, and it didn't take long for that moment of lightness Martha had first experienced on his return from Richmond to wear off. Fatigued, worried, and out of sorts herself, Martha sought restoration of her spirits in the company of her father's even temper. Unable to ride yet, she joined him as he took his morning walk to examine the fall plantings in the garden, and soon they fell back into their old, comfortable habit of conversation. What did they talk of? The blight on the cabbage; the peculiarities of the climate; whether or not to introduce tomatoes to the garden. But as they walked Martha's father also described for her a new system of measurements, expounded on his "Indian project" in which he hoped to categorize the assorted tribes and compile a dictionary of their languages, and calculated the yield of his orchard.

One morning at the end of a week of shared walks, Martha's father paused at the farthest point in the garden and looked down at her. "Tell me, child. You manage?" His face sat as unruffled as ever except for a pair of vertical lines that had bloomed between his eyebrows. If Martha read those lines as honest concern, she might actually confide in him, letting out her worries in hopes of freeing herself of them. What release that would be, if only for this brief minute! *Oh, how I struggle to manage,* she would tell her father. *Tell me how to keep my husband in balance! What am I do with my dull-witted, cantankerous, children? And how do we manage a farm that sinks my husband into greater debt with each crop he harvests?*

But . . . *You manage,* her father had said. It was not, after all, a question.

"I manage," she answered.

Immediately, the frown lines eased. "I must count on you to do so," he said. "For there are those who believe that after the next election I shall become vice president of these United States."

"Oh, Papa! You said you were done with politics and glad of it. You all this week talked of nothing but the joy of your farmer's life."

"We must work to keep this republic we've made, Martha."

"Indeed, I understand this, surely. But you were rarely here when you served as secretary, and I can only think how seldom I shall see you."

"This is why I must count on you and your husband, a man I consider my inestimable friend, to take care of things in my absence."

Martha could find no comfort in those words, for any of them.

THAT EVENING Thomas Jefferson called his son-in-law into his cabinet and no doubt explained his future plans to him. Tom emerged thoughtful, calm, the glimmer of assurance that had come back from Richmond with him again visible. Perhaps Martha's father knew Tom better than she did; perhaps he trusted him more than she did. Night after night the two men closeted themselves in either cabinet or library, Tom electing to share little of the conversation with Martha, her father discovering less time for things like walks in the garden. Martha told herself she didn't mind, that she had enough to do with her fussing infant, her backward older children, the management of the Monticello household that she felt obligated to take back from the Hemingses whenever she arrived, but she missed those far-ranging morning conversations she'd shared with her father that so reminded her of Paris. Perhaps that was why, when she spied a letter from William Short among the correspondence just arrived for her father, she found herself taking undue interest.

In the years since the Jeffersons had left Paris, other letters had come to Martha's father from Short, and with every letter he had apprised Martha of its contents. Greetings from old friends, reports on the French political climate, news of Paris in general always comprised the evening conversation in the parlor following the receipt of such a letter. Martha had long ago recovered from the effects of her parting from the man and took in the news with neither more nor less interest than that of any old acquaintance. The letters always closed with a brief line that her father dutifully transmitted: *My warm regards to your daughters,* which Martha knew perfectly well meant neither more nor less than such lines usually meant, but even so, she always waited for it with a bizarre kind of anticipation, curious to discover if Short would again trouble to include it.

That evening at supper Martha waited for her father to raise the subject of that day's letter. She waited again when they gathered after dinner in the parlor. When nothing was said of the letter, she grew ever more curious about it. What news could it contain that her father wouldn't wish to share with her? Martha had already heard of those of their friends who'd been beheaded or turned into paupers or exiled to other countries by the revolutionaries in France. What worse could follow? What could her father want to spare her?

That William Short had gotten married. It came to Martha in the night, as she lay awake in anticipation of the next disturbance from Ellen. William Short was thirteen years younger than Thomas Jefferson, ten years older than Martha, long past the age when such an event should have occurred; only last winter Martha's father had commented on Short's "ongoing fondness for the state of bachelor." But once the idea of a possible marriage occurred to Martha, she couldn't stop thinking about it. *Had* he wed? And if he had, to whom? In fact, Martha could think of a half dozen possibilities—she'd observed that most females, once they'd met him, made a remarkable effort to keep in his company.

It began to obsess her, that letter, in part, no doubt, because she'd already begun to anticipate her loneliness after her father left Monticello. In part too, Martha would admit it, because the encounter with the gentleman at Warm Springs the previous summer had unsettled her. Martha knew all this and understood it for the foolishness it was, and yet she couldn't leave the matter. Catching her father after a hasty exit one day, she managed to enter his cabinet unnoticed.

The letter wasn't easy to locate, not left among the piles of correspondence waiting to be answered, not filed away with the ones already addressed. She'd come close to abandoning the search when she spied an unlikely bulge in the pages of the book of poems her father kept by his bedside. Martha began to skim over the tightly written words, looking for any hint of the personal, but as soon as she realized the topic she slowed in astonishment and took it up at the beginning. William Short was suggesting to her father that the best hope for emancipation lay in miscegenation, the inter-mingling of black and white, a thing unlawful in the state of Virginia. *The whites would get no darker than some residents of Spain,* Short wrote. *The blacks would grow lighter until there remained no distinction. This would work even in Virginia, and to prove it, I suggest you think only of Mrs. Randolph Tucker and the rich color of her complexion—there is no country that might not be content to have its women like her.* Martha knew this Mrs. Randolph Tucker, had met her at Richmond soon after her marriage; the woman was one of the Randolphs who bore the most visible signs of their Indian ancestor, Pocahontas.

That night Martha lay awake thinking of Short's letter and what likely response her father would make to it. Martha pondered her own conjectured response to it. At first it seemed to her that Short had been away from Virginia a good deal too long if he could in all seriousness write such a letter, but after a time Martha began to think of Monticello, and what Short might in fact know of life as it was lived there; Martha knew her father well enough to know that he would never commit to paper anything that might hurt his or his family's legacy, but what might he have said to Short while they lived in Paris together? *Perhaps your father grieves less than you think . . .* Oh, if only Sally had taken her chance for freedom and stayed behind in Paris! Martha reached for Tom, but for once he wouldn't wake easily to her touch, and a rude waking would do little to soothe either of them.

## CHAPTER 16

IN MARCH 1797, Thomas Jefferson left Monticello for his inauguration as vice president of the United States, and Tom and Martha returned to Varina. With her father now gone, with Tom traveling more and more to the other plantations, Martha discovered that time seemed to fold in over her and her children. What day? What month? Varina seemed always hot and humid and pestilent; the older children seemed perpetually behindhand and little Ellen no plumper or better natured; only the crops going into the ground gave her any sense of calendar.

It took Maria's letter to fix the days. On she wrote with a fever that carried off the page and into Martha's fingers. *I'm to marry Jack! I shall never again be without my dearest person.* Martha shouldn't have been surprised—Maria was now eighteen and their cousin Jack Eppes had figured larger than anyone else in every letter Maria had ever sent from Eppington, and yet Martha *was* surprised. Maria was still a child in so many ways, so full of laughter and nonsense, still running about from here to there . . . Martha stopped herself. At one time *she'd* been the one chastised for running about; *she'd* been the one to charge down the bluff at Tuckahoe with Tom on the eve of her own marriage. She wouldn't do such a thing now, of course, because now she was a wife and mother. As Maria would be soon. Poor little running, laughing Maria! But dear God, what on earth was Martha thinking? Maria wouldn't stop laughing once she married Jack. Martha hadn't stopped laughing when she married Tom. *Had she?*

—————

IN OCTOBER Tom and Martha traveled to Monticello for the wedding. Martha's father had pushed ahead with work on the house, planning a complete redesign of his own creation, and as the horses pulled into the last roundabout, the noise and dust around the brick kiln and joiner shop told Martha construction had not abated for the festivities. She stepped through the debris up the steps and into . . . air. The hall had no ceiling, the east room adjoining no walls, the parlor where Maria planned to wed no single clear space for the bride and groom to stand up in.

Maria gave little evidence of caring. She flew, haloed in joy, to greet her sister, and Jack, an easygoing favorite of all the Jeffersons, greeted Martha with a warm hug, dropping a comfortable arm over Tom's shoulder.

"I had to marry her," Jack said. "She wouldn't leave Eppington. What else was I to do, drop her at the roadside?"

Martha, Maria, and their father laughed. Tom said, "She might have had a home with us if she wished it."

"Which it appears she did not," Martha said, and they all laughed again, except for Tom.

Perhaps Martha didn't laugh as much as she'd like when alone with her husband, but he loved and cared for his wife beyond her every expectation. What matter that he was not by nature a jovial person?

—————

BUT MARTHA UNDERSTOOD it was only natural that her father would respond to each of his sons-in-law in kind, that with Jack he would engage in lighter fare, with Tom the more pedantic; it couldn't be the father-in-law's fault that Tom was sensitive enough to notice and fragile enough to give the disparate treatments another meaning. Nor could it be *Martha's* fault that she found their shared dinner a welcome change, the talk flying around the table with a quickness of wit that carried her with it even as it left Tom lost and silent.

"I'm just a silly bird among the swans," he said to Martha later that night.

She'd been lying a bit removed from him in their bed, having already proved that once she gave up nursing one child, she could expect to become pregnant with another, and Ellen had begun to turn from the breast before Martha was quite ready to move ahead with the next one. She could not, however, stay at such a distance in the face of her husband's remark. She slipped inside his arms, found his mouth, and kissed it till it softened.

"You confuse your birds," she said. "'Tis the swan who sits in quiet dignity while the silly birds all flap and squawk about him. Remember, please, which bird I chose as mate and accept your prize with less humility."

Martha's witticism was too effective in the short term but perhaps not so effective in the long term; Tom wasted little time in taking their new proximity to its natural conclusion, but as soon as he—and she, she must admit to it—achieved their satisfaction, he rolled away from her.

———

MARIA AND JACK MARRIED CHEERILY among the rubble with only family in attendance, but with no sparing over the wedding feast, despite the disordered household. As soon as they departed, Martha felt her sister's absence much the way she felt the loss each time she left Monticello. But with Jack gone, Tom received a double share of his father-in-law's attention, so Martha got to witness a rare lift in his spirits. When Martha's father asked them to stay even after his departure and Tom accepted, Martha's spirits floated to meet his. Little Harriet's sudden death from a throat ailment brought the household low, and it fell to Martha to write her father of the news. The only acknowledgment of the letter came in a brief line in a letter to Tom:

*Please tell my daughter I am in receipt of her missive of the 19th.*

When just after the turn of the year, Sally gave birth to a light-skinned, hazel-eyed, auburn-haired boy, Martha left the news for someone else to carry. Sally named this boy William Beverly, the name of a close friend of the Jefferson family.

———

MARTHA'S OWN CHILD, Cornelia, was born that summer, again at Monticello, coincidentally timed with her father's summer hiatus. What little work Sally had done before had ceased after the birth of her son, and Martha couldn't help but note and compare her own household contributions despite caring for her infant *and* three other children. She remarked to her father one evening, "I've not seen Sally in two days. I do hope she's well," but her father only gave her a single, unreadable look and picked up the newspaper.

By now the rubble of construction had been cleared and the roof and walls had been installed, but a poor start had been made on the interior painting. Perhaps the four Randolph children underfoot were hindering progress. Perhaps Martha's father heard a visiting neighbor mistake Sally's boy for Martha's girl. Perhaps Tom's increasing restlessness had become more obvious. Or perhaps for another reason altogether, Martha's father called Tom and Martha into his cabinet.

"My renovations are far enough along that I may now send my carpenters to help you ready your house at Edgehill."

———————

MARTHA'S FATHER RETURNED TO PHILADELPHIA, but the Randolphs remained at Monticello, keeping a watchful eye as the carpenters began work on their house at nearby Edgehill. The house would be modest, and to Martha's eye peculiar—an unadorned eighteen-foot by forty-foot rectangle—but the Randolphs had no cash to spare on fancy design and trimmings. By now Martha had noticed that Tom's health improved in summer and regressed in winter, but the house project seemed to help him; he managed to keep himself moving through all of January and February and might have sailed straight through into spring if it weren't for the trouble in Richmond.

The news had already spread through Monticello as if on the wind; before Martha knew the fact of it, she sensed something of its nature by the shuffle in Critta's steps, by the way Molly never lifted her eyes above the wainscoting, by the way Monticello's first black overseer skipped his afternoon meet with Tom. A parched horse and rider carried a letter from Tom's Richmond uncle the next morning; Martha heard the frenetic crack of Tom's boots across the hall floor and the smack of the door as he entered the small parlor, holding out the paper in a trembling hand. Martha reached out and took the letter; as she read she felt the hollows of her hands begin to dampen. Nine hundred slaves had been discovered preparing to seize the Richmond armory with the intent to murder every white citizen they encountered; a great massacre was prevented only by one slave informing his master of the plot, and a wholesale arrest of the insurrectionists had begun. Tom closed the parlor door, pulled a chair close, dropped his voice low.

"I've set a guard."

SALLY CABOT GUNNING

"Good heavens, Tom, not here!"

"Just the same. We might trust the house staff, the artisans, our overseer, but I can't say that with any certainty of the men working the ground. I can only think if I were they—"

Yes, Martha thought. She too.

---

THE NEWSPAPERS CARRIED THE LATEST DEVELOPMENTS to Monticello but never as fast as slave carried them to slave; Martha could read in the hollowed-out eyes around her of the wholesale hangings, innocent with guilty. Even so, such retribution did little to calm the fears of white Virginia; curfews were set, patrols combed the hills, one of their Albemarle County neighbors flogged a slave almost to death when he refused to work on Sunday. Tom rose up and spoke indignantly against the flogging, drawing other neighbors to join their voice to his. Martha's father wrote from Philadelphia:

*The Almighty has no attribute which can side with us in such a contest.*

Martha answered her father's letter herself, although it had been addressed to Tom.

*My Dearest Papa, Can you think of nothing to be done? What's to become of them? Of us?*

Martha received no answering letter. If her father sent one to Tom, he chose not to share it with her.

---

IN DECEMBER SALLY GAVE BIRTH to another light-skinned child, a girl she named Thenia, who lived and died so quickly Martha saw her only twice, and yet images of her first, Ellen, began to haunt her. As Sally moved about ash gray and listless, Martha found herself dropping her lips onto Cornelia's silky hair as she suckled, stroking Anne's cheek as she curled in her lap, catching Jeff or her second Ellen for quick hugs as they dashed by. She even began to gather up the neglected Beverly and sing to him, just as she sang to her own children, until a disturbing familiarity began to grow in his hazel eyes, as if he'd known her through a long, former lifetime. She left him be.

# PART II

# Edgehill

*1800–1809*

## CHAPTER 17

IN JANUARY OF THE YEAR 1800, Tom, Martha, and their four children moved into their new home at Edgehill. The wife of Sally's brother Peter, Betsy Hemings, joined them as cook, not as a gift but as a loan, and Martha's father made them promise not to send her any farther from her husband than their property at Edgehill. Martha was thrilled to add the competent Betsy to her household; she enjoyed the lovely south-facing slope before their house; she even admired the sparkling Rivanna River at their feet; but most of all she cherished the distant glimpse of Monticello to the west. Her own house ended as it had begun, awkward in both size and shape, and despite the free labor, the brick and timber and simple furnishings had caused an additional debt they now owed to Martha's father.

As if to compensate for its not being Monticello, Martha's father sent them gifts—books and toys for the children, chinaware, a Turkey carpet, and a pair of chairs upholstered in a lovely rose brocade ordered via William Short in Paris. When Martha's father realized she had no horse to ride, he lent her a gentle bay that Tom would have preferred she refuse, but she couldn't bear to—she no longer needed to wait for the carriage or climb the three-mile ascent by foot to reach Monticello.

Martha's father also paid Varina's overdue mortgage bill.

MARTHA HAD EXPECTED TO SETTLE contentedly at Edgehill, but too soon she found herself plagued by an odd feeling of disconnection. No matter which of her belongings took its place in which cramped room, she couldn't escape the sensation that she was still standing with Tom on that hill at Monticello and looking down at someone else's distant farm. When news traveled down the mountain of the death of Ursula, poisoned by the dosings of the Negro doctor, Martha hadn't felt so untethered since the death of her own mother. Indeed, when Martha thought back on her childhood and its many comforts, it was Ursula's arms she felt around her, not her mother's. Martha traveled up the stark, winter mountain with blurred vision to watch Ursula buried, standing apart at the edge of the grove of trees as was the custom for white mourners at Negro funerals, only causing that feeling of disconnection to deepen further.

For the whole of the next week, Martha worked about the house with heavy feet and heart until she noticed Tom growing more and more unsettled each time he came upon her. She attempted to lighten her air, only at night after Tom had fallen asleep allowing her tears to wet her pillow, allowing herself to whisper Ursula's "Coffee Song." *Oh! Fare ye well, my bonny love* . . . But what *was* this pain? Was she the forsaken or the forsaking? Why hadn't Martha even known Ursula was ill? Had they kept it from her thinking she wouldn't care or couldn't help, or *had* she been told and simply not taken proper notice? And why hadn't she insisted that their own Dr. Norris attend the slave, instead of the Negro doctor who had been suspected of poisoning others before Ursula?

———

Martha had only just begun to reclaim her balance when the news came from Eppington that Maria had prematurely delivered her first child. Two more letters quickly followed, the first carrying the news that the child had died, the second the news that Maria was not well.

"Oh, she is too like my mother!" Martha cried. Frantic to be with her sister, she sat in torment for three days as a rare blizzard whited everything around her and trees, fences, even the Rivanna River disappeared behind a wall of snow. By the time Tom declared the roads safe for travel, Martha had convinced herself she wouldn't find her sister alive.

They left the older children at Monticello and took Cornelia, Molly, and Ned, the horses high-stepping through the drifts, the carriage once almost overturning until Tom ordered Ned to walk ahead checking for rocks and logs under the snow. As they drew nearer to Eppington, Martha's trepidation grew.

"I don't know why she didn't go to Monticello as I did to have her child. Our fine Dr. Norris, so many loving hands and familiar faces, the healthful air."

"She's spent most of her life at Eppington. If those faces aren't yet familiar to her—"

"I'd sooner have any Hemings beside me than Aunt Eppes."

Tom flashed Martha a look. "You don't like your aunt Eppes, do you?"

"Of course I do! I only suspect her judgment. My father asked her to send an older servant to France with Maria, one who'd been inoculated against the smallpox. My aunt sent Sally."

"So you blame your aunt for the Sally trouble."

"I don't know what you mean when you say *Sally trouble*. I only blame my aunt for sending a pox-prone, giddy young girl to France. And I shall certainly blame her for not sending Maria home to Monticello if—"

"Her home is at Eppington. Her husband is at Eppington." But there Tom removed his eyes from the troublesome road and looked at Martha again. "And there shall be no *if*. Maria will be fine."

It was so unlike Tom to think the happier thought, and he said it with such understated conviction that a violent rush of love overtook Martha. She slid closer to him in the carriage.

———————

Maria was not fine but she was much recovered, a fever caused by an inflamed breast at last subsiding, only the still-fresh grief at the loss of her child dulling her eyes and her spirits.

Maria greeted her sister with, "So I'm to be my mother in all things."

"No," Martha answered. "Only the part that ends with two thriving, happy children and the lot of you spoiled by an adoring husband and father."

Maria worked up a thin smile. She took Martha's hand. "You're so like Papa."

"Come back with us," Martha said impulsively. "Build your own house nearby. You mustn't keep so far away."

But Maria shook her head. "I'm not so like—" There she seemed to lose the strength to finish. She closed her eyes.

———————

In the winter of 1801, Thomas Jefferson was elected third president of the United States on the thirty-fifth vote of the House of Representatives, the Electoral College having fallen into deadlock. For Martha the insult was almost too much to be borne, but her father announced it calmly, as if it were how all presidents came to office, as if the men of the House, with whom he'd worked so closely for the past four years, were now perfectly entitled to treat him as a stranger.

Before the new president left for the new capital in Washington, the Madisons came to Monticello to dine, and Tom and Martha were invited to join them. James Madison had finally married a lively widow named Dolley, who had little trouble holding her place in the conversation. Martha loved her too-large nose and chuckling eyes and reined-in smile, as if at any minute she might burst into a wild tale not quite suitable for the company. Martha also caught more than one warm look, enough to give her hope that she might have found a friend. But Martha noticed that Tom seemed little interested in either the Madisons or the talk, until the subject turned to James Hemings. Martha's father had sent word to James that he wished to hire him as chef at the President's House, but James had failed to respond, forcing Martha's father to hire another man.

"What on earth was James thinking?" Madison asked. "As president's chef he would make twice what he could make in any other position."

"Perhaps it seemed a backward move," Tom said, "going to work for his old master."

"I should think he'd be grateful for such a chance to shine," Martha countered.

"Perhaps he doesn't wish to be grateful." Martha heard the new inflection in Tom's voice. No doubt her father heard it. He moved the conversation to the fluctuating temperature readings on his new thermometer.

————————

AT THE END OF FEBRUARY, the president left for Washington. Two months later Sally delivered her fifth child, another Harriet, another pale infant with deep red glints in her hair. Again Sally recovered slowly, and a young girl named Edy was brought to Monticello to help care for the newborn and the three-year-old Beverly, an unheard of thing at Monticello—a slave for a slave.

In July Martha's own dark daughter, Virginia, was born.

————————

THE NEW HARRIET THRIVED. Virginia struggled. She occupied Martha's waking hours and disturbed her sleep, but even when the child finally settled, Martha lay awake, her perverse mind seeking out worries that weren't her own, fixing too often on James Hemings. Tom's remark about gratitude twisted and turned in her mind. Would she expect gratitude for an entire youth spent in slavery? Of course not. Even gratitude for being set free, as every human being should be free from birth? No. But after all that had been done and not done, when nothing was left but to make the best of a future that could not be easy for anyone, to refuse the offer of one of the most prestigious employments in America? *Why?* James Hemings could now say yes or no to Thomas Jefferson as he could not have done before, but it was important to Martha's father—and to Martha—that this man her father had carefully trained and freed did well. It was also important to Martha—and, of course, to her father—that the former slave held them no ill will. When Martha finally slept, her mind continued its twists and turns, mixing up Tom and James, Harriet and Virginia, the President's House and Monticello, until she woke even unsure of her name.

Martha was still puzzling over James Hemings when her father wrote that he would be returning to Monticello for a month at the end of August, and that James had agreed to come with him and cook for a wage. Now, perversely, all Martha could think of was Tom's other word: *backward.*

———

MARIA GAVE BIRTH TO A SON, Francis, named for her uncle Eppes. Martha was unable to attend her sister, due to Virginia's continued ill health, but this time the mother and child at Eppington recovered well. Not only had Virginia kept Martha from her sister, the struggling infant continually kept Martha from her father as well. When he arrived at Monticello in August, Martha sat trapped at Edgehill nursing Virginia through prolonged fevers, rashes, and digestive upsets. Finally Martha's father sent her John Hemings's wife, Priscilla, as nurse, perhaps now realizing that having brought

in Edy to help care for Sally's *two,* he could at the least offer someone to assist Martha's *five.* Besides, there would be little work for
Priscilla and the other slaves at Monticello once Martha's father
returned to Washington, and Priscilla would remain within three
miles of her husband; so Martha told herself, concluding—at least
to herself—that it was a fine solution for all.

---

IN DECEMBER Tom entered the small parlor wearing a face that
looked as if someone had drawn a bleach-soaked hand over it,
every feature sagging and pale. He held a letter that Martha saw
at once was written in her father's hand. Virginia hadn't quite finished her meal but Martha eased her from her breast and handed
her to Priscilla. The slave was already occupied with Cornelia and
Ellen, but however unreadable Priscilla's face remained, she appeared to read Tom's; she took charge of all three children and sped
them from the room. Or perhaps Priscilla knew the information
her new master carried to his wife beforehand.

Tom handed Martha the letter. She read through the request for
books, the talk of a new waterproof cloth, a report from Eppington, and came to it near the end.

> *By now you have likely heard of James Hemings's tragic end in
> Baltimore. It has since been confirmed an act of suicide. I am told he
> was delirious for some days previous to his having committed the act,
> and it is the general opinion that drinking too freely was the cause.*

The page shook in Martha's hand. She thrust it at Tom, not
wanting it near her, but Tom wouldn't take the letter or look at her.
"Is there no hope for it then?" he asked, but he didn't wait for
Martha's answer, supposing she'd been able to form one. He left the

room. At first Martha wasn't sorry that Tom had gone; it allowed her a rare chance to sit alone and puzzle out the meaning of such weighted news—but it was December and Tom's annual winter descent into misery was almost upon them. She closed down her own despair, took up a thick shawl, and went out the door after her husband.

---

Tom wasn't hard to find; Martha followed the path he'd already worn that led down to the river and found him standing on the low bank, staring into the tumbling water. She drew close, laid a hand against his wide back, and leaned her cheek against his shoulder.

"My poor father."

Tom shrugged away from her. "Your father lives. James Hemings does not." He turned and started off for the path, but stopped only a few feet away from her. "Do you know what they'll say now? Do you? They'll say they can't be freed. They'll say they can't manage without the direction of their masters. James Hemings has killed more than himself." He strode but a few yards up the path before stopping again. "*Why?* Why did he do it?"

"Perhaps, as you said before, he felt coming back here was a step backward. Yet for him to leave here, he had to leave his family behind in slavery. Only think of the choices that left him."

"I don't wish to think. I can think no more on the subject. There's nothing more to be thought that I haven't thought already." He turned again for the path, but Martha caught him by the arm before he could escape her.

"Tom. You *must* think. What more could be done? My father gave him an excellent trade. He freed him. He offered him paid work."

But Tom was staring over her shoulder at the river, not listening, leaving Martha to speak to herself. To argue to herself.

## CHAPTER 18

T{OM MANAGED THE EDGEHILL PLANTATION} that first year with few additional slaves, only those he could spare to move out from Varina, but by the second year he'd taken on ten more, again on credit issued in Thomas Jefferson's name; by the start of 1802, Tom told Martha that he could not run the plantation without increasing his slaveholdings further, that he must write again to his father-in-law. Martha took note of Tom's distress over the next few weeks, but she had her own concerns to occupy her: organizing her household; enrolling Jeff in the neighborhood school for boys; setting up her own classroom for her oldest daughters in the small parlor. She could *not* get the seeds of the French language to germinate in Anne. She pulled the door closed—again—and looked at Anne expectantly. "*La porte est—*"

Anne gazed back, her face blank.

"*Ferme!* The door is closed. *Ferme.*"

The door flew open and Tom beckoned to her from the other side. Martha stepped through and closed the door behind her. *Ferme.*

"I had but a single goal," she told Tom. "To educate my children to a higher standard than has formerly been offered in Albemarle County. It would appear this is not to be."

"Come," Tom said.

Martha followed him down the hall. He entered his study ahead of her, hurried behind his desk, and began to push papers toward its edge, toward Martha. "Cotton," he said. "'Tis far more lucrative than tobacco now, and much easier on the Negroes."

"Tom, we can't grow cotton here."

"No, we can't. This is why we must move to Mississippi and take up the crop there. The land costs nothing, we'll sell our holdings in Virginia to pay off our debts, we'll bring our Negroes with us. We start again, but ahead, for the first time since our marriage."

"You mean to say you would move us to—" Had Martha heard? He would move them to *Mississippi*?

"Mississippi. The Virginia tobacco industry is done. I've run out the numbers for the first two years of cotton—see the enormous gain."

Martha picked up the paper, her fingers clumsy and fumbling, but even the quickest glance told her the new numbers were considerably higher than any she'd seen at Varina. She knew she must think, and she knew she must do it in calmness, that she must present her thoughts in a way that didn't run wholly counter to Tom's own. But how could they not run counter? *Take life by the smooth handle* was all very well, but too smooth a handle right now and she and her small children would end up many hundreds of miles away from her family. Her world. The world she trusted. Of course she trusted Tom, but . . .

*No.* If Martha were to think this through with a clear head, she must be honest in her thinking. She *couldn't* trust Tom. She couldn't count on any steadiness of mind or persistence over his labors. It was her father who supported her family, paid their mortgage, gave them gifts that in fact provided the majority of her children's books and clothing. She might see to her daughters' education, no matter the French door being open or closed, but the rest she could not do. For the rest she must rely on a husband or a father.

Her father.

"You must write to my father," Martha said. "Send him your figures. He'll comprehend them better than I do." He'll comprehend in them the tale of daughter and grandchildren removed from him forever.

————————

WHEN MARTHA RETURNED to the study two hours later, a half-drunk bottle of brandy and a half-finished letter sat on the desk, while Tom slept in the chair. Martha crept around the desk and looked down. The numbers she had glanced at earlier had been neatly copied on a fresh sheet of letter paper, another sheet blackened in a close, tight hand that little resembled Tom's older, freer style of writing.

> *This list tells you the practical reasons for us to go, never forgetting the gentler labor of cotton vs. that of tobacco, but now I list the other reasons. I'm sure by now it's become eminently clear to you that I am so essentially and widely different from all within the narrow circle around you as to look like something extraneous, fallen in by accident and destroying the homogeneity. The sentiment of my mind when it contemplates yourself alone is one of most lofty elevation and unmixed delight. My heart overflows with gratitude and affection. More, when I attempt to esteem the value to the whole human race of the incredibly, inconceivably excellent political system which you created, developed and, at the last I think, permanently established, I cannot find its bounds. All this only proves the more that I have not earned that place at your side.*

Martha stood gazing at her husband, his torment washed away in childlike sleep, and realized how seldom she saw his waking features in such a state of peace. Everything she'd thought through so meticulously earlier in the day now seemed nothing but a gross betrayal. How hard he tried! How much he loved her! What was

Mississippi but the evidence of it, however erroneously applied? Martha pushed back her hair and felt the knobs in her own brow; she took a deep breath and forced the knobs to smooth out, but by the time she'd returned to her room, they'd rebuilt themselves, this time as if in stone.

———

THE LETTER WAS SENT. Martha watched for the answer, but when it came Tom gave no sign of having received it and made no offer to share it with her. Perhaps another wife, perhaps one with another husband or with less at stake, might have kept to her own affairs and allowed her husband his, but his affairs *were* hers, and the path his mind traveled was not a safe one to leave him to wander alone. Add to this, by March Martha had begun to suspect she was pregnant again, even though she was still nursing Virginia. Virginia, far more sensitive to the timbre of the household than were Martha's other children, fussed with every raised voice and grew distracted from the breast by every unfamiliar sight or sound, looking again and again at Martha for reassurance that her mother was still there. Martha need only gaze into those trusting eyes to understand how much responsibility she owned.

Martha found her chance to read the letter, or rather she made her chance, even though it meant invading Tom's study as soon as he rode out, digging the letter out of the battered leather portfolio into which it had been stuffed. *The shade into which you throw yourself, neither your happiness nor mine will admit that you remain in,* Tom's father-in-law had written.

> *In matters of interest, I know no difference between yours and mine. It would appear I hold the virtues of your heart and powers of your understanding in a far more exalted view than you do. If*

*you would grant me leave, I shall endeavor to return to Monticello before month's end to convey some information possibly useful to your plans.*

*—TH Jefferson*

TH Jefferson. Her father. Martha smoothed the letter and returned it to its portfolio, clear in her specific task now: She must only delay Tom's leap to Mississippi till the month's end.

———————

THE PEAS WERE SPROUTING and the buds on the fruit trees were near to bursting when the president returned to Monticello; this time Martha, Tom, their five children, Maria, Jack, and their boy were all there to greet him. He stepped out of his carriage and stood a moment, as straight and fit as ever, looking around him with an air of relief, as if surprised to find it as he'd left it. His eyes swung to the steps where they all stood waiting and held his arms wide, as if to say, *Here is what I return for.* Soon he was among them, hugging and kissing his daughters, clapping their husbands on the shoulders, scooping grandchildren into his arms, tossing Jeff in the air until his squeals roused Virginia. Martha's father turned to Virginia at her cry, tousled her head, and moved on to greet the Hemingses; after he'd gone around to each of them, he retraced his steps until he found Tom, put an arm around his shoulders, and led him into the house ahead of the others.

For most of the afternoon, Martha's father remained out of sight in his room. At supper he showed the talent that it was already rumored Washington had begun to thrive on—his ability to bring together disparate personalities and advance them toward a common goal.

"Tom, you must tell Jack what you wrote me of opossums," he began, and just as Tom's dissertation began to veer into the arcane, "That calls to mind my French sheepdogs. Jack, how is that pup of yours performing?" Before Jack could become a little too entertaining, Martha's father interjected again. "Perhaps you'd all like to hear this latest from Washington." And so it went around. But as they left the table, it was again Tom who was singled out with the arm across the shoulder.

"Perhaps we might have a word." This time he added, "Martha, would you care to join us? I have so little time to see my family." Martha, her blood surging, followed the two men into the library.

The most recent alterations had brought the library to the first floor, just beyond the greenhouse, where her father had already found time to discharge half a dozen books from their shelves. Through the far door lay his cabinet and bedchamber, but Martha was seldom invited even as far the library. The reason that they settled in the library rather than the parlor soon became clear, however, when Martha's father pulled a large map off the shelf. He waved Tom and Martha into the matching armchairs, and pulled a third up to the table between them.

"Mississippi," he began, spreading the map out on the table. "This idea intrigued me, Tom, as soon as you broached the subject, so I took the liberty afforded me by my position and inquired of those who'd recently been there. I've brought home this new map as well. Let me share with you some of the concerns of those who've been there." He pointed to the area near the southwestern edge of the boundary. "Here's where you find the most available land." He looked up, his eyes glancing past Martha's, fixing on Tom's. "Choctaw country. This should be our first concern; the Choctaw are beginning to rise up. We must fear for the safety of your family, number one." Martha's father drew a finger over the western edge of the map again. "Next I don't believe we should discount the French in Louisiana. They rumble; they beat their chest. Were you to invest in land only to have it occupied—"

"By the *French*?" Tom attempted a laugh. "They might like to try."

"I only pass along the fears barreling around Washington just now." Martha's father sat back in his chair. "You've made so thorough an analysis of all the farming data, I knew you should want the political too. Tell me, what are your thoughts on the lowland climate?"

"'Tis no greatly different from Varina."

"Ah. Yes."

"But you were sick so often in Varina," Martha said.

"I'm sick here."

"But not as you were. You can't have forgotten those fevers, the rashes. And with five children to acclimate—"

Martha's father stood up, effectively silencing Martha without words. "We're all tired tonight, but I didn't like to wait in offering up the little information I'd managed to acquire in case it proved useful to your deliberations. I'm so very glad to have you both here. Indeed, the most difficult part of this job of mine is that it keeps me far from everyone who matters to me." He kissed Martha's forehead, grasped Tom's hand, and disappeared through the far door.

Tom rose and exited through the near door, not looking at Martha. She stared at the map. The nightmare. She sat a long time, after a while forgetting the map, looking around at her father's books, at the mind-boggling diversity of his interests. Government, of course, and architecture, and philosophy, and the arts, but there were also numerous books on plants, animals, rocks, shells, the Greeks, the Egyptians, and many books on the American Indian.

"Excuse me," a voice said behind Martha and she jumped. Turned.

Sally. "I thought everyone gone."

Sally made to leave, but Martha raised her hand.

"No, please. Hold." But why? Why had Martha stopped her? James, Martha thought. She wished to speak to Sally of James; it would be unconscionable not to do so.

"Your brother," Martha started. "I was so stricken by this news of your brother."

Sally dipped her head.

"But why, Sally? Why did he do it?"

Sally lifted delicate shoulders. A slave's shoulders and arms— even a woman's—were usually thick and strong, but Sally looked as if she rarely lifted anything beyond a needle and thread. " 'Tis not for me say, ma'am."

"To say or to know?"

Sally lifted her shoulders again.

"My father could not be more distressed. You do know this, Sally?"

"He's spoken to me of his distress."

*But did you believe him? Do you blame him? Or are you mocking him? Or me?* Oh, that look in her! What was it? If Martha could only see into those amber eyes and know. But know what? What *would* she want to know? Sweet Sally. Dashing Sally. These were the names the girl bore on both white and black sides of the mountain, but now Martha could see only the dash and none of the sweet. What if under that dash there lurked a vein of hatred so thick and rich it might burst through to the surface in the night and murder them all in their beds? Yes, that was how white Virginia always said it: *We'll be murdered in our beds.* Here they were, taking these people into their homes, allowing them— demanding of them—every intimate kind of contact; *help me out of this dress, bring me a soak for my feet, fix this bolster for my neck—*

and suddenly one uprising, one suicide, one sale, and the night comes when the bolster is lifted out from under the neck and brought down over the face . . .

Martha rose from her chair until she towered over Sally, waiting for the slave to turn and go back as she'd come, but Sally stood as she was, waiting for Martha to pass *her,* no doubt because she wished to continue on to her master's chamber beyond the far door. Oh, the affront of it! Martha considered sending Sally on a last-of-day chore in the kitchen, but if Sally refused, it would mean she knew her privileged status to be inviolable, that Sally's power and Martha's had become equal somehow. *Somehow.* Dear God, why couldn't they just get rid of her? Why couldn't they just get rid of them all?

———————

THEY'D TALKED OF IT IN PARIS. Martha had just been removed from the convent, Dr. Franklin had been asked to dine, William Short was of course at hand. It was the kind of talk that might normally have happened after Martha had excused herself, but the wine had been excellent, according to Dr. Franklin, and her father had continued to pour it out, and Dr. Franklin had continued to engage Martha, giving her little chance to make her habitual gracious exit. Of course she hadn't *wanted* to make her exit, despite the fact that she'd been angry with her father—she remembered it so distinctly because it was such a rare occurrence. She'd wanted to join the convent, and instead her father had removed her from the convent school, unable or unwilling to hear her objections. That was her father's way—to smile as if attending her every wish and go on as before, overseeing packing her trunks into the carriage, carrying her off to buy her new clothes, hats, shoes. Incentive versus disincentive.

When the dinner talk had moved on to recent news from Virginia—a new owner for a neighboring plantation, his addition of thirty Negroes to those already living on the property, Martha had burst out, "Dear God, have we not enough Negroes already? Why aren't they just *freed*?"

The table—slave owners all—fell silent. Martha's father looked at her as if surprised to see her there. "Martha, child, what are you still doing among us? Say your good nights and leave us."

But William Short interjected, his eyes fixed on Martha with new interest, "I should like to hear what ideas Mademoiselle Jefferson might have on the subject of emancipation. What is it, do you think, that continually stalls our efforts?"

"Why, bigotry," Martha said.

"Economics," Dr. Franklin added.

"Fear," Martha's father said. "In Virginia, on our isolated plantations, we're vastly outnumbered. Were the Negroes to be freed, were they to be allowed to assemble and arm, were they fixed on revenge, there is no white man who could stop them." He paused. "Or any God who would wish to."

The table fell silent again. Martha's father appeared to notice Martha again. He smiled. "Martha, dear, I've once suggested you pay your respects and leave us. Now must count as twice. Pray don't force me to bore our guests by saying it a third time."

Martha's face flamed. To go from Mr. Short engaging her as an adult to her father engaging her as a child was far too rapid a descent for a single evening. It was also the only instance Martha could recall where her father had humiliated her in front of guests. And to do it in front of *these* guests! She stood up. "You needn't worry, Papa, as I've only learned to count as high as two."

Oh, the balm of Short's laughter as it followed her out the door!

THE NEXT DAY William Short asked Martha to accompany him for a walk in the garden. With little effort he got her to vent her fury at her father's behavior of the previous evening—Martha and Short had grown that comfortable since she'd come home—but somewhere in the middle of her tirade, Martha realized she was not making her case as an adult very skillfully. She broke off.

"Oh, do keep on," Short said. "I've long suspected no father could be quite as perfect as you paint yours. Besides, you're quite lovely when you're fuming."

Was that where it began? Martha wondered. She thought back to that morning in the Paris garden, the elegant Short fitting his step to hers—an easy thing to do as they were of like height—but also effortlessly fitting his conversation to hers. What other man ever spoke to her so naturally? What other man had ever called her *lovely*? Indeed, what other man would have so patiently listened to a daughter's petulant fuming? And then . . .

"Of course your father is not perfect," Short told Martha. "As no other man is perfect. But this I will tell you—he is the man who will solve this slave debacle for us." He pulled out his pocket watch, took a quick look, and shoved it back. "He will also smile at me with that deadly smile of his if I'm not back at my desk in two minutes, and this I do not wish to see. Excuse me, my friend. If we *are* friends?" As he spoke he gripped Martha's elbow with an urgency that erased every bit of ease and elegance and turned him into someone so real, so humble, that Martha could think of only one thing in life she now wanted, and that was to be this man's friend.

## CHAPTER 19

TOM GAVE UP ON MISSISSIPPI. His next idea: Georgia. That lasted only as long as it took him to discover that South Carolina would not allow the transport of slaves across its border.

"Why must we go away to consolidate our holdings?" Martha countered. "Can't we sell Varina?"

"Its sale would hardly clear its own debt and would do nothing for our debt on Edgehill. We might sell Wingo."

Wingo. Martha's security. In fairness, that was the point of *security,* that it rescued you from your *in*securities, insecurities caused by a threatened move away from her family to a swamp full of mosquitoes and Indians. But selling Wingo meant more than selling a plantation, it meant selling slaves, and the one thing worse than adding slaves was subtracting them, displacing them, putting them at risk of being sold away from *their* families. Martha did pause to ask herself why she didn't mind displacing the Varina slaves, but in her mind those were still Randolph slaves; the Wingo slaves were Jefferson slaves, and Jeffersons didn't sell their slaves without the slaves' consent. Or did they? As Martha thought, she recalled some talk of slave sales while they were in France, when her father's income as minister fell far short of his expenses.

Martha pushed France away. It had begun to intrude too much of late. "If you sell Varina you might bring those Negroes here to Edgehill. Surely the increased output could make up some of our debt."

Perhaps the twin defeats of Mississippi and Georgia has so weakened Tom's confidence that he took Martha's suggestion without argument. Or perhaps he knew he couldn't sell Wingo without Martha's signature on the paper and now doubted her compliance. He set off for Charlottesville to consult his lawyer and to put the plan in motion for the sale of Varina. It was a good plan, Martha would always insist; its only difficulty lay in the fact that tobacco prices were falling all over Virginia and planters were attempting to sell land left and right, even land that wasn't toxic to human habitation.

No one wanted Varina.

---

THE PRESIDENT RETURNED to Monticello for the summer. He built an icehouse, reconfigured the garden, planted grapevines from France and peach stones from Pisa. In August William Short arrived from France. Martha had heard the talk the year before and the year before that and even the year before *that*: "Mr. Short writes that he returns to America." "Mr. Short writes that he's booked his passage." "Mr. Short's canceled his passage." She'd long ago stopped paying any great mind to her father's talk of Mr. Short, and now here he was, and here she was, pilfering what looks she could across her father's dinner table, amazed at how changed he was. That was her first thought as she gazed at the stylish short hair swept close around his face, the velvet collar on his coat, the cashmere breeches, the silk waistcoat; by the time the wine had gone around a second time, she realized her mistake. Martha was the one who had changed, her French polish long rubbed off, the dress of rural Virginia now the standard by which she judged others. No matter the pains taken over hair and dress, it was hair pinned by a young slave, a dress hemmed by one. And if William Short glanced at her more than once, it was clearly because of all she'd left behind in Paris, all she'd taken up since she'd come home, all the care that now marked her face. But one thing *had* changed in Short: His smile used to hold all the secrets they'd shared; now, it held only strangeness.

Martha spoke little. Tom spoke none. William Short spoke a great deal, prompted by his host to recount all the news of Paris, but as Critta entered to clear away the plates he broke off.

"And where is Mademoiselle Sally? I must be allowed to pay my respects to Mademoiselle Sally."

A pause, the kind perhaps only Martha would notice, before her father spoke. "Critta, fetch Sally, please."

The talk started and stopped again as Sally entered, as William Short rose from his chair to kiss her hand and speak some foolishness in French. Martha credited Sally with enough good sense to give only a brief, murmured answer before making a hurried exit. Short's good sense appeared to have been jettisoned while crossing the Atlantic.

"She's unchanged," he said. "I can only marvel at it. You're none of you changed."

"And you've changed only in a greater talent for falsehood," Martha said.

Short's eyes fixed on her.

Tom stood up. "Mrs. Randolph, I believe 'tis time for us to depart. Mr. Short, a pleasure to make your acquaintance. You must come visit us at Edgehill, although you'll find nothing as grand as this."

"Thank you, Mr. Randolph; I should like very much to visit. Would the morning suit?"

Tom appeared startled. "Very well. Half-nine?"

"Half-nine," Short confirmed.

W<small>HAT A PREPOSTEROUS FELLOW THAT SHORT IS</small>," Tom remarked
as they jolted down the mountain in his father-in-law's borrowed
carriage. "What on earth does he think he plays at, embarrassing
Sally that way?"

Martha thought of Short's letter to her father, of Mrs. Randolph
Tucker, of Sally's mixed parentage and grandparentage. How fast
a leap from there to Sally's children, so pale they must shout to all
of yet another generation of racial mixing! In Virginia everyone
liked to point to their neighbors' whitewashed slave children, all
the while ignoring their own. What was Short playing at? Perhaps
Martha knew.

But she answered Tom. "I can't imagine."

S<small>HORT ARRIVED EARLY, ON HORSEBACK</small>. Martha greeted him as
she would greet any guest but was glad when Tom hastened him
off on a ride along the river, glad to return to her routine with her
children. When she saw the two horsemen reappear, she called for
Priscilla and dashed to hide in her scrubby young garden, but her
escape plan failed. Tom rode off to his fields, but Short simply dismounted and followed the path which ended at Martha.

"Walk with me," he said.

"I've much to do."

"I'm sure you do. Only walk with me to the edge of the wood,
and afterward I shall leave you to your work." He reached out a
hand, helped her to her feet. "You're not glad to see me here, are
you?"

"I'm always happy to welcome my father's guests."

"Ah. You're always happy. This is what your constant half smile
says, and your cheerful little hum, and I don't believe in either

thing. I'm no longer able to believe what I wish to believe, you see. I once believed in a wild girl with torn hems and no shoes who leaped so boldly across the lawn that surely she could be persuaded to defy her father and stay with me in France." He stopped walking, gazing out at the distant fields dotted with the bent backs of Negroes. "I once believed that a great man I knew had the power and conviction to emancipate the slaves."

Martha whirled around. "Our slaves are better off than half the poor white workers you see huddled in shacks all over Virginia."

"Yes, Mrs. Randolph, I know that argument. But I don't wish to argue. I only wished to say that I'm sorry. I should never have pushed you to stay behind. When you balked I should have respected you then as much as I respect you now. This is all I wished to say."

"And you no longer respect my father. This is also what you wish to say."

"There is no man I respect more," Short said quietly. "This is why—" He stopped. Continued. "Your father is a man of his word. He kept his promise to free poor James. He'll keep his promise to Sally."

*Keep his promise to Sally?* Martha didn't ask. She wouldn't ask. She felt sixteen again, awkward, disadvantaged, dazzled by this confidant of her father's, and yet in so many ways that sixteen-year-old had been bolder than this woman, this wife, this mother of five, this daughter of a *president*. Who was this William Short that he dared accost her like this, that he *dared* to speak to her of Sally?

"When do you return to France?" she asked. "My friends wrote me of a certain attraction, the lovely Rosalie, the wife of the duc de la Rochefoucauld, I believe she is. Or was. I heard a rumor that the poor duc was stoned to death by the mob. If true, this clears your path, does it not?"

Short gazed at her, a new, deep sadness unconcealed, but whether a sadness over the duc or Rosalie or Martha's callousness she could not tell.

"Yes, he was stoned to death," Short said. "So you see it was best you didn't stay. Good-bye, Mrs. Randolph." He turned back toward his horse, but stopped again. "What *is* that song you hum so constantly? I know it."

"The 'Coffee Song.' Ursula taught it to me."

Short laughed but without humor; Martha could note the lack because she knew the other laugh so well. "'Tis the '*Coffle* Song,' Mrs. Randolph. You do know what a coffle is? A line of slaves chained one to the other and driven off for transport or sale."

———

THAT NIGHT THE 'COFFEE SONG'—'Coffle Song'—ran endlessly through Martha's head, or rather, Ursula ran endlessly through Martha's head. Why had Ursula sung such a song to her? Had it meant nothing to Ursula beyond a poignant tune, or had she understood its pain and hoped to teach that pain to Martha? Defiantly Martha hummed the song under her breath, refusing to give up its comfort, but of course there was no comfort in it now.

———

BY SEPTEMBER WILLIAM SHORT HAD LEFT MONTICELLO. Martha's father remained. At first, Martha found time most days to visit the mountaintop, but she seldom found her father alone, and when he was, he was often secluded in his cabinet, forcing her more than once to return down the mountain without a sighting. On those rare occasions when she found him in the garden or on the terrace, there was like as not a servant with him, one or another relation of Sally's. One day she found herself looking at her father differently, as William Short no doubt looked at him, a white man on top of his mountain, ringed by a collection of more-than-half-white servants, while down below lived the black masses who fed and clothed him, who in fact had leveled the very mountain on which he sat and who had built the castle in which he lived. Who was it who had first drawn the line that separated the three colors? Or were there three colors, or four or five or nothing but shades of one? Who had decided that the man at the top should have the fruits of the labors of men of all colors except his own? And why was Martha attempting to sort all this now? Because of William Short. Because he came and saw and asked and wondered and he made Martha do so too. She was glad Short hadn't stayed long; no comfort, no peace, could ever be found in his company.

———

Martha was in her parlor admiring Ellen's slate of practice letters one day when she heard a now-familiar insistent tread in the hall. Ellen had followed her namesake with her own brightness, her own eagerness, her own reaching for anything new, and Martha found her greatest fulfillment in teaching her. But wife coming before mother, Martha turned away from Ellen and met Tom at the door. Martha looked at the *Richmond Recorder* in Tom's hand, at the deep, mahogany flush to his skin, and felt as if she'd read the news already. Tom thrust the paper at her and jabbed at the passage:

> *It is well known that the man, whom it delighteth*
> *the people to honor, keeps, and for many years has*
> *kept, as his concubine, one of his slaves. Her name is*
> SALLY . . .

Tom wrenched the paper from Martha's hand and reversed his course down the hall. Martha followed. "Where are you going?"

"To talk to him. We must get his denial to the paper at once."

"Wait. Please."

"For what?"

"For me."

---

WHILE TOM SAW TO THE SADDLING OF THE HORSES, Martha changed into the riding habit her father had once given her, assembling the pieces with methodical care: first the pleated worsted petticoat, next the matching waistcoat and jacket with the satin-covered buttons, next the hat with the thick ribbon designed to contain her hair in the worst wind. She usually set out less formally for Monticello—indeed, her appearance often drew a particular pinched look from Ursula as she tumbled off her horse into the hall—today, however, she felt it was important to appear who she was: the daughter of a president. But as she dressed a curious sense of having done all of it before again overcame her; just as she'd known what the newspaper would say about her father and the slave concubine named Sally, she knew what would happen when they arrived at Monticello.

Tom led the way, Martha following, the horses picking their own way on a trail as familiar to them as to the riders. Martha noticed little of the route beyond the flamboyant carpet of leaves as she fixed her eyes on the ground, thinking of what she would—and wouldn't—say to her father.

They found him in the vegetable garden with the Hemings grandson he'd been training to serve as gardener, measuring the diameter of the pumpkins. Even stooped, Martha's father appeared larger than life, just as he had always appeared to Martha, and when he straightened, beaming at the sight of them, some of the things she'd resolved in her mind began to waver, just as the surface of the fishpond wavered whenever the mountain breeze touched down.

"Tom! Martha! Come. We've got some lovely cakes and cider."

"We wish to talk to you about the *Richmond Recorder*," Tom said.

Martha could only stand amazed as her father's smile never altered. "Which I do believe we might do over cakes and cider." He put an arm around Tom and led them to the small parlor.

Critta brought the food and drink; her master thanked her with his usual courtesy. "And please close the door," he called after her. Why did a slave never close a door? Martha wondered. Well, of course—to listen better.

"You've picked a fine day to ride up the mountain," her father said. "Is that bay as sweet as ever?"

"Yes, Papa."

"We've come," Tom said again, "to talk about the *Richmond Recorder*. We must make haste if we're to get your denial in the next paper."

Martha's father set down the cake into which he'd just bitten. He chewed; swallowed; picked up the folded, pressed square of linen, and wiped his mouth. He set the napkin down. "I find," he said at last, "that the older I get the less I'm inclined to do anything in haste. In fact, the less I'm inclined to do anything at all."

"But in this particular case—"

"In this particular case especially."

Martha looked from Tom's thunderhead eyes to her father's cloudless hazel ones. What did he mean by *this particular case especially*? What was he admitting? Those cloudless eyes told her nothing. She might ask, of course, but if she did, and if he answered . . .

Martha said, "This story won't stay in Richmond, Papa."

"No, it won't. But it will die the same natural death wherever it lands."

"Perhaps if you send Sally and the children to one of your other plantations till it blows over—"

"It will blow over all the faster if we refuse to send up a cross-wind."

"'Tis not only you this affects, Papa."

Only then did Martha's father's expression alter, the eyes opening wider, the mouth straightening. "My dear child, it will only affect you if you let it."

"*I* shall write the papers!" Tom shouted.

"And if you do so, what happens then? Someone else writes the paper. Another story is written. It becomes a case to be made. Do you think this is the first time someone has written a story about me? Such stories appear, they disappear, they're forgotten. Now, in truth, my greater concern today is that no one has tried this cake, which is a superior cake, I must say." He took another bite.

Tom stood up. "Come," he said to Martha.

Martha hesitated. It seemed much more should be said, but as she didn't know just what, or indeed who should say it, she followed her husband out the door.

———

## CHAPTER 20

M ARTHA'S FATHER RETURNED TO WASHINGTON. The Sally matter plunged Tom low, followed by a press of creditors that sank him lower; he refused to write his father-in-law for another loan, and the creditors pressed harder. When Martha's father wrote from Washington, Martha went in search of Tom and found him closed in his own darkness, alone in his study with the candle long out. Martha entered carrying her own flame, but Tom turned away from it.

"I can't bear to see him tarnished," he said.

Martha, who'd been thinking the same thing since the minute she'd been forced to read the odious paper, could find no solace in the confluence of their minds. "I think—"

"'Tis not what we think!" Tom shouted. "'Tis what others do! And yet your father puts it aside as if it were never written!"

Martha hesitated. "Perhaps he doesn't. I've had a letter." Martha handed it and the candle to Tom. She watched as he read, the words playing through her own head as she did so. *I should like you and your sister, with your families, to join me here in Washington.* Martha suspected she knew the reason for this particular letter coming now: The Sally rumors had worked their way north, and they hadn't died the natural death that Martha's father had anticipated. What could better offset the image of the president's long limbs curled around his winsome slave than a daughter at each side and a grandchild on each knee?

Tom read the letter and pushed it away. "I'm entirely too ill to travel. And you certainly wouldn't carry a sick child to Washington. Why is nothing done about Virginia? Why isn't Dr. Norris called? She can't breathe. She—"

"Dr. Norris has been called. Twice. He tells you and I tell you. 'Tis nothing beyond the usual teething."

"I stand over her at night and listen to her struggling. Indeed, I begin to think I catch something of it; I couldn't capture a good breath for an hour this morning."

"Then of course you mustn't travel."

Tom looked up. This she must say of him—he often knew her mind before she'd formed it. "Go, then," he said. "Leave Virginia and me to manage as we can. Go among the swans. Someone will be sure to send you word should anything befall me or our little chicken."

Martha had heard such remarks many times and each time she'd argued against their gloom, but right now she was tired of it. She was tired of everything. Failed crops. Illness. Hemingses.

*Washington,* Martha thought, as she hadn't thought of it a half hour before; Washington and her father and her sister, and talk of something besides rain and pests and phlegm and indebtedness. Was it not a daughter's *and* a mother's duty to help protect her father's legacy, especially as it grew more and more likely this was all her children would inherit?

Just thinking of her children's futures set Martha's pulse fluttering. The wild thought momentarily possessed her that she could leave all her children behind in the care of Priscilla, that she could have a respite from everything that wore at her, but she soon remembered the likely purpose of the mission, and how useful a few children would be in creating a living family portrait that would charm her father's critics. But she would not bring all of her children. Her timid Anne would get more trauma than joy from the experience, but ten-year-old Jeff could not be left behind, nor could she think of leaving out the six-year-old Ellen; as to the three-year-old Cornelia and the sixteen-month-old Virginia, Tom was perfectly right—they could be left safely in the care of Priscilla. With none but her two most independent children with her, Martha might capture a good breath herself now and then.

———————

Martha's father sent one hundred dollars to pay for their travel. Dolley Madison, who had indeed proved to be a friend, sent the fashionable hairpieces, combs, shawls, veils, and handkerchiefs not worn in the hills of Virginia, which Martha's father also paid for. Martha didn't wince at the expense, as she knew her husband couldn't afford to pay, and if her father requested that they take this trip he *should* pay. He should *pay*. Still, Martha hid the details of the transactions from Tom, doubtful as it was he'd even notice; he spent his days either in his bed or shut up in his study.

Martha tended to Tom with all the meaningless aids she could remember, but the time came when she had to stop trotting down the hall and up the stairs and concentrate on preparations for her departure. She set out her best dresses to be washed and pressed, sewed a new coat for Jeff and a new dress for Ellen, and put Molly to work cleaning shoes and mending stockings.

Although in the end Maria had decided to leave her son behind, Jack Eppes chose to accompany them partway, which provoked Tom to comment, "So it's to be a merry journey, then. Mind he doesn't distract the driver with his piffle and cause him to over-turn."

"I'll mind," Martha said, but she did indeed hope it would be a merry journey, and if it was, she wouldn't care if she over-turned.

JACK AND MARIA ARRIVED to collect Martha and her two children; Martha found Jack and Maria in high spirits, Jack because his were always so, Maria because, like Martha, she wore new traveling clothes. She twirled for Martha. "Am I not fit for society now?"

And did our father have to pay for your clothes too? Martha wondered, but she said only, "You are," and gave her sister a fierce hug.

Jack looked amongst the milling children and asked, "Where have you stuffed your old fellow?"

"He's not well enough to come down. He sends his affection."

"Well, damn the man, tell him 'tis not returned. Lazy old sod." Jack laughed.

Martha took a last trip up the stairs to say good-bye to Tom. She reached to smooth his hair but instead, already feeling merry, swatted it into a tuft. Tom batted it down. "I don't feel at all well. I don't need teasing."

"Of course you do not," Martha said, in answer to the first thing, letting Tom think she'd answered the second. This her father had taught her: What does it matter what they *think* as long as you *know*? She caught Tom's face in her hands and kissed him; at first he remained unresponsive, but he couldn't keep it so; he held her face and looked deep into her eyes as if for the last time. His eyes filled. Martha's filled. It would seem a merry journey could not be bought so cheaply, that the cord that bound them could not be unknotted so easily, even for a month or two.

BUT AS THE WHEELS ROLLED UNDER MARTHA, the pull of all she'd left behind began to lessen. November was a fine month to travel, with no mud or heat and just enough crisp air to freshen the crowded carriage. And they laughed. Oh, to be drunk on laughter again!

When had Martha laughed like this? In Paris, when William Short told her a story about Dr. Franklin that he should never have told, of being summoned into Franklin's chamber to find him pink and naked in the bath, glasses fixed to his nose, going over a letter that Jefferson had asked the senior minister to review. " 'Tis a fine letter," the doctor said, "but our friend Jefferson tends to conceal too much."

Oh, how Martha had laughed!

And Short had told her she was lovely when she laughed.

———————

JACK LEFT THEM as the party transferred to the carriage her father had sent to meet them; from there the trip grew more tedious. Jeff continually pestered to ride "on top" with the driver; Ellen bounced from seat to seat and window to window, no matter if Maria or Martha happened to sit between them; both children lost their fascination with wayside inns and grew quarrelsome. When they arrived in Washington after a five-day journey, Martha's high spirits had already been worn down.

Perhaps the disappointing look to Washington contributed. It appeared as no more than a fair-size village, Pennsylvania Avenue narrow, unpaved, and lined with trees, with workmen's huts scattered along either side, giving little sense of the community Martha had hoped to join. The president's house was spacious but dark, cold, and sparsely furnished. Only the joy in her father's eyes as he came hastening from a meeting to greet them made up for it all; her father, as tall and straight and strongly made as ever, and yet he seemed older than he'd appeared only the month before at Monticello, his naturally soft voice even softer, his eyes watering as if with tears.

"I'm Thomas Jefferson Randolph," Jeff announced to the porter, and the tears, if such they were, evaporated into the familiar, hearty laugh that no one could ever hear without joining. Yes,

Martha would find her laughter here too. She felt her mood lifting and it stayed lifted as the president himself led them above-stairs to large, airy rooms with better furnishings and waiting fires.

---

THE PRESIDENT'S HOUSE WAS STAFFED by eleven servants and three slaves brought from Monticello to serve under the cook; apprentices, they were called. Martha overheard two of them talking together one day about one of the Washington servants, a free black man from North Carolina. "He bought himself. He sold vegetables from his own garden and chickens from his own coop and saved enough to buy himself! It took him fifteen years."

The words haunted Martha.

During the day Martha and Maria were visited by the Washington ladies and returned the visits with the grace they'd learned in Paris; at their father's almost nightly elegant dinners, they helped move the conversation evenly about the table, again as they'd learned to do in Paris. Martha spoke quietly but confidently of matters she knew: the importance of girls' education, her manner of teaching her children, the seasonal challenges of farm life, her years in Paris and what she understood of its subsequent change. When asked, she admitted to an undying enthusiasm for her father's republican principles. After the first of these dinners, as the gentlemen disbursed, the wined and careless words drifted along the hall toward the sisters. For Maria: *Lovely girl . . . so charming and accomplished . . .* For Martha: *Her father again . . .*

No one talked of slaves—at least not to the president's face or in the presence of his daughters—but Martha saw quite enough of the topic in the papers: a cartoon of her father as a rooster, chasing a black-faced hen; a Northern tirade about slaveholders in the presidency; a satirical poem. The poem was too much for Martha to bear. The author, not content to claim the president lay with his slaves, insisted that he lashed them too. Martha tore the poem from the paper and burst into her father's office. Wordless, she thrust the print at him.

---

*The patriot, fresh from Freedom's councils come /*
*Now plea'd retires to lash his slaves at home / Or*
*woo, perhaps, some black Aspasia's charms / And*
*dreams of freedom in his bondmaid's arms.*

---

But Martha's father read the poem and only erupted into the same hearty laugh that had greeted them in the hallway, leaving Martha in confusion. Surely no guilty man could manufacture such a robust laugh when confronted with a charge? She began to think of the Carr cousins, infrequent visitors to Monticello but fond of their visits to the "white man's harem" as some called the slave quarters. But Sally didn't live in the quarters. And the Carrs had not been in France where that first too-pale child had begun.

---

PERHAPS NO ONE TALKED OF SLAVERY at the president's table, but they did talk of religion. After one particular diner insisted on the necessity of the government's legislating in favor of Christianity, Martha's father interjected, "The legitimate powers of this government extend only to such acts that are injurious to others. It does me no injury for my neighbor to say there are twenty gods or no god."

The table fell silent. The president moved the talk on, but after dinner he ushered his two daughters into an adjoining stateroom where a four-foot cheese occupied the only table.

"This was sent to me by some New England Baptists, admirers

of my defense of the liberty of conscience, the right to worship—or
not worship—as one pleased."

"Papa!" Maria cried. "How long has this cheese been sitting here?"

"Why, since I arrived."

"Since a year ago last spring? Why, 'tis molding! And look here,
something's chewed it! Oh, Papa, you must get rid of the thing."

Martha's father gazed down at the cheese as if he'd only just noticed
its decay, as if blinded to all but the great principle that inspired it. "Perhaps," he said sadly. "Perhaps . . . yes, one day soon. Certainly."

But next day, no doubt in anticipation of its pending demise,
the president took time out of his schedule to show his grandchildren the cheese. Maria refused to go along, but Martha accompanied them, if only to listen to her father explain the principle that
inspired the gift, as she knew he would do.

"I wrote a law," he began. "It allows for the protection of a man's
thoughts. No man must be forced to think like another. Some people
who liked the law sent me this cheese as a way to thank me for it."

Ellen wrinkled her nose. "I *hate* cheese."

Martha watched her father as he struggled to maintain his smile,
and even at six Ellen seemed to understand that her remark had somehow wounded him. "But I don't mind if *you* like it," she amended.

"Exactly!" Martha's father cried. He scooped Ellen up and carried her from the room, the two of them chattering like squirrels.
*Do you like maple candy? Do you like baked apples? Do you like cake?*

"*I* like cake," Jeff chimed in behind. Martha's father slowed, dropped
a hand on his grandson's shoulder. "Then let's have some now."

Martha was pulled into the impromptu cake party with them, but
she wasn't in fact a part of it; a new three-way pact had formed. She sat
back and watched and listened as her father asked and they answered,
as they asked and her father answered. *I like . . . Do you like . . . Our
papa likes . . .* The children gazed at their grandfather as Martha had

always gazed at him, as if he stood taller than the trees. He would never shrink for them. Or would he? Martha stood up, brushed away the crumbs that always seemed to seek out her shawl, and made herself a silent promise: She would not allow her father to shrink before her children. She would not allow him to shrink before anyone.

## CHAPTER 21

Martha was in washington three weeks before anyone dared mention the subject to her directly. Celia French, the wife of a Massachusetts lawyer who was in Washington to interview for a post, had been present at a luncheon at the Massachusetts senator's house, and she and Martha had struck up a general conversation that soon turned to the more personal matters of husbands and children. They'd crossed again at a tea at the president's house, where they'd shared their impressions— both favorable and unfavorable—of Washington, finding they agreed in large measure. Now they crossed again by specific invitation: Mrs. French had asked Martha to come for coffee and cake. Alone.

Martha liked Celia French. She felt at ease around her. She vowed to go home and copy the simple knot she put in her hair, the narrower line of her skirt; when Celia moved the conversation to the subject of Thomas Jefferson and her great admiration for him, Martha relaxed even further. She was unprepared for the sudden exclamation that followed.

"I'm sorry but I must ask. You seem a sensitive person and I must know how you manage it."

"Manage what?"

"The slave! That Sally they write of in the paper. They say he has several children by her. Dear Lord, they're your brothers and sisters and he enslaves them!"

Martha set down her coffee cup; it was no great sacrifice, as she'd found it bitter. "You can't mean, Mrs. French, that you believe what they write in the newspapers."

"But they all talk of it. It comes from all directions. I find it difficult—"

"It comes from all directions that lead straight back to a single story in a single paper, written by a low-life opportunist, disappointed not to get a position in my father's government. Ask this 'all' that you seem to trust so implicitly, ask them where they get their tales and you'll find it comes back to this one individual, a man named Callender, who wrote a solitary, falsified, spiteful article in a Richmond paper." Martha rose. "I'd stay to chat longer, but I'm sorry to say that I find our current topic of little interest. Good day." Martha left, not waiting for the servant to escort her, and climbed into her carriage.

All through the ride back to the president's house, it seemed as if everyone stared and whispered. Was she imagining it now, or had she simply blinded herself before? Now she could think back to those dinners and teas and see a dropped eye, a hand lifted to a mouth, the chatter cut off as she entered a room. Or perhaps she imagined that too.

When Martha reached the president's house, she went in search of Maria. She found her on the second floor, playing a harpsichord that had miraculously appeared as if for her sole enjoyment. Martha sat down on the bench next to her sister and took her near hand, clinging to it so fiercely Maria looked at her in bewilderment.

"What, Martha? What is it?"

"I've been to see Mrs. French. It was an unpleasant visit." Martha told Maria exactly what was asked and what was answered. Maria listened with keen attention, as if she were memorizing, not just every word that Martha spoke but every expression that crossed her face, and Martha was filled with even greater affection and gratitude for her sister. Maria understood what was to be said of the matter henceforth. There would be no need to discuss the topic further.

Ever.

———

MARTHA AND HER SISTER STAYED in Washington for six weeks but kept close to the president's house, close to their father. Tom wrote from Virginia:

> *I'm despairing of our daughter's and my health. Dr. Norris came and gave vague counsel only. He had few words of comfort for me, but I shall not fail in my duty to our children.*

Martha answered:

> *This must be a quick note to tell you I am in good health and so are Jefferson and Ellen and Papa and Maria. You are greatly missed and I shall be glad to come home. We hope to leave at the end of December.*

Tom wrote back:

> *My health is so improved, Virginia is so far recovered, I now make plans to arrive at the end of December to escort you.*

———

THE NIGHT BEFORE TOM WAS TO ARRIVE, Martha's father entered her room carrying neatly wrapped parcels for the children who'd remained at home. He unwrapped and rewrapped each to show Martha: carved ivory beads for Anne, a gold-embossed book of fables for Cornelia, a silver cup for Virginia that bore her name.

Martha fingered the satiny cup. "Papa, I fear you will run yourself to starvation if you take every one of our comings and goings as an excuse for an extravagant gift."

"Nonsense. Your children are as dear to me as my own."

Martha flushed. Could he mean . . . no, he couldn't possibly mean any children but Martha and Maria, who were of course no longer children, but just the same . . .

"I shall miss you, child."

*There,* Martha told all those phantom Celia Frenches who might be listening, *he calls me child yet.* She placed the silver cup back in its wrapping and let her father refold the paper, fasten the string. "I shall miss you, Papa. I always miss you."

"'Tis my dearest wish to be back on my mountain with my family and to never leave it again."

"'Tis my dearest wish as well."

Martha's father lifted his eyes, those old, vertical lines popping up between the brows. "Things are well with you?"

"Between nursing sick children and comforting a troubled husband, yes, things are well."

"My dear girl, tell me how I may help you."

"By taking care of yourself. As you fare, we fare."

Martha's father set down the cup, crossed to her, and enclosed her in his arms. She could feel the strength in him, the sheer force of his will, and yet she could feel his gentleness as well. He released her.

"Your welfare is my paramount concern. Yours and Maria's and your families'." And although Martha had said no single word about finances, he added, "I shall speak to Tom on the morrow about the state of his affairs. I'll do all I can."

———

TOM ARRIVED, indeed gaunt and fevered looking, rushing to Martha to collect her to him despite the audience of guests and servants in the hall. After watching her father forge so close and easy a bond with his grandchildren in only six weeks, Tom's awkwardness with his own children stood out the more; he managed to scoop up Ellen and fuss over her new bow, but with Jeff he didn't seem to know the proper pose to strike. He lifted a hand as if to ruffle the boy's hair and then dropped it low as if to shake, finally leaving it dangling unused at the end of his arm. When in the next moment Jeff grabbed his grandfather's sleeve to tell him of the wild turkeys he'd seen on the lawn, Tom seemed to take it as the excuse he needed. He turned to Martha and began recounting all he'd suffered since she'd been gone: The plaster had fallen in the east room; Cornelia had the mumps and the others would likely have it soon; he was fevered himself, he was quite sure.

---

MARTHA'S FATHER HAD HOPED Tom would stay in Washington several weeks, keeping his daughters with him that much longer, but Tom—and Martha now—wanted to be gone. Martha's father insisted Tom accompany him to the capitol building, and Tom returned from the visit thoughtful and subdued, but he refused an invitation to join a group of senators at a president's house luncheon, and remained quiet through their final dinner. As eager as Martha was to get away, the parting from her father the next morning was so melancholy it carried with her through a subdued journey home.

---

HOME. EDGEHILL. Martha stepped through the door with a new appreciation, scooping up her daughters in turn; Anne's responding hug lasted too long, Cornelia's not long enough, and Virginia seemed not to recognize her at all. Priscilla, Betsy, Molly, and Ned gathered around to greet her, and Martha pressed a coin into each hand for the extra work they'd had to do while she was gone. Incentive versus disincentive. She looked around. The plaster had indeed fallen in the east room but little else had changed, surprising Martha; she'd been sure the mountain had tumbled down on them while she was gone.

That night Tom made a passionate application between the sheets in a way that had been absent in Washington; Martha responded with more relief than eagerness, glad of anything that suggested health in her husband, but before she fell asleep, Celia French kidnapped her thoughts, keeping her awake despite the exhaustion of travel. It took Martha a number of hours to realize that the Celia French problem was a Northern one; no Southern woman would dare bring up such a subject. Yes, she concluded: It was good to be home.

———————

THE NEXT MORNING Tom nudged Martha awake and began speaking as if taking up a topic they'd only just left off. "I confess I didn't expect to be so impressed with our capital. A living, working, and yet symbolic place, a place that's changed the world and will continue to change it. I see now why a thinking man should wish to be a part of it."

Martha attempted to rouse herself. "I know one thinking man who wishes to be shed of it."

"A man who's already done his part and more. Dear God, how could I not wish to join him? Martha, I've decided to run for Congress."

Martha sat up, awake now. "You were in Washington five days and couldn't wait to come home."

"I had other matters on my mind. Samuel Jackson Cabell's up for reelection; I shall oppose him. I've made up my mind."

"But Cabell's a strong supporter of my father."

"Do you imagine I wouldn't strongly support your father?"

"Of course I don't. But what kind of reward is that for Mr. Cabell's efforts on my father's behalf?"

"Reward enough, if he wins. And if I win against such a man, my reward must be declared well-earned." Tom couldn't have heard his own contradiction as he added, "Randolphs never lose in Virginia."

"But what of your farms? You can't afford to allow them to lag any further behind."

"Your father manages from afar. Do you think me less capable?"

"*You* manage for my father. Who will manage for you both?"

"You." Tom grinned and attempted to pull her down beneath him.

She pushed him off, although she had little to risk; during her month in Washington she'd begun to suspect that she was pregnant again.

Later, when she found Tom staring at the fallen plaster, another suspicion dawned: that Tom's fascination with Congress was but a means of escaping his failures at home.

———

MARTHA TRIED. She reminded Tom of his health difficulties, she perhaps prematurely announced a pending child, she reviewed their financial ills, but Tom pushed all aside. In the end Martha convinced herself Tom would lose and refused to worry until he won by eighteen votes, a poor enough showing made poorer by Jack Eppes's decision to run for his own county seat and winning unopposed. Martha did succeed in convincing Tom he needed to find a tenant farmer for Varina. She also insisted she accompany Tom to a meeting with the new overseer at Monticello but grew sorry for that last. The man glared at Martha and Tom in turns, barking out one-word answers to her more involved questions, while answering Tom's short ones in detail; she left with a new sort of ache in her head that she feared she would come to know well.

But Martha still didn't quite believe Tom would leave her until she saw him mount his horse and ride off.

———

FOR HER FIRST ACT Martha summoned the overseer to her husband's study, positioning herself behind Tom's desk, holding Tom's pen in her hand. She did not ask him to sit down. He stood before her, unblinking.

"I shall make mistakes," she said. "I shall count on you to point out as many corrections as you choose, to make as many suggestions as you choose. But when I decide which course to follow, the decision will be mine alone. Are there other matters we need to discuss today?"

"Indeed, a great many. Too many for a single day."

"Very well. Pick the two most urgent."

He blinked.

Martha waited.

He chose three. "We must get in the winter wheat and dig the potatoes and wrap the fig trees. In what order do you wish to proceed?"

Martha knew it was a test, but she'd lived at Monticello all her life and knew the subjects well. "The wheat is a necessity and can't be risked long in the field. The figs are a luxury, but so fine a one, and the trees costly to replace. The potatoes will keep underground. "Wheat, figs, potatoes. Would you disagree? I shall listen if you do."

"I do not disagree."

"Thank you. Tomorrow we'll discuss the next two items on your list. Two, if you please, not three, but I promise you I shall work my way up to three soon." She smiled.

The man didn't smile, but Martha liked to believe he frowned less. It would have to do.

———

MARTHA SUMMONED EDGEHILL'S OVERSEER SECOND, an ordering of her priorities she did not wish to defend to Tom, but as Tom wasn't there, she could do as she chose. The problems at Edgehill proved harder: The overseer reported that the granaries were not nearly full enough for the approach to winter, there weren't enough bottles for the cider making, and two of the imported Varina slaves had run off.

"Let me think on these matters."

Martha went to bed overwhelmed and freshly angry at Tom, but woke as if by miracle with answers in hand.

The neighbor to the east had sold them wheat and corn in the past and must be propositioned again. Monticello could loan bottles for the cider. The two runaways had family in Richmond; Martha need do nothing until she conferred with Tom—she knew where the slaves were. She rose and went at once to her husband's desk to compose a note to her neighbor.

> *My husband having gone off to join my father in fulfilling his*
> *duty to our fledging nation I am caught short here at home.*
> *May I beg of you the greatest favor in the shape of wheat for our*
> *granary, should you have it to spare, the charge to be kept on*
> *account, which shall be paid as soon as we receive a return on*
> *our tobacco?*

She took up a fresh sheet and began to compose a letter to Tom about the slaves, but pushed the letter aside after completing nothing but the salutation. If she wrote of her troubles to Tom, he would only answer with a list of his own.

———————

BY WEEK'S END bottles had arrived from Monticello and eight barrels of wheat had arrived from the neighboring farm. Martha made note of both things in a brand-new account book, the fresh pages giving her hope. She also made note of the runaway slaves.

———————

IN NOVEMBER 1803, Martha gave birth to a daughter, but despite her sister's presence, she felt alone enough to incur the expense of both midwife and physician. Perhaps that aloneness made her feel comfortable in naming this child without consulting her husband. *Mary, she is called,* Martha wrote Tom, *for my sister, who remains by my side.*

---

## CHAPTER 22

Martha was busy—a new infant, five other children, her father's and her husband's plantations—and yet she took the Jefferson carriage back and forth to Monticello, with Ned driving and Molly holding Mary, at the end of every week. In November the last of the red maple leaves still sparkled among the gold needles and black pinecones that littered the ground; her father's marigolds, black-eyed Susans, bloodflower, and China aster still bloomed. She'd been three years at Edgehill and had three times set her father's precious gifts of seed in her ground to poor effect, yet her absent father managed to keep something blooming in his gardens nearly year-round.

The sight of the late garden, the forest, and the house were a comfort, but Martha could not walk through the door without feeling the spaces that remained. The doorways appeared empty without Ursula passing through; the large parlor seemed death still without the sounds of her father's violin, his humming, his occasional bursts into Scottish song.

The Hemingses always came to greet Martha—with their master gone there was little else for them to do—but Sally always managed to appear the most idle, even despite two small children, for she had her own "girl" to feed and catch and chase and hold. The first time Martha saw Sally's children after a gap of time, she sang out, "How tall they grow!" until she heard the suggestion in the words. She amended. "How grown up they've become!" Sally gave a smile full of that mother pride that Martha had never quite mastered and moved on with a grace that Martha likewise had never quite mastered. Beverly was a handsome boy, but it was Harriet who captured Martha's attention every time she saw her—the vibrant hair, the golden skin, the complicated eyes that reflected the green of the forest and the smoke of the mountains in turns.

Martha now met the overseer in the small parlor at Monticello; a copy of the Declaration of American Independence honored one wall and a French clock occupied the mantel—both old friends. The overseer always threw as much trouble as he could find at Martha, but Martha followed her father's example—and in truth, the experience gained out of her marriage to Tom—by exhibiting nothing but calm, no matter the turmoil within. *The corn must be got in. The icehouse repaired. New blankets ordered for the Negroes.* Martha reviewed and checked the items one by one. On matters of her own concern, she asked for and mostly took the overseer's advice, requesting explanation where needed—she would not pretend knowledge she did not own—and she had no time for political maneuvering; she had work to do. Martha suspected she would never feel at ease with the man, but at the end of the first month, she felt she could say in fairness that they got on.

Oddly, with the malleable overseer at Edgehill, Martha did less well, being less familiar with the workings of that farm. Where the one man needed more confidence in Martha, the other needed less; when she asked the Edgehill overseer for advice she got a list of choices and seldom more. *We could begin with the roofs on the north cabins. Or chance the roofs one more winter and get up the fences. Or put the men to clearing the far field.* These were difficult decisions for someone not knowing the exact state of the roofs or the fences, or the plan for the field. Martha pressed and chose, pressed and chose, pressed and chose, and in time discovered that her instinct proved good eight times in ten.

Martha ended with little time for letters but managed one a week, rotating among Tom, her father, and her sister. Tom answered the most reliably of the three, missing her, feeling adrift—or so Martha read between his lines. She read in the paper that the president's sons-in-law were a mismatched pair, Tom speaking little and when he did speak always taking the presidential line. Jack was labeled more forthcoming and oppositional, something that Martha could not approve, and yet Jack was always presented as the wiser, the more popular, the more useful of the two.

Tom came home at the end of the congressional session, fevered at the sight of Martha but otherwise uninterested in Edgehill or Monticello, walking around as if muffled and blinkered, even dumb to Martha's requests for his advice. For the first time Martha felt she didn't know him, and this stranger padding around the house as quietly as the servants unnerved her. Several times a day she found him staring out the window at the distant glimpse of Monticello atop its mountain; if she woke in the night she most often found him sitting in the chair in the moonlight staring at *her.* Her touch no longer seemed to soothe him; he thrust himself into her without prelude or postlude or caught at her roughly as she entered the room. Whenever she attempted to engage him in conversation—Anne's skillful reordering of the pantry, Jeff's fine repair of the cradle, Ellen's increasing quickness at her lessons—Tom interrupted and struck up topics of his own.

"Judith's ejected Nancy from Bizarre. She's gone to Richmond to seek a place there. I've promised to send her money."

"Tom—"

"I can do naught else. My sisters received little from my father's estate."

"As compared to you who received naught but debt?"

"You would have my preyed-upon sister starve?"

I would have a new coat for Anne and shoes for Ellen, Martha wished to answer, but she didn't. She too began to look out the window toward Monticello, wishing her father were home.

---

WHEN TOM RODE OFF at the beginning of the next session, they resumed their letters, and in the pen-and-paper Tom, Martha found her husband of old. *I know nothing of real loneliness until I'm forced to be apart from you.* Unable to adapt so quickly to the new-old tone, Martha wrote back in more circumscribed language: *You must take care of yourself for the sake of all here who share such concern for you.* Martha wrote to her father and sister too, but soon she had only two letters to write—Maria was to have another child, and with Jack in Washington, Martha convinced her to come to Edgehill to await her husband's return.

Maria arrived pale, apprehensive, and already missing Jack, "the best beloved of my soul," she told Martha, even as she stepped from the carriage. The words unsettled Martha. Who was the best beloved of her soul? She would not like to choose. She kept her sister close, finding that the comfort worked in both directions, only realizing the degree of her own loneliness now that it was dispelled. Their father wrote:

> *You must be sure to call Dr. Norris at the first symptom, the expense to be mine alone.*

The first symptom came too soon, Jack still in Washington, Martha supervising the cleaning of the Turkey carpet, the furniture pushed against the walls. Without waiting for Maria to object, Martha called Dr. Norris as her father had instructed her to do; she'd seen Maria after the birth of her first dead child and did not want to manage her alone. A tiny, rosy girl was born without great difficulty, and Maria immediately named her Martha; she was unable to nurse her due to an inflamed breast, but Martha, still nursing Mary, had enough milk for two and all seemed well.

Jack arrived just as the fevers set in. He rushed to hold his wife, but it was Martha he looked to, and hastened her outside the room to speak with her alone.

"She battles and wins," Martha told him. "You mustn't worry." What else was she to say?

Maria grew weaker. Martha wrote to her father and Tom. *Come.* Tom wrote back: *I set out now.* Her father wrote:

*Have her carried to Monticello. The fine air and my best sherry will restore her. I shall leave here as soon as I can.*

Martha ordered six slaves to carry Maria the three miles up the mountain and over the stream in a litter, not daring to risk a jolting carriage ride; Jack drove Martha in the carriage. As Maria's litter arrived, the Hemings servants rushed out to ease her into the house, Sally exclaiming, *"Mon dieu!"* at the sight of the once-robust girl she'd accompanied to Paris.

*"Hush,"* Martha snapped at her, but Maria reached out and touched Sally's arm.

Jack and Martha sat with Maria through the night, each urging the other to take some rest, neither willing to leave Maria's side. She grew delirious, thinking her father there, recognizing neither Jack nor Martha; when Tom arrived he declared equal alarm at the sight of both sisters, insisting that Martha rest. He held her through a short, broken sleep, but this time he made no effort to pretend all would be well.

Martha had returned to her sister's bedside by the time their father arrived. He stepped into the room and up to the bed, kneeling to kiss Maria's brow, to take her hand. She opened her eyes and smiled as she hadn't done in days, as if making her final effort to cheer him, but his shock at the sight of Maria's gray skin and shrunken frame appeared too great for an answering smile. "Martha," he whispered, but Martha understood it wasn't a call to his daughter, it was a call to his wife, who'd lain just so before she died. Oh, how Martha remembered that room! Ursula, Sally and her mother and sisters, all standing behind Martha and her father, weeping as Martha and her father wept, until her father collapsed in a swoon.

In the end Maria did as her mother had done, her last breath no different from the one before, dying so silently that only Jack, still holding her hand, realized at once that she was gone. He dropped his head to her chest; Martha gulped tears she thought she'd exhausted long before. Martha's father walked out of the room, silent and dry eyed, his skin as gray and ashen as Maria's.

Later, when Martha and Critta had dosed Jack with brandy and Burwell had eased him into his bed, Martha went looking for her father. His chamber door was closed and locked, but from behind it she heard a soft female voice singing in French, so low it was hardly more than a whisper, each word an ache: "*Ma chandelle est morte, je n'ai plus de feu . . .*"

*My candle is dead, I have no more fire . . .*

———————

SPRING ERUPTED JOYLESSLY. Martha's father returned to Washington. Martha fell ill—violent cramps, spasms in her limbs, trouble breathing, symptoms she attributed to her diet, but Tom, frantic to find his ever-sturdy wife laid low, argued her self-diagnosis.

"'Tis hysterics only."

"'Tis milk and radishes taken together at Sunday's meal."

"One must never succumb to one's nerves."

"Nerves! Pains so severe they make me tremble and you can say nerves!"

"You must rise up and move about. Distract your mind from its torment by engaging in other occupations."

Oh, that Tom Randolph could say this to her! And what other occupations did he have in mind—tending to *his* ills? But Martha had little strength for arguing. She gave it up just as she gave up everything else, handing her children and Maria's child into the care of Priscilla, retreating to her bed and staying in it. Molly changed her linens and helped her wash and eat, Priscilla carted the infants up and down the stairs to be nursed, Betsy delivered bowls of broth. Tom hovered outside the door, but Martha feigned sleep whenever he entered. When he finally managed to catch her awake, she did hear first his concern for her.

"'Tis good you rest," he said. "You've worn yourself down with the nursing of your sister." But soon he decided that Martha was rested enough to hear his woes: Virginia still did not breathe properly; Jeff was growing argumentative; his father-in-law had not responded to his latest request for a loan.

Martha's father wrote her:

*Consider my dear Martha to what degree, how many persons have the happiness of their lives depending on you, and consider it as a duty to take every care of yourself that you would think of for the dearest of those about you.*

That letter affected Martha more than any words of her husband's or any gabble of her children. Her father, who grieved equally for Maria, didn't need such worry over his last remaining child. Martha wrote her father:

> *I shall take every care only that I may dedicate what remains of my life to easing yours.*

Much to Tom's joy, Martha rose from her bed and returned to her duties, but she couldn't discriminate one day from another, one month from another, beyond the most glaring details: Summer and Monticello's riot of blooms. Fall and the mountain's golden light. Winter, nine months after Martha had listened to "*Au Clair de la Lune*" outside her father's door, and James Madison Hemings was born.

## CHAPTER 23

D<small>ESPITE THE PERSISTENT SALLY RUMORS</small>, Thomas Jefferson won a second presidential term with ease. Tom also won another term, by a four-hundred-vote margin this time, but he also lost his entire wheat crop to the Hessian fly. Complicating his legislative tenure, Richard Randolph's brother had now joined Tom in Congress, freely spreading a rumor that Tom's sister Nancy had poisoned Richard. Tom's counterattack was inevitable, but the speed and degree to which the battle accelerated horrified Martha—near the end of what began as a gushing love letter, Tom announced that he was now preparing for a duel. Martha wrote a frantic letter to her father. He answered: *I tell him dueling is not for men with families. He doesn't hear me. You'd best come and remind him what he risks leaving behind.* Martha, seven months' pregnant, still struggling to bat her way out of her cloud of grief, began her preparations for a second trip to Washington, carrying Priscilla and her children with her.

T<small>HIS TIME WASHINGTON OFFERED MARTHA</small> no prospect of escape; this time she carried the full weight of all she was: wife, daughter, mother, and soon to be mother again. Contributing to the cheer-lessness of the visit, winter had not treated the capital well, adding chill without removing the damp, while providing no decorative cover of snow. And Martha had barely taken a breath and settled into the second floor of the president's house when Tom started pacing and ranting in front of her about his pending duel.

Martha cut him short. "You will not duel," she said. "You will not tax my fragile spirits with another loss, the greatest loss I might bear in this life. I know this of you. You are not so cruel. Your courage is bottomless; I know this of you as well. It will carry you to the floor of the House and bring forth the language needed to subdue your cousin, to make the kind of apology that will place you above him in the rolls of honor."

When Tom began a hot answer, Martha refused to listen. "I am not at all well. I've come all this way to say what I just said in the hope of sparing your life; if you wish to spare mine, *and* the life of your next child, you must leave me to rest now."

Tom left her, so alarmed that he didn't raise the subject of dueling again, and two days later he made his public apology to his cousin with such grace it was remarked upon in the papers. Martha, quite rested by then, nevertheless kept to her bed a good part of the time until she was delivered of her seventh child, a boy her father proudly touted as the first child born in the president's house, although Martha had noticed that one of the Monticello slaves had recently borne an infant there.

Tom, delighted as ever with his wife and child, began to ponder names taken from the Randolph family. John. Theodore. Even Richard.

"No," Martha said.

"Shall we honor your father again by allowing him to choose the name?"

"I wish to call him James Madison, after my father's oldest and dearest friend."

Tom looked at his wife in surprise, but Martha watched the surprise melt into understanding, if not accord; he knew first-hand how effectively someone could erase another by usurping his name.

SALLY CALLED HER SON *MADISON*. Martha called hers *James*. In April Martha, Priscilla, and the children traveled home, escorted by Tom, who stayed only long enough to settle in a new overseer at Monticello and upset Martha's hard-won balance with the overseer at Edgehill. As soon as Tom left, the roof on Edgehill's north quarters caved in, and a freezing northwest wind swept down and killed all of Monticello's peach trees. Perhaps the crises were helpful in Martha's forging a quick and sure bond with the new overseer, Mr. Bacon; having worked with them now, Martha better understood why the overseers were changed out so often, but the plantation had seldom seemed to gain by the change until now. She asked for Bacon's help and he responded, perhaps seeing something the former overseer had not seen—that Martha could be of use to him. Soon congenial and useful messages traveled back and forth between them daily.

It seemed Martha had only just set things right when news charged up the mountain, trailed by the foulest rumors: Thomas Jefferson's dear friend and mentor, George Wythe, was murdered by his nephew over a will that left the estate to Wythe's mulatto son. Wythe named Thomas Jefferson as his executor, no doubt confident that his old law pupil would see his wishes through, but of course it caused the Sally talk to bubble up again. Clearly, they said, Wythe named Jefferson his executor because Jefferson had already named Sally Hemings's children in *his* will and knew how it must be done. Others took the supposition further: Not only were Sally Hemings's three children named in Jefferson's will, but Martha and Maria's combined eight children were not! The Wythe case—and by association the Jefferson case—were cited as "evidence" when the Virginia legislature signed into being a law requiring all slaves freed after 1806 to leave the state. The now-

paired cases even encroached on space that should have been taken up by a piece of federal legislation that Tom had successfully sponsored, ending the importation of slaves by the year 1808.

———————

AT THE END OF JULY, Tom and his father-in-law traveled home to Virginia together for their summer hiatus. On Tom's first night at home, Martha was forced to apprise him of a particularly pressing bill come due and an appointment at the bank the next day; that night Tom didn't reach for her as was his usual habit after being away. The next day he sat silent at breakfast before riding off to his appointment; that night the Randolphs traveled up the mountain for a celebratory dinner at Monticello in honor of both the men's homecoming and Tom's new law. They took that ride in silence too.

As the carriage pulled into the last roundabout, Martha spied her father standing on the terrace, talking to a stranger. As the carriage drew closer, the stranger grew more familiar; Martha recognized that odd mix of easy stance and lively gesture, the gentle cadence punctuated occasionally by an emphatic rise or fall. The carriage stopped before the house and the men on the terrace came down the steps together to greet the Randolphs.

"Good evening, Mrs. Randolph," Short began. "My apologies for invading your private party."

"Nonsense," Martha's father said. "Invited guests cannot be classed as invaders."

Short held out his hand to Tom. "Fine work on that bit of paper, Mr. Randolph."

Tom peered at Short as if trying to determine if he'd been insulted. Martha's father put his arm around Tom. "Yes, we're most proud."

Tom addressed his father-in-law. "I must ask for a word in private, sir. Regarding certain circumstances that were only just called to my attention on my return."

Martha noticed her father draw in a breath, the only sign of impatience he'd ever show. "Certainly, Tom." The two men walked up the steps side by side.

As soon as they were out of sight, Short turned to Martha and spoke with a full throat. "I cannot talk of anything else until I express my sorrow over the loss of your sweet sister. I can see the mark of your father's grief still on him. I see it on you."

"Such things don't go away."

"But they soften, surely? I pray so. I pray so for *you*."

"Thank you."

A silence dropped between them. "I can't seem to travel from such a subject to another," Short said at last. "'Tis too great a weight to move."

"I've been longer practiced. Allow me to move it for you. Thank you for acknowledging my husband's role in our newest legislation. You see that better times are upon us."

Short's expression altered. "Are they?" He swept his hand wide to include all he saw: the slave quarters, the slave backs still doubled over in the garden, the homespun-clad slave children just trailing in from the lawn. He swept wider to include all they couldn't see but knew to be there: the slaves at work in the nailery, the joiner's shop, the charcoal pit, and the distant fields, where they would work until the sun set. "What does the new law do to change all this? Your father didn't import his slaves, he inherited them. As you will inherit them when he's gone. Where lies the end to it? This is why I return to France in the fall."

"To France! So soon?"

"This Virginia manner of extracting a livelihood doesn't suit me."

"Perhaps a certain Frenchwoman is more to blame for your return than a certain style of living."

"'Ah. 'A certain style of living,' you call it now. In France you called it something worse. Do you see how it is? Once inside this life you grow blind to its horrors. I must be gone."

"And what would you have us do, Mr. Short? Do you think the solution a simple thing?"

"I do not. But behind me lives a great man with a mind accustomed to solving the not simple things. And in front of me stands a woman of uncommon intellect who once spoke against a thing not caring whether it was simple or not. I only wonder where she's got to."

"Why do you do this, Mr. Short?" Martha cried. "Why do you try so hard to make us at odds over this? Why don't you talk to my father of this and leave me in peace?"

"Do *you* talk to your father of this?"

No longer. It was true that Martha had given up on raising the topic with her father altogether. "I don't talk to *anyone* of it," she countered. "I don't enjoy tormenting my friends as much as you do, Mr. Short."

"I do no such thing. I come here to Monticello alight with joy at the thought of seeing you, of seeing your father, and then I witness again how your life is lived. I grow sour. Despondent. I want so much better for you. And I include your husband in this. He works to stop the importation of slaves and then enslaves his wife in this futile cycle of—"

"Enough, Mr. Short. Go back to your duchess and then write to me of futility."

Martha strode past Short and climbed the steps to the house, but she knew better than to attempt to seek out father and husband.

Tom would be asking for another loan, a conversation as unwelcome to Martha as the one she'd just abandoned on the lawn. She walked to the far end of the terrace and looked out over the mountain as the day left it, cooling herself until she could face a dinner likely to be as difficult as any she'd faced in Washington. She'd eased the way for her father's distinguished guests there, she could certainly do so here, but what if she chose not to? What if she let Short provoke and Tom rage and her father evade? What if *she* provoked and raged and *didn't* evade, just as she'd once done as a girl?

Martha's father's voice rang out from the hall. "Martha! Where have you gone?"

Where indeed? "Here, Papa," Martha called. She stepped through the terrace door and smiled.

And smiled and smiled and smiled.

## CHAPTER 24

Early in 1807 Martha received dread news from Eppington that Maria's little girl had died. Next came news that Tom's brother had died. While the first raised in Martha all the old sorrow of Maria's and Ellen's passing, the second raised in her cold fear. The Randolph family debt reverted to Tom in its entirety, and his creditors began to demand he sell off some slaves in order to satisfy his obligations. It was true that by virtue of natural increase, they had too many young slaves, perhaps too many old ones, but the old ones could not be sold and the young ones . . .

"The slaves I've watched grow up they would have me sell," Tom told Martha, again from the blackness of a dark room.

"We must try harder to sell Varina," Martha countered. "And you must focus your attention on your farms. Your expenses in Washington overbalance your income."

Tom said nothing in answer, but to Martha's surprise her words appeared to sway him. He resigned his seat in Congress and did in fact do better at timing the next market. He again attempted to sell Varina but received only a single offer that wouldn't even clear its mortgage. Martha's father wrote from Washington, offering to sell some of his own land to clear Tom's debt: *I consider it common stock in our joint family; what we retain between us will certainly provide for all.* Martha didn't see how, but she was no easier when Tom refused his father-in-law's offer, deciding to mortgage Edgehill instead. Martha had never developed any great affection for Edgehill's cramped rooms and awkward lines, but to mortgage it only left more debt; why was she the only one who saw the evil end to it? When her father made a second generous offer to send Jeff to school in Philadelphia, however, it was Martha who insisted Tom refuse. She'd come to think highly of her son's common sense but no better of his intellect; additionally, with the offer of land instead of cash she suspected her father must be experiencing some financial difficulty too. Both Tom and Martha did attempt to decline the offer of schooling, but Martha's father persisted in such optimistic tones that Martha acquiesced and packed Jeff off to Philadelphia.

———

MARTHA MISSED HER SON, the more so when Sally Hemings gave birth to her own Thomas, to be known by his middle name of Eston, just as Martha called her Thomas by his middle name of Jefferson. But whenever Martha heard Sally speak the name of *her* child, she thought of a snake hissing; in fact, whenever Martha saw Sally she began to think of her as a snake, lurking among the dark and the damp and the rot, waiting quietly for Martha to step wrong so she might leap up with head high and tongue flicking and bring her to the ground.

———

IN ANOTHER OF THOSE QUIXOTIC ABOUT-FACES that came at Martha unaware, Tom decided to run again for Congress and was defeated by a margin so huge it was as if the last illusion that had supported him finally let go. Martha noted his crumbling into the usual ill health, but she hadn't noticed anything extraordinary in his symptoms until Ned careened into the kitchen one day where Martha stood reading to Betsy from a cookery book.

"What on earth, Ned, who's after you?"

196 · SALLY CABOT GUNNING

"Come, missus!"

Martha took a clearer look at Ned's face, grabbed two fistfuls of skirt, and ran after him, past the barn, past the slave quarter, past the orchard, deep into the wheat field.

Martha saw Tom far out in the middle of the field, pitched forward over his horse's neck, spurring him into the wheat shocks, trampling the shocks to the ground, reining left and right as if he were in the throes of a medieval battle. Martha and Ned ran out into the field and stood side by side before the nearest row of shocks, forcing Tom to draw up. His face purple and shining, his damp hair stuck to his neck and forehead, he sat like his horse, legs stiff and straight, breathing hard.

"Tom," Martha said. "Come in now. You overheat yourself and your horse. 'Tis time for a drink of cider."

Tom stared at her as if he'd forgotten who she was.

"Master," Ned tried. "You look at that horse of yours. Done in. Get down and let me walk him home. Mrs. Randolph needs your arm."

Tom gave Ned the same empty stare he'd given Martha. Martha could hear them all breathing—Tom, Ned, the horse, her—a ragged mixture of tension and exhaustion. No one spoke; after a time Tom threw his far leg over the saddle and slid to the ground. Martha took up Ned's cue, reaching to take Tom's arm as if she were in need of support; perhaps seeing her so close or feeling the touch of her, Tom's eyes came back into focus. "Martha."

"Yes, 'tis I."

Tom's mouth twitched into a gruesome line. "But who am *I*?"

———

Martha dreamed terrible dreams of stampeding horses ridden by wild, black-eyed Indians, wheat shocks burning, Monticello burning. She woke out of the dreams exhausted from her efforts to escape, to save her family, to understand what had gone wrong. She became like Tom, secretly watching him as he watched her, but she discovered only that she'd lost all sense of him, that the man she'd willingly shared mind and body with for so long had moved so far away she could barely make him out anymore. But at other times he seemed too close, so close she daydreamed of packing up all her children and fleeing to her father in Washington; never again would she dare leave any of her children behind.

This dream of escape began to affect Martha's decisions; she could admit this, if only inside her own mind, when Charles Bankhead, the son of an old friend of the Jeffersons, came to Tom for permission to marry Anne. *Anne escapes!* Martha thought, but Tom thought Anne too young.

"She's seventeen—my age at the time of our marriage," Martha countered.

"He'll wait another year."

"Will he? Or will he grow discouraged and decide to look for someone with a real dower?"

Tom flinched. Martha looked away, unwilling to see whatever it was that she'd just caused to further break in him, but she would break it again if it would save Anne from the fate of her mother. She persisted. "Who better do you see for your daughter than—"

Tom cut her off. "Tell my daughter to send Bankhead to see me."

———

TOM GAVE HIS PERMISSION for the marriage and a promise of five hundred acres of land, to be gifted once its debt had been cleared. Martha knew the flimsiness of such a promise, but she said nothing—her father said nothing. The couple married in the newly remodeled parlor at Monticello as soon as the president was able to break free for his summer hiatus. Tom toasted the new couple: "Charles, I give into your care the warmest heart but one that I know. Anne, may you honor and respect your husband as he deserves. To you both, were you to be blessed with a marriage half as rich as mine, you would be rich beyond your deserts."

———

THE SENIOR BANKHEAD HAD SETTLED a large plantation with many Negroes on his son, and as the couple prepared to leave for their new estate, Martha hugged Anne good-bye with as much relief as sorrow. One child safe. Gone. And yet seven children remained in Martha's care at home. After Anne's departure Tom began a new habit of charging off on horseback to places unknown, only returning at the end of the day to hunt out an empty room where he could sit alone. He had little trouble finding such a room, as his children now hid from him. In truth, Martha hid from him.

When Martha's father wrote from Washington outlining his plans for pending retirement, sharing an idea to bring his sister to housekeep for him, Martha rushed at once to pen and paper. *I think little of your plan regarding my aunt. She has neither the skill to keep your house nor the wit to preside at your table.* But there Martha set down her pen. If not her aunt, who? An image of Sally Hemings standing at the door, her pocket bulging with keys to cellar, cupboard, and pantry, caused Martha to close her eyes. Immediately a new image leaped in to replace the old, one Martha surely hadn't consciously summoned, of herself at the door, *her* pocket bulging, but as soon as Martha saw the scene she felt every weight she carried slip from her. Of course. What better answer? Martha's father would be tended with the kind of care only a loving daughter could deliver, a house Martha knew better than her own would be kept to the highest standard, her children would be safe under their grandfather's protection and support, and Martha would again be lodged where her heart had always been lodged. As for Tom, surely such close proximity to a calmer, more deliberate nature would settle him?

Martha rang the bell for Ned. "Have you any idea where Mr. Randolph's gone?"

"He rode off toward the far field about an hour ago. Should I try and fetch him?"

"No, I shall."

———————

MARTHA FOUND TOM lying under a tree at the river's edge in the far field, reading a book of Greek poetry, a bouquet of wildflowers at his side. Martha reined in her horse and slid to earth. If she'd found her husband directing the spring plowing or planting, she might have gone more gently into the subject, but looking at the book, the flowers, the idle frame, the words flew out of her without any softening.

"I should like to suggest to my father that on his return we move into Monticello with him. He needs someone to keep his house. He needs you by his side to help him manage his farms."

Tom's eyes flicked to Martha's face and returned to his book.

Martha pushed on. "It will be best for the children. Papa's books, his art, his collections, his wide-ranging circle of acquaintances—it will expand their educational experience."

Tom's eyes stayed fixed on his book, which again helped Martha to say the next part. "If we're to consider the cost of supporting two households against the cost of supporting one—"

There Tom's head came up. "The cost *to your father* of supporting two households. This is what you wish to say, is it not?"

"Perhaps just now he sees us through, but in future—"

"But here we are in the *just now.*"

"You would agree, then?"

Tom picked up the wildflowers, fingering a small bloom, laying it out singly on the grass. He removed a notebook and pencil from his pocket. "I'm categorizing them. I seem to have missed this lovely periwinkle—a crime." He made a note in his book, returned the book to his pocket. He gave Martha a long look that unsettled her more than any dismissal. "Do you really think your father wishes us to join him?"

"I shall only offer. He'll do as he likes, of course."

Tom laughed. "Will he?"

"I should think he'd prefer to have his family about him." After all, he'd brought them to Washington to keep down the talk—he wouldn't like to settle at Monticello with none but Hemingses around him. *He would not.* As Martha thought this she grew more determined in her course. She considered mentioning the Hemings difficulty to Tom, but he'd already returned to his book; she turned away, but some faint memory of the Tom of old, the partner of old, drew her around. "Would you ride back with me?"

"Not just yet. My favorite poem comes up."

Martha returned to her horse, found her stirrup, and pulled herself into the saddle. She said nothing more. She would say nothing more. She would write her father just as she wished. As she rode away she felt certain this was the right course, but she would admit that something troubled her. She got all the way to the house before it struck her: How had it come to pass that she no longer knew what Tom's favorite poem was?

Martha entered the house to the sound of Priscilla chastising one of the younger children: "You sit or I'll sit you!" She heard James begin to fuss; she heard Ellen playing "Loch Lomond" on the harpsichord; she heard Cornelia—or Virginia—attempting to sing along. Martha didn't stop for any of them, slipping quietly up the stairs to her room to finish the letter she'd begun earlier: *Another solution comes to mind—our family might join you at Monticello, where Mr. Randolph could help you with your farms and I might devote myself to the care of your household with more interest than I could ever take in my own.* There was more she could say—or was there? She could never put into writing the Hemings awkwardness, nor did she see a need to carve into a piece of paper her husband's erratic behavior or their increased financial worries. These things her father already knew.

# PART III

❦

## Monticello

*1809–1829*

## CHAPTER 25

In march, when Thomas Jefferson returned to Monticello, nine Randolphs and four of the Randolph slaves—three of them Hemingses—had already settled themselves into the empty second floor of the now-completed house and the nearby slave dwellings on Mulberry Row. The new Monticello contained nine bedrooms on the second and third floors, as if her father had planned to accommodate the large Randolph family all along.

Martha's first full day on the mountain she walked out into the spring morning and breathed in the mountaintop air that had never tasted quite as fresh three miles below at Edgehill. She looked out and saw a welcome view no matter which way she turned—the town of Charlottesville winking at her in the distance, the peach-blow mist rising out of the Blue Ridge, the rich green forest ringing her, her father's neat horseshoe of multicolored tulips dancing about her feet. Returning to the house, Martha paused in the hall and took in the things that had always meant her father to her—Indian artifacts, fossils, maps, a model of the pyramids. She stepped onto the cherry and beech parquet floor that her father had designed himself and entered the parlor; he'd chosen every chair and sofa, the harpsichord and pianoforte, filling the room with portraits and busts of men he knew and men he only knew of: Washington, Franklin, Adams, Paine, Bacon, Madison, Monroe, Locke, and Newton. While they were in France, the famous sculptor Houdon had created a lovely bust of the even more famous Thomas Jefferson, which was Martha's favorite object in the room. But that night, encased in her bed as if returned to the womb,

Martha had to admit to the lie she'd told Tom concerning her reasons for returning to live in this house. For her father, *yes*—on her first day she'd put out a finer table than he'd have found in a year under his sister's management. For her children, *yes*—she might stand them in the center of any room in the house and they would learn more than they would have learned in the finest museum in Paris. But for Martha too. She could admit inside the new quiet of her mind that only here did she stop dreaming of rampaging Indians. Only here did she feel safe. Only here did she feel at home.

———————

THE DAYS AT MONTICELLO SETTLED into a pattern that seldom varied: At eight o'clock the family and whatever guests were visiting shared a large breakfast. At nine Martha's father retreated to his library and his correspondence as Tom rode off to Edgehill. Martha's father emerged as soon as he could and began his tour of his farms, while Martha and her daughters settled into housework or education, depending on the age of the child. In the afternoon the children always found time for play, usually organized by their grandfather; in good weather he would set up races on the lawn, starting the youngest children first, awarding the winner with his prize figs. If poor weather, Martha would likely find them in the parlor, her father on his hands and knees on the rug playing horse, or seated under a pile of grandchildren playing an alphabet game. Dinner was at four or five o'clock and following dinner came conversation, strolls through the garden and grounds, or music—Martha's father was a skilled violinist and Martha's two oldest daughters excelled at the harpsichord and pianoforte—all could sing. *Mademoiselle voulez-vous danser,* Martha's father would sing, and the girls would sometimes answer, but sometimes, wise to the trick of being forced to practice their French, they would divert their grandfather to the more lively Scottish tunes he loved, and "Smash the

Windows" or "Fisherman's Hornpipe" or "Road to Lisdoonvarna" or his favorite, "Money Musk," would fill the air. Oh, the joy of hearing such music again! More than once Martha caught up a small daughter's hands and danced while her father clapped.

Once the candles were brought in, the family settled into a quieter vein, the youngest children going off with Priscilla and the adults and the older children picking up their books. At nine o'clock, after the children were in bed, there would be tea and fruit from the Monticello orchards and more conversation; this was the point where Tom always excused himself to his books and papers, declaring himself unaccustomed to so much talk.

Tom was unaccustomed to a number of things. Soon after their arrival at Monticello, the five younger children fell ill with the deadly malignant throat and Tom sat up night after night tending them with Martha, but he appeared at a loss when it came to a healthy child, taking little interest in Martha's daily efforts toward educating their daughters. "An accomplished woman cannot be an ignorant one," Tom had declared with enthusiasm when Martha first set up her school, but he'd then paid slight attention to his children's individual progress or, indeed, in their individual selves. A child like Cornelia, painfully shy and therefore most in need of encouragement, seldom received it from her father, but her grandfather, sensitive to her nature early, took special care to find time for her. Once he discovered her artistic bent, he set up his instruments for mechanical drawing and taught her how to manipulate them. Recognizing Ellen's quickness, he taught her to play chess. He bought the musical Virginia a guitar. When little Mary dissolved into tears over a torn dress, her grandfather "mended" it, that is to say he bought her a new one.

Tom appeared particularly inept with his now-sixteen-year-old son, already home from a single year at school that had proved just as disastrous as Martha had predicted. Jeff had grown into a young man as darkly handsome as his father, with his grandfather's height but none of his intellect or temperament. After Jeff's poor showing at school, his grandfather made an effort to continue his education in a more practical vein; he took him with him as he toured his farms, instructing him, using praise and gentle correction where needed. Tom used impatience and interference as his guide, and the father-son programs usually ended in shouting; so natural a thing, then, for Jeff to gravitate to his grandfather's side. But natural too—Martha understood this—for Tom's resentment to build. Martha attempted to intercede for a time, encouraging Jeff to ride off to Edgehill with his father each morning, but after one too many days of closed, thunderous faces returning, Martha realized that the best thing she could do for her son was to send him into his grandfather's company as often as possible.

That spring Jeff and his grandfather oversaw the planting of sixty-eight peach stones, sixty-nine plum stones, and sixty-eight apricot stones, both grandfather and grandson making careful note of the tally in their journals. They went on to plant a new kind of squash from Maine, a pumpkin from South America, and an African pea that would yield three crops a year. Martha's father discussed other ideas with the boy—perhaps expanding the nail factory, or resurrecting the manufacture of cloth. Sometimes Martha was present for these conversations; she was impressed with the way Jeff listened, asked thoughtful questions, and then listened to the answers. Too late, Martha understood her own error with Jeff's education—give him the means to understand any immediate, practical application of a topic and he would thrive.

All the children thrived at Monticello; Martha's father thrived: His utter happiness was evident in the foolish songs that burst from his throat when he thought no one could hear—*When first I saw Betty and made my complaint/I whined like a fool and she sighed like a Saint.* And with the extra Hemings hands allowing her to focus on educating her four girls, Martha regained her sense of purpose. If Tom didn't thrive, it couldn't be said that he fared worse—he rode down no more crops; he wandered off less; he remembered who Martha was. It had been the right thing to do to remove the family to Monticello; Martha had no doubt of it.

One thing—and only the one—troubled Martha awake or asleep. She stood on the terrace and watched four of her children and three of Sally Hemings's running over the lawn in a comingled herd and knew what any stranger would think looking over the lot: three red-haired children that no doubt belonged to the Jefferson clan alongside four black-haired children that belonged to someone else. Martha couldn't bear it. She could *not*. Martha made casual mention of the Carr cousins whenever she found a guest peering too hard at Sally's children, but when another newspaper story about the slave concubine appeared, Martha decided that something more must be done. She carried the paper to her father's study door and knocked.

"Papa, 'tis I."

"Ah! Come in, child." Martha's father sprang from his chair as Martha entered. Surely Martha and her family had had a good effect on him, she thought, if he could leap so youthfully to greet her.

"I do hope I don't interrupt."

"You do not. I only answer more foolish letters and annoy Sally by pulling loose another thread on my waistcoat." He pulled again on the thread.

"Papa, I come on that exact subject."

"My waistcoat! Why such fuss over a little fraying? If I don't mind, I don't see why anyone else should."

"I come about Sally, Papa. You see that the papers have started again." Martha held out the piece.

Her father kept his smile. "You mustn't trouble yourself over such things. They come and they go."

"I only think you might help yourself if you don't keep Sally and her children so close. I've suggested before, if you sent them to live at one of your other farms and brought another family to live here in their place—"

"Disrupt two families for no reason but to satisfy some gossips? But of course it would only satisfy them as far as they could take credit for provoking such an act."

"I only think—"

"On this matter 'tis best not to think; it will gain nothing of use. Now come, my dear, and look at this lovely hibiscus that your Ellen plucked and gave to me as a gift. I confess I enjoy the fact that she believes the flowers hers to give as much as I enjoy the gift itself."

"Papa—"

His expression changed. She'd seen such a change before, and would not call it unpleasant, only a signal that the subject at hand was closed. Martha could push on, but if she did, if he objected, how strongly would he object? And what would it mean if he did? That was the thing—that was the *only* thing—Martha truly could not bear to find out.

"I must get the children in," she said.

———

MARTHA FOUND THE CHILDREN as she expected to find them, out on the lawn in a confusing mix of colors and sizes, everything around them spring green and fresh and full to bursting with young life. James—her James—tumbled to the ground and began to whimper. Harriet, the nearest, turned around and tugged him to his feet, but Ellen, already the young mother, rushed up and brushed the bits of grass and dirt from her brother's knees, pushing him up the hill ahead of her. Martha closed her eyes and opened them again. This time she saw Thomas Jefferson's grandchildren trudging up the hill to the house and his slaves trailing along behind. Henceforth she would see nothing else.

Later—a good deal later—Martha remembered what her father had said about Ellen believing the flowers to be hers, as if to remind Martha that in fact the flowers were not hers, that she and her husband and her children were, even now, his guests.

———————

TWO CRATES ARRIVED FROM FRANCE. One crate contained Italian cheeses and a sack of Calville Blanc d'Hiver apple seeds, Thomas Jefferson's favorite apple. The other crate contained a fluffy white cat with eyes the color of pale jade. A note from William Short explained: *A Turkish Angora, to keep you company in your lonely retirement. Angoras like high places.* Ellen picked the cat out of the crate, but it somehow scrambled from Ellen's arms and onto Martha's shoulder.

Martha's father laughed from his chair. "'Angoras like high places,'" he quoted, but even when he stood up to his full height, the cat seemed to prefer Martha. "Very well then, you must name her, my dear. She'll accept no name from anyone else."

*Bibelot,* Martha decided. Curio. But whenever Martha's father wanted to find the cat, he would ask the children, "Where is Mama's little friend?"

———————

PARADOXICALLY, Tom seemed to do better with his Edgehill farm now that he was no longer in residence. He brought in a new type of onion that yielded two hundred and forty barrels to the acre; his new method of plowing saved his corn from the washout suffered by the rest of Albemarle County; he put in place his father-in-law's system of incentives in the form of extra food rations and increased his tobacco yield by two percent. It made for a good year but wasn't enough to keep up with what they owed. No doubt realizing that the Randolphs needed another source of income, Martha's father gave Tom the lease of the grist mill on the Rivanna River, and now Tom rode off to the mill each day on his way to or from Edgehill. It helped their pocketbook and offered Tom something of his own to report at the evening meal, but he continued to disappear once the plates were cleared and the talk spiraled.

Oh, the things they talked of! Martha listened, participated, and reveled in this richness that had come back into her life. When they had guests they might talk of the American Revolution or the American character, what her father described as a natural aristocracy based on virtues and talents instead of wealth and birth. When they were alone they might talk of gardening or landscaping or furniture design, or the children's progress with arithmetic, or Martha's irrational fear of root cellars, or her father's distrust of the Anglican priests. Sometimes her father wished to retire to his bed, but Martha egged him on. Sometimes Martha would start up at a sound from one of her children, and her father would ease her back into her chair with a reminder that the capable Priscilla would be sure to fetch her if one of her children was in fact in distress. Eventually Martha would climb the stairs, relieved when she found Tom asleep, which he was oftentimes, but not quite often enough.

Once again, Martha was pregnant.

———————

TOM BEGAN TO SHOUT. The shouting itself was not new, but the fact that he now directed it at Martha was.

"Why have you got Ellen a new saddle? Do I leave you such excess in your purse that you decide to go off buying saddles, even as you whimper for more this and more that?"

"The saddle was a gift from my father."

"You must think well of yourself if you think you may decide such matters as saddles in this house."

"Tom. My father bought Ellen the saddle. One day she mentioned she was waiting for me to return from my ride so she might borrow my saddle and my father—"

"So he has money to spend on a girl's pleasure riding. After claiming the presidency put him in debt."

"It did. He felt he should entertain his official visitors in a certain style, which came at his own expense."

"And no doubt he considers the thirty thousand dollars I'm in arrears as a result of my extravagance."

"Thirty—"

"Go away. Go shame your father with your stares, not me; I care nothing of what you think."

———————

IN FEBRUARY TOM SOLD WINGO for eighty-four hundred dollars. Martha could hardly object, knowing the state of their affairs, even if she knew that the eighty-four hundred dollars would disappear like a stone in their sea of debt. Perhaps Tom knew it too; he began to spend less time at his farm and mill, to spend more time shouting, at both Jeff and Martha. Martha, thinking of her father's smooth handle, put her own twist to that old method, calling it the diagonal approach: don't oppose but don't agree; veer off in a direction as near as practicable to the destination. It began to work. It also began to exhaust Martha even more than her husband's moods exhausted her. For the first time in the twenty-one years of her marriage, Martha would look out the second-floor window, see Tom riding up to the front door, put a quick word in Priscilla's ear, and exit out the back to explore the "little mountain," as her father called his Monticello. *Her* Monticello.

## CHAPTER 26

Mᴀʀᴛʜᴀ ᴀɴᴅ ʜᴇʀ ꜰᴀᴛʜᴇʀ ꜱᴀᴛ on the terrace after dinner, watching the children play robber on the lawn, watching the dusk thicken, both father and daughter reluctant to give the signal that it was time to return to the house. Despite numerous calls to Grandpapa to join them, he stayed as he was, talking of his plans for the garden, for the laying out of a cloth factory at his Legos plantation, of sending Beverly to the joinery to apprentice with his uncle John Hemings.

"And I mustn't forget to write William Short and order twenty-four cases of wine; 'tis rumored he's to return to Virginia for good."

Martha's father said something else that she didn't catch; a rocker might have creaked, or a child called, or a wave of nausea distracted her; Martha was finding no joy in this latest pregnancy, and every rise of bile only made it that much worse. Her daughter Anne had delivered a premature infant who had died soon after birth and Anne had fallen ill, continuing the family tradition that only Martha seemed to have escaped. Anne continued in another tradition; her husband had turned out an inferior crop of tobacco that he was unable to sell, and already the Bankheads had fallen into debt. Charles had come to Tom asking for his cosignature on a note to the bank, and Tom had signed.

"Why does the bank take your signature when you already owe them?" Martha had asked.

"Because of the value of my disposable property," Tom said.

Disposable property. Slaves.

A voice called her out of her ruminations. "Martha, dear?"

"I'm sorry, Papa, the children distracted me. They must be got in. What did you ask me?"

"I asked if you wanted anything of Mr. Short. This may be our last chance."

"No," Martha said. "No, I do not." Bibelot was quite enough. No matter her father's feeding the cat crumbs of cheese from his plate or cutting a hole in the door to the attic eaves for better access to the mice, Bibelot always sought Martha's lap, Martha's touch, Martha's voice. And against her best plan, Martha had given in to the cat's claim on her, comforting the animal as it curled on her lap and in turn receiving her own kind of comfort in the touch of the luxurious fur, the devoted gaze in the jewel-like eyes. Had Short suspected she would take to the creature so? No, of course not. He'd sent the cat to his friend to keep him company in his "lonely retirement"; he hadn't even known the Randolphs now resided at Monticello. Or had he? If so, had the remark been meant as a joke? And if it was, did it refer to the Randolphs or to . . . someone else?

Apparently Martha's father had fallen into his own reverie about William Short. "I find it curious that Mr. Short's never married," he said.

"There are those who say that of you."

Martha's father smiled. "But I did marry. There lies the difference between us. I believe you're right, the children must be got in; my shirtsleeves grow damp."

Martha's father rose, and without raising his voice or clapping his hands, by simply lifting one palm as if to wave or declare a halt, first one and then another child came streaming en masse toward the house, indistinguishable from one another in the growing dark. And there in that gray interlude Martha thought of William Short again, specifically of his theory that admixture would provide the solution for the human race. The last time she'd looked at this odd lot of children coming across the lawn she'd struggled to separate them and keep them separate—master's child and slave's child; Short would have her look at them as they appeared now—one no different from the next. What Martha wanted to know—and did not want to know—was what her father thought of Short's view, what answer, if any, he'd made to Short's letter, but of course Martha could never ask.

Oh, the things they didn't talk of!

———

THAT EVENING THE FAMILY WAS SITTING in the parlor playing their favorite alphabet game when Tom entered, slapping a newspaper against his thigh, clicking his boots across the floor as if in an effort to outrace his own announcement. "I gave my love an APPLE," Martha's father had started, and now five-year-old James shouted back, "I gave my love a BEE." Virginia and Cornelia fell back on the rug in laughter.

Martha looked at the newspaper. *Sally,* she thought. Another story about Sally that Martha would have to deny and deny and deny, as her father would not, or else the snake would rise and bite. The snake. Oh, Martha knew how unfair it was to blame Sally for a newspaper story, but somehow it did seem in part her fault. Indeed, as Martha thought on it, much of it could be deemed Sally's fault. She might ask to be moved in the same way the rest of her family kept asking to be moved to suit their own purpose. She might, from time to time, do her share of the household work, or at the least tend to someone else's chamber and waistcoats! She might keep her pale-skinned, red-haired children out of sight.

Tom clapped his hands and shooed the children out. He closed the door behind the last of them, turned, and thrust the newspaper at his father-in-law, but it appeared he'd already memorized the words and was glad enough to spew them out.

"Your nephews, sir. My wife's own cousins. Isham and Lewis Gilburne. They chopped a slave to pieces and threw the pieces on the fire. The dog pulled out the head and dragged it into the yard, else they'd never have been found out. It would seem Lewis had the sense to kill himself after it got about, but Isham lives yet."

"I know," Martha's father said. "I've heard from Isham." He reached into his pocket and withdrew a much folded and refolded letter. He dropped his head as if to read, but his eyes remained fixed in space. "He pleads drunkenness. Begs forgiveness. Asks for a loan to aid his defense."

"A loan!"

"Which I have refused." Martha's father leaned forward and thrust the letter into the fireplace, but as there was no fire, it lay there, fluttering.

Martha stared at the letter. She couldn't draw up the faces of these cousins of hers, it being so long since they'd moved west, but she now flushed hot with rage at the pair of them, living and dead. That they could treat a human being as if it were a piece of wood, that they could lay such a stain on her father by even the slimmest of connections to him!

"When did you learn of this, sir?" Tom asked.

"I received the letter a fortnight past."

Tom slapped the newspaper against his leg again. "And you say nothing of it to us?"

Martha's father looked up at Tom as if looking at a stranger. "Why would anyone wish to repeat such news? Why would anyone wish to hear it?"

"So as not to hear of it in town, as I did!"

Martha's father winced. "Yes, Tom. I see. Of course I should have mentioned it, but I suppose I could think of no words to introduce such an execrable subject." He stood up. "I should like to say good night to the children—they're unused to being so abruptly dismissed." He walked out.

Martha looked at Tom, a man possessed of a sensibility so fine he struggled each time the subject of whipping a chronically tardy nail boy came up. She pushed Bibelot off her lap, stood up, and crossed the room, reaching out to comfort Tom and perhaps be comforted herself, but Tom caught her by the shoulders and pushed her back so violently she stumbled and almost fell to the carpet, only catching herself by grabbing hold of a chair back. A raw, black anger overtook her. She started forward again under the terrifying power of it, but Tom's face had already crumpled.

"Oh dear God, Martha, do you see what they do to us? We *must* . . . we must leave this place!" He reached for Martha, ready now to take her in his arms for that shared comfort, but Martha no longer wanted or trusted those arms. She picked up Bibelot, stepped wide around her husband, and walked out.

---

THOMAS JEFFERSON MADE NO FURTHER MENTION of his nephews' villainy. Tom Randolph made no further mention of it. And yet Martha felt the weight of it whenever a pitcher was slapped on a table too hard or the napkins came out of the laundry stained or loud voices rumbled up from the kitchen below. In the shadow of the Gilburnes, Martha now felt surrounded by strangers. She'd returned from France noting every face around her, but she realized now that somewhere in the intervening years she'd stopped seeing them. She forced herself to look now and noticed the way Molly's hair sprung out of its bun each afternoon around three, the way Priscilla's lips pursed when she listened, the way Betsy always smelled of flour and something sweet, like honey or molasses.

She began to take closer note of Sally.

*Sally* now hummed Thomas Jefferson's Scottish tunes as she wandered about. *Sally* wore a new dress while Molly sat retrimming Martha's old one. *Sally* rushed to Martha's father when he fell on a broken step and reached him before Martha did, slipping her hand inside his coat and feeling his injured ribs with practiced fingers. *Sally,* who had aged every single day that Martha had aged, walked about with unlined face and shimmering hair and nimble steps. Where once Martha hardly saw Sally in the course of a day, now she appeared everywhere, strolling from here to there with one of her children, busy at nothing.

———

BUT SOON MARTHA WAS FORCED to turn her attention to Tom. He'd begun to spend less and less time at the mill and at Edgehill, instead walking off into the forest with his cane, slashing wildly at whatever growth intruded on his path, shouting at whatever child—or slave—happened to cross his route. He continued to shout at Jeff and Martha, and more than once started toward Martha in fury, only checking himself as he drew near. Perhaps Martha's growing unease worked its way to her womb, to yet another child who would be forced to depend on its grandfather for its food and clothing. In Martha's fourth month she miscarried a boy for whom she grieved only as long as it took a flash flood to wash away their mill on the Rivanna River.

## CHAPTER 27

In the quiet of winter 1812, Molly and Ned "married" in a ceremony held behind the Hemingses' slave cabins on Mulberry Row. Martha contributed cloth for Molly's dress, Tom gave Ned a made-over coat and read a Bible verse, Martha's father ordered up a quarter barrel of whiskey. As the festivity wound down, William Short arrived at Monticello, newly returned from France for good, or so his letter to Jefferson had said. Martha had doubted he would ever actually give up Paris until she'd received word from her friends that his duchess had wed a marquis; apparently an affair with an untitled American was acceptable, but a marriage to one was not.

Again, Short had changed little in the few years since Martha had last seen him, his features perhaps softened, his hair perhaps lighter at the temples, but another fine suit still fit superbly and he stood at his usual ease inside it. He hugged his old mentor, shook Tom's and Jeff's hands, bowed to Martha and the girls, saluted the little boys. He proclaimed great joy at being reunited with his old friend Bibelot as he scooped him from Martha's fingers. Through dinner he brought out his Paris diplomat best, inquiring after everyone's health, asking after the children's interests, telling amusing tales of France. When Tom turned the subject to his favorite topic, a possible war with England, William Short attended with all politeness, but his eyes strayed more than once to Martha's face.

And why shouldn't they? Again, Martha was the one who had changed. Since Short's last visit she'd given birth to three more sons with her usual non-Jeffersonian efficiency, but if she wasn't nursing, she was pregnant, and at forty years of age her body was beginning to show the strain of such constant efforts. Each glance in the mirror she'd carried from Varina to Edgehill to Monticello showed new lines at the corners of her eyes, but those were the lines that started her smiles and drew them upward. She needed those lines, especially now, especially as Short continued to gaze at her in search of . . . what? Whether she attended her husband's convoluted speech? Of course she did; she was no French wife. To prove it she turned to Tom. "It would seem by your studied analysis that war is a sure event," but Tom acted as if he hadn't heard her. Short gave Martha another long look and turned to address her father.

"My good friend, as I sit here in the heart of your family circle I recall your last words to me as you prepared to leave France. You urged me to come to America soon, declaring how lonely you would be without my company, especially once your dear daughters were gone from your house. And here Mrs. Randolph sits, and the fine Mr. Randolph, and their many children to entertain you. Clearly I could not have been missed, which leaves all the regret to none but myself."

"Regret is of little use to a man," Martha's father said. "I rejoice now in your presence, and I hope to see you at this table so often it necessitates the holding of a regular place."

"I shouldn't dream of becoming such a nuisance to Mrs. Randolph," Short answered, "assuming she keeps your house for you. Or perhaps Mademoiselle Sally—?"

Of course. Of course he would start again with Sally, needle them with Sally! "I keep the house," Martha said, "and as I do, you'll excuse me, please, as I see to it."

The gentlemen rose. Tom retired to his room, but the two

friends carried their wine to the library as Martha busied herself supervising the settling of the house for the night, preparing it for the morning. Once she paused outside the library door and listened to the gentle rise and fall of the men's voices, hearing nothing but the contented ripples of old friends talking, with none of the sharp counterpoint that Short always brought out in her. Or did she bring it out in him?

Martha thought back to France, to her first time alone with Short. Martha had fled to the garden in an effort to avoid the latest round of visitors and had attempted to scramble through the hedge; she'd lost her shoes and half her hem, but Short had somehow managed to appear on the far side of the hedge not only unmarred but carrying her shoes. He'd helped her tuck up her hem and offered to accompany her back to the house.

"Do you think me so silly as to go to all this trouble to escape only to return now?"

"I don't think you silly. In fact, I don't think you silly enough. How old are you now?"

"Old enough to know you stand here talking to me only to avoid those foolish Cosways yourself."

Short had laughed—a lovely, clear bell of a laugh. "They are quite foolish, aren't they?" And on hearing voices emerge from the house, Short had ducked down with Martha behind the hedge.

The same, bell-like laugh rang out from the library now, answered by Martha's father, and a wave of loneliness swept over Martha that for a minute—but only a minute—made her long to be curled up knee to knee with William Short behind that Paris hedge.

---

Short left early the following morning. It was so unusual for a guest to leave after only a night's stay that Martha wondered if late in the night Short and her father had gotten into some sort of disagreement. She believed she did note a brief depression in her father's spirits and a distracted gaze at table; at first she believed, but later discounted, that the distracted gaze had landed on Sally more than once. Whatever Martha saw or imagined she saw, it didn't last; nothing dispiriting could ever last when spring came to the mountain.

Spring meant that Martha's father joined his gardener out of doors, fixing the sticks and running out the twine as the boy set the peas, asparagus, potatoes, strawberries, artichokes, and carrots. Planting always set Martha's father humming and she found herself joining him as she worked around the house, pushing the "Coffee Song" into that part of her childhood best forgotten, picking up her father's favorite "Money Musk" to replace it. Did she hum because she was happy or did humming turn her happy? It little mattered; despite William Short's theories on the topic, she *was* happy—as long as she could keep certain thoughts pushed into the dark and apply her attentions to her children, who, it must be said, seemed to need it more the older they got.

At nineteen Jeff had grown strong and handsome like his father, but he could rage like his father as well, and brood just as dramatically over troubling questions. "I confess to a struggle," he told Martha one day, on the rare occasion of finding her alone in the small parlor. "A slave being person and property, I fear any feelings for the person might impair the value of the property." Martha tried and failed to think of the proper words with which to answer her son, but indeed, there were none. The person *was* property.

The fifteen-year-old Ellen was the closest to her grandfather, his best correspondent whenever he was away, the one who would answer his every call to read or play the harpsichord or engage in a game of chess. She was also nearest to her grandfather in intellect, but too easily crushed by a word or a look; here again Martha longed for the words that might help her daughter to navigate life unscarred, and here again she couldn't find them.

Cornelia at twelve was already clearly destined to be tall and lovely; she had also grown even shyer, and no efforts on Martha's part had thus far succeeded in drawing her out. She preferred books to conversation, comfort to style, and could seldom be persuaded to change for dinner. "Why must I, when soon after I'll change again for bed?" Martha had yet to find a sensible answer for that.

Virginia was much like Cornelia in looks and devoted to her sister; easier at chat, she often spoke for Cornelia, and already at ten took better care with her dress. She was active, as Martha had been, preferring outdoors to indoors, but far too averse to any form of housework to happily survive her likely role in life.

Mary was the only girl still truly a child, still unformed, still in need of every educational tool Martha could muster. She was bendable, amenable to every scheme of her grandfather's, always first at his knee and last to leave it, but like Anne, little interested in her schoolwork.

The youngest boys were a mix of dark and light and cheerful and ornery, occupying more of Martha's time than she might have liked. They were coming into the stage where they needed a father's guidance more than a mother's, but thus far Tom barely noticed them, even as they attempted to trail him about the house.

And Tom was . . . Martha stopped her musings, aware that she'd almost included Tom among the tally of her children, the last and neediest on the list.

## CHAPTER 28

I<small>N JUNE OF THE YEAR</small> 1812, the United States of America declared war on Great Britain for the second time in its young life. The issues, as Martha, her father, and Tom debated them, included untenable trade restrictions, impressment of American mariners, and Britain's support of American Indian insurrections that were foiling American plans for expansion. Two other issues remained unexpressed in print, but were talked of at table: America's interest in annexing the Canadian territory and a sense that the United States had never been accorded the respect it had won so honorably in its war for independence. The former president opposed military involvement on principle, preferring the application of economic pressures, but his embargo having been foiled by the New England federalists, he was now resigned to "James Madison's War," as the newspapers called it. Tom was ecstatic.

Martha had left her father outside with her children and had slipped into the small parlor to sort out her overdue household accounts. Tom came into the room and rounded the desk. He lifted the stray hairs from Martha's neck, caressed her exposed skin, and kissed the part at the top of her head. There was nothing new in any of this, traditionally nothing unwelcome, but now Martha felt in Tom a secret purpose and she flinched.

Tom drew back. "Martha, my love, I plan to ask President Madison for a military commission."

"Certainly he might do such a thing. An honorary rank for a member of so honorable a family—"

"I should never dream of asking for such an honor. What have I done to deserve it? I have yet to fight."

Martha whirled around. "You can't mean to *go*."

"I can. I must. Others fought for me last time. 'Tis my turn now."

"You're forty-five years old. You have nine children in need of you yet and numerous plantations to run, both yours and my father's."

Tom's mouth twisted in a way that Martha had seen before and had grown to dislike. "All of which will do just as well—if not better—in my absence. The overseer will tend to Edgehill. Your father now rides his plantations with Jeff."

"He relies on you. We all rely on you."

"No, Martha, only your father—and you—pretend this is the case. You have a role here and are content in it. I do not and am not."

It was true. He was not content. Martha could see this, had seen it, supposed she might have predicted it, and yet it hadn't mattered to her—or it hadn't mattered enough. Would her mother have thought so little of her father's well-being? No, but neither would her father have avoided his duties to his family, worked so hard to keep himself apart, forced his wife to think alone about how best to manage all of it, how best to keep a large family fed and safe. Her father had never dreamed of leaving to her mother the management of anything beyond the keeping of the house. But then again, Martha was not her mother.

She tried once more. "Disregarding, if you like, Jeff's independent spirit, you still have three younger sons in need of your guidance."

"And what kind of guidance might I give them? How not to succeed at law? How to embarrass themselves as politicians? How to fail at raising their crops?"

"You're not. You haven't. All the Virginia planters suffer in a like manner. And what of me?"

"You managed quite well when I went away to Congress."

"I'm far busier now."

"With your father's household, yes. But your father would be the first to agree that we must all sacrifice if we're to keep our liberty."

Martha studied Tom's face, infused with fresh blood, locked on its course, ready to burst if challenged. She knew that look well enough by now, knew enough to keep away from it, and yet suddenly another kind of knowing roiled in her, surprising her with the fear it set loose. War meant battles. Battles meant death. Easy or hard, Tom Randolph had been part of Martha's every thought and feeling for thirty years, and to be so abruptly confronted with the prospect of his loss unbalanced her in a way she had not anticipated.

Perhaps Tom was not so caught up in his war fever that he couldn't read Martha's thoughts. Her reached down and touched her face; Martha covered his hand with hers and clasped it to her cheek. What could she do but support him? Was it not her job in life? "You've always been a man of courage," she said.

———————

BUT BY THE TIME TOM WAS LEAVING FOR CANADA, Martha was again pregnant and thinking another thing about Tom's courage, seeing this new venture as an attempt to run away from his responsibilities, leaving Martha alone—once again—to cope. He came to Martha to present his new will to her and read it out in all pride:

> *With full confidence in the understanding, judgment, honor,*
> *and impartial maternal feeling of my beloved wife, I direct her to*
> *distribute among her children for their and her own use as she may*
> *see fit, after paying all my debts.*

You great, bloody fool, Martha thought—as if there would be a thing to distribute after the debts were paid. As if the debts would even be paid. As if your father-in-law wouldn't then officially take on your family's care as he'd unofficially taken it on for most of her married life.

————

THE NEW WAR, no different from any other, asked things of those who stayed behind as well as those who marched. Jeff took on the management of the rebuilt mill, and with English trade again disrupted, Martha's father decided to settle his cloth factory at Monticello, asking Martha to oversee it. She said no—she was sick, exhausted, consumed with worry—but Martha's father persisted.

"You're needed, Martha," he said. "And forgive me, child, but I think you need to do it for yourself. You need to step aside from those things which burden your mind. You can't allow yourself to be unhappy."

*Allow* herself to be unhappy? Indeed, that would be how Thomas Jefferson saw it, the pursuit of happiness easy enough if one only ignored the things that stood in the way of it. But however illogical it seemed to Martha to give an overburdened person more burdens, her father was right; as soon as Martha threw herself into the factory, her fatigue left her. The weaver's cottage was larger than the usual quarters at Monticello, it had more and bigger windows, and the work was light by slave standards; indeed, Martha had operated her own spinning jenny since her father's embargo had taken effect and took considerable pride in turning out yard after yard of homespun fabric. Martha took just as much pride in the amount of fabric the slaves turned out, and found her own satisfaction in their work. But soon Martha's father sent the now-thirteen-year-old Harriet Hemings to the factory to learn to spin and weave, and

Martha's equilibrium tottered. She couldn't keep her eyes from the girl, couldn't stop seeing the family ghosts in her. Where Sally so resembled Martha's mother, Harriet resembled Martha's sister, Maria, who in her turn had taken after their mother, so in Harriet both dead women were represented. Maria, though, was also part their father . . . Martha pushed the thought aside.

But Martha could not push Harriet aside. How lovely she was! Like Sally at a similar age, Harriet appeared mature beyond her years, her body already grown into a like symmetry and balance, but she was taller than Sally, her skin lighter than Sally's, so light she caused many visitors to Monticello to mistake her place. Her eyes were not Sally's amber, however, but hazel, and seldom averted; Martha found it difficult to meet the challenge so evident in them, and yet she couldn't look away from the girl. She watched as Harriet played at her new task, more interested in the learning than the producing, and in this too Harriet reminded Martha of her sister—so Martha thought and immediately chastised herself for thinking it. Oh, Maria! What Martha wouldn't sacrifice to have that playful nature beside her instead of this willful child of a slave who seemed not to understand the future that awaited her.

"Harriet!" Martha called above the clatter of machines and voices, which might have explained why the girl took no notice of her. Martha considered calling again, or walking up to the girl and clapping her hand down on her shoulder, but just then the girl did look up, straight at Martha, causing again that double—or triple—jolt of recognition. Martha looked away from her.

## CHAPTER 29

FALL CAME AND MARTHA'S FATHER SET ABOUT the season's tasks in the garden, overseeing the slaves as they dressed borders; set out bulbs; covered the most tender plants; cut back overgrown trees, vines, and shrubs. As the weather worsened, Tom, far to the north, wrote less and less often, and the letters that did arrive grew more and more melancholy; Martha longed for and dreaded them in equal measure. Alone, overburdened, she felt Tom's moroseness creeping into her own nature, exacerbated ten-fold when Mr. Bacon hinted to her one day that some economy might be in order at Monticello. Add to it a newly intensified apprehension over her pending confinement, and Martha decided that she must act on her own to secure the future of her family. President James Madison was a dear friend, his wife even dearer; Martha believed her family had done enough for their young country to warrant asking a small favor.

Martha labored over her request, going sideways and even backward before she could bring herself to ask what she wished to ask, but the final draft of her letter to the president was straightforward and absent of excuses. She asked that her husband be appointed to the new position created by the drain of war on the country's treasury—federal collector of taxes. Such a position would pay four thousand dollars a year, albeit only for the duration of the war, but as Tom would be collecting among his neighbors, he would be safe at home. Martha only mentioned the letter to her father after it was written, not wishing to appear to pressure him into adding his plea to hers; whether he chose to do so after Martha's letter had gone she would never know. She only knew that her request was granted.

Martha wrote Tom. Tom raged in answer. *I am now to leave my post and accept a position gotten on the application of my wife?* But Martha could absorb Tom's rage quite well at a distance. With little sympathy for his damaged pride—good God, how long ago had her own pride disintegrated?—she answered,

> *You must take this post. Mr. Bacon hints at concerns over my father's financial situation; we must take on more of the burden.*

---

IN JANUARY MARTHA GAVE BIRTH to her eleventh child and seventh daughter; the number seemed so significant that she named the child Septimia, whom they immediately began to call Timi. For the first time Martha's recovery was long, spotted throughout with random fevers; she missed the support of her sister, and Ursula, and Tom. She received word that Tom had marched on Canada, participating in the successful seizure of Fort Matilda, an insignificant outpost that few had heard of and drew but brief mention in the papers. Tom's next letter reported an altercation with his commanding officer and his resultant decision to resign; Martha saw it for the excuse it was, allowing Tom to take up the federal position without admitting the choice was forced on him by his wife. Martha awaited his return with new anxiety, but he came home with his old joy intact at the sight of her. "I can never again live separate from you," he told her. Martha cried when she saw him, cried as he held her, cried again as he rode off to Charlottesville to accept his new position. Who *was* this crying woman? She blamed the ravages of birthing and nursing Timi.

232 · *SALLY CABOT GUNNING*

M<small>ARTHA AND EDMUND BACON WORRIED</small> over the Monticello finances; Martha's father didn't. He ordered a new landau. He bought more live carp for the fishpond. A new violin appeared, and almost nightly he accompanied Ellen as she played the harpsichord. The next day Martha heard some considerably inferior playing, and concerned, followed it into the garden, where Beverly Hemings sat frowning over an old violin. He'd grown into a handsome boy, tall and slender with russet hair and peeled-almond skin, well mannered and well spoken, as were all Sally's children. His clothes were clean and well made and of better stuff than those provided the non-Hemings slaves; Martha, who had Molly and Priscilla to help with her own large brood and still spent many hours over her needle, understood what care it had taken, but she also understood whose pocket it had come from, whose pocket was more shallow than it had once been. And now, a violin.

"Where did you get that instrument?" Martha asked.

"Master Jefferson gave it to me."

"Who taught you to play?"

Beverly rose to his feet, his eyes now level with Martha's, his gaze direct, his demeanor composed, nothing in him hinting of the slave.

"Master Jefferson," he answered, but this time Martha heard it, the slurring of the *a* so that the word sounded more like *Mister,* commanding less respect for the man thus mentioned but more for the mentioner.

B<small>Y SUMMER TOM HAD GROWN RESTLESS</small>, unhappy in his new role of asking his neighbors for money, frustrated with the continued poor return from his labors at farming. He joined the militia at

Richmond, this time bringing Jeff along with him, heedless of the burden this placed on Martha and her father. Tom stayed until the militia disbanded, but Jeff came away earlier, concerned for the mill and the crops, in marked contrast to the lack of concern in his father. Martha noticed this new maturity in her son; she also noticed his new attentions to a young woman of their acquaintance, the daughter of the current governor of Virginia, Jane Nicholas.

One evening Jeff came to Martha where she sat alone in the large parlor, lingering after her father had retired, enjoying her book and the fire and the quiet. She saw her son and her heart cracked at the dejection in his features.

"How am I ever to acquire a home, to marry?" he cried. "My prospects from my father are blank, from my grandfather little better. Monticello will consume itself if not better managed. And what good will my meager education offer?"

Meager education! The words cut into Martha like thorns. Had she not tried her best with the boy? Or had she? She'd discouraged her father sending him to school, and perhaps Jeff had heard of it. If she'd supported the endeavor, if she'd believed that Jeff would succeed, might he have done so? But as Martha ruminated, Jeff continued to talk.

"Even the one thing I might have hoped to count as an asset—my family connection—now appears to work against me. Jane's mother in particular has made it quite plain to her daughter that she considers a connection with me to be beneath her."

"Beneath her! The wife of a garden-variety governor thinks the grandson of the president, the author of this country's founding principles, should fall beneath them?"

Jeff laughed. "'Tis not Grandpapa they object to. 'Tis this wild tribe of Randolphs they find fault with, and in that tribe you must now find yourself included. Mrs. Nicholas even criticized your dress. No cap, she says, hair flying every which way, and once she saw you running across the lawn barefooted!" There Jeff seemed to take his first good look at his mother's face. "Oh, Mama, don't look so. I only pass this along to you because I know how amusing you'll find it, how you'll only admire Jane the more because of how she answered it—'I've no doubt that if Mrs. Randolph eschewed cap and shoes there must have been little sense in wearing them.' She then told her mother that she'd long thought caps silly, and with a lawn as soft and green as Monticello's, it would be criminal not to put her naked feet in it. But what is this? You don't look amused."

With a great effort of will, Martha rearranged her features. "I've always thought Jane a sensible girl," she managed.

"And Anne's husband does little to enhance our position—'brawling in taverns and breeding slaves to support his family,' as Mrs. Nicholas put it."

Martha was so enraged she couldn't speak. Of course Charles Bankhead did nothing to enhance their position. Of course Martha had already come to regret the fact that her oldest daughter was now trapped in a life with a man no more successful than her father; Anne's letters depressed Martha for weeks each time she received one. As to the breeding of slaves, Martha had heard the rumors and denied them, as she'd been forced to deny so many things. But now here was her son, her poor love-lost son, with so little to offer a bright young woman whom Martha could have eagerly welcomed into the family, and yet what could Martha do for him? What her husband had always done.

"You must go to your grandfather."

"I did. He offered me a position as manager of his properties and the lease of his Tufton plantation when the current tenant's lease expires. Until then he promises a room at Monticello after Jane and I are married."

"Jeff! Then why so troubled?"

"I worry what my father will say to it. I worry he'll think he should be offered the position of manager."

Martha considered, but briefly. "You must take the position," she said. "All of our fates now hang on the fate of Monticello; we can't risk it to your father. You do see that?"

Jeff peered at Martha. "I do," he said softly. "I didn't expect that you did. I should have, I suppose." He rose and squeezed the hand that lay gripping the chair arm. At the door he paused. "You did a fine job with the mill and with Edgehill while we were off warring. And don't hate Jane's mother or my life shall be torn in half between the women I admire most and least."

"Mrs. Nicholas is beneath my hatred," Martha answered. "But I'll be sure to leave off my shoes when next she calls on me."

And why should William Short intrude on Martha's thoughts just then? The shoes, of course—the shoes left in the Paris hedge— and the heart-shaking thrill of that first catapult into love.

---

AFTER THE HEDGE, William Short had managed to find Martha alone in the garden a second time, and a third, and a fourth. It was during the fourth encounter that he'd caught her hand in an effort to direct her silent attention to a redwing blackbird; before he let her go his thumb brushed across her knuckles as if to say he released her only under duress. That minute—that touch—undid Martha; she could no longer conceal all that she felt. In fact, she would have melted against Short's smoothly fitting waistcoat right then if he hadn't stiffened his arm and held her back. "Your father," he whispered, and indeed, her father had just stepped out of the house and started across the lawn toward them. "I shall ask permission to take you promenading in the Luxembourg Gardens," he said. "What say you to that?"

"Yes," Martha said.

"Yes to what?" Martha's father asked as he reached them, smiling.

"The Luxembourg Gardens," Short answered.

Had Martha's father looked relieved? What did he fear she'd agreed to? Perhaps all the things she silently agreed to after that. Their first embrace, their first kiss, the first time Short dropped his mouth to her throat, her breast—but none of it undid her as did that first touch in the garden.

## CHAPTER 30

W HEN TOM HEARD OF JEFF'S PROMOTION, he rode off to Williamsburg on some supposed errand to do with his sister Nancy and didn't return for a month. When he did come home, he continued to walk out daily, sometimes returning to Monticello to dinner and sometimes not. When William Short arrived at Monticello in April, Tom made an effort to be present at dinner, but he remained quiet to the point of sullen at table, and excused himself for his bed long before the fruit and nuts. To compensate for such rudeness, Martha stayed up late, or so she told herself at the beginning of the evening, but in truth, something had happened to William Short. His talk was different this time, the kind of talk that Martha could feed herself full on, a communal revisiting of their shared lives in France. As Short talked, Martha watched her father's face soften and glow, felt herself soften, heard herself laugh over images of Maria and Martha sliding over the waxed floors of the Hôtel de Langeac in their stockings. Oh, how lovely it was to have Maria alive among them again! How lovely to be laughing!

At length, near one in the morning, Short said, "Enough. Return to those loved ones warming your beds or I shall be blamed for your absence."

Martha was so revitalized by the talk, the tone, the sheer joy of the evening, that she didn't even realize until she was in her bed and curled next to Tom what Short had said. He spoke to her *and* her father. He spoke of loved *ones*. Warm *beds*. Tom warmed hers, but who did Short think warmed her father's? As if she even needed to ask it. The burning of her mortified skin kept her awake long into the night.

————————

By midmorning, already exhausted by her usual labors after so little sleep, Martha had constructed enough resentment against Short to power their grist mill. She said little at breakfast and drew repeated looks from Short; she was unsurprised when he found her at her little factory. The place was noisy, rowdy, and without Harriet Hemings—word had come to Martha via Edmund Bacon that Harriet would not be returning—Martha was both relieved and resentful, although she said nothing to Bacon about it. Saying nothing should have grown easier by now. It had not.

William Short came up behind Martha and watched the laborers in silence; the girls who worked the jennies and looms were either too young or too old for the fields, but until that moment Martha had never questioned whether that might not make them too old or too young for work at the jennies and looms.

"Excuse me, please," she said after she could bear Short's silence no longer. She made her way out of the building, but Short followed her. She'd planned to return to the house but took a sharp turn and headed for one of the woods trails instead, thinking to shed him, but again, he followed her.

At length Short said, "You're quiet today. Too lively an evening?"

"We have a great deal of company and a great number of lively evenings."

"Your father is much sought after."

"Yes."

"Even I couldn't stay away, although I was in some doubt of my welcome from the mistress of the house. But all the while I was in France, I missed your father more than I missed my own. He fuels me."

Martha looked sideways. Short's eyes were cast down, his hands locked behind him, his stride perfectly matched to hers. He looked up and caught her looking. "I missed *you*. I would like us to be friends. Could you find a way to make that be? Life is such a quirk. I come here and feel your missing sister as I feel this missing molar at the back of my mouth; I don't want to lose another tooth. I speak too freely with you; I know this. I say too many things that cause you distress. 'Tis only that I've known you when you were distressed for other reasons—may I say for better reasons? But you see, there I start up again. My excuse can only be that my age puts me halfway between you and your father, so it can be no great surprise if my behavior toward you vacillates halfway as well; one minute I preach to you as if I had a father's right, the next I speak to you as if I had another kind of right. I have neither. I know this. Let me try one last time to talk as I should talk; let me find a neutral subject to which no one could take offense. Here, what is this shrub? Let me begin with that. And what is that flower?" He lifted his eyes and gazed at the distant view of Edgehill toward which Martha had inadvertently walked them. "And how does that lovely farm of yours? 'Tis a hard thing these days to survive as a farmer in Virginia. Even your father struggles."

"Did he say so to you?"

"He did, but only in passing. He won't dwell on anything unpleasant. But there can't be anything new I can tell you of your father." Short's eyes had swiveled from Edgehill to Martha and hung there, no doubt, until he was quite sure she caught his meaning.

"No. There isn't."

Short let out a great sigh. "What a mad world we live in. And yet none of us thrown together in it dare speak of the madness.

You see, I forgot how it was, and now I'm forced to remember, and now I'm forced to keep silent. I'd had such great hopes. I thought it might start here at this famous place, and with your father's name behind it, we might combine our efforts to move it out. We talked of such fine things—of setting the Negroes on their own parcels to work for a wage, of compensating those skilled at a trade, of pressing through law for the gradual emancipation of all, but your father tells me it's not to be the work of our time. He now prefers other subjects. And you as well, I see this. Will you change the subject for us? I seem to fail again at it. Or shall I turn back to the house and leave you in peace?"

Peace. Was there such a thing? And even if there was, what chance of finding it at that house? Only the day before, Martha had overheard her father pushing the three youngest boys to better attend their studies if they wished to succeed at their future work.

"Oh, we shan't need to *work*, Grandpapa," James had answered. "We only educate ourselves to make intelligent conversation with other wealthy gentlemen."

"Then you'll lose all you own to the fellow who does work," their grandfather had countered, and all three boys had laughed.

*Laughed.* What on earth had Martha taught them? What had Tom demonstrated by his example?

"That shrub is quince," Martha told Short. "My father planted it four years ago. The flower is witch hazel. Surely you know it."

"Of course. I only needed reminding. You see? This is the use of friends."

"Sometimes friends don't want reminding."

"I know. I'd only hoped . . . Ah, Martha, you know all my hopes—do leave them be and talk of yours. What are your dreams these days?"

"For my father's legacy to remain untarnished. To remain beside him as he enters whatever infirmity lies ahead and to care for him as he's cared for me. For my husband to find peace. For my children to grow up healthy and useful and secure. My oldest girl, Anne, I had such hopes of her marriage but now I hear of Mr. Bankhead's fighting in the taverns, of debts worse than her father's, of—" Martha stopped. Restarted. "You can't know how it wrenches me to hear that my eldest daughter's husband lives off the breeding and selling of slaves."

Short's hand brushed Martha's, as if he wished to catch it up but changed his mind. Or perhaps his hand didn't brush hers; perhaps the breeze that fingered her hair only made her think it.

Again Short left Monticello earlier than he'd planned, this time claiming a forgotten appointment in Richmond.

———

EDUCATION HAD ALWAYS BEEN of greatest importance at Monticello, but now Thomas Jefferson took it up as a thing nearer to an obsession. He laid out a plan for Virginia that began with free elementary education, complemented by a secondary program funded by tuition, culminating in the establishment of a state university in Charlottesville. He charged off to meetings, wrote letters, entertained even more than previously, and at last a plan was approved for the University of Virginia. He surveyed the lines himself, found the Italian stonecutter, designed the buildings, and watched their construction through a telescope from his favorite spot on the north terrace. Martha couldn't have been more delighted with her father's interest and plan, but she would confess to missing the hours lost to her and her children. She would confess to wanting her own part in it. Had she not successfully educated all—or most—of her children? She began to hover at doors as shamelessly as the Negroes. She spoke to her father of the lessons tried with best success in her parlor schoolroom. Her father listened in all politeness but enlisted her in nothing.

———

AT THE END OF THE YEAR, Martha returned to Edgehill with Tom to host their annual harvest feast for the slaves. The house had grown no more accommodating; Martha and her older girls worked awkwardly in the small kitchen directing Betsy and her helpers, bumping hips and elbows as they carried platter after platter to the long tables set out on the lawn. Roasts of chicken, goose, beef, mutton, and pork; stews of squash, turnip, cabbage, potatoes, and onions; meat and fruit pies; and loaf after loaf of bread disappeared almost as fast as they were delivered. Tom and Jeff minded the jugs, and on the surface they appeared to get on, but as Martha looked closer she could see that both men were more at ease conversing with the Negroes. Tom even started a fine speech, thanking the slaves for their hard efforts toward "our shared cause," mentioning a good number of them by name, but soon he began to lose his thread, rambling about another time when the crooked would be made straight and the parched would be sated.

That night Tom, topping off a liquored afternoon with several more draws from his own private bottle, insisted that Martha join him in their old bed at Edgehill despite a kitchen still in a state of upheaval. He made a brief attempt at their usual bedtime endeavors but soon fell off to lie so still beside her that Martha believed him asleep, until his voice rolled over her out of the darkness. "What a hideous monster is our Southern system. The greatest white dastard among us may hold the bravest Negro entirely in his power, entirely dependent on his whim."

"Yes," Martha answered. "And so we must work to even it—as

my father says, to make sure we ask nothing of our slaves we wouldn't ask of a free laborer."

"So all will appear well as we sell away their children?"

"We don't sell away children!"

Tom rolled away from her.

———

MARTHA BETTER UNDERSTOOD that liquored deep-night conversation two weeks later. Their son-in-law forfeited on the loan Tom had cosigned, and Charles's—and Tom's—creditors began pressing harder, in competition with one another for what remained. Mr. Randolph must liquidate assets, either property or slaves, they told him. But Tom still couldn't find a buyer for Varina—the state was overrun with land-rich, cash-poor gentlemen farmers—and to forfeit Edgehill meant Tom must give up all hope of being anything other than his father-in-law's dependent. Martha had managed the farms in Tom's absence and felt she understood something of the problems with farming; Tom's failure had been not in raising the crops but in getting the crops to a well-timed market. He needed to stop losing himself in books and soldiering and politics and melancholy; he needed to *focus*.

But now there was no time.

Tom spoke to Martha again from the dark of their bed. "We must sell one."

Martha didn't need to ask what Tom meant.

"Mr. Bacon offers me five hundred dollars for Mavis."

Mavis, Ursula's fifteen-year-old granddaughter, born at Edgehill, where she lived yet with her mother and father and sisters and brothers. "Not Mavis. You can't sell Mavis. Give him Aggie." Aggie, who'd been caught stealing a ham. Edmund Bacon could manage Aggie.

"I offered him Aggie. I offered Suke. He wants Mavis, for he knows the quality of that family. Besides, she's of child-bearing age. 'Tis the most money I'll be offered for a single slave, Martha. Better to sell one than several."

Yes, one was better than several. And Martha could easily spare Mavis. Indeed, another kind of household would have sold Mavis, Aggie, *and* Suke long ago. Martha was not happy to be forced to this—of course she was not happy—but at forty-six she'd just been delivered of her eleventh living child whom her father had requested they name George Wythe after his murdered friend; Tom, usually at his most supportive at the birth of a child, had continued to disappear most days and well into the evening; Jeff had informed her that her father had cosigned twenty thousand dollars in banknotes for Jeff's father-in-law; Ellen had dashed in aflutter over an invitation from Dolley Madison to visit her at the capital, but Martha had no money to outfit her daughter for such an entree into Washington society. It was too bad about Mavis, but she would remain a well-treated house slave in the neighborhood she grew up in, and at least her mother could know she'd be properly housed and clothed and fed.

Such Martha could say—and repeat—as Edmund Bacon arrived to collect Mavis and her bundle of clothes, while Mavis and her mother cried as if the girl weren't to be seen again in this life. Martha had planned to give Mavis a hug and a shawl but changed her mind at the onset of the torrents; she turned her back on the scene and retreated to her bed, which she should never have left in the first place—she had *not* recovered from George Wythe, as Tom might have observed if he were present.

## CHAPTER 31

A RARE FALL OF SNOW ERASED THE BLUE RIDGE, whitewashed the forest and lawn, and capped Monticello's dome. In the midst of the new chill, Martha struggled to find her old warmth, her strength. For the first time in her many birthings, she had difficulty regaining her legs, difficulty nursing George Wythe. It little helped that Madison Hemings had now taken up the violin, and the inexpert shrieking seemed to come at Martha from every corner of Monticello. The violin, the insatiable new infant, ate at Martha like two worms in the same ear of corn; why must her father choose this particular moment to teach a slave to fiddle? Why must he choose to name her child *George Wythe,* the man who had bestowed his estate on his mulatto child? Even her father's gift of one hundred dollars to finance Ellen's Washington junket distressed Martha after Bacon's and Short's hints at her father's financial worries.

Martha would also admit that she'd run out of patience with her husband. Could he not look about him and see that someone else suffered, perhaps as much or more than he did? Could he not spend less time idling about in the forests and fields, until his sons thought this was the extent of the effort required of a *gentleman?* Except for Jeff. Jeff, who carried all. Jeff, who had also run out of patience with his father.

Jeff followed Tom into the house, dusted in snow and yet saturated with sweat. He accosted Tom in the hall. Martha, hearing in her son's voice that note of impatience, stepped out of the parlor.

"I should like to speak with you," Jeff said to Tom.

"I'm on my way out," Tom answered.

"You just came in. I've been looking to speak with you for three days now."

Tom picked up a newspaper off the hall table. He didn't turn around. "Speak, then."

"I wonder when you were last at Edgehill, Father."

"When I go to Edgehill is my business."

"I mention it because the cistern appears cracked; if it isn't repaired soon, it will drain its contents."

"'Tis my business."

"Indeed. 'Tis *your business*."

Before Martha's brain could catch up with her eyes, Tom dropped the paper, whirled around, lifted his cane, and brought it down on Jeff's shoulders, Jeff too stunned to move. Tom lifted his arm again and Jeff's face became suffused with rage; he stepped in, caught the cane, and twisted it out of his father's hand. Martha rushed forward, but before she could reach either man, Jeff swung around and strode from the room, shaking like a child. Martha ran after him.

"Jeff!"

He neither answered nor turned. Martha started toward the stable after him but he'd already ridden off by the time she got there. She turned back to the house, shaking as Jeff had been shaking. She must speak to Tom, she knew this, but her legs wouldn't seem to carry her into his orbit. Instead, they turned back toward the stable.

As Martha approached the building, Peter Hemings came hastening out, but Martha waved him away, heading for the farthest bay and the young mare her father had recently purchased. The old bay had died, and Martha's father had instructed her to consider the mare her own; Martha had taken an instant liking to the horse, and as it had arrived with a hot foreleg, it gave Martha the needed excuse to visit the stable. She knelt to check the leg and decided it had cooled, but she was not yet ready to leave the dim, quiet building; she picked up a piece of sacking and began to burnish the mare's coat. Soon the work, combined with the touch of the horse, began to soothe her, and after a time she found herself humming. *Oh, say bonnie lass, can you lie in a barrack, and marry a soldier and carry his wallet?* She stopped humming. By the simple act of loosening her will, her knees folded and she sank into the straw.

―――――

TOM HAD BEGUN A NEW CUSTOM—or perhaps it was an old custom formerly overlooked when Martha had been more inclined to overlook things: He retired to his study each night with a bottle of brandy and didn't reappear until the negotiation of the bedroom doorway had become problematic. If Martha was awake, Tom sooner or later found a subject of contention that provided him with a satisfying rant; if Martha gave him no specific subject, he picked at her faults in general. *Why do you let your hair fly about all day and braid it so tight at night? Why can't you do a simple thing like keep a stocking mended? Why must you spend so long at the table talking?* Martha soon learned to appear heavily asleep as soon as Tom banged through the doorway. This served the double purpose of preventing a scene *and* a twelfth child, the one thing now as unwelcome as the other.

―――――

MARTHA SAT IN HER SMALL PARLOR with her girls around her, the older ones reading, the younger ones attending their slates, Martha focused on nothing but the image of Tom's cane coming down on Jeff's shoulders. She'd just resolved to abandon the classroom when

Critta entered and announced a visitor, Virginia's suitor, Nicholas Trist.

"Mr. Trist would like a private word with you, missus; I sat him in the big parlor."

Ellen and Cornelia giggled. Martha turned to look at them and caught Virginia's wild blush. So. "He wishes me and not Mr. Randolph?"

"He asked for you, missus."

Martha stepped out of the small parlor into the larger and found the young man she'd come to know while he was tutored at law by Martha's father. His usually delicate skin had flushed as bright as Virginia's and his eyes burned as he erupted into his speech. How deeply he loved her daughter. What great care he would take of her. He was to leave for West Point soon, but he—and Virginia—had hoped to settle on an official engagement before they parted.

"My daughter is but seventeen," Martha interrupted, hearing in her voice Tom's words when Martha had pushed for Anne's marriage to Charles Bankhead.

"Indeed, yet she professes herself firm in her mind. I know myself firm in mine."

"She's too young to be entangled by an engagement. If you both feel the same after you complete your schooling, come speak with me again."

Oh, how the light died in the boy! But how gracefully he submitted! "If this is your wish, I shall cherish the hope that on my return I may find the heart of Miss Virginia as free as mine shall be devoted, and that I may one day be entitled to the appellation of your son."

Martha could only nod at Trist, her throat suddenly too constricted to form words. After he left, however, she sat long, reflecting on many things. Why had young Trist sought her out instead of Tom? Had he already observed that Tom Randolph was no longer in command of himself and therefore no longer in command of the family? If there had been any question of a marriage settlement, of course Martha would have been forced to refer Trist to her husband, but as there was not, as Nicholas Trist apparently knew there was not, Martha could speak as she wished. And the fact that she'd spoken as she'd spoken, knowing her penniless daughters had little chance of receiving any offers of marriage, let alone any from young men like Nicholas Trist, meant what? That she acknowledged her error in allowing Anne to marry so early, or that she now regretted her own young marriage?

Martha got up from her chair and strode from the parlor, but she didn't return to the schoolroom; dusk had begun to roll in across the lawn and the anonymity of it called her. She continued out the door and along the first roundabout toward the stable. Ever since the incident with the cane, the stable had become Martha's refuge, but on this day Martha never quite reached it. Looking out past the dormant vegetable garden she spied Harriet Hemings, just coming up the rise toward Mulberry Row, and the brick mason Davy Bond approaching her from behind. Like Virginia, Harriet was now seventeen and as lovely as it was possible for a young woman to be, black or white; Martha could admit this even as she saw something off-putting in that hair, that skin, those eyes. She watched Harriet as the girl walked at a dreamy pace, oblivious to the presence of the brick mason behind her, until he dashed ahead and caught Harriet by the arm. Harriet whirled around and pulled back so violently that Davy Bond released his hold; Harriet sprinted toward the house, barreling past Martha as if she were nothing but a fence post, open rage burning her features.

"Harriet!"

The girl continued ten more feet before stopping. Another second passed before she turned.

"What are you thinking, wandering about alone at this hour?"

"You're alone."

"I'm alone! You would compare my condition to yours? I asked you what you're doing out here alone so near dark."

Harriet breathed hard. A few more breaths and it seemed to calm her. She pointed down the mountain. "I feed the deer in the deer park. They wait for me at evening."

"And so does someone else, apparently. Get in the house and keep close to it henceforward or I won't answer for your safety."

"Yes, ma'am," Harriet said, but with a lift to her chin that had not come from her mother.

Martha gave up on the stable and followed Harriet's course, returning to the house, intending to find her father and speak to him about the brick mason, but the episode had unsettled her. *Harriet* had unsettled her. When little Timi raced to Martha as she entered the hall, giggling with delight for no reason other than joy at the sight of her mother, Martha stooped to pick up the child, this seventh and surely last girl. Timi would not grow up with that edge Martha saw in Harriet, distrusted in Harriet, disliked in Harriet; she would not walk about pushing a false pride before her or slashing others with her resentment. If Beverly and Madison carried such feelings in them, they hid it as Harriet did not, and Eston was still too young to comprehend what his life was and was not; perhaps this was the thing that bothered Martha the most, that Harriet comprehended but refused to admit, that she didn't acknowledge the difference between her place and Virginia's. Or more accurately put, more disturbingly put, she didn't acknowledge the difference between her place and *Martha's*. Oh, why wouldn't her father put these Hemingses away and out of sight?

No, she could not talk to her father of the brick mason. She would mention the episode to Edmund Bacon, she decided, but as

Harriet was now safe inside, there was no need to do so that evening. Martha hugged Timi closer as the girl chattered some joyful silliness in her mother's ear. Ordinarily Martha would call to Priscilla to put the child to bed, but this night Martha carried Timi up the stairs herself, touching the nursery door as she passed through it, taking comfort in its solidness, its weight. She touched the silk-smooth plaster, the simple molding, the sturdy bed; all this would shelter Timi just as it had sheltered Martha. She carried Timi to the window in hope of showing her a last look at her world, her mountain, her refuge, but it had already melted into dark.

## CHAPTER 32

JEFF KEPT AWAY FROM MONTICELLO, and Martha spent the long days avoiding Tom where she could, taking solace in her father's company as he permitted. Word of the altercation between the two men had miraculously failed to reach Martha's father, but she lived on edge in the constant fear that it might. A sense that Martha should be doing something about something—or everything—pervaded her, and yet she couldn't sort out how or where or what to do. She needed someone to confide in and yet there was no such person for her; her father had a talent for making and keeping friends, but Martha seemed to have shed most of hers. She would admit she'd begun to avoid invitations that included Tom, fearful of the growing number of inappropriate outbursts, and since she'd returned from Washington—or she might as well say France—the women of her former acquaintance seemed to have grown shy of her. Besides, she could no longer speak freely to any of them of her private worries— she was the daughter of Thomas Jefferson, and above all else she must protect his reputation and the reputation of his house.

Perhaps that was why—of course that was why—when spring brought William Short back to Monticello, Martha found herself greeting him with more than her usual warmth. She noted it and Short noted it, as evidenced by his returned warmth, but he also noted other things, and wasted little time in sharing his thoughts. Although the mare's leg had healed, Martha continued to use it as an excuse to escape the house, and on Short's second day on the mountain, he caught up with her on her way to the stable.

"You see your husband daily," he said as they crouched together examining the mare's leg for the nonexistent heat. "But I come and go, and each time I come I note a greater change in him. He was always meticulous in his dress, more so than either you or your father. He always paid some degree of homage to the rules of civilized society. When I came upon him at this visit, I took him for a poor tenant farmer, not only because of his dress, but because he brushed past me without a nod or a glance; the distinct smell of brandy trailed after him, and it was but ten in the morning. The next I saw him he was raging at poor Priscilla, who couldn't move her old knees fast enough to keep up with . . . the devil knows who she couldn't keep up with—one or another of your children."

Martha stood up. Short stood with her. "And this isn't the worst of what I see. The way he speaks to you. The way he thrashes about with that cane. I've known men like this and they only go on in one way. I must say to you that I fear for your safety."

Martha hadn't meant to change her face, but something in it made Short peer hard at her. "Dear God. He *has* struck you."

"Of course he hasn't. He lashed out once at Jeff. 'Twas nothing, 'twas over in a minute." Martha turned away, but Short caught her arm and turned her back.

"So is murder over in a minute. Martha, you must listen to me. You mustn't keep here with him. I've no doubt he was a fine man once—"

Martha pulled free. "He's a fine man now. And he's my husband. Must I remind you, Mr. Short, that this is not France where one moves about from husband to husband and wife to wife? We apply no such remedy here."

"Perhaps you should. You could come with me to Philadelphia. I've given up on Virginia and its slaves. In Philadelphia—"

"You know me little if you think I'd leave my father as he enters that time of life when he'll have most need of me."

"He has no need of you. He has Burwell who would thrust his hand through flame for him. He has Sally who's kept faithful to him for over thirty years. But I see you make no mention of the wrench of leaving your husband."

"I speak only of that which I believe important to *you,* so you might better hear me."

"Then come with me to Philadelphia. We'll visit Monticello once it's cleared of your husband. Of course you must bring your children; how many do you have now, six, seven?"

"I've nine still at home. Shall I name them for you?"

"You squabble over details; this tells me you have no argument against the main case. I shall learn your children's names; will that convince you I'm sincere?"

Martha stared at Short. He was in jest, surely, but he didn't look it. She turned away, admittedly flustered, and hurried for the house.

Short followed. "Martha!"

She whirled around. "Mr. Short, you may think you know all there is to know of my life. You do not. This place *is* my life. If you cannot allow me to live it, then best you go back to Philadelphia. Or Paris."

———————

BUT THIS TIME SHORT DIDN'T GO. Two days later he managed to catch Martha alone again by joining her in chasing after Timi at the far end of the terrace. He beat Martha to the child and plucked her from the rail, handing her off awkwardly.

"I should like to apologize for my presumption the other day," he said, speaking low. "I'd be grateful if you'd allow me to leave it behind, along with all the other embarrassments I carry about from my past. I must say, they do seem to crop up extraordinarily frequently in stables."

"In stables!"

"Perhaps I never shared with you the story of my first romance. A clumsier boy never lived. But even now, whenever I get near the smell of hay I become . . . shall I say enthusiastic?"

Oh, how could Martha help but smile at the man? And how gratefully he smiled back at her! And how quickly he took note of the success of the new tack. Thereafter, at least once a day Short managed to provoke a laugh in her. But at the same time he began to accompany her from house to terrace to lawn and even from room to room where decorum permitted. In truth, there were times when decorum surely wouldn't have permitted, but he kept close just the same—when she was brought her infant to nurse, when she sat drying her hair in the sun, when she walked again to the stable. And day by day they fell back into the old, comfortable way of speaking to each other.

One aspect of Short's behavior didn't change, however. Martha came upon him in the hall, talking to Sally in French.

"Now see here," Short said as he spied Martha. "Mademoiselle Sally informs me she begins to forget her French. You must make a point of speaking to her in that language."

"Whatever for? Her duties don't require it. Now excuse me, please, I'm in hunt of my father."

"He's resting in his room," Sally said. "I'm just now taking him his aperitif." She moved off down the hall.

Again Short seemed to read something that came unbidden into Martha's face. He looked at her and burst into laughter.

———

MARTHA'S FATHER SENT JOHN HEMINGS, along with his nephews Beverly and Madison Hemings, to work at the University of Virginia. No better compliment could have been paid the three men, for it had become clear to Martha that her father now counted the university among his greatest achievements. He spent long hours searching for tutors, selecting books, writing letter after letter enforcing his argument that the university should have no religious affiliation, should, indeed, not include the topic in its curriculum. The position was not popular, but Martha's father persisted, until his rheumatism grew so severe he had trouble mounting his horse to ride to the necessary meetings. Peter Hemings devised a method of positioning his horse alongside the terrace so his master could ease himself down into the saddle, but after a few weeks of such effort, he decided that it was time to try the famous Warm Springs cure for himself.

Against the advice of his daughter and his three oldest grandchildren, Martha's father traveled by horseback with only Burwell to accompany him; his departure signaled that it was time for William Short to leave as well, and although Martha would give her father's departure the credit for her sinking spirits, she could admit this time that she would feel William Short's absence too. Martha didn't need Short's bodyguarding, but she did need his willing ear. That it came with a ready and at times unwelcome freedom of speech only allowed Martha that same freedom, something she denied herself so often at Monticello.

"When do you return?" she asked.

Short made something of a study of her before replying. "I don't know."

Once Martha had urged a young Tom Randolph to return to her soon if he wished to please her, but those had been a young woman's words. An unmarried woman's words. "Very well," she answered. "I would ask you to beware, however. If you take too long, you'll return to find us toothless and crippled."

"I would ask *you* to beware," Short burst out. "You and your father together, you ignore anything that distresses you. You trust to reason where none exists. You cannot live so! I must make you understand—"

To Martha's equal relief and annoyance, Short stopped midsentence, pivoted, and strode indoors.

———

As vehemently as Martha denied the need for Short's protection from Tom, she took to watching him with care and didn't like what she saw. He did neglect his personal care; he did thrash about more wildly with his cane, graduating from shrubs to fence rails; he began to shout at the servants; he shook Martha out of false and real sleep and accused her of abandoning him.

"I'm here, Tom," she said. "I'm exactly where I've always been," but he never seemed able to hear her. One night she actually did get up and walk out on the terrace to look at the magnificent umbrella of stars, needing a closer touch with the mountain, with the greater world, needing to shrink her own fears. On her return she found Tom standing at the foot of the stairs, a looming patch of black against the lesser dark. As Martha drew closer, she saw he was holding Timi against his shoulder, her head lolling at an awkward angle, stopping Martha's heart with fear.

"What's happened!"

"She woke calling you. I told her you were gone."

Martha grabbed Timi and found her deep asleep. She jostled the child till she woke and cried and clutched her mother. Martha carried her to the nursery and settled her again, sitting in the dark and quiet long after the child had fallen back to sleep.

———

Martha's father returned from his treatment covered in such festering boils he could barely sit in his saddle. Dr. Norris was sent for, but the mercury treatment he prescribed only further debilitated the patient; he retired to his bed, but he would allow only Sally and Burwell to attend him. When Martha forced her way into his chamber, she found her father propped on his side with pillows, his usually rosy complexion waxy, his always cheerful air absent. "I'm afraid I'm in no state for visiting, child."

Sally was just coming in the door as Martha exited. "My father doesn't wish to be disturbed," Martha said, meaning *Sally* was unwelcome, but Sally apparently saw something in Martha's face that told her *Martha* had been found unwelcome. "'Tis only that he dislikes his family seeing him when he's not himself," Sally explained.

*Sally* explained. To Martha. "I've known this of him since I was a child," Martha snapped. "And my father knows this of *me*: I cannot rest until I know how he fares. I shall return in the morning."

———

INCONVENIENTLY, Martha's daughter Anne, hearing of her grandfather's illness, decided to visit Monticello, bringing her husband, Charles. Martha had seen her daughter little; Anne wrote happy letters that Martha disbelieved as soon as rumors climbed the mountain of Charles's tavern altercations, of his living off the sale of slaves. Looking at her daughter's once lovely, now drawn and colorless face, Martha's trepidation increased, but worn down with concern for her father, she hung out her own smile and went on with her preparations for a special dinner of Anne's favorite Parmesan macaroni to welcome her. Cook knew the recipe well but disliked the machine that made the noodles; Martha's father had brought it home from France and Martha liked to oversee its use to make sure no harm befell it.

A distant, catlike shriek, cut off too soon, caused Martha to look upward seconds before Molly came tearing into the kitchen. "You must come!"

Martha took the stairs on Molly's heels, bursting into Anne's room to find a drunken Charles standing over a crumpled Anne, kicking her in the legs. "Get up! Get up, I say!"

Martha flew at Charles and caught him by his coat, hauling him backward. Charles pushed her off. Tom and Ned burst into the room, Tom's face black with rage. He whirled and snatched up the fireplace poker, whirled again and swung. Charles dropped.

Martha and Molly eased Anne to her feet and helped her to the safety of Martha's room. Ned and Burwell dealt with Charles. Between them they managed to keep Charles from Anne, Tom from Charles, and any news of the disturbance from the master of Monticello; they ministered to Charles only long enough to see him conscious and on his horse and pointed down the mountain.

"You'll keep here with us henceforward," Martha told her daughter. Such was Martha's plan. Anne's was another.

Within a week she'd left to join her husband.

———————

MARTHA WAS TOO STUNNED from that first blow to feel the full effect of the second until weeks after it struck. A bank panic forced Mr. Nicholas to default on his loans, depositing his twenty-thousand-dollar debt on the shoulders of its cosigner, Thomas Jefferson. Tom's affairs were affected, of course, but Martha had long ago given up on the possibility of the Randolphs becoming solvent. Her father was another thing. When Martha at last absorbed what had happened, it felt as if the thinning bed of needles under the cracked branch on which they perched had blown away. Such was Martha's first reaction; Tom's first reaction put hers to shame.

"He can never free them now," he said.

Tom sold Deany, age fourteen, born at Edgehill, to Edmund Bacon. This time Martha didn't even contemplate appearing to say good-bye to the girl; her father needed her at home. *Home,* she said and meant Monticello.

———

How fast deany was erased, how fast even her absence was erased! Being of Edgehill she was little missed at Monticello, and Martha allowed herself to forget her as she'd forgotten Mavis, as she'd forgotten Harriet and the brick mason Davy Bond. Martha saw Harriet running on the far side of the garden one day; she saw a shadowy form disappearing behind the slave cabins that might—or might not—have been Davy again. Martha watched until Harriet had almost reached the house, watched as she slipped into the dependency under the house where she slept with her mother. Martha went inside, but as soon as the scene was at her back, she began to doubt that the man had been Davy, or even white, and if he wasn't white, it was a matter of two slaves meeting up behind the cabins; nothing Martha need disturb Edmund Bacon about after all.

## CHAPTER 33

Mᴀʀᴛʜᴀ'ꜱ ꜰᴀᴛʜᴇʀ'ꜱ ʜᴇᴀʟᴛʜ ɪᴍᴘʀᴏᴠᴇᴅ. He returned to his terrace and his horse and his dinner table and his family evenings in the parlor; Tom seldom appeared at either dinner or in the parlor. In fact, Martha paused when she entered the parlor one evening after dinner to find her father and Tom sitting in the room alone, one on either side of a newly kindled fire. The fall had come in mild, but Martha's father had reached an age where he enjoyed a good pine blaze in the evening, one that would start bright and die without overheating the room. He waved Martha into a chair between them and leaned forward, hands on knees, eyes alight— all signs of the kind of excitement that would require no preamble.

And so it proved. "What think you of your husband's taking a turn as governor of Virginia?"

Martha looked from father to husband to father again, now in grave doubt over the state of *both* minds. She'd taken care to shield her father from Tom's increasingly unreliable behavior, but surely her father must have seen enough to know? His countenance wore an unreadable smile; her husband's wore a combined air of hope and doubt. Martha could have said things to that first countenance that she wouldn't wish to say to the second—that she doubted Tom's ability to get elected, but if elected, she doubted more his capacity to serve. How could her father not know this? But as Martha struggled to form her response, another thought occurred. If Tom did manage to get himself elected, the income that the position generated would be most welcome; that this might outweigh her other concerns appalled her, until her father spoke from a like mind.

"The annual salary is upward of three thousand dollars," he said. "I've made inquiry in private circles; it would appear we've some influence yet, that no other likely candidate would be viewed as strong. His military service has enhanced his position, and the general feeling is that if Tom put himself forward, he would be elected." Martha's father leaned toward her. "Think what this means. Tom would have a chance to open new discussion regarding issues dear to us all."

Martha looked at Tom. His expression had not changed. Yes, she thought, there *were* other things besides the money to consider. And when had she last seen anything like hope washing over her husband's features, even shadowed as it was by doubt? She recalled Tom's past history of focusing best when given the most to do, of her own history of finding strength in the distraction of new tasks, of the fact that her father would be near to guide him.

"I think it a fine idea," Martha said.

The shadow, the doubt, vanished from Tom's features.

———

TOM PREPARED FOR HIS CAMPAIGN by leaving off the brandy till after dinner, getting a haircut, buying two new suits of clothes, talking endlessly with his father-in-law, and at the end of each night, as he lay in bed close to sober, with Martha. She would admit he seemed much improved, his plans for Virginia sound. As fiercely as Martha resisted assumptions of success, she found herself falling into Tom's dreams, something that allowed them to share the kind of talk they hadn't shared in a long time. Ever since the episode with the cane, or perhaps her talk with Short, Martha had been unable to take any of the old physical comfort from Tom, or to give it in return, and as a result there existed a constant state of physical stress between them. The talking helped that too. And yet when Tom left for Richmond to campaign, Martha luxuriated in the empty bed and undisturbed sleep; she found her old joy in the sounds of the mountain night: the wind and the owls and the fox and the gentle creaks and whispers of a house as it slept.

———

But often in the night Martha woke thinking of Anne. Martha had fled to Monticello in part in search of protection for her children, and now she wanted desperately to draw Anne inside its sheltering walls. Martha wrote again and again asking Anne to come, and Anne finally wrote back accepting the invitation but for a visit only, with Charles. Martha understood it was best that Tom wasn't at home to complicate the visit, but she couldn't entirely defeat her resentment that she'd been left to manage yet another difficulty alone. In the end she decided to tell her father of what had transpired at the last visit so she might engage his help in persuading Anne to stay behind, or at the least to conspire with her to protect Anne from Charles.

Martha watched the clouds sweep over her father's features as she relayed the scene between Anne and Charles, but he offered practical suggestions that hadn't occurred to Martha; they would declare that he was no longer indulging in spirits due to health concerns and lock all the liquors in the wine cellar. They would station Ned on a pallet just outside the Bankheads' door. During the day they would busy Anne in the kitchen learning French pastry cooking and in the evening they would enlist her to perform on the harpsichord.

They made provision for everything but Jeff.

Jeff and his wife, Jane, had taken up the lease at Tufton and had managed to turn a profit within the first twelve months. They'd also managed to produce a child every year and a half, outpacing their parents. Busy as they were, Jeff hadn't seen his sister in two years, and when he heard that she'd come to Monticello, he decided to ride up the mountain to visit. He arrived soon after his sister; his look of alarm at the sight of her mirrored Martha's. Anne had lost color and weight, as if she'd shriveled inside her skin; she stood hunched in a shawl that she gripped as if it were the dead of winter. Charles had clearly found his drink along the way, but Jeff had barely greeted him when he announced that he was heading back to the tavern, "as there's nothing worth swallowing here." He strode out.

"Perhaps I'd best mind him," Jeff said and rose to follow, but Anne leaped up and grabbed her brother's arm.

"No, please, he'll only think I sent you. Do stay and visit with me. How long it is since I've seen you!"

Jeff turned to Anne and took her by the shoulders to give her a hug, but she flinched and drew back. Her shawl drooped; Jeff scowled and took a step closer, drawing the shawl away; Anne was black and blue from neck to elbow. Martha leaped out of her seat. She gripped her daughter's arm and turned it, seeing the clear mark of fingers; she lifted the awkwardly held chin and found more. Jeff's face suffused as his father's so often did; he turned and strode from the room.

Martha's father came to Anne and touched her cheek. "My dear child," he said. "We can't have this. You must keep here with us where we can see you safe."

"And have my father kill my husband? He nearly did so once."

"Your grandfather means that you must keep here alone," Martha said.

"Yes," Martha's father added. "And Charles might keep with *his* father; the elder Mr. Bankhead should have a moderating influence on his son. And as I understand Charles's farm is in danger of going to the banks—"

Anne looked from mother to grandfather. "You *talk* of this? Together? You plot to take me from my husband? To shame me? To shame all of us?"

Martha felt her fury rising. *Foolish girl!* She took Anne by the chin and turned her neck to the light. "You think this doesn't shame all of us, to have our daughter and granddaughter treated so?"

Anne's eyes filled. Her grandfather stepped up to her and took her in his arms, holding her as she cried.

———

AFTER DINNER MARTHA ATTEMPTED to talk to Anne again about keeping at Monticello, but Anne would only shake her head. *No.* Her grandfather tried it another way, talking of day-to-day affairs on the mountain: of how well his fig trees came on, of a new litter of sheepdogs due in May, of how desperately the garden needed Anne's eye. As the evening drew down, it appeared that Anne's grandfather had at least convinced her to stay on and help plot out the garden while Charles attended a slave auction the next week. Martha insisted Anne keep with her in her room that night, and after a time she managed to see her daughter into an exhausted sleep.

———

MARTHA WAS STILL AWAKE when a pounding on the front door roused them. Someone—Burwell, no doubt—had gone to the door, and now Martha heard loud voices in the hall. She threw a shawl over her nightdress.

"You keep where you are," she told Anne, but indeed, Anne already sat pressed against the bedstead, clutching the bolster in front of her, as if she'd experienced this type of alarm before.

Martha flew down the stairs with Molly at her back; Burwell, bizarrely clad in nightshirt, boots, and coat, was just closing the door on a stranger's back. Martha's father appeared, shirt loose over his breeches, feet bare, candle in one hand and boots in the other, with Sally trailing behind in nightdress and shawl. Burwell rushed up to his master.

"Mr. Jeff rode down the mountain with a horsewhip to attack Mr. Bankhead and Mr. Bankhead stabbed him. Mr. Jeff's grievously wounded." Burwell's eyes began to shine excessively in the light.

"And where is Mr. Bankhead?"

"Run. They don't know where."

"Rouse Peter and tell him to saddle my horse."

"I'll ride with you."

"No, we need you and Peter here in case Mr. Bankhead returns. Martha, keep your daughter out of sight. Sally, I rely on you to keep the house quiet."

"Papa!"

Martha's father turned to her, his face streaming with tears. She'd meant to say *you mustn't* but found she could not.

———

Martha suffered every form of torment and self-recrimination until near daylight when her father dragged himself back up the mountain. Martha rushed to him in the hall, appalled at the aging that appeared to have overtaken him in a single ride.

"He'll live," he said, but he could add no more till he'd collapsed into his chair in the parlor. "A fire, perhaps—"

Ned rushed to kindle a flame. Burwell arrived with a glass of dark liquor he'd resurrected and held it till his master could grasp it in a steadier hand.

"How severe . . . ," Martha asked when she could wait no more.

"The wound is to the ribs. The doctor who treated him declared the necessary organs had been spared. Jeff's been carried home into his wife's care; I've sent for Dr. Norris to attend him there."

"And Charles? What of Charles?"

Martha whirled. Anne stood at the door, fully dressed and shawled as if ready to leave.

Her grandfather turned to her with tired eyes. "Charles has been found and jailed."

Anne began to weep, but for husband or brother? Martha feared to think.

———

MARTHA, HER FATHER, AND THE OLDER GIRLS took turns traveling to Tufton to see Jeff every few days until he told them he'd been hovered over quite enough and it was time to be gone. Word came that someone had posted Bankhead's excessive bond and that he had gone to stay at his father's house. The news seemed to settle Anne, which again alarmed Martha.

"We can't let her go to him," Martha told her father.

"No."

"How soon the trial?"

"There will be no trial."

"No trial! *Why?*"

"Best leave it be."

Martha studied her father, her sphinx of a father. She could unearth nothing more. Later, as she lay in bed awash in a tangle of nerve ends, she thought perhaps she understood. Hadn't her father said it? He was not without influence in Virginia. Hadn't Anne said the rest of it? No one would want to shame Thomas Jefferson or his family.

Unless he was of the opposite political party.

———————

THE FIRST LETTER FROM CHARLES ARRIVED, full of remorse; another arrived, and another after that. Next the senior Bankhead wrote his friend Jefferson.

> *My son has put away all drink and only wallows in regret for past acts. He begs to be reunited with his wife, with every promise of proper behavior. I would be willing to have the pair here under my guidance and protection.*

Anne thought it the perfect plan. Her grandfather thought it acceptable. Martha thought it mad. By September Anne was back with Charles, living at his father's house. Can this be us, Martha wondered, this family of canings and stabbings? Why could she do nothing about any of it? Why could her father do nothing?

It was some time before Martha realized she'd never once considered an appeal to Tom.

CHAPTER 34

―――――――――

In december tom was elected governor of the state. They decided together—or rather Martha decided and Tom eventually
agreed—that when Tom traveled to Richmond, Martha would
stay behind at Monticello. Martha cited the expense of keeping a
wife and their many children in Richmond, the concerns over her
father's health, the management of the Monticello household.

"And Edgehill," Tom reminded her.

"Yes, Edgehill." But in fact all these reasons were reasons
dredged up in haste to disguise Martha's real reason: She dreaded
being in far-off Richmond with Tom. As for Edgehill, Martha had
already counted it lost to the banks.

Tom departed for Richmond. His first letter arrived five days
later. *They would consume me with their society if I would permit them.
How desperately I miss you.* The following week he left Richmond
Saturday night, rode all night, arrived to spend Sunday with
Martha, and departed Sunday night to land in Richmond on
Monday morning. He did this so often he began to lose weight,
to grow sallow, to define time in Sundays, eliminating the weeks
between. *When I saw you yesterday,* he wrote on Wednesday, and *I
make an early start tomorrow* his Thursday letter declared.

But to Martha's surprise she found herself looking forward to
Sundays, if only for the chance to talk over Tom's plans for Virginia, to take part in it all. He talked with his father-in-law, of
course, but always he found time to talk to Martha alone, as they
used to do. His biggest dream: gradual manumission of slaves as

they reached adulthood, controlled quotas taken in equal measure from each part of the state to lessen the economic burden.

"And after they're freed?"

"The law dictates they must leave Virginia. The slave colony already established in San Domingo might serve."

"But using this method, how long till slavery is eradicated?"

They sat on the terrace. Tom looked off toward the quarters, the fields. "I have little hope of lessening the evil to any sensible degree in my lifetime." He returned his gaze to Martha, black eyes alight. "But a just responsibility to posterity requires that I begin. Would you not agree?"

Martha would agree, and more so on her next trip to Edgehill where she discovered Aggie in the act of making off with a chicken. Martha found a switch and struck the girl until welts appeared on her bare arm, until Martha's anger ebbed, until the shame that had subdued the anger began to bring the anger up again. Was this how a man could flog a slave near to death, she wondered, all in an attempt to beat out his own shame?

———————

Tom's GRADUAL EMANCIPATION PROPOSAL came to a vote in February and was immediately tabled, Tom vilified in every newspaper. When Tom arrived that Sunday, his father-in-law told him, "I commend your courage in putting the bill forward," but he could offer no practical suggestion for advancing the plan. Indeed, Martha could not. In their own quiet talk together, she moved the conversation to his other causes.

Tom had many: plans for canals, for greater representation for the western counties, for educating the poor—both white and free black—with a literacy fund paid directly to the teachers in order to eliminate any embarrassment for the families requiring assistance.

He pushed for popular election of juries and for better training for militia, issues that came directly from his own experience, but as with his plan for emancipation, he couldn't seem to win supporters. His father-in-law identified the problem: Tom continuously shunned the Richmond social life that so dictated the political; in short, Governor Thomas Randolph had not succeeded in making friends in Richmond the way President Thomas Jefferson had in Washington.

Her father may have found the problem, but Martha offered the solution. By now she'd perfected the role required by her marriage of rounding Tom's sharp edges with a simple modifying adjective or adverb, of softening his tone by softening hers, of skewing a rocky conversational path a hair left or right as needed. Martha still didn't want to live in Richmond with Tom, but in truth his new mission seemed to have steadied him. She very much wanted his programs to succeed, and she felt she knew how to make that happen.

Martha wrote to Tom, *Thinking again of our relative situations and what might be gained most overall, perhaps I should join you in Richmond.* Tom answered, *My greatest earthly wish has now been answered.* Martha didn't write to Tom of the rest of her plan: to borrow money from Edmund Bacon to outfit not only herself but Virginia and Cornelia for entry into Richmond society. Ellen had her chance in Washington with Dolley Madison; now it was time to give Cornelia and Virginia, twenty and eighteen respectively, a chance to meet suitable husbands—husbands who would not spend their lives weighed down by unproductive, slave-filled plantations.

———

THE TWO-DAY CARRIAGE RIDE only proved to Martha what lengths Tom had gone to in order to make the trip in a single night;

she further discovered another reason why he may have troubled to make the trip so often: Richmond suited Martha even less now than it had on her honeymoon. The quiet of Monticello had now become Martha's solace, and where she'd once been used to a city's pace in France, that way of life now trailed so far behind her, she had trouble even crossing a Richmond street without getting hit by a carriage. Cornelia and Virginia, unused to a population made up of anything other than well-trained slaves and equally well-trained Virginia ladies and gentlemen, disconcerted Martha by gawking at the unkempt workmen, unwashed children, and questionably clad women. If her daughters were to adjust to any life other than one lived on a plantation, Martha had brought them to Richmond none too soon.

———

BUT MARTHA AND HER GIRLS had little time to adjust; on their second night in Richmond, the governor hosted all the key political figures at a fine dinner, for the sole purpose of introducing his wife and daughters. Martha saw at once that she'd prepared well— the white Grecian gown she'd bought made her stand out among the Richmond ladies, making her feel almost Paris smart. Nearing fifty, she still drew eyes from both men and women as she crossed the room to join her husband. Virginia captured even more eyes, stunning in a low-cut blue silk, but Martha had been unable to persuade Cornelia to accept a certain degree of discomfort for the sake of fashion; she'd chosen a dull gown of pearl gray that hung too loosely on her frame. Martha wouldn't like to admit as much to Virginia, who'd taken such pains, but she was perhaps most proud of Cornelia, standing tall and unapologetic in her unremarkable gown, defying any in the room to dismiss her.

And Tom. He stood at his presentable best, handsome inside his new suit, even remembering not to scowl at those he was trying to woo to his platform; Martha could even squeeze his arm to elicit a smile, a thing she did often during the first half hour of the reception, but soon thereafter something un-Jefferson-like happened to her. The men and women who continually approached, anxious, as Martha assumed, for an introduction to the wife of the governor, took less pains, or took no pains, to greet the governor; it soon became clear that the person they'd come to meet was Thomas Jefferson's daughter. Sunday upon Sunday Martha had listened to Tom's repeated complaints that the Governor's Council in fact ran the state of Virginia, that the governor was considered little more than a figurehead, but she hadn't expected the council members to treat him so rudely, to do it in a public reception, and to do it in front of his wife and daughters.

For a time Martha continued to smile and nod and return barbs with pleasantries until one particularly overfed, soft-palmed council member approached her. He bowed low over Martha's hand. "Good evening, Mrs. Randolph. 'Tis my very great pleasure to make your acquaintance. Your presence here has gone a long way to justifying the existence of the office of the governor."

As Martha looked into the man's eyes, she saw again what she'd seen too often already that evening: the man's sense of his own entitlement, his disinterest in the fates of others, his stubbornness, his stupidity. She saw that no matter what she said or did, there was no hope for her husband's programs. Seeing all those things at once depressed and exhilarated her. Freed her.

"Perhaps you haven't read it, sir, but in fact the state constitution justifies the existence of the office of the governor." Oh, the lovely sight of a self-satisfied face as it went slack with surprise! Martha tucked her arm inside Tom's, and didn't remove it until she'd been seated by his side at the dinner table in defiance of protocol and to the consternation of the councilor's wife whose seat she'd usurped.

Martha didn't care. It was as if someone had jabbed her with an elbow, knocking her off the track she'd spent a lifetime traveling, and she couldn't climb back on. She responded to a loud critic of her husband's canal plan: "Well then, if you dislike the bill so much, we must both hope you're in your grave when it comes to pass." To a skeptic of Tom's education bill: "Do I understand you? You fear some impoverished child ending better educated than the members of your council?" And to one who made unveiled reference to Tom's financial difficulties, questioning his ability to manage the state coffers: "Dear me, I see your foot and that loaf have strayed into your mouth together."

Oh, poor embattled Tom! He couldn't decide whether to look embarrassed by or proud of his wife's behavior. At one point in the evening, it did occur to Martha that her father would very definitely *not* have approved of her manners, but it also occurred to her that if William Short had been there, the hall would have rung with his laughter.

*CHAPTER 35*

———————

MARTHA AND HER DAUGHTERS RETURNED to Monticello after a month spent in Richmond that had only proved to Martha—and to Richmond—that she didn't belong there. One effect of her visit was the change it caused in Tom; witnessing the uselessness of Martha's frontal assault on his council, he saw the uselessness of his own. He continued to put forth his ideas in the hope of at least a single seed falling to receptive earth, but he no longer wasted his energies writing long diatribes to the papers or thrusting his shoulder against locked doors. Was Martha glad or sad over this change? She remained unsure. She *was* glad Tom spoke forcefully in support of his father-in-law's stand that religion had no place in a state university, even though it caused him to grow even less popular than ever.

And governor or not, his creditors continued to press him.

When Tom returned to Monticello at the end of his term, his son Jeff requested an appointment with him. Whenever Martha saw Jeff after a time apart, she took new pride in him; despite the banking crisis, Jeff's farm thrived and he carried no debt. He strode into the small parlor with the air of a successful man, which at once convinced Martha she must keep in the room; fresh off repeated failures at Richmond, Tom already looked as bristly as a wild boar.

Jeff made no attempt to disguise his visit as anything but business. "Surely you know, Father, and I'm certain my mother knows, that your financial ruin is not far distant. I've thought on your situation at length, and I've come here to offer what I believe to be the least objectionable solution. I'll assume your debt. You understand that I have my own wife and family to provide for; in exchange for assuming the debt, which I calculate at thirty-four thousand dollars, I think you'll find it fair if I ask for the deeds to Edgehill and Varina as security."

Tom leaped to his feet.

"Tom," Martha said. "Only listen to the plan."

"Only consider the alternative," Jeff countered. "Selling off slaves. And when the slaves are reduced, how do you work your plantations? I've thought on this, Father. I can think of no other solution."

"You take everything."

"I take the deeds only as security. I would take less were it less dangerous to my family to do so."

"And what of my family?"

"Remember, please, your family is mine too—my mother and brothers and sisters—and I offer this for them, in hopes that by erasing your debt, they'll have better prospects going forward. Having no debt, you might begin to work your farms at a profit."

"Leave here," Tom said.

"Thank you, Jeff," Martha said. "Leave us to ponder this, please."

"Ponder what?" Tom shouted. "You mark me—he'll sell us out in a year!"

Jeff rose. "I sell nothing that turns a profit, Father. So you see it rests on your shoulders." He left them.

———

MARTHA TALKED TO TOM, but he would not see his own salvation in Jeff's plan. She talked to her father, who could find no better answer for Tom's situation than Jeff's. Martha talked to Tom again.

His father-in-law talked to him. At the end of five days, Tom left off shouting and succumbed, without choice, as he saw it, because son, wife, and father-in-law had aligned against him. Tom signed over the papers, and was, in his mind, almost immediately proved right.

———————

MARTHA CLAIMED, to Tom or to anyone else who questioned, that Jeff did his best. He consolidated all the debts and made periodic payments, but the drain proved too great and Tom's half-hearted efforts came too late; Jeff's own strong position began to suffer. It became clear to Jeff—and to Martha—that something must be sold at once, and a closer look indicated that both Varina and Edgehill must be sacrificed—Varina to clear the debt put on it by Tom Randolph Senior, Edgehill to clear the debt incurred by Tom Randolph Junior.

Jeff had laid out a meticulous plan, but Tom never stayed long enough to hear it. At Jeff's first words Tom leaped up, grabbed the arms of Martha's chair, and shook it.

"Did I not say! Did I not warn you!" He bolted from the room, the house, the mountain.

———————

IT TOOK THE WHOLE OF THE DAY for Jeff to locate his father, sealed inside a vacant cabin in Milton, a few miles south on the Rivanna River, property still owned by the Randolph family. Tom would not allow Jeff to enter; he ordered him to keep his siblings and all Jeffersons—"In which I include your mother"—from trespassing on his property or he would not answer for the consequence.

Martha wrote Tom. *You can't think this is how I wish us to be.* Tom sent back ugly and bitter words that Martha struggled—and failed—to answer: *You care for nothing but Monticello. I am as nothing to you, you and your son together. You would sacrifice me for your father. I shall not stay for the fatal blow, to discover which of you holds the knife, or whether you put a hand to it together.* Martha sent Ned to Tom, but Tom sent him back.

"He says I'm not his anymore. He says he's not married anymore and doesn't have any children." Now a father himself, this last declaration seemed to strike Ned the hardest. "No children!" he repeated.

Martha decided to leave Tom alone for a time, in part because she didn't know what else to do, in part because others matters pressed her. Tom could withdraw from life for months if he wished; Martha could not. Her children still demanded her time, the household demanded her time, the steady stream of visitors—or gawkers, as Martha called them—continued to arrive, faceless and nameless, there to lay eyes on the visage, to hear the voice, to touch the hand that wrote the Declaration of American Independence.

"Who *are* they?" Martha asked her father.

"Americans," he answered. "And they think me theirs as much as you do."

Martha might not have minded so much if her father's health had been better. He stood as tall and straight as he had as a young man, but his legs grew weak, limiting his walks, and vague "digestive troubles," as he called them, kept him to his room for days, during which time he again insisted that only Sally and Burwell tend him. More and more often Martha made his excuse to the visitors, and if she'd had her choice, would have sent them away, but her father insisted they be welcomed with the usual attention. This forced Martha to serve as hostess in her father's absence, greeting his guests, arranging for their comfort, growing more and more alarmed at the cost of such heedless generosity. Night after night

Martha's father insisted the best food and wine be brought to a full table, whether or not he could attend it; no guest was ever discouraged from staying as long as he desired and no cost-cutting measures were ever practiced. Even Edmund Bacon's attempt to reduce the ration given to the guests' horses was countermanded as soon as his employer learned of it. Gifts continued to come Martha's children's way, less when it was decided to sell Edgehill and Varina and it appeared money might be coming in, more again when Tom roared his way off the mountain, leaving the older children round-eyed and the smaller children tearful. Martha began to fear that even selling their two properties would not offset their constant drain on the resources of Monticello, that something else must be done, and who to do it now other than Martha?

One evening, after Martha's father hadn't managed to come to table, Martha knocked definitively, defiantly, on his door. Sally opened it. Perhaps coming on her at such a late hour accounted for Sally's appearance, but it seemed to Martha that she had undergone some kind of recent internal and external devastation. The once-gleaming hair appeared dull, the delicate hands were dry and cracked, the face looked drawn with fatigue. Or worry.

"What is it?" Martha cried. "Is he ill?"

A look of annoyance crossed Sally's face, come and gone like a turkey vulture's shadow, but it chilled Martha to her gut. "Your father is old," Sally said.

"Do you think I don't know this?"

Sally's face closed up. Her tone changed from assertive to meek so fast, Martha could only think of it as mocking. "He's retired to his bed. He fatigues earlier now. Would you like me to—?"

"Martha? Is that Martha? My dear, be so kind as to ask her to step in here."

*My dear?* Had Martha actually heard her father using the endearment usually reserved for Martha with *Sally*? Of course he hadn't. *Martha?* he'd said. *My dear! Be so kind* . . . Martha collected herself, stepped through her father's cabinet, into his bedchamber, and up to the bed he'd designed himself, nestled into a two-sided alcove to save space and create a better circulation of air while sleeping. He sat propped on a bolster with his books nearby, on a stand he'd specially designed to hold five open at once.

"Are you quite well, Papa?"

"Of course. I do grow tired. But you look weary yourself. You must take care of your health, child, so many of us depend on it daily."

*We all depend on* you. You *must take care. You mustn't expend your resources so wildly.* This was what Martha had come to say, but as she looked at her father, his face now worn down to its essence, she knew she would never say it. Was he not entitled to live the last of his life as he'd led the first of it, generous to all, perhaps pampered himself, but who on earth more deserved a little pampering?

Martha's father lifted his candle to study her more closely. "What troubles you, Martha? The sale? We can do naught to stop it. Tom? Let me write to him. Perhaps I might persuade him to return."

"'Tis not that, Papa. Or not only. 'Tis too late for the Randolphs to remedy their situation, but what of you? You give far too much to too many."

Martha's father patted her hand. "We've set ourselves back; this is true. But Jeff takes care of us; we now consolidate our resources. I know Tom feels we sacrifice him only to save Monticello, but Monticello is his and yours as much as mine. He'll understand that eventually. It will all come right, my dear; please, you mustn't worry."

*My dear.* For a second Martha's heart lightened, as if confirmation of this endearment were all she'd come for, but the lightness didn't carry her through her next breath. Were endearments all she might expect of her father now? Martha kissed the paper-thin flesh on his brow and left him in peace, but she made her own resolutions as she brushed past Sally and out the door. She would speak to Cook about one roast only at dinner; she would reduce the numbers of different wines served; she would speak to Edmund Bacon about possible reductions elsewhere on the plantation. She needn't worry her father about any of it, and if he discovered her efforts, if he complained . . . Well, she'd have to worry about that as she came to it. Worry. It seemed to Martha as she climbed the steep stairs to her room that the worry was hers alone now.

───────────

MARTHA'S FATHER WROTE TO TOM: *Can you not leave off your affecting concerns and restore yourself to the society of your family?* Tom neither answered the letter nor returned to Monticello. In his absence Jeff managed to engineer a quick sale on Varina by including the near-worthless land and the valuable slaves together, taking far less than the total was worth and barely enough to clear its debt, but the act itself went some way to appeasing his creditors. He then set about a thoughtful plan for the sale of Edgehill, deciding that in such a stressed economy it would be best to divide the land into five smaller parcels, but to get the best value for the slaves, they should be sold at auction separately. As detached as Martha had remained from Edgehill, as much as she understood Jeff's challenge and the need to take that particular action, she could find no way to make her peace with it. The thing Martha had sworn the Jeffersons and Randolphs did not do—auction off slaves—was about to take place. All their efforts to ameliorate conditions for those in their care were about to be erased; Martha's father could still sit atop his mountain above the rest of slave-holding Virginia, but the truth was that the Randolphs were now no better than the rest.

## CHAPTER 36

WINTER DROPPED DOWN OVER THE MOUNTAIN, the wind tearing at Monticello and stripping the sheltering trees around the great house, leaving Martha feeling raw and exposed. Nothing bloomed. The grass cracked with frost under her feet. Inside, the fires never seemed to reach beyond Martha's knees and the windows shuddered. Martha's own health began to trouble her. Her courses ceased, but the anticipated relief brought on by the event was tempered by the onset of headaches, heart palpitations, fevers.

Perhaps the single light was her father's improved health, as evidenced by his emergence from his room to visit her in hers where she lay in bed pampering a headache. Seeing her father alone, uncluttered by servants, she realized how he'd changed, even as she feasted on the sight of him—his hair was now all white, the last hints of sand vanished; he was thinner, the angles of nose, cheekbones, and jaw more finely drawn; the color in his cheeks less vivid, but his lovely hazel eyes remained warm and alive, that half smile as unreadable and yet as soothing as ever. He walked across the room straight and tall, but the right leg hitched slightly each time he moved it forward. His hip? His knee? Both? Martha would have asked, but her father seemed to have his own plan for their conversation. He pulled a chair near the bed and settled himself, his hands on his knees, his back straight.

"I hear you're not well."

"I'm well, Papa, 'tis just a headache, already passing."

"You take mine from me, then. I've not had one of my periodical headaches since I left Washington."

"You're where you should be."

"And you?"

"I am also, Papa."

"I know Tom—"

"Please, let's not talk of Tom. We can do nothing. 'Tis his struggle now; all we might do for him is to hope he'll soon win it."

"If I'd managed to come up with the needed sum—"

"There would only be another needed sum. You have your own difficulties. Jeff takes the only course."

"Jeff. All your boys. I'd so hoped . . . Martha, dearest, the land I'd set aside for your sons must be sold. I wish you to know this so their expectations might be altered accordingly. You can't know how it saddens me to take this step."

"Perhaps 'tis for the best. Let them start a new way of living. 'Tis no easy life, this Virginia farming."

"I was not suited to it. Not with this system of labor. But Jeff succeeds. He would have saved it all, were it not for the banks."

"Yes, the banks."

"I intend to see your sons educated, Martha."

"I'm grateful, Papa."

"It will be up to them to plot another course from this point forward. I must plot another course. I cannot . . . we must . . . *you* must—" His voice trailed off, his mouth grew tight, the vertical lines between his brows reappeared.

"Papa?"

Martha's father regained his smile, his ease. "We'll talk of these matters another day, when you're in health." He rose, dropped a kiss on her forehead, and left her.

Jeff set the slave auction for January 2 in the new year of 1826, as far off as he could while still appeasing the banks. No matter how Martha tried to ignore it, the date sat there, eating at her, until she decided she must do something to stop its gnawing. As soon as the weather eased, she rode to Edgehill—forced herself to ride to Edgehill—and reined in the mare at the edge of the wood by the side of the river, where a half dozen Negroes were cutting ice. She recognized Solomon and Daniel wielding saws, and Gawen and Stephen loading the blocks into the wagon. Solomon had grown slow and his hair had gone gray, which would reduce his price on the block. If he wasn't bought at the auction, would he be allowed to remain with the Randolphs or would he be led off in coffle chains for sale farther South? Daniel had twin boys just starting work in the fields and once word of the sale got out, he would spend every minute of his days and nights in fear of their separation; Jeff would certainly try to sell them as a lot, but all three were prime Negroes and the price would be high for even one of them.

Martha looked at the two remaining slaves who worked covering blocks of ice with straw and was shocked to realize she didn't know their names. Mounted above these men by the side of the field, this seemed to Martha her greatest sin, that she didn't know the names of these fine, strong young men the Randolphs had long owned and were about to sell. She must know who they were. Did they not deserve this much of her? She slid to the ground and took a step forward, perhaps three steps forward, leading the mare behind, but that was as far as her shame took her; learning names at this hour was a penance that would help no one and nothing except her conscience, and her conscience didn't deserve a salve of any kind; better she carry with her always the fact that she sold away these human beings without even knowing who they were.

Martha rode back up the mountain, blind to all but her dark thoughts. As she drew closer to the house, she lifted her head and saw a man on horseback riding toward her; Tom, she thought, and felt only dread. He eased his horse into a slow canter and something in the seamlessness of the gait change told her it wasn't Tom; Tom would have spurred his horse ahead in a violent burst, he wouldn't continue to ride toward her at this steady pace. But almost as soon as Martha had realized the rider wasn't Tom, he'd drawn close enough for her to recognize William Short, and her misplaced relief at the sight of him made her turn her face away.

Short slowed his horse and swung it around to her side, riding next to her in silence until they reached the stable. He slid to the ground first and took the mare's reins with one hand, reaching to help Martha dismount with the other. An earthy steam generated by animal flesh greeted Martha as she entered the stable; she remembered Short's tale of his first romance and blushed, the blush forcing her to turn her face away a second time. Peter hurried toward them to collect the horses but Short waved him off and began to remove the horses' leathers himself.

"Have you seen my father?" Martha asked.

"I have. He's resting now. I was told you'd gone to ride, so I took a chance on guessing your route, as I wished to speak to you in private." He paused. "I received word of the pending sale."

Yes, he would have. All Virginia would have. Thomas Mann Randolph, ground to dust.

Short peered at her. "Are you—" But he seemed unable to settle on the proper way to finish his sentence. "Here." He handed Martha the mare's reins, led his horse into an empty stall, and began to rub him down with a piece of sacking. Martha led the mare into the next stall and picked up her own piece of sacking, but she'd only just begun to dirty her hands when Short appeared and took the cloth from her. As he leaned into the mare, coat pulling at his shoulders as he worked, Martha found she could speak to his back much more easily than she could speak to his front.

"I've borne the discomfort of slavery all my life," she said. "But its sorrows—and their bitterness—I never fully conceived of till now."

Short slowed his stroke, but somehow he understood he should neither stop nor turn. "They all go on the block? None can be spared?"

"'Tis the banks that dictate it."

"Have you no dower right?"

Dower right? *Dower right?* "Why yes, I do."

"Equal to life use of one third your husband's properties?"

Oh, dear Lord, what kind of lawyer's daughter *was* she? What kind of wife? "Does this mean . . . Might I take my dower in slaves?"

"No creditor's claim can supersede it."

Martha's thoughts tumbled over each other. How fast could she do this? Would the banks wait? How many could she save? Which ones? But already Martha knew which ones. Priscilla, lame in the hip from chasing after Martha's children, and Betsy, her hands now shaking with age, must never be forced to stand on a block. Molly and Ned and their little daughter must also be kept from such humiliation. But if she took a few strong, young women who could be hired out for a wage, that wage would provide Martha with some income. She would see them safely assigned to a location nearby, she would keep careful watch over them, she would do better for them than the block, but she must look out for her own family. Thinking this, resolving this, Martha should have felt better, but the abhorrent tears came.

Short had by now turned around and hung his piece of sacking

over the stall door. Martha picked it up and went to dry her eyes
with it, but Short took it from her and used his own handkerchief
to wipe her face with brisk, businesslike movements, one slash for
each cheek, just the kind of matter-of-factness required to stop the
flood.

"We'd best get up to the house," Martha said, collecting herself.
She turned to leave, but Short captured her arm.

"Hold. Please. I must ask you of this other news I've heard. That
Mr. Randolph has left his family at Monticello and goes to live
alone at Milton."

Martha tasted the bitterness of her smile. "I'm sure you did
hear. He tells all who'll listen how his wife and son have sold his
birthright from under him only to save Thomas Jefferson's precious
Monticello."

Short said nothing, but that silence Martha could read well
enough. "And what would *you* save?" she cried. "Edgehill, a rundown, mortgaged farm which its owner ignores while he reads his
poetry? Or would you prefer Varina, a debt-ridden piece of swamp
overrun with mosquitoes? Yes, we save Monticello. *Thomas Jefferson's* Monticello. Only a fool would choose otherwise. A fool or a
madman." Martha looked away, took a great breath. "But of course
this is just what they say. Thomas Randolph *has* gone mad, just as
his father did." She expelled a long breath, which was a mistake,
as it cost her the last of her rage, which in turn cost her the last of
her strength. Why was it all crumbling around them so fast? Why
could they do nothing to slow the fall if not to save themselves
from it entirely? If they could have held out through her father's
life, if they could have allowed him to expire without seeing any
Randolph slave go on the block . . . Oh, her father! To anyone else
Martha would have kept the thought unexpressed. To Short alone
did she dare to say it.

"My father . . . my father is grown old."

"I know. I saw him. And Sally looks worn through. But how much in her is fear—"

"Fear!"

Short took Martha's hands in his, gave them a shake. "Martha. Don't allow the blinders your father's so skillfully constructed for himself to fool you too. I grant you, there are no slaves better treated in Virginia, but they're still *slaves*. Your father's property. What happens to one's property when one can no longer afford to pay the bill? It gets sold. Sally sees the tragedy that's happening to her friends and family at Edgehill. Surely it must occur—"

Martha pulled her hands away. "What would you have us do? Open the doors and let them go?"

"A while ago perhaps. Now the banks would never allow it. You'll keep your dower's worth, and no doubt when your father's turn comes—"

"*When* it comes! He sells his lands in order to *save* Monticello."

"Very well. Even if he can save it. You say yourself your father is no longer young. He's not well. Should he die before he's kept his promise—"

"What promise? Why do you talk always of this promise?"

Short studied her, puzzled. "You can't mean he's told you nothing of it? I thought surely—" Short considered her a moment longer. "'Tis not my place. And yet, if something happens to him, it will fall to you to keep this promise. Very well, let me go beyond the bounds—'tis not the first time, is it? The promise was made in France. Sally wished to stay behind with her brother as a free woman, according to French law. Your father had since come to . . . he'd come to value her company. He wished very much for her to return to America with him. He made her certain promises in order to entice her, among them extraordinary privileges at Monticello for herself and freedom for her children when they turned twenty-one."

"He told you this?"

"James told me. He was unhappy with Sally's decision to give over her freedom; he didn't trust your father quite as much as Sally did. But James was eventually persuaded to return to America too, under the promise of his own freedom once he'd trained another cook to replace him."

Well yes, this promise to James Martha *had* heard of, and she'd witnessed its fulfillment. James had gone free. But not Sally.

"My father never promised to free Sally?"

"Would that not defeat the purpose? He wished to keep her by him while he lived; what he's done in his will I can only ponder. But if I know him, I believe Sally has a right to fear. If your father frees her in his will, the talk would start again, at the very moment when your father would least want to distress his family, and when he must hope the country would be focused on his legacy. No doubt Sally thinks of this. Maybe she's even been told of this. I've been giving a lot of thought to Sally of late. And to you, of course. For a similar reason, as it turns out."

"Why on earth—"

"Both of you are bound to this place by a single man."

" 'Tis more than one man binds me."

"Indeed? With Randolph gone from you?"

"It changes nothing."

"It changes everything. Or it could."

Martha peered at Short, waiting for the usual jest, but none came. He took a single step closer, but that left another step between them, one that she could easily take if she wished it. And oh, how she suddenly wished it! How she longed to step into Short's warmth, his strength, his certainty! How tired she was of being worried, of being responsible, of being lonely! But she was the daughter of Thomas Jefferson, the wife—without remedy—of Thomas Randolph, the mother of still-young children. She stepped back.

Short smiled. "And here I was dreaming of tupping the mother of eight in a stable."

"I'm the mother of eleven."

"Good Lord. You visit this stable often, then."

Martha was in such a state she actually began to contemplate her number of visits to the stable before she caught up to his joke. It was inappropriate to laugh, Martha knew this, and yet the relief of it was just too overwhelming. She began to laugh and couldn't stop, didn't want to stop, for fear of never having another chance.

## CHAPTER 37

SHORT LEFT MONTICELLO TWO DAYS LATER without seeking Martha's private company again. This time Martha was glad to see him go; while he was at Monticello, she couldn't look at a single beloved view without new fear, couldn't look at her father without new worry. She couldn't look at Sally at all. And the next time she came upon Harriet crossing the lawn and saw what she'd seen in her—and resented in her—all along, she understood its cause. Harriet knew she would not be a slave forever, that one day she would stand equal to Martha in the eyes of the law.

Yes, Martha was glad to see Short go—she couldn't remain in his presence without experiencing a confusion in her that didn't belong—but as soon as he left, her head cleared. She was, without remedy, the wife of Thomas Randolph, and it was past time she acted so. She sent word for Peter to ready the mare; Molly helped her into the same riding habit she'd worn years ago to visit her father, and as the girl applied the brush Martha studied her. What agony did Molly suffer over the rumors of the slave sale? Martha wanted to speak of her plan for her dower right but didn't dare until she'd talked to Jeff. To Tom. She traveled through the same mental tunnel when she went outside and found Ned mounted and ready to ride with her. "Ned, please, this is a trip best done alone."

"No, Mrs. Randolph. I've seen him and you haven't. This is a trip best done with someone waiting outside who can hear you if you call."

Martha studied Ned, the thickened arms inside the old coat, the solid legs, the strong hands on the reins. When had he turned into this *man*? "Very well," she said. There wasn't a thing Ned didn't know of the Randolphs by now, and perhaps he would prove a help if difficulties arose; Tom had always gotten on well with Ned. In fact, he got on well with all his Negroes; Martha had only thought of what the pending sale was costing her—and them—and never considered what it must be doing to Tom. If Martha could have shut herself away at Milton, wouldn't she have done so too? They shared this wound. They shared eleven children. This is what she would say to Tom.

———

THE MILTON HOME where Tom Randolph had chosen to reside was little more than a cabin, sitting on its own land next to a grander house that his family had once owned and since sold. Ned dismounted, took the mare's reins as Martha slid to the ground, and led the horses far enough away to be invisible through the windows, but near enough to hear Martha should she need him. Martha strode up to the door and knocked.

"Tom! 'Tis I."

The voice that answered was barely recognizable. "I don't know this 'I.'"

"'Tis your wife."

"I don't know this thing called 'wife.'"

The door was unlatched; Martha pushed it open and walked in, absorbing in a single glance the unmade bed, the lone chair, the desk piled with books—books Martha recognized as gifts Tom had received from his father-in-law over many years.

"You may look as you like; I took nothing from Monticello that I didn't own." Tom pulled at his shirt. "No Monticello slave made this; I bought it in Richmond. And the breeches and coat as well."

Martha looked at Tom's clothes as directed, but with another purpose in mind; she saw they were in need of laundering and mending. Tom's hair, once cut short in the newer fashion, had grown long and greasy and been pushed back behind his ears. An empty bottle—not of her father's expensive brandy but of cheap rum—sat on the desk beside a crusted glass.

"I don't know why you do this," Martha said. "No one at Monticello or Tufton welcomes this arrangement. Everyone wishes you home."

Tom shot up out of his chair and leaned over Martha. Martha stood as she was as Tom thrust his face close and hissed in her ear, almost as if he knew of Ned, waiting outside. "You rob me. You scheme with the banks. You push me aside and take your son's part over mine."

"Tom. Look at me and recall who it is you speak to so. I am your wife who loves you."

"You could say this to me?" He looked wildly around the room, breathing hard. "What have you done to the air in this place? Do you try to suffocate me? Is not even my breath my own?"

"Monticello is your own. My father says so. 'Tis yours as much as it is his or mine. He wants you back by his side to help him manage it."

"He has Jeff to manage it. He makes his choice and he must keep to it. Go and leave me alone." He began to cough, visibly struggling to hitch some air into his lungs.

"Why, you're ill."

"God in heaven! Have I not told you this enough times? And now you choose to believe me, when I'm near gone? This is the last time I tell you. Go."

When Martha didn't move Tom picked up the chair he'd been sitting in and heaved it across the room. It came nowhere close to Martha, but behind her she heard Ned, already through the door. He made no attempt to speak to Tom, directing his effort to Martha, taking her arm and pulling her backward. "Come along, Mrs. Randolph. They need you at home."

At Ned's words a new pain crossed Tom's features. He fell onto his bed and turned his face to the wall.

---

MARTHA STOPPED SLEEPING. During the day she struggled to keep alert as Timi read aloud from her history in the small parlor; Martha had turned over the boys' education to the tutors her father had selected and paid for, but Martha's greatest pride lay in the fact that she'd managed to educate four clever, well-read, erudite girls, and she did not plan to rest until she could add the fifth. There were times when Martha pondered how much of Anne's misfortune in life had stemmed from her mother's failure at educating her, what more Anne might have expected for herself if she'd managed to comprehend more of the world outside Monticello. At one time Martha had thought she'd failed Jeff as well, but it would be the practical workings of Jeff's mind that would save them all.

Except for the slaves.

Except for the slaves.

Except for the slaves.

As if Martha's black thoughts had called him, Burwell knocked on the door. "Missus, your father asks to see you in his cabinet."

When Burwell had first gone to work in the nailery as a boy, and Tom had found his only recourse with the chronically tardy ones had been a lash with the whip, Thomas Jefferson had sent Tom a note: *Burwell is never to be whipped.* After Burwell had been brought into the great house to serve as Thomas Jefferson's personal servant, the special considerations continued, until, as Short had said, Burwell would have thrust his hand into flame for his master. Martha had long chosen to read in this particular slave's face an honest affection for her father that was returned in kind; now she doubted. Burwell's daughters were part of the Edgehill estate now; Burwell's daughters would be included in the slave sale.

Martha followed Burwell down the hall to her father's rooms, but Burwell left her to enter alone. Martha's father stood up from his desk. "Come," he said. "Sit here." He pointed to the chair in front of his desk. He returned to the chair behind it. Some papers and his farm book lay neatly side by side on the desk's surface; he picked up the farm book and opened it.

"I've just been forced to make a difficult entry here," he said, his eyes on the book's open page. "I've made note that Beverly Hemings has run away."

"Beverly! Run away!"

Martha's father lifted his head and gazed evenly at Martha. "Yes. Beverly."

"Do . . . do you have hope of recovering him?"

"I do not." Again, the level gaze. "He's quite light skinned, I expect he'll disappear into the white world and leave no trail behind." He unlocked the desk drawer and set his farm book inside. He picked up the papers on the desk. "But here is what I wish to talk to you about. My will."

"Papa—"

"Let's not be foolish, child. I'm in no danger, but as I've already outlived many a man's expected course, there are matters that you and I must discuss which should not be delayed. First, I've made two decisions that won't sit well with your husband. One is that I've made Jeff executor. My reasons—"

"You needn't explain the reasons to me, Papa."

"Very well. The second decision I've made is to circumvent

your husband and leave all my property in trust for your maintenance, again with Jeff as trustee. 'Tis the only way to keep my assets out of the hands of Mr. Randolph's creditors. You understand this as well?"

Martha nodded.

"I fear, however, that Mr. Randolph will not understand, that his sensitive nature will cause him to doubt my affection and respect. I've therefore written a codicil explaining what and why I've done what I've done, but I felt you should be prepared ahead of time."

"Thank you, Papa."

"Now I should like to speak to you of the other contents of the will. Please note I use this word in all its many senses: my will as my document; my will as my desire; my will as my choice; my will as my compulsion; my will as my wish."

"Papa, please—"

He raised his hand to silence her. "I'm afraid I've failed to provide for my family as I'd hoped. A division of lands was to be made among my grandsons, handsome settlements provided for my granddaughters. Now there will be little property beyond this plantation, which must be kept for your maintenance. It simplifies my instructions considerably, however; first I order that my debts are paid and that each grandchild receives a gold watch as a remembrance. The rest, as I said, falls to you in trust. There are, however, certain other obligations that must be met." He paused. "There are certain promises that must be kept."

*Promises.* Martha's father shifted in his seat, but it seemed to ease him little. Martha could now read pain in his face, but physical or emotional? Whatever he intended to say to her, it taxed him to do so. He resumed. "In my will I free Burwell and John Hemings. I additionally give John free use of the labor of his two apprentices until such time as they turn twenty-one, when they will also receive their freedom. I'll petition the legislature to make an exception to the rules of this state regarding freed slaves and ask that these four men be allowed to remain in Virginia; as all are highly skilled and already have experience working outside Monticello, I expect this request to be granted."

Burwell. John. Their long and faithful service required no explanation for this act. But the apprentices? With Beverly gone, John's apprentices were Sally's remaining two sons, Madison and Eston Hemings; no logical reason existed for Jefferson to free them over older, trusted slaves like Peter Hemings, unless William Short was right. Unless Martha's father had promised Sally in France.

But there was a fourth child. The old Martha would never have asked it, but now Martha was ready to give up this game they'd played for so many years.

"And what of Harriet?"

Something gave way in Thomas Jefferson's eyes; the grimness around the mouth eased. There would be no need for more pretense. "I greatly fear that Harriet too will run away."

"To live as white?"

"I would imagine were she to join her brother, wherever he might be, it would be easy for her to do so."

Yes, Martha thought, it would. Beverly and Harriet were the palest of the four—red haired, freckled, educated in the ways and mannerisms of the white world; now so many things Martha had observed and not wished to admit observing in her father's treatment of the Hemings children made sense. But not all. "I only wonder why you don't simply free Beverly and Harriet in your will along with the others."

Martha's father leaned forward in his seat, his face and form straining with the effort to explain a thing he'd worked so hard *not* to explain for so long. "Because they made another choice. Were I to free them it would leave a record of a life of slavery, a life to which they could never admit. This was a difficult choice for them—they leave here and never see their family again, or do so only at great risk and under the utmost concealment. But they chose this course believing it the best chance they would get in this country as it exists today, and I could not in good conscience argue against them. I've long felt were we to emancipate our slaves en masse the only way to prevent a civil war would be to settle them in a foreign country. I would not want—" Martha's father worked to collect himself. It was such a rare thing to see her father discomposed that it caused Martha to shift uncomfortably.

"There is one more I would see well situated at my decease."

Sally. The single name, thus far absent from her father's list but nonetheless foremost in Martha's mind, would finally step out of her shadow to stand present between them. William Short's words flooded Martha's thoughts. What *would* become of Sally at her master's death? The names of two Hemings apprentices would hardly cause a stir, especially as their names were unknown outside the immediate neighborhood. Sally Hemings's name was known to all America. If Thomas Jefferson freed Sally Hemings, it would appear to confirm every rumor ever written about her.

Martha's father sat and waited, watching Martha, as if expecting Martha to say the name of the slave who now filled the room, but this was a name Martha could not speak. Would not. At length Martha's father came to his own understanding, the moment signaled by a half smile, half grimace. "As all my property becomes yours in trust, Sally will remain your property. It is her wish to live with her sons Madison and Eston, but were I to formally free her, she must leave Virginia. Were I to petition for her to remain, were I to put her name forth in so public a manner—"

Martha's father stopped and this time Martha understood that he would wait as long as needed until she responded. Very well, she would respond. Had not William Short prepared her?

"If you free Sally it would start the talk all over, Papa. It would discredit you and your family and it would take attention from your true legacy."

For a long moment Martha's father said and did nothing. He didn't nod or blink or cast his eyes away, but they were the old eyes, the ones that gave no hint of the thoughts hidden behind them. At length he resumed. "This, then, is my wish. At the proper moment, when the attention has turned away from me, I ask that you quietly send Sally to take up residence with her sons. She will run a certain risk. She will remain your property in trust; she will have no legal standing. But this will be the best resolution when considering all parties. Again, I ask you to take the word *trust* in all its meanings."

Martha said nothing.

"Tell me I'm understood, Martha."

How was Martha to understand a thing that her father had never explained? But what if she asked and he *did* explain? No. Martha would never ask. She rose from her chair. "I understand you, Papa."

"We must keep faith with those who put their trust in us."

But now, it would seem, Sally must put her trust in Martha.

## CHAPTER 38

MARTHA WAS NEVER SO RELUCTANT—and so glad—to see William Short when he returned at the end of August. The mountain was hot and damp but not as hot and damp as Philadelphia, and Martha knew the forest he rode through would be cool, the summer lushness still evident, the air sweet with the last stages of summer life. The terraced vegetable garden would greet him with its second crops of lettuce, endive, spinach, and turnip; black-eyed Susans, China aster, bloodflower, and heliotrope would salute him from the flower gardens.

And yet as Martha walked down the steps to meet him, Short could only remark, "The road's rutted. The tobacco's sun blasted. The corn's wilted."

"Why can you never find a single lovely thing to say about our mountaintop, Mr. Short?"

"I find loveliness in the bloom in your cheek, the spark in your eye, the smartness that comes out of your mouth. This spinster life appears to suit you."

"How I pity any spinster with eleven children. Come, let me take you to my father; he rests in his chamber."

Short caught Martha's arm. "May we not pause here a minute? May we not walk together to the stable? Peter's gone off with my horse before I could tell him; the animal has a hot foreleg that will require a daily inspection."

"It will?"

"It will not. Come anyway."

Martha went. Because she longed to talk to someone. Because she didn't want to return to the house on such a lovely day. Because she was vain enough and starved enough to follow the least compliment, even if it led nowhere but a stable.

"What news?" Short asked as they set out, and in one long rush, against her every intention, Martha told Short of her conversation with her father. Martha knew it was not a good subject between them, but it was the first subject on her mind, and till she'd cleared it out she could find no other.

Short listened in silence, contemplated in silence. "So he frees John and Burwell too," he said finally. "'Tis far less than I'd wanted, but I'm sure he calculates that in the end every slave he frees takes from his family's ability to pay his debts. In the end, of course, I'd hoped such an extraordinary intellect would find a way to cast aside calculation and take up the larger principle, but alas—"

And Martha and her family were to end beggars so that Thomas Jefferson could free his slaves; this was the world that William Short would choose if he could. Martha attempted to visualize the world she would choose, and although she could see the end, she could not see the means; she could not choose her slave over her child, just as her father could not. Martha felt the beginnings of a headache forming, the rising nausea that signaled a severe bout ahead. They'd reached the stable, but Short kept walking toward the wood, heading for Martha's favorite path to the spring. She placed her hand on Short's arm to slow him, to tell him she needed to return to the house, but Short covered her hand with his, adjusting hers till it had settled more comfortably into the crook of his arm, and continued to walk. Martha's brain attempted to send a signal to her hand that it should draw away, but somehow the signal never reached its target.

"Indeed, your father might have done more than he did," Short continued, "but he could certainly have done no less; he considers himself as close to Burwell and John as he ever was to me. As to Sally's children, he only does as he promised."

"But he doesn't free Sally."

"You may consider it his parting gift to you."

"To me!"

Short only looked at her. Yes, she realized, to her. Her father would not leave her to suffer the consequences of a freed Sally Hemings. Self-interest versus their interest.

"Even so, your father proved Sally was right to place her trust in him; he kept his word for over three decades—not every man would."

"He kept his promise to my mother longer."

"The promise not to marry? The promise that back in Paris you insisted on seeing in the light of romance, while I saw it in the light of cruelty and selfishness?"

Martha pulled her hand away, turned back toward the house, and stretched out her stride, but Short only spun with her and matched her pace.

"Sally should have stayed in Paris," Martha said.

"You did not."

"It wasn't the same!"

"No, it wasn't. You wouldn't have been alone."

"Nor would Sally! She had her brother with her."

Short looked sideways at Martha. "It would appear she saw greater promise for herself and her children in someone besides her brother. Consider also that she was as young as you were, and that your father is a persuasive man who wished very much to keep Sally with him. In a case of real affection—"

"Real affection! You would use those words!"

"I would think it real enough. I can't pretend to know all your father felt for Sally in France, but perhaps the better measure is what he feels for her now, when she's no longer so young and beautiful."

Oh, she was still beautiful enough, Martha thought. But a Thomas Jefferson feeling real affection for a Sally Hemings? No. *No.* And yet as Martha walked in silence beside Short, she found unwelcome images forcing their way out of the past and into the present, images Martha had barely acknowledged then and could not welcome now: Sally standing in the doorway, looking more like Martha's mother than her own mother; that heartaching rendition of *"Au Claire de Lune,"* the birth of James Madison nine months afterward; and perhaps an even more troubling image from a day earlier that summer: Martha's father in the greenhouse crouching over his lemon tree, Sally coming in to bring him a cool cider, her master looking up at her as if she were the first sun of spring, or perhaps the last sun of fall.

Looking at her as he'd so often looked at Martha's mother.

As if she'd spoken the thought, Short said, "Why does it distress you so to consider that your father might have genuine affection for this woman, or she for him?"

"Because it diminishes him. Because Sally is his slave."

"And being his slave makes her less capable of loving and being loved? What of your father? Do you think he exists on some barren plain devoid of these emotions? Your father made that death-bed promise to your mother and decided—most foolishly in my view—that it was a promise that must be kept; what honorable choices did he have left? Surely you see how this lovely, clever young woman might have answered for him, how he might have answered for her, once her bargain had been struck. Only think of her courage. How many young slaves would dare to bargain with a man as powerful as Thomas Jefferson? And look what she worked. How else do you suppose she might have secured freedom for her children?"

"She might expect that if he cared for her as much as you seem to believe he did, he would free her *and* her children, before her life was spent."

"And they would have lost each other forever. Slavery was the only cover they had; by law they could never marry, even had they possessed the courage to do so."

"You assume Sally cares as much as you presume my father does."

"I at least admit the possibility exists that she might care enough not to wish to leave him."

"Or perhaps my father never gave her the chance."

Short looked again at Martha. "Perhaps he didn't. If you wish to diminish him, diminish him on the basis of that supposition, or for accommodating himself to the habits of slavery, or for spending irresponsibly, or for promising us all too much. Don't diminish him for having feelings for Sally. Respect him enough—and her enough—to grant them that. Respect their faithfulness to each other for over three decades."

"You can't know a thing of their faithfulness!"

"Can't I? Have you seen your father engage with any other woman since he engaged with Sally in France? As for her, she's given birth to no other children but those who happen to possess a most remarkable resemblance to your father, born at intervals that coincide exactly with his sporadic trips to Monticello. I know—oh, how I know—that if they didn't care for each other, the circumstances could have remained the same; your father could do with Sally as he wished simply because he owned her. He *owned her.* He could have forced her to—"

"He would *not.*"

"No, he would not. No one knowing him could imagine he would. But does this absolve him of the sin of owning her? It does not."

Martha pressed her feet harder over the ground and attempted to surge ahead of Short, but he caught her up. "Stop," she said. "Stop talking to me of this. Why? Why do you do this?"

"Because you shared with me a conversation you had with your father, and that conversation tells me that it rests with you what happens next, what turn this particular piece of our history takes. You want to protect your father's legacy. I only ask you to think what your father's true legacy could be and find the courage to honor it."

They'd reached the house. Martha pushed ahead and climbed the steps into the confusion of children and servants and guests and father and all the things that made up the facts of her life, the tradition of her life, a life William Short couldn't know. This, then, was what she must honor: this life.

## CHAPTER 39

T HE MOUNTAIN HAD BEGUN to take on that lush palette no other place on earth could claim—smoke-colored shadows from below the cloud line, gold-tinged purple from above, the many shades of green found in lawn and field and orchard, the colors deepening and enriching themselves as if after a week of rain. Martha had seen Paris and New York and Philadelphia and Boston and yet she'd never seen anything like the way the mountain could sharpen and soften her world together, blurring the details while better defining the shapes, clarifying motions. Meanings.

The smoky hour of night caused Martha to temporarily confuse what she saw. Even during the day she could never testify to the color of the girl's skin, but in this queer mix of dark and light she *could* still testify to the shape of her—tall as Martha was tall, but rounded where Martha was angular, with Martha's same thick, red hair flying out behind her like a hawk's wing. Perhaps this was why the girl so disconcerted Martha, repelled her—Harriet served as a mirror to something in Martha that she didn't care to face. And had she not told the girl to keep to the house at this hour? Here she was coming across the field and there was the brick mason trailing her and again Harriet appeared unaware, or at the least unconcerned; she made no effort to increase her pace until the brick mason was but a few feet behind her. Oh, enough of this!

Martha started toward the pair, but long before she got there she saw Harriet reach into her pocket, saw her turn and raise her arm high over her head and bring whatever object she carried down on the brick mason's skull. He staggered, grabbing the girl by the hair and yanking her head back, but the arm swung again, going wide this time, now catching the man at the temple, sending him toppling sideways to the ground. He rolled once, his feet scrabbling in the dirt as if trying to rise, but the arm came down again for a third blow, again to the skull, and the feet stopped scrabbling. At some point between the first and second blow, Martha had started running, but Harriet now lifted her eyes, looked straight at Martha, dropped whatever she'd held, and ran in the opposite direction.

"Harriet!" Martha shouted, but Harriet disappeared around the south pavilion, and presumably, into the trees beyond. Martha yelled again but received nothing in answer aside from the objections of a disturbed crow. She charged forward, stumbling over the rough earth of the vegetable garden, slipping on the rise that banked the terrace, until she'd reached the ground behind the charcoal kiln where the brick mason had rolled after he'd fallen. He lay still and silent on the grass, Harriet's improvised weapon—a sharp-edged rock—lying beside him. Martha knelt down and put her fingers to the man's lips, feeling for a whisper of breath. None. She rested her palm against the shirt above his heart and felt nothing. She turned the head sideways and back; the blows to the scalp were camouflaged by the thick hair, but the blow to the temple had mangled flesh and bone together. The man's right hand was clenched as if frozen in the act of grasping at the last straw of life, or, as it proved, a dozen strands of Harriet's hair, coarser and wirier than Martha's but just as flamed with red, the proof, some would say, of Thomas Jefferson's blood in her veins. Of course right now it made no difference *who* Harriet was, as long as she was *what* she was; by the laws of the state of Virginia, Harriet Hemings was Thomas Jefferson's slave, she'd just killed a white man, and as no Virginia law protected a slave's virtue, Harriet would be charged with a capital crime.

Martha stood up, twisted Harriet's hair around her fingers until it formed a small red ball, thrust it into her pocket, and began to run again, this time toward the house. What would happen after she got there and reported to her father was as clear in Martha's mind as if it had already happened: Sooner or later Harriet would have to emerge from those woods, and once she did she'd be easy enough to hunt down, her first crime being that she was far too distinctive, not just in her coloring but in her loveliness. Her second crime was her rashness, her openness of temper. No slave could survive on the run who hadn't yet learned to erase all emotion from its face, all passion from its limbs; that Harriet Hemings could bring her slender arm down onto the brick mason's skull in such a way exhibited a demented rage that could not be contained. Harriet must be found soon and dealt with as the law dictated; with such fury on the loose, no white person could count himself safe.

As Martha reached the gentler footing of the lawn she looked toward the house, the first floor aglow with welcoming light, the hallway crisscrossed by more light-skinned servants, more Hemingses. Oh, how tired she was of them! Martha hastened toward the steps and the parlor door where she expected to find her father and a good number of her children playing, reading, relaxing after dinner. Over the past weeks, since William Short's visit, or perhaps since his talk with his daughter, Martha's father had rallied, and as much as Martha enjoyed witnessing him up and about with the family, she'd continued to slip outside for her usual quiet interlude with the mountain, the same interlude Harriet enjoyed, the same interlude Martha had warned her to enjoy at her peril. That Martha could take such a moment in safety and Harriet could not was simply a fact of life. A fact of slave life. For a second Martha pondered how events might have played out had she spoken with Edmund Bacon about the brick mason's behavior as she'd intended, but even if the man had been discharged, another would have come along to take his "entitlements." Martha had warned Harriet, Harriet had ignored the warning, and now a man lay dead; there lay the fault of it.

A man lay dead. Indeed, why did Martha rush so to break apart the happy scene she knew she would find inside the house? The brick mason was already dead. She paused at the foot of the steps, and as she paused she heard a sound; no, not a sound but a cry; no, not a cry but an involuntary release, as if from a creature in pain. Martha turned from the steps and followed the sound through the dependencies under the house to the steep stairs that the slaves climbed many times a day to reach the main part of the house. The closer Martha drew to the stairs the clearer the sound came until it led Martha to Sally's door. Martha paused. Tapped.

"Is all well?"

The noise stopped. Martha pushed open the door and stepped into the tiny room, where the bloody Harriet stood tall and silent in front of her weeping mother. Yes, it was Sally, not Harriet, who sobbed in such pain as she clung to her daughter's arm and swabbed and swabbed at her hands, arms, face, dress.

Harriet had spun about at the sound of the door and torn the cloth from her mother's hand. She met Martha's eyes full-on, but it was Sally's eyes that transfixed Martha. *How much in her is fear?* William Short had asked of Sally. Martha had never seen fear like she saw now in Sally's face, but she'd felt it as she'd looked at her own dying Ellen; there could never exist a fear as cutting as a mother's fear for her child's life.

Sally began a stream of desperate gibberish in a voice Martha had never heard in her before: *She's fallen . . . cut her hand . . . bruised her cheek . . .* and Martha, understanding what lay ahead for Harriet, understood what lay ahead for Sally, what had always lain ahead for Sally, what had lain ahead for every slave woman, what fear for their children went to bed with them each night and rose with them each morning.

But Harriet. Even now, Martha could see no fear in Harriet. "Hush, Mama," the girl said. "'Tis no use. She saw what I did."

"Yes, I saw." And squirreled away in Martha's pocket sat a ball of red hair to prove it.

But Sally, quiet, demure Sally! She would not hush. She grabbed Harriet's arm and shook it. "You tell her! You tell her *why* you did it!"

Harriet lifted her chin in Martha's face. "She knows that too, Mama."

"He's dead, Harriet," Martha said. "Do you know that?"

"I know it."

"But you didn't run. You came here."

The girl shrugged. Perhaps she'd never understood there was no such crime as the rape of a Negro woman. Perhaps she thought she'd actually tell her story in court, that it would be heard, that whatever she said would be weighed equally against whatever Martha said. Perhaps she knew nothing of Richard and Nancy Randolph, a white man and woman in a white man's court, the black evidence discounted, unheard, and the pair released.

"I must speak to my father," Martha said. She left the room without looking at either Hemings.

Martha found her father in the parlor, surrounded by a large number of Martha's children, all listening with varying degrees of attention as Ellen played an Irish tune on the harpsichord. Martha bent down to her daughter. "Take them to bed."

"Oh, pray, hold!" Martha's father cried. "We've only just settled to our music."

Martha held, taking the interlude to study her father. Almost eight decades of life may have washed the fire from his limbs as well as his hair, but his eyes still lit with the same old joy whenever he was with her children, and indeed, whenever he looked at Martha. As she studied her father, she realized that he probably succeeded far better at the art of reading Martha than she ever had at the art of reading him. What did she know of her father, really? He had never denied Sally; in fact, if Martha added up all his commissions and omissions, he'd never obfuscated in any way on the subject of Sally *or* her children. Start with the namings, the resemblances; continue with their special attentions, gifts, privileges. How could he have risked it? How could he ride out all the Sally rumors essentially unscathed? Perhaps by concealing Sally and her children in plain sight they'd become invisible. Or was it simply that people believed what they wished to believe?

And what did Martha wish to believe? That her father was worthy of every last honor his country might bestow on him; that he'd caused intentional harm to no living creature; that he'd done what he could to ease the plight of those in his care; that he was trapped, as they all were, in a vile system that could not be righted in this life. She looked at her father's hands, disfigured from writing, working, forming words, ideas, governments that would last for all time, for all mankind. But with what codicil attached? Martha pushed the thought aside. That was her work for tomorrow. Today's work was to tell her father what Harriet had done. Thomas Jefferson was, of all things, a man of law, just as Tom Randolph was a man of law; as Tom had urged Martha to tell the truth no matter the harm to his family, so Martha's father would do—she was sure of it.

But . . . *his family*. The words. The sudden awareness of the awful choice Martha was about to inflict on her father struck her. A thundering pain began to split Martha's head between the eyes, to surround her eyes, to travel over her temples and down into her neck. Again, she thought. Now it would all be talked of again. As if it weren't salacious enough that a man lay dead behind Monticello's charcoal kiln, they would have to talk about who this girl was or wasn't, about her hair, her color, the Jeffersonian symmetry of her face. Oh, if only her father had done the sensible thing long ago, as Martha had begged him to do, and simply put all these Hemingses out of sight! Well, now Martha would put Harriet out of sight. But of course she would have been put out of sight eventually. *I fear she too will run away . . .*

And why, just then, for a second time, did Nancy and Richard Randolph intrude on Martha's thoughts?

Because white law had denied the existence of a murdered white infant when no white person would admit to seeing it. Why not the same with a murdered white brick mason? After all, who did Martha think to help? Who to hurt? What was the right of it? What was the wrong? Oh, dear God, so much was wrong, Martha could never in her lifetime right an eighth of it.

But perhaps she could even up a small piece.

Martha signaled Ellen. Ellen herded the children from the room and Martha crossed to her father, took up his hands. "Papa, I bear ill news. There's been an accident, the brick mason in his drink again, falling and striking his head on a rock."

Martha's father began to struggle upright, but Martha put out her hand to settle him. "'Tis too late, Papa. 'Twas a rock as sharp as a blade; by the time I reached him, he was gone. I'll speak to Mr. Bacon. He'll see to it."

As Martha left the room for Mr. Bacon, she considered her words. After all, none were untrue. Or unlikely. And even if they were, who would question? The white woman would be believed.

## CHAPTER 40

Martha always knew deep night when she woke in it, the dark darker, the quiet quieter, no children rustling, no servant up yet to start a fire or begin a chore. Sometimes Martha woke at such an hour without prompting, but this time when she woke she knew her waking had followed a noise; she sat up and listened and in time she heard the shuffling of a horse, the creak of leather, the thud of a boot hitting ground.

Tom. This was just how he would choose to come home— riding up the mountain in the dark to avoid any explanation or fuss—and who else would dare to arrive at Monticello at such an hour? Martha wrapped herself in her robe and picked her way down the stairs, feeling her way through the hall by the touch of the chairs that lined the walls in an effort to accommodate their endless visitors. She pushed open the heavy door but stopped at the first steps; this was no horse and rider but a horse and carriage, and by now her eyes had adjusted sufficiently to the dark to be able to identify not Tom at the reins but Edmund Bacon.

Bacon saw Martha and leaped down. "Mrs. Randolph! Please, you must go inside."

"Do you go to fetch Tom?"

"No, I do not. Please, go inside." But as Bacon spoke he looked behind her, drawing Martha's eyes around; the cloaked figure would have been unrecognizable in the dark if she hadn't seen Martha and pulled her hood back in her usual defiance.

Harriet.

Two months had passed since Edmund Bacon had quietly seen to the interment of the brick mason, two months during which Harriet had equally quietly turned twenty-one years of age. Now she passed Martha without a word and got into the carriage; Edmund Bacon closed the door after her, reclaimed the reins, and drove off. Martha watched the carriage to the first bend, her mind jumping one way after another, but when she turned around, it focused at once on a small, dark shadow standing at the hall window: Sally, come to watch her daughter's exodus. Martha started back up the steps, but Sally slipped away long before Martha reached her.

Martha went inside and headed for the stairs, but halfway there she made a forceful turn and took the hall to her father's chamber door. She knocked. "Papa?" She waited.

He came to the door fully dressed, alert, his face lined and shadowed by his candle.

"I saw her," Martha said. "Harriet. I saw her being driven off."

Martha's father drew her in and closed the door.

"What will happen to her?"

"She goes to her brother."

"But what *happens* to her?"

"She's a lovely young woman well trained in the domestic arts. I expect she'll marry."

Yes, the solution one always sought for one's daughters. "And if she does not?"

"She'll be with her brother. He's found work in the joinery trade. She was—they both were—given . . . a sum."

"But she's so alone, her family now lost to her!"

"She goes to her brother, Martha. Do you think I'd send a young woman such as Harriet to live alone?"

No. But how little it seemed! And yet Harriet had chosen this over remaining behind enslaved, and Sally, who had once made another choice, had chosen to let her go. Thinking of the strength of the two women made Martha tremble with her own weakness. She returned to her room and went to her case of drawers— wrapped in a handkerchief at the back of the bottom-most drawer sat a ball of wiry red hair. Martha picked it out, thinking to throw it in the fireplace, but instead she returned it to the drawer, for reasons she couldn't name.

———

J UST AS NO ONE TALKED OF BEVERLY'S LEAVING, no one talked of Harriet's; the only mark of their absence lay in the changeable cast to Sally's features, her face raw and puffy one day, gray and hollow the next. Harriet Hemings's absence rattled Martha, in part because it forced her to realize how constantly the girl's presence had rattled her. Edmund Bacon's departure caused something equally as distressing in Martha, but the reason for her distress was much more visceral; Bacon had abandoned her. So many overseers had come and gone at Monticello—and Varina and Edgehill—that Martha hadn't even cataloged their names. Edmund Bacon had been different. He and Martha had formed the kind of partnership—the kind of understanding—that would be impossible to duplicate; they had shared a common cause in Monticello, and Martha had fully expected Edmund Bacon to help her safeguard it forever. To help her safeguard her father. Instead, as soon as he'd accumulated enough slaves, he'd purchased his own plantation in Kentucky and taken them far away from their families, carrying Martha's last excuse over the slaves' sales with him. But when Martha tried to speak to her father of the loss of his best overseer, he said only, "Jeff manages," and diverted all Martha's subsequent efforts from the topic.

———

AFTER BACON LEFT, Martha began to walk around Monticello touching things: the "magic" double parlor doors her father had designed that were linked by a chain under the floor, allowing both sides to swing open when only one was pushed; the special double-paned glass in the north-facing tea room that kept them warm in winter and cool in summer; the enormous gravity clock in the hall that chimed the nearest hour so all the plantation could hear; the telescope on the terrace that her father kept positioned just so in order to watch the construction advancing at the University of Virginia. And each time she passed it, she found herself touching the Houdon bust of her father, needing to feel it solid and cool beneath her fingers, always afraid she'd find it crumbling to dust.

## CHAPTER 41

M ARTHA LINGERED IN THE BIG PARLOR after the others had gone to bed, the flame of the lamp turned low, revisiting the shadows she knew so well, searching for the beginning of her spiraling gloom. She chased it lower and lower until she found her thoughts back in the ground with her poor, dead Anne.

Oh, Anne! She'd insisted in her letters that all was well, that Charles was devoted, that Charles's father was as kind as Martha's own. She'd announced the news that she was to have another child as evidence of her happy married state, but Martha was too familiar with the way those things got done to believe it proved anything beyond a single night's confluence. She'd worried Anne with letters, begging her to come to Monticello to have her child, restating her unchanging faith in the healthful mountain air, the Hemingses, the aging Dr. Norris, but in fact, Martha could simply not believe her daughter safe until she'd seen her so. Perhaps Anne divined that her mother's fears had come near disabling her; perhaps she too preferred to give birth at what Martha would still call Anne's home; Anne wrote promising to come, and that letter had almost convinced Martha that all *was* well, that perhaps all would remain well. The next letter came from Charles's father, claiming Charles too devastated to write himself: Like Martha's mother and sister, Anne had died giving early birth to her last child.

Martha had succeeded in bringing Anne home to Monticello at last—they laid her out in the parlor and followed her coffin to the Monticello graveyard, burying her next to Martha's mother and the first Ellen. As the family moved away, Martha turned for a final look and saw Tom slip out of the trees to drop to the earth that now covered his daughter, his sobs following them as they moved back up the mountain. Had her father seen Tom? Martha doubted it; he was too dulled by the loss of Anne to even notice the grandchildren who hovered around him, seeking or giving comfort, each according to their comprehension and needs. The family returned to the parlor and ate their funeral meats and drank their funeral wine, but no one lingered—in twos and threes they drifted off to their rooms, giving Martha wet kisses and trembling hugs. She busied herself with the lamps until they'd all gone and she was able to return to the parlor alone.

So many pieces of the room were missing now. Anne had taken her piece, the seat next to her grandfather's where they'd talked over their garden plans each spring—but other pieces had gone before. Nicholas Trist had returned from West Point as devoted as when he'd left, never leaving Monticello until he and Virginia had stood before the mantel as man and wife. Tom had ridden up the mountain for the ceremony, groomed something better than he'd been at Martha's last sighting, making a fine toast that brought tears to Virginia's eyes, before turning and speaking low words to Jeff that drove him from the house. Nicholas Trist had carried Virginia off to Washington, where a position as state department clerk awaited him, taking with him Virginia's special piece of the room—her perch on the embroidered stool on which she'd played her guitar.

When had Bibelot died? After Virginia's departure or Ellen's? Martha couldn't recall, but he'd outlived two sheepdogs and owed her nothing more. And Ellen. Martha had sent Ellen to Washington and Richmond in hopes of her meeting young men from outside the planter class, but in the end the husband who had carried her off had found her at Monticello. Joseph Coolidge arrived from Boston on a pilgrimage to meet the great Thomas Jefferson but discovered the greater treasure lay in his granddaughter Ellen, or so he explained to Martha when he asked for Ellen's hand. Martha could find no argument against Coolidge, a successful merchant, a non-slaveholder, and indeed, a kind and engaging young man. Ellen and Joseph Coolidge stood before the bedecked mantel as Virginia and Nicholas had, as Anne and Charles had, as Martha and Tom had, and Ellen had gone off to settle with her husband in Boston, leaving empty the chair in which she'd sat playing chess with her grandfather. When Martha wrote asking if Ellen had experienced any difficulty in finding a suitable maid in the north, Ellen replied:

*We dress ourselves here.*

Tom had not attended Ellen's wedding, sending a long, rambling letter blaming his absence on vague, subversive attempts by Jeff to destroy him. Edgehill had not sold, even in small parcels, so Jeff gave over his own lease and bought the farm for a dollar an acre more than had been offered on the open market. Martha believed this to be a generous act, but Tom saw this as evidence of a long-conceived plot to confiscate the property. Jeff also bought what slaves he could—those with connections to Monticello, those he'd grown up with—and Martha's dower right rescued Burwell's daughters as well as her own domestics, but the rest had gone in the sale.

The sale.

Martha pushed herself out of her chair and headed for the stairs. The dead Anne, her absent daughters, the missing pieces of the room; that was enough for this day. She could not think of the sale.

———————

THE SALE, FOLLOWED SO CLOSELY BY the death of Anne, seemed to take the last of Thomas Jefferson's will. He began to speak of Maria; he sat for long hours on the terrace with a blanket over his knees, scanning the lawn east to west as if looking for something lost. Even with the assistance of four slaves and the elevation of the terrace, he could no longer mount his horse for his daily ride; in early June he became so weak he retired to his bed and never rose again.

Martha wrote to Ellen and Virginia: *Come.* She wrote to William Short. *My father slips away—best come if you wish to make your farewell.* She asked Peter to saddle the mare and this time asked Ned to accompany her down the mountain one more time.

Tom had failed even more since Martha had last seen him at Virginia's wedding, his flesh loose on his limbs, his eyes slow in focusing, his mind tracking aimlessly from topic to topic. Martha persisted until she was understood. "My father is dying. You must come."

"No," Tom said. "Let his regrets comfort him. If he has none, let him die uncomforted."

Martha stood and stared long at her husband. As she'd ridden down the mountain, she'd convinced herself that Tom had caused her all the pain he could possibly cause her; she'd entered his cabin with a dreary kind of hope that with no further wounds to inflict, they might settle at last into a kind of hollow stasis. All such hope now lay fractured amid the shards of this new pain, this final denial of what had once been. She said no good-bye. She rode away, the bite of her anger propelling her forward. The man who lay behind her was the one who was dead, the one who would die uncomforted.

But as Martha rode she couldn't help but relive every year of wasted care and worry and love. Or *had* it been love? She could no longer say for certain. She could think back to that terrible time when her father had announced he was to leave for New York, when Sally had walked into the parlor so visibly with child, when a life at the dread Eppington plantation awaited her. What a charming diversion Tom Randolph had been! Of course she would have become infatuated. Of course she would have wished to think it love. And if she only considered the state of her heart before he'd first disappointed her, before he'd first frightened her or betrayed her . . . Indeed, she could think of no single minute when she'd begun to feel alone, but she could look over the vast years now and see clearly how lonely she'd been. Was still.

Diversion, love, infatuation, disappointment, fear, betrayal— whatever it had been, today was the last of it. Martha rode on, letting it all trail away behind her.

———

PERHAPS IN ONE WAY TOM HELPED MARTHA by allowing her to put him aside, by allowing her to focus on her father; she'd told William Short she wished to be at hand to care for her father as his life waned, and this wish—as devastating as it was—would now come true. The door was barred to Martha no longer; she spent each day beside her father, reading to him, talking of Paris and Washington, listening to him talk of the wild days of revolution. He knew the fiftieth anniversary of the signing of the Declaration of American Independence neared. "I should like to see that dawn," he said. "After that, I exit the scene in peace."

"Of course you shall see it," Martha said, but behind her she heard Sally's failed effort to abort a sob, heard the sweep of her skirt as she hurried from sight. Fear or love? Martha no longer cared. She switched the talk to their beloved mountain, what flowers had burst to life thus far in the season, which vegetables had come to table, which were likely to come in the days ahead. Martha's father talked of what he'd like to see planted the following spring; there Martha excused herself to tend her children, barely making it through the door before her own sobs overwhelmed her.

Jeff came and didn't leave again, spelling Martha at her father's bedside. Cornelia tried, but sat in such tragic silence Martha found it better to send her to the kitchen to oversee the efforts making the broth, jellies, and teas that her father never tasted. Ellen had written: *We leave on the morrow for Monticello,* but it was a long trip from Boston. Virginia and Nicholas arrived, both faces glazed with tears even before they reached the bedside; the middle children took turns reading aloud to their grandfather each day, and Timi and George collected and refreshed the flowers, their lesser understanding cheering the room even more than their offerings.

Madison and Eston Hemings found reasons to enter the sickroom that Martha saw as contrived by their mother but did nothing to block them; in fact, when Madison came to tighten a chair rung and Eston to replace a smoking lamp, Martha stepped outside and left her father to them.

But Martha could not bring herself to leave him to Sally. The slave was always there, fussing over this or that piece of bed linen, wiping up invisible spills, moving books from one pile to another. Sometimes her master's eyes followed her but sometimes they closed as if exhausted by her; at least this is what Martha liked to think as she sat in a chair by the bed in what she also liked to think was a soothing stillness. No, she could not bring herself to leave her father to Sally, until the day she happened to notice Sally trembling as she wiped fingerprints off Thomas Jefferson's inkwell. *Love or fear?*

Martha rose from her chair. "Sally, I must see to my children. Will you keep my father company till I return?"

Sally continued to stand by the desk.

"Sit here in this chair, Sally. Rest. If he wakes, I want him to see a familiar face."

Sally went to the chair, carrying the inkwell with her, clenching it tight as if to still her hands, her eyes fixed on her master's face.

———

STILL MARTHA'S FATHER REMAINED LUCID, his thoughts clear. "Do not imagine for a moment that I feel the smallest solicitude about the result, my dear. I am like an old watch, with a pinion worn out here, and a wheel there, until it can go no longer."

He requested the grandchildren attend him. "Pursue virtue," he told them. "Be true. Be truthful." After they left he turned to Martha. "George does not understand what all this means."

At a later hour he remarked on his bed curtains. "They came in the first cargo that arrived after the peace of 1782." After a period of silence he continued, "My mind seems to turn to those days now. To those scenes of revolution."

On the third of July he said, "This is the fourth of July," and no one corrected him. When the doctor arrived to administer his laudanum he said, strong and clear, "No, Doctor, no more." Without the medicine he slept fitfully, waking to go through the mime of writing. "The Committee of Safety must be warned."

Somehow Thomas Jefferson willed himself into the real dawn of the fiftieth anniversary of the signing of the Declaration, but not six hours beyond. The last words he spoke were understood only by Burwell.

"What, Papa? What?" Martha asked, while Burwell stepped in to make the requested adjustment to the pillow. She watched her father's chest rise and fall, rise and fall, and stay fallen, unwilling to believe, continuing to watch him, until Jeff led her from the room. She remembered that: her son's insistent hand under her arm. She remembered all in the household, black and white, sobbing as she climbed the stairs to her room. What happened afterward Martha could not recall; it was as if a great hand drew the shades down over her senses at the same time it drew them down over her father's.

---

MARTHA SURFACED WHEN TOM APPEARED AT THE FUNERAL, apparently only to strike up a violent argument with Jeff before bursting into exaggerated weeping; when he approached Martha she turned away. Tom had once declared he had no wife; Martha now declared it in her own silent vow: She had no husband.

---

LATER, ALONE IN HER ROOM, Martha came upon her father's poem, tucked in among her sewing. How had he gotten it there? Who had done this final errand for him? Oh, that he should worry for *her* at his end! She read the poem once only and put it away; already the ink had blurred with her tears.

> *A death-bed Adieu. Th:J. to MR.*
> *Life's visions are vanished, its dreams are no more.*
> *Dear friends of my bosom, why bathed in tears?*
> *I go to my fathers; I welcome the shore,*
> *Which crowns all my hopes, or which buries my cares.*
> *Then farewell my dear, my lov'd daughter, Adieu!*
> *The last pang of life is my parting from you!*
> *Two Seraphs await me, long shrouded in death:*
> *I will bear them your love on my last parting breath.*

---

## CHAPTER 42

M̲ARTHA SAT IN THE SMALL PARLOR ALONE, waiting for Jeff. Ellen had arrived after the funeral and spent her time wandering about Monticello in a stupor, picking up this and that of her grandfather's, staring as if waiting for his hand to interrupt her. The next-oldest girls stayed busy attempting to sort and disburse their grandfather's clothes, the boys by helping to cope with the neglected gardens; Priscilla had taken Timi and George away as soon as Martha told her of Jeff's note requesting a moment alone to "discuss matters of import," but Martha didn't know what important matters those might be. Jeff had already sat with her and taken her line by line through her father's will.

Burwell was freed with three hundred dollars. John Hemings was freed with his tools. Both men were granted life estates in houses near their still-enslaved wives, plus an acre each of land. As promised, John Hemings was given "the service of his two apprentices, Madison and Eston Hemings, until their respective ages of twenty-one years, at which period I give them their freedom; and I humbly and earnestly request of the Legislature of Virginia a confirmation of the bequest of freedom to these servants, with permission to remain in this State, where their families and connections are, as an additional instance of the favor, of which I have received so many other manifestations, in the course of my life, and for which I now give my last, solemn, and dutiful thanks." Also as promised, Sally Hemings's name did not appear.

Jeff arrived an hour past the appointed time, a delay that ordinarily would have knotted Martha with anxiety but now barely moved her. He came to her chair and kissed her forehead. "How do you fare, Mama?"

"I'm well," Martha answered, but in truth she wasn't well; her head and stomach pained her day and night and the world seemed dull, even absent, as if she floated through nothing but empty air. Her children's departures had left empty corners; her father's departure had left an empty house. An empty mountain. An empty heart. Oh, how much of it he'd filled!

"Ellen wishes you to return to Boston with her in October."

"Just when the cold weather comes."

"'Tis best you go then."

Martha looked at her son. "What more has happened?"

Jeff looked away. "You know, or surely you might guess, Grandfather died with debts."

"How great?"

"Over one hundred thousand dollars."

Three times the sum Tom lay in arrears. She remembered how William Short had warned her. And where *was* Short? Hearing nothing in response to her first letter suggesting he come, she'd been forced to send another informing him of her father's passing. An answering letter *had* come then, but its sentences were as stiff and hollow as an old log. *My deepest sympathy . . . May time prove itself your friend . . . With my old affection perpetually renewed . . .* There had been no acknowledgment of the enormity of Martha's loss, no single word of Short's own grief, no tribute to her father's contributions to the world. Martha hadn't answered.

"All must be sold, Mama," Jeff said now. "Monticello. The slaves. This is why 'tis best you go north. The slave sale is scheduled for October."

Oh, how many questions Martha might once have asked, how many arguments she might have made! Now she asked but a simple question. "How many?"

Jeff didn't pretend to misunderstand. "One hundred and thirty."

Martha felt that hated, wet pressure behind her eyes as it began to rise. It seemed a pitiful response, an excuse of a response, but after all, she'd been making excuses for so long, why quibble over a few tears now?

Jeff came and knelt by her chair, collecting her hand. "What good would it do to remain here and watch them go? You can accomplish nothing."

"In his will . . . Your grandfather wished to free some."

"And they will be freed, I've seen to that. This much the banks will allow."

"And what of—" Yes, now she must say the name. "What of Sally?"

"She remains your property."

"But all the others—?"

Jeff said, "We might salvage a few more. I'll make every effort to keep the price low, especially on the older slaves, in hope that their families may buy them. But you see why I say 'tis best you go."

"So you and Ellen have conspired toward this journey of mine."

"We all do. We're all self-sufficient now, except for Timi and George, and they'll travel with you."

Oh, what a cowardly thing to do, Martha thought, to run north and hide while her father's slaves were auctioned off, but she knew she would go. She studied her son. Tall. Strong. Contained. She'd heard that he had a problem with runaways as her father and husband had not, that when he recaptured a slave he whipped him, as her father and husband did not. Would he be the one to survive in this world? Would she even want him to? But what other world could she see for him?

"Believe me, Mama," Jeff said now, "if I could have saved them, if I could have saved Monticello—"

"Save Monticello for what? Why? So it might ruin your children too? Has it not ruined enough of us?"

"Mama, please, I don't mean to upset—"

Martha waved away the rest of her son's words. "When does it get sold?"

"I've appointments at the banks. I hope to arrange some time for you to—"

"What of the contents? Does it all get sold?"

"The main of the furnishings must be sold, but I've instructed the family to submit requests for their favorite pieces."

Martha stood up and left the room. She walked through the sunroom where her father's lemon tree had just sent out fresh green orbs full of a false promise of fruit—and life—to come. She passed through her father's library where several books still perched open on the chair, as if her father would appear any minute to scoop one up and call out to whatever guest had engaged him in argument over some point of government: "Here, sir, you see I make my case well!" She passed through her father's cabinet, passed his chair, his desk, his bookstand, his copying machine, to the bed where he'd died. She pulled the quilt off the bed and folded it neatly in four. It had been the last, closest thing to him, and this was all she wanted from Monticello now; she would use the quilt that had covered her father to cover herself against the New England cold.

Martha returned to the parlor and found Jeff still waiting. "May I assure Ellen you'll come in October? With Timi and George?"

"I'll think on it."

"Mama. I didn't like to upset you further, but you must know that my father only grows worse. He blames you as much as me for his ruin, saying if you hadn't sided against him, he'd still be the master of Edgehill."

"He may blame me and be happy in it. He's my husband no more. I care nothing for the law now; I divorced myself from him at my father's grave."

"Mama. I'm afraid the law cannot be entirely ignored. It sides with my father when it comes to his children. In the law they're his, not yours."

"Then let him feed and clothe them."

"He threatens to take the two not yet of age."

Martha came up straight in her chair. "He would take Timi and George?"

"This is why we urge you to go north and take them with you. I'll watch over the others, but you must keep those two out of his hands or it will be the end of all your hopes for them. And what peace will you ever find if he holds this threat over you day after day?"

Martha sat silent. "So this is how God evens it," she said at last. "Thomas Jefferson's daughter and grandchildren must flee north for their freedom."

"Mama, I've done what I can."

Yes, Martha thought, this is what we've all said. We've done what we can.

———

AFTER JEFF LEFT HER, Martha sat for some time in the growing dark until Molly came in to light the candles, or so Martha thought in her fatigue and despondency until the girl drew close to her chair: not Molly, but Molly's daughter, Jessie, a girl nearly the age Molly had been when she'd been given to Martha. Of course no one had to give Jessie to Martha, because from the minute of her birth, Jessie was already enslaved as Martha's property, a fact every slave mother must surely contemplate as she faced her travail.

Every slave mother.

Martha turned to the girl. "Jessie, fetch Sally please."

Whether in the coming or the going, it took some time for Sally to appear. When she entered the parlor, new cracks in her demeanor were evident, but Martha felt she could understand them; Martha too felt unmoored. She began it where it was to end. "Your sons are to be freed. You were told this. I only wish you to understand that whatever happens to others at Monticello, this does not change."

Sally said nothing, watching Martha.

"A petition has been entered asking that they be permitted to remain in the state; they're both skilled in a sought-after trade—my father had no doubt that the petition would succeed."

Still Sally said nothing.

"At the right time, when the move will attract least notice, you'll be free to join them."

A lift. A light. "Free?"

"*Free,* no. You remain my property." Martha needn't have said more—surely she needn't have said more—but she found herself continuing. "Were I to free you, there would be a manumission document with your name on it, there would be the petition to the legislature with your name on it; your name, which has been tossed about quite enough already, would only be tossed about again." What Martha didn't say, but meant, was that the talk of Jefferson's concubine would start again, now considered confirmed by the fact that Jefferson's daughter had freed the slave, the only female slave to be so freed. Instead Martha continued, "Consider too that the result must be in doubt. Your sons are young, talented artisans, easily employable, with no risk of becoming a burden to the state. This is not the case with you. You could be required to leave Virginia. So I'm sure you can see why I cannot free you, Sally."

Sally turned to go.

"Sally!"

Sally turned back, but only partway, her hand still on the door.

"What do you hear of Beverly and Harriet?"

"I will not hear of Beverly and Harriet," Sally said. "In the world they've chosen to enter, they can be my children no more."

## CHAPTER 43

M ARTHA DISMOUNTED from the carriage at Philadelphia, gripping George and Timi each by a hand. In the past Martha had much admired Philadelphia—the wide streets, the paved sidewalks, the streetlights, the tidiness, the cleanliness—but now she only took note that little had changed, except for the presence of the man coming toward her. William Short pushed forward through the crowd and took charge of the luggage; Martha was not glad to see him. Why had he refused to visit her father? In time he'd written a second letter, from which Martha did indeed manage to take a modicum of comfort:

> *It has always been demonstrated to my mind that your father's greatest illusions proceeded from a most amiable error on his part; having too favorable an opinion of the animal called Man. He was too sanguine in his nature, too easily deceived in the result of things; in this way he was able to deceive himself as long as it could possibly be done as to his affairs . . .*

Martha *had* answered that letter but what she'd said in her answer now escaped her; she must have mentioned her pending trip north, for in Short's next letter he'd insisted on engaging her rooms in Philadelphia, where she would break her journey. Martha, unable to organize the effort to refuse, had acquiesced. Within five minutes of their meeting, however, Short himself proved to be too much of an effort.

"So you see I wait and you come," Short said. "And with only two children in hand now. *Two* names I might remember." He smiled. Could he not see that she was in no humor for smiles and innuendo?

Martha pointed to the house before which the carriage had stopped. "Is this Mrs. Hill's?"

"The best rooms in town. She has a bedchamber and a sitting room for you and a girl who will mind the children while I take you to dine."

"I'm tired." Martha pushed past Short toward the door of the inn.

"Mrs. Randolph!"

Martha turned.

"You're angry with me."

"I am not. I'm only shocked you could imagine me in a mood for jest."

"I thought it best to pretend lightness. I promise you, I'd more easily weep at the sight of you, so heartbroken and worn."

"I would think you would weep for my father."

"Ah." Short stepped back. "You're angry I didn't come."

"I am not. You may make up your own definition of *friend*."

"I wonder if you would better understand if I said to you that I couldn't bear to discover that he knew."

"That he knew!"

"That he knew it was all to be torn apart and sold away. That he was to leave his family near destitution. I couldn't bear to look at him and see—"

"And afterward? When you knew all was lost, did you not think to inquire as to how I got on?"

Short blinked. "I couldn't bear to discover that either."

Martha walked away. Short called after her, "I shall come for you at five."

THE DINNER WAS A QUIET ONE, served in the private dining room of the City Tavern, a place Thomas Jefferson had frequented while attending the Continental Congress; this Martha knew from the stories so many of their guests had told. Had Short picked the place to honor him? Yes. He said in quiet reverence, "If you listen you can hear the talk that formed the nation echoing from these walls."

Martha did listen, in the main because she and William Short appeared to have little to say to each other. He seemed to have thought better of the false cheer with which he'd begun and attempted to get Martha to talk of her father's last days, but she could not; nor could she talk of Monticello, or answer his questions about the slaves. But after they'd spooned up the last of the pudding, she accepted his offer of a walk through the streets, making no objection when he drew her arm through his and pinned it to his side; Martha could make use of that arm. She *was* tired.

After a time Short began to talk of her father, but of her father in Philadelphia and Paris and Washington, never on his mountain; nearing what should have been the end of the walk, he urged her on another block by asking of Tom. Martha, her anger and bitterness still fresh, found that she could talk of this at length: Tom's refusal to see her father, his antagonism toward Jeff, his behavior at the funeral, his threats to take the children.

As Martha ran out of venom, she expected Short to make another remark about its clearly being time for Martha to leave Tom to his own sick mind; he did not. "Tell me of the children," he said, again urging Martha to walk on. Martha began—and found she must end—with Anne. All that had happened, all the stress of travel, all that hovered unspoken had exhausted her. "Please, I should like to return to my room."

Obligingly Short turned, almost colliding with a young couple also walking arm in arm, the woman tall, auburn haired, and so stunning Martha could feel the effect of it in the sudden alertness she felt in Short's arm. The man who accompanied the woman was hard to notice in such company beyond the fact that he was of like height, pink faced, and blond.

Martha looked at the woman again. "Harriet!" she cried.

The woman looked blankly at Martha and gripped tighter to her companion's arm. He hurried them on.

———————

SHORT ARRIVED AT THE INN the next morning to see them off. Again they seemed to have little to say—a comment on the fineness of the day, a hope for a safe journey, a request for letters, a promise of answers. Short helped Martha into the carriage, grasped the door to close it, and paused.

"I would say many things," he said, "but right now I ask only one question. Will you remember I'm here?"

Martha nodded. Short closed the door.

———————

MARTHA FOUND BOSTON of even less interest than she'd found Philadelphia. She couldn't rouse herself or rejoice in her daughter's family or find the concentration to attend to her own children's lessons. Joseph Coolidge found a school in Cambridge for George and insisted on paying the boy's fees; when he informed Martha that they would take girls as well, when he gently urged her to let Timi take a place beside her brother, Martha didn't resist. Neither did she resist this new way of living, with ill-mannered servants who came and went on a whim, a free black community shunned as no slave owner could ever shun his slaves. The only thing that roused her from her deep melancholy were the letters that came from home, eagerly received and opened only to plunge her into melancholy again.

Jeff wrote:

*The sale is done. I managed to buy back Ursula's family, including all seven of her grandchildren, and have reunited them here at Edgehill, although my mother-in-law accuses me of putting this slave family above my own. Maria's son purchased Critta and sent her to live with her husband. Some of the families have managed to keep together under new owners but some are divided, the children sold on. I've hired on Burwell at wages and allowed his mother to remain in her cabin on the mountain; she was priced at no value, and besides, she's refused to move. Burwell visits her daily; he takes his keys to Monticello and makes his daily round as of old, checking windows and doors. John and his apprentices live in Charlottesville. In accordance with your instructions, John's sister resides with her sons now.*

John's sister. Even in a letter between family members, Sally could not be named.

That night Martha lay in bed playing portions of Jeff's letter over and over in her mind. *Some are divided, the children sold on.* She tried to soothe herself with the many memories of her father's kindnesses to his slaves; he'd been well known as the last, best recourse for a slave facing punishment or even sale. They would find a way to him at the great house knowing all would be forgiven— even a runaway had been forgiven his crime and returned to the nailery—it had become such a trial for Mr. Bacon that he'd gone to great lengths to keep the petitioners from her father's door. In only one instance had it worked in the opposite way, when one of the nail boys had struck Burwell a near-fatal blow; Martha's father had instructed that the boy be sold so far away that it would be as if he were dead to those left behind.

Perhaps no wonder Burwell, now freed, would continue to patrol the house as if it were his own.

———————

MARTHA HAD INTENDED TO STAY in Boston for three months. She stayed for eighteen, most of it passing unnoticed as she descended into a gloom too deep to swim through. She knew her father was gone, Monticello was as good as gone, the slaves were gone, and beyond those three thoughts she could not seem to go. But in the spring, when Ellen was delivered of a son, Martha surfaced, not into the present but deep into the past, when *her* first son was born, during the days with Tom that now seemed their happiest times, before the weight of debt and illness and slaves and children had worn them down. As a single, scrawny band of red tulips bloomed in Joseph Coolidge's garden, Martha began to think of Monticello, and all that would be flowering there unseen by those who had most appreciated it. She remembered Tom's youthful, eager plans: *perhaps a hundred acres, just enough to provide for my family's needs, without dependency on the Negroes.* It had sounded such a fine plan to Martha, and yet somehow it had slipped away from view as they stood with their eyes fixed on the mountaintop. Or as *Martha* stood with her eyes fixed on the mountaintop. Oh yes, she would admit this now. She began to think, for the first time, that perhaps they had been wrong to jettison all else in favor of saving Monticello, a ship so riddled with its own worm that it too was destined to go down. But what was left to cry over? It was done. Gone. Such was Martha's state when Tom's letter arrived.

O<small>N THE OUTSIDE COVER</small> Tom had written "Mrs. Martha Randolph," but the letter inside was addressed to "My Dear Timi." *I have loved your mother and only her with all my faculties for thirty-five years next December. I live in hope of spending some happy years yet, in the decline of life, with her.* But the letter was too long; it could not maintain the elevated tone. Tom lapsed back into blaming his son for turning Martha against him, blaming his father for the loss of his inheritance, blaming his son and wife and father-in-law for the loss of Edgehill and Varina. *I will reconcile even with my son, however, if it will now return my wife to me.* Tom then informed Timi that he had found employment translating foreign agricultural manuals into English. His closing fervent hope that it would all come right yet brought Timi to tears.

The letter from Jeff that followed also struck a conciliatory tone.

*I have heartening news—all signs from my father convince me he has surrendered his claims to Timi and George, that he wishes reconciliation with all. He has asked my forgiveness and I have given it. He is most anxious for you to return home, although he declares he would not attempt to live as part of the family again, requesting only a bed in his old office in the North Pavilion. Mama, he is not well and can no longer get his meals at the tavern, so we deliver his sustenance now. The banks have agreed to postpone the sale for two years so as not to rush your departure from Monticello. Should you wish to return, therefore, you still have a home.*

A home. But what kind of home? A ghost home. A ghost life. And a ghost husband? For weeks Martha agonized over Tom's and Jeff's letters, listening to Ellen and Joseph counsel against her return, but in the end Martha's answer to Tom was her own. *Acknowledging that the heat has dimmed, we must only take care that no chill takes hold.* She could not live with him as his wife again, but she needed to see him. She needed to see Monticello.

---

## CHAPTER 44

FOR A SECOND, as the carriage rounded its last turn, Martha thought all was as before—the new bursts of life on mulberry and honey locust and sugar maple and pecan, the living fences of peach trees, the magnificent copper beech at the corner of the terrace. All this was as it had been, and Martha took back some of her life from it, until the neglected garden came into view. Thomas Jefferson was gone, the gardener was gone, the cook was gone; who now cared what grew? Of the rows of treasured peas and beans and tomatoes and eggplant and peppers and asparagus, many of the vegetables introduced by her father to America for the first time—what remained? Cabbage and kale, some chive and lavender, no more.

And the house—how quickly it had lost its glow, the brickwork crumbling, the paint peeling, its graceful lines still holding their power but somehow taking on the look of a displaced monarch at the same time. Perhaps the most shocking of all was the absence of the usual commotion coming from Mulberry Row—no chattering or crying or singing from the servants' houses; no smell of lye from the washhouse or hot metal from smithy or nailery, no smoke from the charcoal kiln; no symphony of hammers or saws or planes from the joinery and carpentry shop. The only relief to the scene came in the swarm of her children, mostly grown now, tumbling down the steps to help her from the carriage and inside. But even their reunion sounded of anguish and joy intermingled, the gaps in the noise louder than the talk, no one mentioning the house's owner or the missing slaves or the man who lay ill down the mountain.

Martha hugged every child and grandchild as her father had done so often on his return from Washington; for him a sanctuary had waited, for Martha a tomb. As soon as she could she slipped away into the small parlor, the room that had always been considered her own, but she was taken aback to find it peppered with the books, work baskets, stray hats, and shawls of others, as if with few servants to pick up after them, her children had forgotten how to do for themselves. But of course they'd never had to do for themselves.

The door opened and Jeff slipped in, closing the door after him. Before he could speak Martha said, "I should like to see him."

Jeff nodded. "We'd best go soon."

THERE WAS LITTLE REMAINING of the Thomas Mann Randolph that Martha had once known. His rich skin was now pale, his thick black hair a long gray whisper, his sharp eyes filmed and glassy and inundated with tears the minute she approached the bed. Jeff escorted Martha into the room but made to leave; Tom called him back. "Jeff, my son, come here please and tell your mother all is harmony between us or she won't stay a minute in this room."

"Papa, I've told her; all is forgiven."

"Martha, you see? I've put myself right with my family, and all for you. For *you*."

Martha only nodded. She seemed to have lost her speech, while curiously, her hearing seemed to have grown more acute; she listened to Jeff's boots as they retreated behind her, to the cabin door as it opened and closed, to some sort of tick in the wood floor as if termites were at work below. She crossed to the bed and perched on the edge, now the only place to sit in the room. Tom smelled of old soap and fresh liquor; he lifted an unsteady hand as if to touch her face, but Martha caught it and lowered it to the coverlet, although she didn't let it go. She'd been wrong about Tom's eyes— the tears had been blinked away and now she saw something in them that she did know, or had known, warm as hot, dark rum and as familiar—more familiar—than her own. Riding down the mountain in the carriage, Martha had remained unsure of whether she could have Tom at Monticello with her and the children; now, looking at him, knowing him, she could only think again of Anne Randolph's letter to her daughter Judith as she pleaded for permission to wed. Indeed, marriage was without remedy. Tom was Martha's husband, still.

"I have too much to say to you, Martha, to know where the beginning lies, or indeed, the middle or end, and yet I lie here in fear that I must say it all this minute, as I'm unlikely to see you again."

Martha had long rehearsed other words to say, but in the end the new ones came more easily. Simply. "Of course you'll see me again. Jeff and I are taking you home."

----

MARTHA WOULD HAVE PREFERRED time, stages, perhaps another visit to the Milton cabin, perhaps next a day's visit at Monticello where they might discuss the rules and desires of all parties involved, but at the initial sighting of her husband, Martha understood that if Tom were to return to Monticello at all it must happen now and it must happen all at once; he would never survive such a trip a second time. Jeff transported his father up the mountain in his carriage and eased him into his first clean, comfortable bed in months. Tom had specified a place be made for him in his old office in the North Pavilion and this after all seemed the best spot for him—a single, familiar room above its own kitchen and away from the commotion of the larger household, bathed in the mountain light and air, sufficiently furnished with fireplace, canopied bed, a settee, and a pair of reclining Campeche chairs.

The North Pavilion's twin, the South Pavilion, was perched at the end of the south terrace as if to form a welcoming pair of arms. The South Pavilion was the first structure completed on the mountain, the spot where Martha's parents had spent their first night at Monticello, and indeed, all the following nights until after Martha was born, snug in their abode as Monticello rose up around them in accordance with her father's plan. Martha had heard the story from her mother many times—they'd set out in a rare snowstorm that had ended up depositing three feet of snow on the mountain, forcing them to abandon their phaeton at a friend's and continue the last eight miles on horseback. They'd arrived at the tiny brick house long after the fire had gone out and the servants departed, but the bridegroom had outfitted the single room with a large bedstead festooned with expensive bed hangings, comfortable chairs, candles, and a bottle of fine wine secreted behind the books. He resurrected the fire, poured the wine, and they spent their first night at Monticello in warmth, laughter, and song.

When Martha first saw Tom settled into the mirror version of her parents' bolt-hole, a wave of envy overcame her. Could she not tuck herself away in the South Pavilion with her own fire and her own bottle of wine, leaving Tom to the North Pavilion, leaving the children, servants, visitors and other vultures to roam in the huge, crumbling hall between? The image grew in all its absurdity until Martha almost laughed out loud.

———

ONCE ESTABLISHED IN HIS OWN SPACE AT MONTICELLO, Tom grew peaceful, grateful, kind to Martha and his children. He no longer talked of what he was and wasn't owed but instead called up their happiest times—his early infatuated visits to Monticello; their late-night talks when all their plans still seemed about to be fulfilled; he talked of his and Martha's deepest connection, the births of their children. One by one the children came and made their peace with their father, taking Jeff's example as their own, but it was Martha who sat with him every day and Jeff every night; at the end of one of those days, when Jeff had just arrived and Martha prepared to leave, Tom opened his eyes and held hers. "Stay," he said. He said nothing more. Near midnight he made one final, violent struggle for air and stopped breathing. Stopped being.

Martha sat on.

———

JEFF EXECUTED HIS FATHER'S ESTATE, which consisted of the books that Thomas Jefferson had given his son-in-law, valued at six hundred dollars, and a horse valued at twenty dollars. When Jeff set the list of her husband's effects in front of Martha, she stared at it a long time, thinking of what might have been on the list: Tuckahoe. Edgehill. Varina. Wingo.

Slaves.

## CHAPTER 45

MARTHA RODE DOWN THE MOUNTAIN ALONE. Over a year had passed since Tom's death; a new spring had decorated Monticello and danced into summer; summer had announced its pending exit and stalled. Monticello had been sold, but the new owners had not yet evicted its present, illustrious occupant. Martha would have been happy to go—she had come to that, she knew—if only she knew *where* to go.

*Edgehill,* Jeff said, but his mother-in-law was already in residence, and Martha didn't relish her disapproving looks across the dinner table. *Boston,* Ellen said, but Boston was far from the rest of Martha's family, and Martha's joints had suffered much in the cold. *Washington,* Virginia said, and indeed, Dolley Madison and numerous other friends appeared anxious to draw her back into the political scene, but Martha could only think of the epitaph her father had requested: *Here was buried Thomas Jefferson, Author of the Declaration of American Independence, of the Statute of Virginia for religious freedom, & Father of the University of Virginia.* He requested no mention of his four years as secretary of state, his four as vice president, his eight as president of the United States. For him, the man who had helped bring it into being, Washington held no charm. He would not have approved of Washington.

Besides, Martha was not yet through with Albemarle County. She rode into Charlottesville and took her first turn in the direction of the university to which her father had dedicated his last years. Martha could see his hand everywhere—in the lovely lines of the buildings he'd designed; in the shape and form of the campus, with students and faculty intermingled rather than segregated as they were in most schools; in fact, in every blade of grass and flowering vine or shrub. Perhaps this was to be Thomas Jefferson's physical legacy, as the crumbling Monticello could never be now.

Martha rode on, leaving the main road for the side street where she'd been directed by Burwell, with a warning—a recent census had listed the three people dwelling in the house Martha now approached as free and white. Martha knew the family as well as she knew her own and would, if asked, agree that two of them were free and white. If asked, she would say nothing contrary about the third, but she—and only she—knew different. The woman who resided in the neat, two-story brick-and-wood house with the effusion of flowers in the front yard was neither free nor white; she belonged to Martha, and her quarter of Negro blood had not been as thoroughly washed from her as it had been washed from her children with that final Jefferson cross.

As Martha drew close she heard the sound of a violin playing her father's old favorite, "Money Musk." The music stopped when she knocked and Eston opened the door; not having seen him in some time, the shock was considerable—perhaps the sound of the familiar tune had conditioned her, but it was, indeed, as if her young father stood at the door.

"Mrs. Randolph," Eston said with a bow, folding his tall form at the waist, wrapping his arms around his chest, even that gesture like Thomas Jefferson's. "Come in, if you will."

*If you will.* Martha stepped into the room as Madison entered through a far door; he greeted Martha as politely as had his brother, but they stood on obvious alert, waiting to hear the purpose of the call. What must they be thinking, Martha wondered, that I'd come to take away their freedom? Did they even imagine she could if she wished it? She could think of no other reason for their wariness, and then she could, of course she could; she'd even come to it herself as she rode. Someone in this house was *not* free, and Martha could call her back into slavery at any time.

"I hope you're both well," Martha said.

Madison answered. "We are."

"And your mother is well?"

Yes, there, the heightened sense of tension. "She is well."

"I've come to speak with her, if I may."

The brothers exchanged a look. Eston left the room and returned; without a word spoken Madison seemed to know what had transpired and waved Martha before him into the adjoining parlor.

Sally sat in a chair by the window, leaning toward the light, working a needle in and out of a sleeve of blue wool. She didn't look up as Martha entered, completing her stitch first; once she'd completed the stitch, she set the work down and gestured to the opposite chair.

Martha remained standing. On the mantel were two objects she recognized: the bell her mother had used to call her servants and the inkwell her father had used to write the thousands of letters that had occupied his last years.

Sally followed Martha's gaze. "They were given to me," she said.

"I've no doubt they were." Martha approached Sally's chair, holding out a folded paper, the weight of it heavy in her hands, because Sally didn't take it from her right away. "I should like you to have this too."

Sally reached out and took the paper, but she didn't open it; her eyes stayed fixed on Martha.

"In that document I formally relinquish all future claim to your labors. I give you back that portion of your time that still belongs to me. You can never be called back to work by me or by anyone anymore. In this way I release you, but I also evade any issue of manumission, any requirement that you leave Virginia." And, hopefully, any unwelcome notice in the press or on the street, but for the transaction to go unnoticed, Sally must decide to keep it so. Martha must put her trust in *Sally* now.

Sally opened the paper and looked at it but said nothing.

Was she to stay silent to the end? "My father—" Martha began, but there Sally spoke.

"Say nothing to me of your father, please. This is all I ask."

Martha paused. She should leave, she knew, but after all this time she found she couldn't leave without broaching the question she'd never dared ask her father. "I only wish to understand what you were."

"Why? You'll deny it, will you not?"

"I will."

"And if others don't deny, what will it matter? People will believe what they wish to believe."

Had Martha not said those same words? But here, in this room, how unsatisfying they were!

Martha turned to go.

"Mrs. Randolph."

Martha turned again.

"Where do you go now?"

The question startled Martha, not only that Sally should ask it, but that Martha still didn't know the answer. Where *would* Martha go? Edgehill? Boston? Washington? Each of those places stank of an old, unwelcome dependency. She looked at the paper Sally had set down on the table beside her. Martha's father was dead. Her husband was dead. Monticello was gone. Her oldest children were settled and her youngest were receiving a better education up

North than Martha could manage to give them. Martha had just given Sally back all that remained of her time in servitude. Sally *and* Martha were free now.

Where would she go? "Wherever I choose."

Sally peered at Martha for some time. She nodded. Had she even smiled?

Martha would never know.

Outside the room, the violin started up again. Sally set down her sewing and closed her eyes. Had she listened just so as her master played? Had he soothed her with his violin music as Sally had once soothed him with her song?

This too Martha would never know.

———

PHILADELPHIA APPEARED FRESH TO MARTHA, NEW. He came to
meet her as before, pushing through the crowd in front of Mrs.
Hill's, but this time Martha saw him as if *he* were someone new.
Or perhaps someone old. From afar his step appeared as lively as it
had in France; as he drew close his eyes—still warm, still brown—
held her in them as they'd perhaps always held her, or if not always,
what did it matter? He'd had his duchess. She'd had her Tom. Neither had ended as planned, but so little of it mattered now.

"Mrs. Randolph."

"Mr. Short." He took her hand and led her a few paces away from
the carriage, away from Mrs. Hill's door. "You do me a great honor—"

"Please, Mr. Short. Is this how we speak to each other after all
these years?"

Short laughed. "Very well, then. You do me no honor. You do
me no favor. In fact, you've taken your sweet bloody time in deciding to visit me again. Where are you off to now?"

"In fact, I come from Washington; my son-in-law found some
reasonably priced rooms there, and President Jackson seems to
think me of use. It would appear that the chance to meet Thomas
Jefferson's daughter still draws a certain kind of person to his table."

"And the chance to converse with Martha Jefferson Randolph
draws them back again."

Martha peered at Short. She could admit that what he'd said
was not untrue. How the idea lifted her! "Where do we dine this
evening? City Tavern?"

"If you wish it."

She did not. How odd, the realization in that single beat of her heart that she did not wish it. "If you have no objection, I'd prefer someplace new."

Had he always smiled so? First she thought *yes,* but then she thought *no*; this particular smile was freer than the old one, more optimistic, or perhaps better put, more realistic in its expectations. In the intervening years Martha had often thought of William Short and their many conversations on slavery; she wondered if, after all, she or her husband or her father could have done as she'd told Short they could never do—open the door and let them go. Martha's family would have lost their slaves first and their property next, but they'd lost those things anyway. What would have been different in the end? One hundred and thirty Negroes would have been free. Thomas Jefferson's legacy would have shone brighter. But Thomas Jefferson had not emancipated his slaves as Short had wished him to do; Martha had not publicly freed Sally and declared her father's admixed family to the world. Short's vision would not happen—if it happened—with the help of either of them.

In her father's papers Martha had finally found that answer to Short's old letter on admixture, written six months before he died: *I consider that the expatriation to the governments of the West Indies of their own colour as entirely practicable, and greatly preferable to the mixture of colour here.* Martha had sat long with that letter in her hand, pondering the man who could write and live ideas so violently opposed until she'd looked around and seen her father's mountain as it really was, for perhaps the first time. This little mountain, her father's world, was not a real world at all but a world her father could see or not see as it suited him, a world he had managed to pretend he could create and control down to the last perfect bloom, without ever tallying the cost. And what was that cost?

Everything.

In her father's papers Martha also found a letter written in response to another from Short in which he'd begged Jefferson to join again in the fight to emancipate the slaves.

> *This, my dear sir, is like bidding old Priam to buckle the armor of Hector. This enterprise is for the young. It shall have all my prayers, and these are the only weapons of an old man.*

Martha remembered Tom quoting her father to her, Tom so in awe of her father's belief in the rights of *all* men. When had her father given up on turning that idea into law? Long before this last letter to Short. Martha looked at Short, himself no longer a young man. Had he given up? Martha thought no. She believed she could see a new excitement in him, as if the disappointments of the past were indeed past, and whatever came next might turn out to be the truest part of the tale. But what might Short see in her? Martha hoped that Short could look beyond the tragedies she still dragged after her and see her own hope. But perhaps the fact that she was here, that she'd found the strength and desire to face the challenge he must always present to her was enough.

For now.

# *Author's Note*

---

I STUMBLED INTO *MONTICELLO* THE WAY I've stumbled into all of my historical fiction—the research for one book left a loose thread that I followed into a new story. *Benjamin Franklin's Bastard* ended in 1776, with Franklin departing for France, where he is eventually met by Thomas Jefferson and his young daughter. As soon as I came across a letter the fourteen-year-old Martha Jefferson had written to her father: "I wish with all my soul that the poor Negroes were all freed . . ." I was hooked. I read all of Martha's letters to her father and his to her. I read her biography. I read his biographies. Running through it all I found a multifaceted woman who had played a much larger role in her father's—and our—history than I'd previously assumed. I also discovered that Martha had spent her life doing something I'd spent a fair portion of mine doing: attempting to figure out her father.

Martha Jefferson Randolph struggled throughout her life to reconcile her roles as wife, mother, daughter, slaveholder, and educated thinking woman. She struggled with the issue of slavery in general and Sally Hemings in particular, and consequently the issue of slavery became an integral part of this novel just as it was an integral part of Randolph's life. Most of the quotes deploring the institution of slavery that are attributed to Martha Jefferson Randolph in these pages (and to her father, husband, and William Short) are historical fact; it's also an historical fact that the Jeffersons and Randolphs bought and sold and relocated human beings throughout their lives. I make no excuses for these families; I explored their struggles in an effort to better understand how intelligent, conscience-ridden people could accommodate such an institution for so long.

Even after definitive DNA evidence, combined with convincing circumstantial evidence, essentially proved that Thomas Jefferson fathered Sally Hemings's children, the argument continues: Was the relationship nothing but an abuse of power, following the pattern of any master-slave relationship, or did it manage to transcend those dynamics in any way? I believe it did. There is no evidence that after Jefferson began his sexual relationship with Sally Hemings in the late 1780s he ever had another relationship with any other woman, or that he fathered any other children. There is no evidence that Sally Hemings ever had any other relationship, and her child-bearing having been well-documented, we know that no other children were born to her but those who came along nine months after Thomas Jefferson's often sporadic presence at Monticello. The testimony of Jefferson's own family indicates that the resemblance between Jefferson and Sally Hemings's children was strong. No matter what else the Jefferson-Hemings relationship was or wasn't, the evidence suggests that it was a monogamous one that lasted for thirty-eight years. The evidence also suggests that the trust Sally placed in Jefferson was not misguided; all her life she received extraordinary privileges at Monticello, and three decades later Jefferson honored the promise made in France, ensuring that all her children went free when they reached the age of twenty-one.

But although Sally Hemings achieved the treasured goal of freedom for her children, this could hardly be considered a "happy ending"—it left three of those children ultimately making the agonizing decision to "pass" into the white world, disappearing from their black family's lives forever. Nor should we call the Jefferson-Hemings relationship a romantic one; if there was or wasn't true feeling between the pair, the circumstances would—or could—have remained the same. But I hope this book reminds us that both master and slave were real people with real feelings who lived real and meaningful lives; that the "abomination" of slavery, as Jefferson called it, tainted and diminished *everyone's* lives, white as well as black, but it did not negate those lives. Were there happy endings for anyone? You decide.

---

FOR THOSE INTERESTED IN TRACING the historical threads found in this novel I recommend six works of nonfiction (note that Martha was sometimes called Patsy and Maria's legal name was Mary): *Martha Jefferson Randolph, Daughter of Monticello,* by Cynthia A. Kierner; *Thomas Jefferson: An Intimate History,* by Fawn M. Brodie; *Thomas Jefferson: The Art of Power,* by Jon Meacham; *"Those Who Labor for My Happiness"*—Slavery at Thomas Jefferson's Monticello, by Lucia Stanton; and *The Hemingses of Monticello: An American Family,* and *Thomas Jefferson and Sally Hemings: An American Controversy* by Annette Gordon-Reed. This last author, a Pulitzer Prize–winning historian, earned my eternal gratitude when she wrote in a later essay: "In the end, it will probably be left to novelists, playwrights, and poets, unencumbered by the need for footnotes, to get at the ultimate meaning of this story." This is why I write historical fiction.

# *Acknowledgments*

---

I AM DEEPLY GRATEFUL to two amazing people on my team who each in her own way helped to make the book better—editor, Jennifer Brehl, and agent, Kristine Dahl. I am also grateful to Anna Berkes, reference librarian at the Jefferson Library; Anne Causey, reference assistant at the University of Virginia Albert and Shirley Small Special Collections; Peter Drummey, librarian at Massachusetts Historical Society; and Bob Hughes at Monticello for their patient assistance with my research.

My heartfelt thanks to my early readers, Diane, Jan and Nancy Carlson, and—as always and for everything—to my husband, Tom.

## About the Author

A LIFELONG RESIDENT OF NEW ENGLAND, Sally Cabot Gunning is active in her local historical society and creates tours that showcase the three-hundred-year history of her village. She is the author of the critically acclaimed Satucket novels—*The Widow's War, Bound,* and *The Rebellion of Jane Clarke*—and, writing under the name of Sally Cabot, *Benjamin Franklin's Bastard*. She lives in Brewster, Massachusetts, with her husband, Tom.